THE
SOUND
OF
ECHOES

ALSO BY ERIC BERNT

The Speed of Sound

THE SOUND OF ECHOES

ERIC BERNT

Jefferson Madison
Regional Library
Charlottesville, Virginia

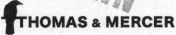
THOMAS & MERCER

Published by Thomas & Mercer, Seattle

www.apub.com

Amazon, the Amazon logo, and Thomas & Mercer are trademarks of Amazon.com, Inc., or its affiliates.

ISBN-13: 9781503904545
ISBN-10: 1503904547

Cover design by Mike Heath | Magnus Creative

Printed in the United States of America

For my wife, Laurel, the light of my life.

Autistic children have the ability to see things and events around them from a new point of view, which often shows surprising maturity . . . This ability, which remains throughout life, can in favorable cases lead to exceptional achievements which others may never attain.

—*Hans Asperger*, 1944

Echo. Echo. Echo. Echo. Echo. Echo. Echo. Echo. Echo. Echo. Echo.
Echo. Echo. Echo. Echo. Echo. Echo. Echo. Echo. Echo. Echo. Echo.
Echo. Echo. Echo. Echo. Echo. Echo. Echo. Echo. Echo. Echo. Echo.
Echo. Echo. Echo. Echo. Echo. Echo. Echo. Echo. Echo. Echo. Echo.
Echo. Echo. Echo. Echo. Echo. Echo. Echo. Echo. Echo. Echo. Echo.
Echo. Echo. Echo. Echo. Echo. Echo. Echo. Echo. Echo. Echo. Echo.
Echo. Echo. Echo. Echo. Echo. Echo. Echo. Echo. Echo. Echo. Echo.
Echo. Echo. Echo. Echo. Echo. Echo. Echo. Echo. Echo. Echo. Echo.
Echo. Echo. Echo. Echo. Echo. Echo. Echo. Echo. Echo. Echo. Echo.
Echo. Echo. Echo. Echo. Echo. Echo. Echo. Echo. Echo. Echo. Echo.
Echo. Echo. Echo. Echo. Echo. Echo. Echo. Echo. Echo. Echo. Echo.
Echo. Echo. Echo. Echo. Echo. Echo. Echo. Echo. Echo. Echo. Echo.
Echo. Echo. Echo. Echo. Echo. Echo. Echo. Echo. Echo. Echo. Echo.
Echo. Echo. Echo. Echo. Echo. Echo. Echo. Echo. Echo. Echo. Echo.
Echo. Echo. Echo. Echo. Echo. Echo. Echo. Echo. Echo. Echo. Echo.
Echo. Echo. Echo. Echo. Echo. Echo. Echo. Echo. Echo. Echo. Echo.

Echo. Echo. Echo. Echo. Echo. Echo. Echo. Echo. Echo. Echo. Echo.
Echo. Echo. Echo. Echo. Echo. Echo. Echo. Echo. Echo. Echo. Echo.
Echo. Echo. Echo. Echo. Echo. Echo. Echo. Echo. Echo. Echo. Echo.
Echo. Echo. Echo. Echo. Echo. Echo. Echo. Echo. Echo. Echo. Echo.
Echo. Echo. Echo. Echo. Echo. Echo. Echo. Echo. Echo. Echo. Echo.
Echo. Echo. Echo. Echo. Echo. Echo. Echo. Echo. Echo. Echo. Echo.
Echo. Echo. Echo. Echo. Echo. Echo. Echo. Echo. Echo. Echo. Echo.
Echo. Echo. Echo. Echo. Echo. Echo. Echo. Echo. Echo. Echo. Echo.
Echo. Echo. Echo. Echo. Echo. Echo. Echo. Echo. Echo. Echo. Echo.
Echo. Echo. Echo. Echo. Echo. Echo. Echo. Echo. Echo. Echo. Echo.
Echo. Echo. Echo. Echo. Echo. Echo. Echo. Echo. Echo. Echo. Echo.
Echo. Echo. Echo. Echo. Echo. Echo. Echo. Echo. Echo. Echo. Echo.
Echo. Echo. Echo. Echo. Echo. Echo. Echo. Echo. Echo. Echo. Echo.
Echo. Echo. Echo. Echo. Echo. Echo. Echo. Echo. Echo. Echo. Echo.

CHAPTER 1

I-76 West

New Jersey/Pennsylvania Border

June 1, 11:47 a.m.

As she drove across the Delaware River on the Walt Whitman Bridge, Skylar took in the Philadelphia skyline. It was reasonably impressive, she thought. The longer she admired the view, the more comfortable she became with the idea of calling this place home.

Skylar had made up her mind, on one of her recent drives home from Harmony House, that she needed to move out of Jacob's apartment as soon as possible. Everything about his place reminded her of him. The closetful of his slightly wrinkled dress shirts, which she had started sleeping in. The art made by friends, works he had collected over the years, which she suddenly found herself appreciating after having loathed them for ages. The scent of his Nautica cologne, which she'd taken from the medicine cabinet and had been spraying onto her pillow at night to help her fall asleep. She had even started drinking the cold-brew espresso he had made just before his murder in the New York subway system. Skylar had started to imagine this as "drinking of him" and wanted it to last as long as possible, so she would only sip a little at a time. But it was his toothbrush—which she had started using instead of her own, along with his Colgate instead of her usual Crest—that made her realize she had to get out of there.

She hated Colgate.

There was also the practical reality that the commute from Greenwich Village to Harmony House was too long. She had moved in with Jacob only recently, just before interviewing with Dr. Marcus Fenton, the now-deceased founder of the government facility. *The evil bastard.* She was glad he had killed himself, as uncomfortable as this was to admit.

Even before the tragedy had befallen Jacob, Skylar had known she was going to have to move closer to work. It was a conversation she'd been trying to avoid. She realized how much she would give to be able to have any conversation with him now. *How were your classes today? Want me to pick something up for dinner? Do we really have to go to this thing? Which dress do you think looks better on me, the red one with the skinny shoulder straps or the frilly lace black one? Are you sure I can't convince you to blow it off?*

Skylar had considered remaining in the city, specifically the Village, for a host of reasons. One was that she simply liked the area. It was vibrant. It was alive. And the thought of the occasional meal at Shu Han Ju, Jacob's favorite Chinese restaurant, was a comforting one. The smell of chow mein would probably remind her of Jacob for the rest of her life. But she also recognized what a bad idea staying in the city was. Given the hours she intended to spend at Harmony House for at least the next several years, there was no way she could sustain a two-hour commute. She had to find a place within reasonable proximity to Woodbury, New Jersey.

As she saw it, that left her with only one choice: Philadelphia, just across the Delaware River. She had several friends from the University of Virginia and Harvard Medical School who had settled there and seemed to like it well enough. None of them raved about living there like her friends in New York or Boston, but she knew it was her best option, at least for now. The distance to Woodbury would make the commute less than thirty minutes long, which was ideal, as far as Skylar was concerned.

Skylar continued following the Google Maps directions as she continued north along I-76. The pleasant female voice told her: *Use the left lane to take exit 346A for South Street.* From there, it took her less than five minutes to reach her destination in the 1700 block of Locust Street, two blocks from Rittenhouse Square. The location was less than three miles from the childhood home of Eddie Parks, Skylar's uniquely gifted autistic patient who had recently become the focus of her professional life. They had visited the site only four days earlier. That had not gone so well.

She managed to find street parking right in front of the building. Skylar decided her good fortune must be a sign from God. Today was her lucky day.

She entered the small but bustling offices of Fox & Roach Realtors, which was apparently a regional division of Berkshire Hathaway. The windows and walls featured photos of available properties, several with *Sold!* handwritten in red Sharpie across them. A young receptionist, answering an incoming call, motioned to Skylar that she'd be right with her, and to have a seat in the waiting area. She pointed to the Keurig machine in case Skylar wanted a coffee.

Before she could even sit down, she heard a familiar voice say, "Skylar?"

She recognized the voice as the one she had spoken to on the phone the night before. He looked exactly like the photo on his web page. "You must be Jared."

He shook her hand warmly. "I am. So nice to meet you. How was your drive into town?"

"Nice. I never realized what an impressive skyline the city has."

He nodded as if that was something he heard frequently. "Before we head back to my office, did you want anything to drink? Coffee? Water?"

"No, thanks, I'm good."

"Well, get ready to be great, because I have some wonderful units to show you." He led her down the hallway to his office, the second door on the left. As they entered, she was surprised to find it empty except for a video camera connected to a laptop computer, which sat atop a folding table. There was no desk; there were only two stackable plastic chairs. There was nothing on the walls. The only decoration was on the table next to the laptop: a rubber Albert Einstein mask, the kind a child might wear on Halloween. *Strange,* she thought.

Before Skylar had time to register the danger she was in, Jared turned toward her and jabbed a syringe into her neck. "What the hell?!" She tried to shove him away, but to no avail.

The man calling himself Jared was incredibly muscular. After removing the syringe from her neck, he grabbed her by the throat and started choking her. "Not another word. Do you understand?" His voice was now completely different. It was cold and utterly emotionless.

She couldn't breathe. His hands were strong and much too rough for a real estate agent. Terrified, she nodded yes, she understood, just before she attempted to knee him in the groin as hard as she could. Her thrust would have landed squarely, doing considerable damage, had Jared not anticipated it. He twisted his torso, raising his thigh to block her knee before it could land. He squeezed her neck even tighter, practically crushing her larynx. She felt the muscles in her body start to go limp. The drug was taking effect.

Her hands dropped, and her knees felt weak. Her panic began to subside, as did the pain in her neck from being choked. He loosened his grip, allowing her to breathe. She sucked in as much air as her lungs would tolerate. "Why . . . are you doing this?"

"You'll find out soon enough."

Skylar's legs gave out and she lost consciousness.

(((•)))

Jared positioned her in one of the chairs and started duct-taping her arms and legs to it. He checked her pulse, which was steady. She would be out for as long as he wanted her to be. He left her alone in the office to join the young woman who had played the role of dutiful reception-ist in the front area. Her name was Carla. He had worked with her several times previously, always in the service of the American Heritage Foundation. She had already removed the realty company signs from the door and windows. The property photos had also been taken down, and she was about to unplug the Keurig machine.

"Hang on, I want a cup."

She held up two choices. "French roast or Sumatra?"

He took the French roast single serving and popped it into the machine. "You want one?"

"No, thanks." Carla held up a Starbucks cup, which had been hid-den behind her receptionist's desk. "You update Stenson yet?"

"Just about to." Jared took out his phone and speed-dialed the only number he was ever to call with that device.

CHAPTER 2

American Heritage Foundation

Alexandria, Virginia

May 31, 5:58 p.m.

Skylar had Googled *Philadelphia apartments for rent* several days ago, not thinking too seriously about it—and that was what had tipped off those assigned to keep tabs on her from within the American Heritage Foundation, which had recently come oh-so-close to acquiring the echo box. Their only problem was that they had acquired a nonworking version of the device. Unbeknownst to them at the time, Eddie had reverted his prototype to a previous version that included faulty algorithms. And only he knew what he had changed. Whatever was wrong with the code could be fixed only by the device's inventor. This had utterly infuriated the director of the AHF, Bob Stenson. He had been outplayed by not only a civilian, but one whose neurological profile placed him on the autism spectrum. It was humiliating, he thought.

This time, Stenson and his foundation were going to be even more resolute in their efforts. They intended to make certain that absolutely nothing interfered with their goal of acquiring this game-changing intelligence technology. Outside of Harmony House, only they knew that the device worked. Or, more accurately, that it was capable of working. They had heard the evidence.

No matter what they had to do, the AHF was going to become the only entity in the world with the ability to utilize the science of acoustic archeology and re-create any conversation ever held. No one else in the intelligence world would have any idea how they got their information. They were going to have a superpower, but nobody outside their inner sanctum would know its source.

By the time Skylar had decided to get more serious about finding a new place to live and emailed several friends for Realtor recommendations, her watchers within the American Heritage Foundation had intercepted the queries and replied on behalf of the friends, who never received the requests. The fabricated responses, each written in the individual's particular style, recommended several firms and names, but only one name appeared in each email: *Jared Himmelstein.*

In less time than it takes most people to make a turkey sandwich, the technical team at the AHF had created the fictional Philadelphia Realtor's website, which made him appear both impressive and approachable. He looked like somebody Skylar would be comfortable with. She dialed the number on his website, which was routed to the phone of a man who was not a Realtor. He was an independent contractor who performed a unique service for a very select clientele that included the American Heritage Foundation. He had been told to expect Skylar's call, but to let the call go to voicemail so she could hear a friendly recording of his voice to go along with the welcoming face on his website.

His voicemail recording ended, *I'll get right back to you just as soon as I can.* Skylar left a rambling message that included who she was, who had recommended him to her, and the best number at which to reach her.

((•))

"Jared" called her back within fifteen minutes. "Hey, Skylar, this is Jared. I got your message and would love to help you. I checked current inventory and happened to find a couple places that just became available, that I think you might really like. How soon are you interested in relocating?"

"Immediately. I need to get out of my present situation as soon as possible."

"Then time is of the essence. Got it. Unfortunately, things have gotten crazy busy for me and I'm booked solid through the following week, but I just had a cancellation tomorrow at twelve thirty, and I was wondering if there's any way you could—"

"I can make twelve thirty work. Text me the address and I'll be there." The address arrived seconds later.

"Terrific. I'll see you tomorrow." As she clicked off the call, she felt good about beginning to move on with her life.

How short-lived that feeling would be.

CHAPTER 3

Harmony House

Woodbury, New Jersey

June 1, 12:39 p.m.

Eddie walked briskly down the hallway toward his room with Nurse Gloria. His pace was much faster than usual, because he was scared. So scared that he had forgotten to count his steps, which was something that always soothed him. That and slapping himself—but while every doctor he had ever seen had discouraged self-slapping as a coping mechanism, none had ever suggested that he stop counting. Eddie correctly assumed this was because his slapping sometimes left marks, but counting never did.

If only he had remembered this time to count the ninety-three steps it took from Dr. Skylar Drummond's office to his room.

"Do you know who put it in my room?" There was an urgency in his voice bordering on panic.

"Eddie, I honestly don't know what you're talking about." Nurse Gloria's voice was soothing. Even motherly. Eddie's own mother had died giving birth to him, which had been the primary motivation behind Eddie's devotion to acoustic archeology and the development of his invention, the echo box. He had wanted to hear his mother's voice.

So many people had told him as a child that his mother had the voice of an angel, yet sadly, no one had ever bothered to record her.

Eddie had made it his mission to hear the voice of that angel. His angel. He had thought of little else until finally accomplishing his goal three days ago. And the moment was everything he had hoped for. His mother's voice was truly angelic. He had repeatedly listened to the sound waves re-created from the decayed, inaudible energy waves still present in Saint Christopher's Episcopal Church in Saylan Hills, Pennsylvania. And they were now permanently etched into his memory, which explained the smile that hadn't left his face for several days.

At least, not until a few minutes ago.

((•))

Earlier that morning, Eddie had confronted his doctor, Skylar Drummond—the person he trusted more than anyone else he had ever known—with a heartfelt question during one of their "walks to nowhere" in the Harmony House yard.

Eddie loved these strolls in the yard, which had only recently become part of his daily routine. "Skylar, if I don't want to share the echo box with anyone, do I still have to?"

She considered her answer carefully. "As far as I know, nobody else even knows it works. You made the rest of the world think it doesn't."

Eddie smiled the devilish grin of someone who had gotten away with something for the first time in his life.

"If nobody knows it works, it's unlikely that anyone would ask you to use it."

"I agree that it's unlikely. But what if they do?"

She paused, studying him. "That's a very good question. I honestly don't know the answer. Would you mind if I thought about it for a while and got back to you?"

"How long do you mean by 'a while'?"

She had forgotten the importance of specifics with Eddie. "No more than forty-eight hours."

He took a moment to consider her proposition. "No, I would not mind if you took no more than forty-eight hours to think about it." He then tilted his head, listening to two dogs barking in the distance. It was a small dog and a large dog. The smaller one barked much more ferociously than the larger one. Over the years, he had noticed this was almost always the case. Little dogs, it seemed, had something to prove.

"Eddie, why don't you want to share the echo box?"

"The only sound I ever wanted to hear with it was my mother's voice. I have heard it now. Last week made me realize that there are people who might use the echo box in ways I don't want them to."

"What ways are those?" She knew the answer, of course, but wanted to hear what he was thinking.

"The echo box could be used by bad people to do bad things, Skylar."

"I suppose that's true. But it could also be used by good people to do good things." The possibilities presented by being able to listen to any conversation ever held, via re-creation of the original sound waves from the minuscule, decayed, but still-existent energy waves bouncing around any given space, were mind-boggling.

There truly would be no more secrets.

"I suppose that's true." He mimicked her perfectly in terms of tone and pitch, but the inflection sounded mechanical. In his regular voice, he asked, "There is no way to control how the echo box will be used by other people, is there?"

She shook her head. "Not if you are not present when they use it, and even if you are, they would still probably do what they want with it."

"Please let me know after you've had enough time to think about it, as long as it doesn't take more than forty-eight hours."

She nodded reassuringly. They walked for five minutes without saying a word. These silent portions of their walks had become the doctor's favorite part; she enjoyed watching her patient use his heightened sense of hearing as he took in the world around them. The sound of each of their steps. The wind rustling nearby leaves. A distant plane twelve thousand feet overhead. She barely paid attention to any of it, but she knew he never missed a single detail.

Eddie stopped abruptly, suddenly looking concerned. "What do I do now?"

CHAPTER 4

PATIENT YARD

HARMONY HOUSE

June 1, 10:44 a.m.

Skylar paused next to Eddie, nodding with the understanding of someone whose life had also been recently upended, although hers was due to loss, not gain. Only the week before, her boyfriend had been brutally murdered by an employee of the founder and former head of Harmony House, Dr. Marcus Fenton. It was Fenton's former office that she now occupied, which gave her some small comfort. Well, that and Fenton's suicide following his ouster from this facility.

"I would start by continuing to put one foot in front of the other," she said to Eddie, motioning toward his shoes. Joking had only recently become a regular part of their communication.

Eddie rolled his eyes. "I don't mean in this instant. I mean *now* as in the rest of my life. For as long as I can remember, the only thing I wanted to do was hear my mother's voice."

She paused, seeming to need the advice herself as much as her patient did. "Well, you figure out what you want to focus your efforts on, and then you figure out how to accomplish it."

"I don't know how to figure out either one of those." He looked bewildered.

"That's okay, you don't need to. One of the things I know I want to do is to help you."

"How do you know that's what you want to do?"

"I knew from the first time I met you." She held his gaze for as long as he would tolerate.

"You didn't answer my question."

"How did you know you wanted to hear your mother's voice?"

Eddie paused to consider the question. It was something he had never contemplated. "I don't know. I just did."

Skylar nodded. "That's because it's something you felt."

He had to think about this. "So there are some things you know because you feel them?"

She nodded again. "I think of this as knowing something with my whole being, more than with just my brain."

"Some people would say you are referring to the soul," he said, repeating something he had heard without having any idea what the person was talking about.

Skylar had an expression like she had just heard something incredibly insightful, which seemed to be the response Eddie was hoping for—to make her think he understood what she was talking about, when the truth was, he was merely guessing. The subjects of soul and spirit confused him because they were so unknowable. He could feel his discomfort start to rise and knew to change the subject before he got too anxious. "Are you sure you can help me, Skylar?"

"I wouldn't say that I'm sure, but rather that I'm confident I can. I know that I want to. And I believe that I can because I'm determined to. I also studied for a number of years before meeting you, so I have a fair amount of preparation."

"But you don't know what I want to do yet, so it could be anything. And you couldn't have studied everything. That's impossible."

"You're right. That is impossible."

"What if I want to do something you can't help me with, like become an astronaut? Or build the tallest building in the world? Or genetically engineer a more nutrient-dense carrot?"

"I will either learn what I need to learn to help you, or I will find someone who already knows how." She seemed to sense he was already thinking of something. Something he wasn't quite ready to communicate. "What's on your mind, Eddie?"

He looked upward. "Nothing is on my mind."

She had forgotten not to use metaphors. "Sorry. I mean, what are you thinking about?"

He hesitated. "Nothing."

She imitated the BUZZER sound he often made when hearing someone deliver a false statement. Eddie had learned the sound from watching game shows. It was a playful attempt at letting him know he was not being forthcoming; she clarified by adding, "Not true."

"There is no way you can know what I'm thinking. There is no way to read someone's mind. At least, not yet."

"I didn't say I know what you're thinking, but I do think there's something you're not telling me."

"Why do you think that, Skylar?"

"I can feel it." She put her hand high on her chest.

He hesitated again, looking up to the sky and then the trees. A gentle breeze blew across his face. "Were you in love with Jacob Hendrix? I mean, before he died on the train tracks in the subway station last week?"

Skylar momentarily stopped breathing, trying very hard not to reveal how devastating the question was for her. Turning her face away from Eddie, she clenched her jaw as tightly as she could. *Keep it together!* Eddie didn't know to ask the question gently, or how fresh the pain still was for her. Jacob hadn't even been laid to rest yet. The funeral wasn't scheduled for another two weeks, to allow extended family members time to make the necessary travel arrangements. "Yes, Eddie, I was."

"How did it happen?"

"Do you mean, how did I fall in love with Jacob?"

"Yes—could it have been anyone, or did it have to be him?"

She smiled, satisfied that she had uncovered what her patient wanted to discuss. "That's a great question. Boy, do we have a lot to talk about."

((•))

Immediately following her "walk to nowhere" with Eddie, Skylar left the grounds of Harmony House. She explained to Stephen Millard, the assistant she had inherited from her deceased predecessor the week prior, that she had a meeting outside the office but would be back later that afternoon. He promised to hold down the fort, then watched her pull out of the parking lot in her Accord. Stephen took out the new phone he had recently received and pressed the speed-dial button for the only number he was ever to call with that device.

Bob Stenson answered with a single word. "What?"

"Dr. Drummond just left Harmony House grounds for an outside appointment. She said she will return this afternoon."

"That is unlikely." Stenson hung up.

CHAPTER 5

Residential Wing

Harmony House

June 1, 12:41 p.m.

Before Skylar had entered Eddie's life, Nurse Gloria had been the only person who'd ever been able to effectively calm him down when he reached a certain point. She had a soothing, nurturing manner—but mostly it was her motherly voice, which explained why Eddie responded so readily to her. It really didn't matter what she said. Her tone was a tonic for Eddie and had been from the first day she started working here, and he preferred her to every other nurse in the facility.

"We're talking about something that doesn't belong in my room!" he screamed. They paused outside his door. He balled his hands into fists, preparing to let loose on himself. He was hyperventilating. His hands were shaking. This was a level of fear he had never known inside these walls, which had been his home for the last sixteen years, one month, and eighteen days. Harmony House was his sanctuary. The world outside this government-run facility made him feel unsafe—especially since his recent adventures in New York and Philadelphia—but Eddie had never felt that way inside these confines. Not until now. And it was terrifying.

Nurse Gloria put her hands on his shoulders. He flinched slightly at the physical contact but did not move away from her. There was only one other person he felt comfortable enough with to let them touch him, but Skylar wasn't here. "You know all I want to do is help you, right?"

He nodded. His voice quieted. "I don't want it in there. I want it out of my room."

"Eddie, whatever it is, I'm going to take care of it. I promise." She was searching his face, hoping to further reassure him, when she felt the phone in her pocket buzz. Not her regular phone. Her special one. It was the newest iteration of the device she'd been given twelve years ago, when she started working for the people whose names she didn't know. The ones she reported to by text on a nightly basis, giving them a status report on the development of Eddie's echo box.

This was the first time they had ever initiated contact with her. Even more unusual, it wasn't just a text. They were calling her, whoever "they" were. Nurse Gloria answered her phone with trepidation. "Hello."

The voice on the phone spoke clearly and succinctly. "Do not enter Edward Parks's room."

"Excuse me?" She seemed to think her ears had betrayed her.

"Do not enter the patient's room under any circumstances. Is that clear?"

Gloria looked stunned. She glanced around her, looking for the security cameras that she assumed must be staring down at her. But if there were any, she couldn't see them. What she could see was Yancy Packard, the new head of Harmony House security, standing at the end of the hall. *My God, he works for them, too.* The look on his face told her so. "Yes, it's clear."

"Go about your regular duties," the voice on the phone said. The instructions weren't exactly barked but might as well have been. The caller hung up.

Nurse Gloria took a deep breath. "Eddie, I'm sorry, but there's something urgent I have to attend to."

He made his BUZZER sound. "Not true." His skill as a walking lie detector remained as sharp as always. The government had yet to test anyone more accurate. As far as Eddie knew, this was the first lie she had ever told him. "Nurse Gloria, why did you just lie?"

Tears welled up in her eyes. She looked genuinely pained, like this was a moment she would never forgive herself for, and hung her head in shame. "I'm sorry, Eddie, but I have to go." She started to walk away.

Watching her hasty exit, Eddie called after her, "Nurse Gloria, why are you sorry?" But she raced around the corner without answering. Eddie turned toward the new head of security standing at the end of the hall. "Will you get it out of my room?"

Yancy Packard did not respond.

"When somebody asks you a question, it is impolite not to answer. Dr. Fenton told me that several times. Did you know him?"

Packard still said nothing. His face remained expressionless. Eddie had observed the man having several conversations with other personnel earlier in the week, leading Eddie to believe there was nothing wrong with the man's hearing. Or perhaps he required hearing aids that he had forgotten to wear this morning, or they had broken or been misplaced, which would explain why the man was not responding to him now. That meant Eddie was going to have to walk down the hall to get directly in front of the man so he could read Eddie's lips. But the thought of standing so close to anyone made him uncomfortable. Eddie's right hand twitched.

He turned back to look inside his room. He reached a decision. After the recent events he had managed to survive, on his adventure beyond the perimeter of Harmony House, he decided this was something he could take care of himself. He marched inside his room with all the courage he could muster and surveyed his possessions. Everything was in its place. Except the one thing that didn't belong in his room, which must have been brought in while he was at lunch after his walk to nowhere with Skylar. He stared with alarm at the thing.

It was another laptop, a second one, sitting on his desk next to his own. The computer was open and turned on. Eddie inspected it closely without touching it, almost like he was afraid to. Like it might have been a bomb. Or coated with neurotoxin. But the technology of the machine was first-rate. The screen appeared to be 4K Ultra HD, because the resolution was superb. The machine's built-in camera glowed red, which meant it was on.

Somebody was watching him.

On the laptop screen he could see a blank wall in a nondescript room. There was nothing remarkable about it. The wall was painted a muted yellow. A faint, muffled voice could be heard in the background, but the voice could not be identified, not even by Eddie.

He leaned in to the screen. "Hello?" There was no answer, so he asked again, "Hello? Is anybody there?"

CHAPTER 6

AMERICAN HERITAGE FOUNDATION

ALEXANDRIA, VIRGINIA

June 1, 12:46 p.m.

Bob Stenson was only the third director in the forty-three-year history of the American Heritage Foundation. Founded in 1975 by like-minded operatives from several different United States intelligence agencies after the debacles that resulted in the Church and Pike Committees, this organization quietly thought of itself as the savior of the Great American Experiment. Its members were the ones pulling the strings and shifting the tides that kept the United States from going astray or collapsing upon itself. And no one outside of a select few even knew they existed, which was perhaps their greatest trick of all in today's hyperconnected world.

They seemed to know everything, but no one knew a thing about them. They were invisible, an unseen hand in so many events over the last four decades that had shaped American policy, steered judicial rulings, and directed military funding. Their record was unparalleled in getting their chosen candidates elected. The AHF was thirty-seven and zero. Not one of the candidates they had supported had lost. That was because they were incredibly selective. They were also extremely careful in how they conducted their business. They were methodical, rational, and utterly ruthless. They worked only with people they had known for years and vetted from a variety of sources. There were never any direct ties to them, so in the rare instances when things went sideways, such as during last week's events involving the pursuit of Edward Parks and his echo box, nothing could be traced back to them.

The debacle was only a minor blip in Stenson's long and distinguished career, and it was a stumble that he was in the process of correcting. The incoming call from a particular independent contractor confirmed it. The GPS transmitter in the man's phone allowed the AHF director to see his current location, a block east of Rittenhouse Square in Philadelphia. The building was one of many owned by the foundation in various major cities around the United States. In fact, the last time Stenson checked, the value of their real estate holdings exceeded $720 million. They used the buildings for a variety of purposes, including "pop-up" offices like the real estate branch they had formed to ensnare Dr. Skylar Drummond.

Stenson answered his phone. "Yes?"

Jared, whose real name was Tristan Barlow, replied, "Audience has been seated. Waiting for the show to begin."

Stenson turned to one of the computer monitors on his desk, which featured a split screen. On one side, Eddie Parks's room in Harmony House was visible. It was currently vacant. It had only been a few minutes since Stenson had ordered Nurse Gloria not to enter Eddie's room. On the other side of the screen, he saw Dr. Skylar Drummond. She was slumped in the chair, bound and unconscious. "Yes, I see."

"How long until we connect with the other party?"

Stenson glanced at his watch. "Not long."

CHAPTER 7

Eddie's Room

Harmony House

June 1, 12:48 p.m.

A man wearing an Albert Einstein mask appeared on the screen of the unfamiliar laptop. He sat down in front of the camera. There must have been a chair just below the frame. The rubber mask concealed his identity. "Hello, Edward."

Eddie's concerns about the device appeared to be confirmed. "You're not the real Albert Einstein. I know because he is dead."

"No, I'm not." He sounded like he was in his fifties and from the Midwest. Eddie guessed northern Ohio but would need to hear him talk more before he could narrow it down further.

Eddie stared at the man in the mask who had appeared on the unfamiliar laptop. "How do you know my name?"

"I know a great deal about you. Including that you reverted your recording device to a nonworking state after using it to hear your mother's voice."

Eddie required a moment to process the information. "The echo box is not a recording device."

"Call it whatever you want."

"The echo box is a device for reconstructing sound waves."

"Goody for you."

Eddie started to feel uncomfortable. And when he felt uncomfortable, that was never good. His hands clenched tightly. "If you know a great deal about me, you should know that I don't like to be called Edward."

"I don't care what you like to be called." His voice was cold and emotionless.

The hair on Eddie's arms stood up. His face became flushed. His body was responding to what his head could not yet process. "This computer is not supposed to be in my room. I don't want it here."

"That's too bad."

Eddie paused, struggling with what to say next. "Why did you put it here?"

"I didn't." Surprisingly, the man behind the mask was telling the truth. "One of my associates did."

CLICK-CLICK. Eddie heard the door to his room being locked from the outside.

Eddie walked over to it, confirming that the door would indeed not open. He was locked inside, which to his knowledge had never occurred in all his years at Harmony House. He had not even known that the door could be locked, because from the inside, it could not.

He BANGED on the door in desperation. "Help! Somebody help! Let me out!"

The man on the computer screen showed no reaction to his pleas. "Yelling won't do you any good, Edward. No one can hear you. Your acoustic tiles make sure of that."

Eddie glanced around the room at the 335 custom-designed tiles he'd had installed on the walls and ceiling when he first moved in, to reduce the echoes produced in the space. This was the first time he could remember wishing he had never installed them. Eddie returned to the laptop. "How do you know about my acoustic tiles?"

The man in the mask answered coldly. "I already told you, I know a great deal about you."

"Why did one of your associates put this computer in here?"

"So you and I could talk."

"I don't want to talk to you. You are a stranger, and I do not talk to strangers." He grabbed the laptop screen, about to close it and end the conversation.

The man in the mask responded quickly. "Before you do that, there's something I want to show you."

"What is it?" Eddie let go of the laptop.

"I will ask you just one time to return the echo box to its fully functional condition."

"I'm still waiting for Skylar to give me her answer about whether I have to. It has not been forty-eight hours yet. I cannot give you an answer until I receive her response."

"I think you will change your mind."

On the laptop screen, the view panned away from the man in the mask to someone else sitting in the room. She was bound and gagged and utterly terrified.

((•))

Eddie screamed at the top of his lungs. "Skylar! Are you okay?! Why are you tied up like that? Where are you?"

It was clear that she could see and hear him, because she reacted to every word. Skylar looked directly into the camera, making it appear like she was staring at Eddie. She desperately tried to communicate something to him, but whatever she said was unintelligible.

On the laptop screen, the man in the mask stepped behind Skylar and grabbed her by the hair. His voice remained perfectly calm. "Edward, I am going to torture her unless you fix your echo box."

"Stop it! You're scaring her!"

The man's voice didn't waver. He sounded like an elementary school teacher standing in front of a class. "It's up to you, Edward. Only you can stop it. You either get your machine to work properly or your doctor will suffer more pain than she has ever experienced, and you will have a front-row seat."

"I don't want a front-row seat!" Eddie pressed his fists to his head, which felt like it was going to explode.

The man in the Einstein mask revealed a knife—it looked to be nine inches long and serrated. The carbon steel glinted in the harsh light pointed at Skylar.

Eddie spoke with all the authority he could muster. "Put that knife down. Don't you know that knives are dangerous?"

"Yes, I do." The man in the mask dragged the blade across Skylar's neck, drawing a small amount of blood. Her face contorted as she screamed in pain through her gag.

"Stop it! You're hurting her!"

The man answered with a discomforting calm. "Yes, I am. And I will continue hurting her unless you fix your box, Edward."

"Stop it! Stop it! Stop it!" Eddie cried as he started hitting himself repeatedly. His fist was closed, making the blows more like punches than slaps. There was a vengeance to the self-mutilation because of the intensity of what he was witnessing. A clinical psychologist would have said that he blamed himself for what was happening to Skylar. Unconsciously, he was intent on experiencing at least as much pain as she was.

And there was no one there to stop him.

Skylar screamed in muted desperation. Tears streamed down her face as her cheeks turned bright red. Her expression made it clear that watching Eddie suffer was worse for her than anything that could be done to her.

Her captor, on the other hand, appeared to have a different reaction. He did not look away or blink. He leaned in closer to the monitor he was watching to get a better look at Eddie's self-inflicted brutality. This screen also contained a camera, so his moving closer gave anyone observing him a close-up view of his reaction. While his Einstein mask concealed most of his face, Tristan's eyes and a portion of his mouth could be seen through the openings in the molded rubber. He was smiling ever so slightly. He was enjoying the show and seemed to hope it wouldn't end anytime soon.

The same could not be said, however, for some of the other parties watching the proceedings.

CHAPTER 8

LIEUTENANTS' SHARED OFFICE

AMERICAN HERITAGE FOUNDATION

June 1, 12:51 p.m.

One hundred and thirty-nine miles away, just outside Alexandria, Virginia, in an office park unremarkable except for the incredible array of sophisticated antennae perched atop one of the buildings, three subordinates of Bob Stenson watched their own monitors inside the American Heritage Foundation offices. They were watching both sides of the conversation in split screen, just like their boss was. After all, it was the AHF who had hired the man to hold Skylar hostage.

Tristan Barlow was an independent contractor they used only for "special assignments" like this. "Special assignment" sounded so much better than kidnapping and torture, which were this man's specialties. He had received his training from the Central Intelligence Agency and had performed this type of duty at various black sites around the world, more times than he could count—including carrying out a majority of the 183 waterboardings of Khalid Sheikh Mohammed, who eventually confessed to masterminding the September 11 attack on the United States.

Of the three AHF employees observing the proceedings, Daryl Trotter, the true genius among the trio, remained the most dispassionate. He could have been watching a chess match—that was his game of choice prior to joining the foundation—for all his face revealed. He was making hash marks with his pencil in the margin of a notepad each time Eddie hit himself. There were currently thirty-seven marks in the margin.

Jason Greers, the heir apparent to one day take Bob Stenson's place and run the AHF, gritted his teeth. He was made uncomfortable by the proceedings but seemed to be trying hard not to show it.

Caitlin McCloskey—the legacy, whose father was one of the original founders—was visibly upset. As the only female among them, she often tried to conceal reactions that might be viewed as too emotional by her male counterparts. However, this time, it was obvious she felt that they had crossed the line and that an emotional response was warranted. "This is wrong."

Greers retorted abruptly, "So this is wrong, but the contract killers you hired last week were right?"

"We've never done anything remotely like this to an innocent."

"Edward Parks is not an innocent."

"What the hell is wrong with you? Look at him." She pointed angrily to Eddie on-screen. Trotter's hash marks were now up to sixty-one. Eddie's cheek was bleeding. His scars were going to have scars.

"His technology is the single most important advancement in intelligence in over fifty years, possibly ever. Whatever his personal limitations are, he is not an innocent."

She stared at him defiantly. "You can't possibly believe that."

It was clear that he didn't, but also that he wasn't about to relent. "What would you have us do? We tried a more politically correct way. Look where it got us."

"There are more than two choices." She said it sharply, her anger now clearly coming through.

Trotter had grown tired of the conversation. "That's true. There are. But it's not me you need to convince."

He was right. If she had been seeking consensus, or moral support of any kind, she didn't get it. Clearly, Caitlin was on her own, and she considered what she was about to do. On any number of occasions she had questioned Bob Stenson, the foundation's director, *before* a certain course of action was taken by an AHF team or one of its subcontractors—but this would be the first time she had ever asked about an action already undertaken. It would come off either as second-guessing or like she hadn't thought the plan all the way through. Neither was good. And if she wasn't very careful, it could sound insubordinate. Or even worse, like she was losing her stomach for this line of work.

All of which meant that she should just keep her damn mouth shut. She knew it. Almost spoke the words out loud. The problem was, she kept thinking of her father, Lawrence Walters, and his private instructions to her upon being hired. These included a famous quote from Winston Churchill, from a speech he gave long before he became prime minister of England.

In 1906, he held the title of undersecretary of state for the colonies, making him responsible for the treatment of the British South African colonies after the Boer War. The thirty-two-year-old Churchill declared, "Where there is great power, there is great responsibility." Lawrence emphasized to his daughter that Churchill didn't become Churchill by being elected prime minister; he became prime minister because he already was Churchill.

Caitlin took a deep breath, knowing what she had to do. Alone, she marched down the hall to the office of her superior, Bob Stenson. His door was open. As she knocked lightly, she could see the director was also watching Eddie Parks exhaustively self-mutilate. Of course he was.

From his expression, Stenson looked like he could have been watching bowling. "Yes?"

"Do you have a moment?"

"I do." He did not appear surprised by her visit. He almost seemed to be expecting it; he waved her in to join him watching the drama play out on the split screen. Stenson never took his eyes off the monitor, apparently not wanting to miss a single moment.

CHAPTER 9

Harmony House

Woodbury, New Jersey

June 1, 12:57 p.m.

Still locked in his room, Eddie Parks finally stopped hitting himself. He was brutalized. There was blood on his face and hands. It was also smeared on his clothing. On his Batman bedsheet. On the floor. He looked helpless, like a wounded animal. Only it was hard to imagine a wounded animal self-mutilating to this extent.

On the laptop screen, Skylar Drummond's eyes bulged as she watched him from her Philadelphia location. She breathed hard through the cloth stuffed into her mouth, apparently trying every way she could to communicate with Eddie. Small streaks of blood trickled down her neck onto her shirt collar from where she had been cut as a demonstration. Her bloodshot eyes were wet from crying, as were her cheeks.

Eddie spoke weakly, almost inaudibly. "Okay."

On-screen, the man in the Einstein mask nodded ever so slightly. "Okay, what?" he asked pleasantly.

"Okay, I will fix the echo box."

Skylar screamed as loud as she could into her gag, which didn't produce much audible sound, but did turn her face a deeper shade of red.

Ignoring her, Tristan cupped his hands to his ears and addressed Eddie. "I'm sorry, I couldn't hear you. What was that?"

Eddie took a long, defeated breath. "I am sorry they are hurting you, Skylar. It's my fault. But now I am going to make them stop."

Skylar vigorously shook her head no. It was hard to tell if she didn't want Eddie to feel responsible for the predicament she was in, or if she didn't want him to do what they were asking of him. Either way, it didn't matter, because Eddie could no longer bear to even glance at her. He looked everywhere but at the laptop screen.

He spoke to the man in the mask, enunciating as clearly as he could. "I said, I will return the echo box to working condition."

Tristan nodded, now speaking as if to an old friend. "Good. I'm glad to hear that. How much time do you think you will need?"

Eddie caught his breath. "Approximately two hours."

Skylar again screamed as loudly as she could. It was now clear that she didn't want him to fix the box. Tristan glanced over toward her with annoyance. SLAP! He smacked her hard across the face with the back of his hand. If she hadn't been tied to her chair, she would have been knocked off it.

"Stop it!" Eddie pleaded.

Tristan paused, speaking coldly from behind his mask. "Fix your box, or I will do much, much worse."

((•))

Inside Bob Stenson's office, Caitlin couldn't watch any more. She turned away from the screens, finding it increasingly difficult to hide her emotions.

Stenson never looked away from the monitors as he turned down the volume. "You seem upset."

She thought she was presenting a better poker face. "I'm more concerned than upset."

Stenson studied her. "You are your father's daughter, aren't you?"

She couldn't tell if he meant it as a compliment or not. "Sir, with all due respect, he would never have sanctioned this."

"You'd be surprised at some of the operations he authorized." Stenson smirked knowingly.

Caitlin now realized that her father may have been trying to help her learn from his mistakes. *After all, if power corrupts, absolute power corrupts absolutely.* "There are other ways we could have convinced Edward Parks to repair his device."

"He prefers to be called Eddie." He smiled briefly at his own joke. "Of course there are other ways. But none are as expedient. After last week's debacle, I am not about to allow any further public exposure of the device or ourselves."

She exhaled deeply, signaling her resignation. "Eddie Parks is an innocent." Meaning "out of bounds." Not part of the game. An element of unspoken American Heritage doctrine her father had taught her was that they treat innocents differently. There are players in the game, there are spectators watching from the sidelines, and there are those who are unaware that a game is even being played. Those are the innocents, and they deserve gentler treatment than those involved in the game. Caitlin could justify playing rough with participants, or even with those observing from a distance, but never with those who didn't have a clue.

"What you don't seem to recognize is that Eddie Parks is terminal." He said it like an oncologist reviewing a biopsy. "Once we are in possession of the device, he is far too great a liability, innocent or otherwise."

Although barely able to breathe, Caitlin nodded with understanding. Not about Stenson's reasoning, but about what she needed to do. It was Stenson's last phrase that did it. *Innocent or otherwise.* He had admitted that Eddie was an innocent but they were doing this to him anyway. And worse, they were going to kill him as soon as he had repaired his precious device and outlived his usefulness.

She looked at the floor, shaking her head, as if coming to terms with the truth of the situation. "Every now and then, this is a very ugly business we are in."

"Just be thankful it doesn't happen more often."

"Indeed," she said, looking at him. She needed him to think she understood, which couldn't have been further from the truth.

Stenson clasped his hands across his knee as if preparing to offer some fatherly advice. "In ten or twenty years, do you honestly think you'll remember this moment? Or even this day? No, you won't. What you will remember is the incredible advantage Eddie's box gave us, and all the good we accomplished because of it. Caitlin, there is nothing we won't be able to know, and no one will have any idea how we got our information." He paused for emphasis and spoke with absolute certainty. "Whatever it is you are feeling now, trust me, in due time, you will get over it."

She nodded again convincingly, though she had just one overriding thought: this was wrong. Very, very wrong. But she was also now beginning to doubt her objectivity, which was exactly what Stenson had wanted. She recognized the possibility that she had, indeed, lost her stomach for this—but she couldn't be sure. She needed some perspective.

And there was only one way she was going to get clarity.

CHAPTER 10

Seminary Road

Alexandria, Virginia

June 1, 1:03 p.m.

Caitlin declined Stenson's offer to join him for lunch, claiming she had already committed to plans with her father. What made this such a perfect excuse was that she was overdue for her weekly visit to his nursing home, and Stenson revered him almost as much as she did. After all, her father had hired and trained him. Stenson visited him several times a year just to pay his respects, and he asked her to give him his best, which she promised to do.

She drove her 2014 Subaru Forester south along Seminary Road, which became Janneys Lane south of Interstate 395. She had NPR on the radio as she absentmindedly picked up her cell phone. Just before dialing, she stopped herself, realizing what a colossal blunder she was about to make.

Putting the phone down, she reached into her center console without taking her eyes off the road. She fished around for something at the bottom of it. When she finally reached the desired item, she pulled out a prepaid cell phone still in its original plastic case. She had purchased the phone in cash for ten dollars at Walmart several months ago, when something told her that such a device might one day come in handy.

That day had come.

She used her teeth to rip open the plastic case and turned on the phone, or tried to. Whatever charge the phone had been packaged with had dissipated in the intervening months. Fortunately, she had also purchased a charging cable, which she plugged into a USB outlet next to her. The phone powered right up. After waiting for the device to get a signal, she dialed a number she had committed to memory one week earlier.

((•))

Detective Butler McHenry had just arrived at the Ridgewood YMCA for a good hard workout. Having been placed on temporary leave from the NYPD for his recent involvement with federal fugitives, he now had lots of time to pump iron. And he was certainly taking advantage of it.

Once upon a time, Butler had been in wicked shape. Five hundred sit-ups per day was just his starting point. He could whip off twenty-five pull-ups before breaking a sweat. The military had a way of sculpting even the most unwilling of physiques into biological machines capable of feats of strength and endurance most people could only dream of. This was particularly true of the covert-operations branches that cherry-picked only the finest specimens from the rest of the services. And they had cherry-picked Butler.

It was his fourth day in a row here. His body hurt in a variety of places, especially his joints, but it was a good kind of pain. At least, that's what he'd been telling himself. *Pain is good. Pain is good.* He had chosen this gym because it was not a place where people went to exercise in nice outfits and to be seen looking glamorous doing so. This was where they went in stained gym clothes to push tons of iron and sweat their asses off.

It could have been located on a military base.

Which was why he looked so annoyed when his phone rang. It was not a number he recognized, but that wasn't unusual. Privately, he was hoping the call was from somebody on the departmental review board saying they'd made a big mistake; that this was all one giant misunderstanding and that he was being reinstated immediately. "This is McHenry."

"Detective McHenry, someone you know is in grave danger."

This was the last thing he was expecting to hear. "Who is this?"

"I can't give you my real name."

"Why not?" He didn't intend to sound demeaning, but he'd gotten so many crazy calls over the years that he did it subconsciously.

"I'll get to that. Please, you've got to listen to me."

"Well, I need to call you something."

"Then call me Eleanor."

"Why Eleanor?"

"Because Eleanor Roosevelt is one of my heroes."

The caller might be crazy, but at least she was educated. "Okay, Eleanor, how about we start with you telling me how you got this number."

"It doesn't matter how. What does matter is that Dr. Skylar Drummond is in terrible danger, and you're the only one who can help her."

She now had his complete attention. The entertainment portion of the conversation was over. "Look, I'd like to help you, but I'm currently on suspension. You should call the police."

"If you don't help her, she will be dead by this evening."

Now he listened with laser focus. "What's this all about?"

"The echo box."

McHenry stopped cold. He no longer thought she was crazy. He was also certain that he would no longer be getting in his workout, so he picked up his gym bag and walked out the door. "What do you know about the echo box?"

"I know that Eddie Parks played it for you. I know that you understand its potential."

The detective couldn't believe what he was hearing. "Who told you this?"

She ignored him, continuing, "But what you don't know is that Parks disabled the machine so that it no longer works, because he became afraid of what people might do with it. This upset some very powerful people who are willing to do anything to get their hands on the technology. Including kidnapping and torturing Skylar Drummond unless Eddie gets his machine to work."

Frustration crept into Butler's voice. "Tell me how you know all this."

There was a pause on the line. "My employer hired the man who is torturing her."

McHenry shook his head. This was too much. All he wanted to do was get his job back. He had left the world of shadows and secrets a long time ago, and for good reason. It was too convoluted. There were too many agendas and too many conflicting interests to know if he was even on the right side. He had moved on to the simpler life of a being a cop—where there were still good guys and bad guys, at least on most days. "I still don't know what you think I can do. You should really call the police, or one of the federal agencies."

She exploded. "Detective, stop playing games with me! I've read your military files, including the parts that were supposed to be redacted. You were an Army Ranger from '98 to 2004. During that time, you were involved in seventeen covert ops, including missions in Baghdad, Panama, Ukraine, and Mexico City. You are credited with fourteen official kills. I need your skill set, and I need it now. Please cut the bullshit."

Every hair on Butler McHenry's body was standing up. His blood ran cold. He was utterly dumbfounded, because the details mentioned by the caller were accurate. "No one is supposed to have access to any of that information."

"You want to know how I have access? There was no way you could have known this at the time, but on most of those ops, you were working for us."

McHenry felt a wave of nausea come over him, as questions long ago buried were suddenly brought back to life. *Does this mission make sense to anyone? Isn't this illegal? What the hell have we gotten ourselves into?* He paused to collect himself. "Who in God's name do you work for?"

"All I can tell you is that we're not military. We're not intelligence, or any other part of the government, but we have access to everything, and sometimes even more than official channels do. Which is why you must believe me. If I contact any federal agency, Skylar Drummond will be dead within the hour. And if you don't help her, she won't live through the day. Am I being clear enough for you?"

He considered the risk the caller was taking. No wonder she wouldn't identify herself. "Tell me you're calling from a burner." He didn't want any trails leading back to him.

"This isn't my first rodeo, Detective."

Butler paused. "If you work for these people, why are you telling me any of this?"

"Because a long time ago, I made a promise to someone I care about. If things got out of hand, I would do something about it."

All McHenry could think was: Eleanor Roosevelt would have done that. *Shit!* He paused, staring at the cement, frustrated by what he was about to ask. "Where do I find Skylar Drummond?"

CHAPTER 11

Harmony House

Woodbury, New Jersey

June 1, 1:19 p.m.

Eddie's fingers were a blur above the keyboard of his laptop supercomputer, which was connected to the echo box. Some of the keys were streaked with blood, which had also dried on his hands. Eddie didn't seem to notice. He was "gone," as various members of the Harmony House nursing staff used to say. So focused, he appeared to be in a trance, which was why he didn't hear the question the first time it was asked.

From the other laptop, the man wearing the Einstein mask repeated his question. "What are you, deaf? I said: How much longer?"

Eddie finally came out of the trance but didn't look away from his computer. "No, I am not deaf. I could not hear you if I was deaf. Most people say I have an unusually acute sense of hearing. Like the golden ears of William Tuthill."

"Who the hell is William Tuthill?"

"He was the architect who designed Carnegie Hall."

"Well, Tuthill can kiss my ass."

Eddie looked up, clearly confused. "Why?"

Tristan shook his head in disbelief. "Are you trying to piss me off?"

"No, I'm not trying to piss you off. I don't understand expressions, and that is one I've heard on many occasions and it has confused me every time, including this one." He kept his eyes focused on the revised computer code in front of him.

Tristan stepped behind Skylar, putting his blade to her right ear. The terror in her face heightened as he said, "Ask me why again and your doctor will lose the ability to hear in stereo." He said it like this was something he'd done before.

Eddie grimaced, closing his eyes. "I will try extra hard not to do that. Please don't hurt her. Please don't hurt her." He repeated his desperate pleas several more times.

The masked man lowered his knife. "How. Much. Longer?"

Eddie's fingers resumed flying across the keyboard. "I cannot give you an exact answer."

"Approximate."

Eddie thought carefully. "Thirty-seven minutes. But if you keep interrupting me, it will take longer because I lose my concentration."

Tristan shook his head. "Hurry up, or your doctor may lose her hearing completely." He caressed both of Skylar's ears gently. She was clearly repulsed and frightened but seemed determined not to show it. Not to her captor, and especially not to Eddie as the camera zoomed in on her face. She stared directly into the lens to make Eddie think she was looking at him. Her eyes were still bloodshot, but they were now steeled with purpose. She had not given up, and she wanted Eddie to know it.

Eddie glanced at her, seeming empowered simply by being able to see her. When he turned back to his laptop, he moved with renewed determination. Skylar smiled ever so slightly.

CHAPTER 12

Kelman Nursing and Rehab Center

Alexandria, Virginia

June 1, 1:37 p.m.

Caitlin drove up the facility's driveway faster than usual. Gravel sprayed as she skidded into a parking space next to an Oldsmobile Cutlass. The 130-bed skilled-nursing facility was built in the late sixties and was long overdue for a makeover, not that any of the residents would have noticed. The youngest was seventy-three. They all seemed to think the decor quite contemporary, which was why they had never complained, at least according to the home's chief operating officer at their last board meeting.

Caitlin removed the battery from her burner phone and pocketed it as she approached the Formica-covered front desk, where she was immediately recognized by the day-shift clerk, Quentin James. He had worked here longer than any other employee and knew more about each resident. He had his favorites, of course, and Caitlin's father happened to be one of them. "Your dad's in his room."

Caitlin nodded her appreciation. "How's he doing?"

"Same as always." It was the refrain Quentin gave to most relatives who asked about their loved ones in this facility. Because it was the truth. In the final phase of life, the only time things really changed was when the person died. "See if you can get him to eat some of his lunch."

"I'll do what I can," she answered, glancing over her shoulder as she continued down the hall. She walked past several other patient rooms and heard the familiar beeping of medical monitors as well as a few moans. Discomfort was part of everyday life here. Most of the residents were hard of hearing, so the sounds never bothered them—it only bothered their visitors. Perhaps that was why so many had poor impressions of the place. Well, that and somebody died here almost once a week.

Caitlin knocked on the door to her father's room, which was cracked open, but there was no answer. She wasn't expecting one, but she waited a moment anyway because it was the polite thing to do. "Dad?" Again, no answer. She opened the door slowly and entered to find him in his easy chair, staring out the window. This was how he spent most days lately, sitting quietly, looking at his view of the parking lot. His left hand quivered uncontrollably—one of the more obvious symptoms of his Parkinson's. She leaned down close to him to make sure he could hear her. "Hey, Dad, how are you?"

Lawrence looked up at her and smiled sweetly. "I'm doing just fine. How are you?" His cadence was slow and methodical, giving him time to find the right words.

She pointed to the untouched meal tray next to him. "Aren't you hungry?"

"For edible food, yes. Not for that. Have you seen what they consider egg salad?"

She picked up his sandwich and cringed. She couldn't blame him for not eating it. "If I give you some contraband, would you promise to keep it our secret?" She reached into her purse and offered him a Milky Way bar.

He gladly took it. "Milky Way's my favorite. How'd you know?"

She studied his face, fixing hair that had fallen over his eyes. She had given him a candy bar every time she visited—at least once a week for the last three years. "You don't know who I am, do you?"

"I most certainly do," he answered indignantly.

She smiled lovingly. "Okay. What's my name?"

He paused, trying to remember. "It's right on the tip of my tongue. I promise you. Raquel?"

"It's Caitlin."

"Right, Caitlin. Of course. I was going to say Chloe, but I knew that wasn't right." He took a bite of chocolate, relishing the taste. Of his many bodily functions that no longer worked completely or at all, taste was not one. While he no longer craved a great many things, like the glass of Louis Royer XO cognac he used to enjoy while puffing on a Cohiba Siglo, he clearly still loved the taste of this candy bar.

She kneeled right in front of him so he could get a good look at her. "And how do you know me?"

Lawrence studied her closely. "You look very familiar. We've known each other a long time, haven't we?"

She nodded. "My entire life."

"I knew your mother, didn't I?"

Caitlin chortled. "I'd hope so. You were married to her for forty-seven years."

"I was? That means . . ." But he still couldn't quite connect the dots.

"I'm your daughter, Dad. Caitlin."

"Right, of course. Caitlin, so nice of you to visit." He reached up and hugged her warmly. "Is mother coming?"

"No, Dad. Mom died four years ago."

He nodded, clearly trying to make sense of it all. "Is that why I'm in this godforsaken place?"

She smiled sweetly. "Well, that, and you have Parkinson's."

He spoke thoughtfully. "Don't get it, this Parkinson's. It'll kick your ass."

She took his shaking hand and held it lovingly as he continued eating the chocolate bar. "Dad, there's something I need you to try and remember for me. Do you think you can do that?"

Lawrence nodded again and took another bite of candy bar. "I can try."

"Do you remember what you told me when I started working at the foundation?"

"Which foundation is that, dear?"

"The American Heritage Foundation. The one you started."

"I did? Sounds impressive." He sat a little more upright.

"It was. And still is. But you told me that if I ever felt those you had left in charge let the power corrupt them, I was to inform you immediately."

"Do you know why I said that?"

She shook her head, realizing this was pointless. It was a mistake to have even asked. "I wish I did. You clearly had a plan, but you never told me what it was. All I knew was that I should come to you, but I guess it's too late."

There was a long, uncomfortable pause. Lawrence's hand shook even more severely. He started to look frustrated. "I'm sorry to disappoint you, Caitlin. I wish I could remember. I really do."

She felt bad, putting pressure on him like this. "I know, Dad. Don't worry. I didn't mean to upset you. I can come up with my own Alpha Reset Protocol."

He immediately let go of her hand, looking at her curiously. "What did you say?"

"Never mind. I shouldn't have—"

He interrupted her with a sudden intensity that hinted at the man's former character. "What did you say?"

His ferocity didn't scare her. In fact, she found it comforting to be reminded of the man who had raised her. "You called it the Alpha Reset Protocol. That's all I ever knew."

He turned toward the window, nodding almost imperceptibly. It was hard to tell if he'd just drifted off or might be remembering something. He repeated the words slowly and methodically. "Alpha Reset Protocol."

A glimmer of hope flashed across Caitlin's face. "Does that phrase mean something to you, Dad? Anything? If there's anything at all you can remember, it would be a great help."

He tried to answer but had difficulty forming the words. All he could get out was "I . . . can't . . ." He struggled to raise his hand, as if to make a point, but it was shaking terribly.

"Dad, it's okay." She knew his infirmity embarrassed him. After all, the man had once wielded nearly unimaginable power. He usually tried to avoid the movements that made his weakened physical condition so apparent. She placed her hand on his to help him lower it.

"Stop." He gave the command with absolute authority. She was taken aback by the edge in his voice and watched him slowly reach inside the collar of his shirt. It was not clear what he was trying to do until he revealed a necklace he was wearing. On the end of the necklace was a key. It looked like the key to a safety-deposit box. With considerable effort, he pulled the necklace up over his head and handed it to Caitlin. "Alpha Reset Protocol."

She held the key tightly in her hand as she stared lovingly at what was left of the man who had been her role model. Her inspiration. And training instructor. She was among the very few who knew that he had been responsible for placing four United States presidents, five Supreme Court justices, and nineteen senators. It was a hell of a legacy, but one she intended to live up to.

Tears welled in her eyes as he stared back vacantly. She didn't know what the key meant but knew where to start. Caitlin now had the clarity she had come for. "I love you, Dad."

"I love you, too."

((•))

Caitlin left the nursing home but did not return to her Subaru Forester. She unlocked the car next to it, the Cutlass, and got inside. The car was still registered in her father's name, although she had paid the annual registration fee for it since his arrival at this facility. He didn't even know he still owned the car, or that it was parked anywhere near him. Every time she visited her father, Caitlin had taken the car for a spin around the neighborhood, gassing it up when necessary. She had always figured there was a strong likelihood that her Subaru had some kind of tracking device in it, and if she ever had to disappear, she would need an alternate vehicle.

The Cutlass was it. She put the key in the ignition, and the car started right up. She backed out of the parking space and pulled into the street, beginning a journey from which there was no returning. She had almost certainly seen her father for the last time.

Tears streamed down her face.

CHAPTER 13

Rittenhouse Square

Philadelphia, Pennsylvania

June 1, 2:22 p.m.

Butler McHenry parked his Chevy Tahoe in an alley several blocks away from Locust Street. The drive to Philadelphia had taken considerably less time than the usual hour and a half. But he had also never averaged ninety-three miles per hour on the route before. It had saved him a good twenty minutes. He paused before getting out of the car, making sure he really wanted to do this. It would place his entire fourteen-year career with the New York Police Department at risk. Hell, the truth was it could do a lot worse than that, but only if he was caught. He shook his head, realizing how much he was thinking like a criminal. No wonder so many crooks became cops, and vice versa.

He wasn't a religious man, but there had been moments in his life that made him believe there was something bigger going on that he would never understand. There was the sniper's bullet meant for him in Panama, which had missed killing him only because he had tripped over the decapitated body of a fallen comrade. There was the IED in Baghdad that should have blown up his entire team, but only threw off a few sparks because the would-be bomber hadn't wired the pressure-sensitive detonator properly. And then last week, he happened to be in the immediate vicinity of the Christopher Street/Sheridan Square subway station when Skylar Drummond's boyfriend, Jacob Hendrix, was thrown onto the train tracks in what was now believed to have been a murder and not a terrorist attack.

The question he often asked himself was *Why?* His friends in Alcoholics Anonymous often said that "coincidence" was merely a synonym for "God" with more syllables. While Butler might not go that far, it did seem that when he acted on what fell before him instead of fighting against it, things worked out for the better. Which was why he was here. His investigation into Jacob Hendrix's murder had led him to Skylar, who then brought her patient, Edward Parks, and his echo box, to Butler. Yes, he was currently on suspension for helping them, but he'd felt like it was something he was supposed to do. Something he had to do.

It was the same feeling he had now. And if there was one thing Butler McHenry was not, it was a coward. If he felt he had to do something, he did it.

He got out of his SUV and walked around to the back. Opening the hatch, he folded down the left rear seat and removed the plastic cupholders, revealing a hidden compartment that contained a weathered backpack. Among former military specialists, it was known as "a bad-day bag." Not unlike survivalists' bugout bags, it contained all the required essentials for when the shit hit the fan. But where a bugout bag held merely tools for survival, a bad-day bag included equipment for conducting an offensive.

Removing the backpack, he checked the contents. The first item was a United States Army–issued bulletproof vest. It hadn't been worn in almost fifteen years. The next two items were a generic black baseball cap and hoodie. Neither had a logo or any other writing on them. He put them on, along with the backpack, and started to walk the four blocks to the address the woman he knew only as Eleanor had given him.

He kept his head down, walking neither too fast nor too slow but at the pace of the other pedestrians, who all seemed to have pressing business of their own. As he spotted the address he'd been given, he could see a young woman through a plate-glass window packing up a coffee maker and other office items. The office had no signs in the windows, nor any other identifying features. If the temporary realty office was already being broken down, that meant Skylar might no longer be there. He could already be too late.

For all he knew, she was already dead.

Butler approached the office door, relieved to find it unlocked. He opened the door, startling the woman as she carried a cardboard box toward him. "Oh," he said, "I am so sorry. I didn't mean to startle you, but I think I may have the wrong address. Is this 1737 Locust Street?" He checked his pockets, as if looking for notes he could no longer locate.

She responded sharply. "No, this is 1731. This is a private office, and you are trespassing."

He looked around quickly, assessing the location. "Oh my goodness, well, don't I feel as dumb as a doorknob. If I could trouble you to point me in the right direction, I'll be leaving."

The woman pointed south, to the left. "Seventeen thirty-seven is that way." She reached into the cardboard box.

Butler shook his head. "Are you sure? I swear, I was just there and—" He never finished the statement because he slammed his elbow so hard into her temple that she lost consciousness immediately. He grabbed her and the cardboard box as she crumpled to the floor. Neither made a sound. As her hand fell from inside the box, her fingers still clenched a Ruger LC9 9 mm handgun. He no longer needed to wonder if he had made a terrible mistake. Butler quickly pried the weapon from her hand and checked the other contents of the box. Among the office supplies was a particular type of fighting knife called a SOG SEAL Pup fixed blade, which happened to be his favorite, so he kept it.

He checked out the windows to see if any passersby had caught the action, but there was no one in view. He removed his backpack and withdrew several items. The first were black leather driving gloves. They were worn from use, and not from driving. He put them on, then grabbed a couple of zip ties and used them to hog-tie the woman. Next was a Steyr M40-A1 handgun, which no longer had a serial number—it had been filed off when McHenry first prepared his bad-day bag. He'd known that if he ever needed to use this gun, he wouldn't want to leave a trace.

He checked the weapon's magazine. It contained twelve hollow points with the latest technology: OTF, or open-tip frangible, which created a wound channel five times the size of the bullet's diameter. It was damn lethal. He also grabbed two extra magazines from the backpack, which contained at least six more, and put them in his front pockets. If he lost the upcoming battle, it would not be due to lack of ammunition. He pocketed several other items and put the backpack on.

McHenry moved down the hallway, stepping carefully. The right side was an exterior brick wall that lacked any type of decoration. The left side was a series of offices. He paused outside the first one. The door was ajar. The room was vacant. As he continued down the hall, he heard two male voices coming from the next office. One sounded older and menacing. The other he recognized instantly. It was Eddie Parks.

At least for the moment, he was still alive.

CHAPTER 14

Harmony House

Woodbury, New Jersey

June 1, 2:58 p.m.

Locked inside his room, Eddie stared at the incredibly dense computer code that filled the screen of his laptop supercomputer. His fingers had stopped typing. The blood on the keys had dried and mostly flaked. His arms drooped at his sides. He was spent. "It's fixed."

The man in the Einstein mask, who appeared on the other computer screen, looked up from his iPhone, on which he was repeatedly swiping left. "Prove it."

Eddie took a deep breath. "How would you like me to prove it?"

"Play something that includes your doctor's voice."

"Which doctor?"

"Which one do you think?" he asked sharply.

"Skylar Drummond, who I am fairly certain is still sitting next to you even though I cannot see her," he said.

"You know, for a supposed genius, you're a real idiot."

Eddie turned to him defiantly. The mask allowed him to address the man directly. "I am on the autism spectrum, not an idiot. That is not a nice thing to say. Nice people don't say things like that. Has anyone ever told you that you are not a nice person?"

"Yes, they have. And you know what, Edward? They're right. And I will remind you how not nice I can be unless you prove to me your box is working right now." He held up his knife directly in front of the camera lens, which made it look even larger and more menacing.

Eddie immediately clicked "Initiate" on his screen. The echo box sprang open, and the eight incredibly sensitive microsatellites started performing their synchronized dance as they acoustically mapped the room, recording the decayed and barely perceptible energy waves that had once been audible sound waves, still bouncing around the room. A three-dimensional acoustical map appeared on his screen as a "percent complete" counter started climbing to one hundred. Eddie turned his laptop so the man in the Einstein mask could see the progress. It took forty-five seconds for the process to finish.

Eddie scrolled through the timeline, looking for a particular date and time, which he located in short order. He hit "Play." The only sounds were low-decibel HISSING and WARBLE.

Tristan shook his head. "I'm not impressed."

Eddie reacted defensively. "That is because you don't understand acoustic archeology or the basis for sound-wave retrieval."

"That may be. But what you need to understand is that I'm going to kill her if I don't hear her voice coming from that box of yours real soon."

Eddie was about to ask how long "real soon" was but realized that asking the question would only further delay him. He worked his laptop as fast as he could, running the reconstructed waves through a harmonic filter. "Now listen." The first voice to be heard was his own.

EDDIE: *Dr. Drummond, why are you just sitting there?*

Courtesy of the acoustic tiles Eddie had installed around his room, the reproduction of his voice was nearly perfect. It was astonishing.

SKYLAR: *I'm actually doing far more than just sitting here.*

EDDIE: *What else are you doing?*

SKYLAR: *For one thing, I am nonverbally communicating with you.*

((•))

Tristan was stunned, immediately recognizing Skylar's voice—as well as the problem the device posed for him. Every sadistic act, every bit of torture, every cruel and unusual punishment he had ever inflicted upon his victims could now be replayed. The notion was unsettling. There would be no more plausible deniability. For anyone.

The reconstruction of the previously unrecorded conversation continued.

EDDIE: *What are you communicating nonverbally?*

SKYLAR: *That I care about you and want you to know I'm here for you.*

Tristan said, "That's enough. Stop it."

Eddie did so, looking confused. "I did what you asked. Let Skylar go."

Tristan did not respond. He was distracted by a sound in the hallway. A creaking floorboard. He immediately thought how nice it was that these old Philadelphia office buildings always let you know when someone was coming. "Carla?" There was no response. The torturer quickly reached for something duct-taped beneath the table: a .357 Magnum. He clicked off the safety and aimed it toward the door.

Eddie stared angrily from the monitor. "We had an agreement, which is a type of promise. And a promise is a promise."

"Edward, shut up." Tristan kept his eyes trained on the door.

Eddie ignored his request. "You said it was up to me. And that was the truth, because I would have known if you were lying." Eddie continued speaking but could no longer be heard because Tristan had muted the volume on the laptop. He was focused on the creaking in the hallway, which was coming toward him. Whoever was in the hallway stopped moving just outside the door. Tristan positioned himself behind Skylar, dropping to one knee, using her body as a shield. To shoot him, the trespasser would have to shoot her first.

((•))

The door slammed open abruptly, but no one came through. There was an unexpected moment of silence, which both Tristan and Skylar knew wouldn't last long. Feeling his breath on the back of her neck as he aimed his weapon over her shoulder, Skylar leaned her head forward as if looking for something in her lap. She then snapped her head backward as hard as she could. *Crack!* The rubber Einstein mask gave him no protection whatsoever. The back of her head impacted Tristan's nose, breaking it instantly.

The pain momentarily blinded him. He couldn't see the stun grenade being rolled in through the door. The device was roughly the size of a can of beer and painted army green. *Delay: 0.5 seconds* was stenciled on its side. There were eight ten-millimeter holes drilled into it, through which an intense amount of sound and light was about to be released.

Skylar had seen enough television cop shows to know she should close her eyes as tightly as she could, but there was nothing that would protect her ears because her arms remained taped to the chair. The ammonium nitrate packed inside the canister ignited, producing a bang of 170 decibels. By comparison, listening to a jackhammer from a distance of one inch produced only 130 decibels. The bang immediately ruptured her tympanic membrane, which regulated balance. If she hadn't been bound to the chair, she would have fallen to the floor, just like Tristan did. For the moment, all she could hear was a constant ringing.

She was temporarily deaf.

The "flash" part of the device was caused by a subsonic deflagration of a magnesium-based pyrotechnic charge inside a thin aluminum case. It released a burst of light of over five million candela. The effect was temporarily blinding, eyes closed or not. Which meant Skylar neither saw nor heard what happened next.

((•))

Butler quickly stepped through the doorway, searching for his target in his gun sight. He first saw Skylar bound to the chair, looking terrified. Behind her, the kidnapper was writhing in pain on the floor. The man wearing a rubber Einstein mask clutched a Smith & Wesson, desperately trying to fire off a shot. Butler fired first. Twice, in fact. A double tap, hitting his target center mass like he'd been taught in Ranger School. *Just like riding a bike* was a refrain several of his former colleagues had repeated at their most recent reunion four years ago.

The ammunition performed exactly as promised in the manufacturer's promotional brochures. The bullets expanded immediately upon impact and exploded out Tristan's back. His heart and spinal cord were obliterated. Death was instantaneous.

Butler moved swiftly to Skylar. He took her hand in his and held it firmly. "It's over. You're okay." He knew she couldn't see or hear him, but it made him feel better saying it. She might not be able to recognize him, but at least she would know someone was there to help.

It was only now that Butler saw the video camera mounted on the tripod, its red light glowing. *We're being watched.* Someone had witnessed him kill the man in the mask. *Shit!* Butler had seen a video setup like this when he took part in a bust at a Brooklyn pornography studio early in his career with the NYPD, when he could still be shocked at the depravity some people engaged in.

He moved to the camera and disconnected it, then turned to the laptop on the table next to it, which seemed to show another location. It appeared to be an empty room. He returned to Skylar and used his newly acquired combat knife to cut through her restraints. She clung to him like a terrified child.

She sobbed uncontrollably as she pleaded, "Butler, tell me it's you!"

He took her hands and placed them on the sides of his face so that she could feel him nod. "It's me."

She breathed through her nose. "I've never been so glad to smell that lousy cologne you wear." Unable to hear herself, she spoke loudly. She then pointed blindly toward the laptop screen on the table. "Is Eddie okay? Can he hear me?"

Butler turned toward the laptop. All he could see on the screen was a vacant room. "Eddie, you there?" There was no response. The detective knew it would be several more minutes before Skylar could hear him, so he took her finger and drew large letters on his own chest: *N-O-T T-H-E-R-E.*

Skylar reacted with alarm. "Not there? What do you mean, not there?!"

CHAPTER 15

American Heritage Foundation

Alexandria, Virginia

June 1, 3:13 p.m.

Bob Stenson clasped his hands in front of him, with his elbows on his desk, and watched the proceedings. The moment Eddie began to play the echoes from inside his room, verifying the device's operational status, Stenson felt validated. Taking the gloves off was not a decision he'd made lightly. After all, he wasn't sadistic. He might employ contractors every now and then who were, but he himself was not. Vengeful, perhaps on occasion, but never without a genuine measure of control. Make no mistake, he had been terribly embarrassed after being outmaneuvered by a special-needs civilian who resided in an assisted-living facility, but that was not his primary motivation in ordering the kidnapping of Dr. Skylar Drummond. It was expediency. The action was merely a means to an end. And now that the objective had been achieved, Stenson sought to close the matter as quickly as possible. He wanted to move on to the bigger fish he intended to fry, and there were a lot of them.

First on the list was the biggest fish in the land.

He dialed the new head of Harmony House security, Yancy Packard. "Show's over. Bring Parks and the device here."

((•))

"Copy that." Packard was standing down the hall from Eddie's room as he hung up the phone. He glanced at a subordinate, C. J. Clementine, whom he had hired only days earlier. Clementine was fifteen years younger, five inches taller, and fifty pounds heavier, with considerably less body fat.

Packard had been his CO during his time in Delta Force, and Clementine jumped at the chance to continue reporting to him in the civilian world. The two men walked briskly down the hallway to Eddie's room, practically marching in step. Old habits, and all that. As Packard unlocked the patient's room, using a key that only he possessed, they heard the sound of gunfire from the second computer. If he didn't know better, he might have thought Eddie was watching a true-crime TV show.

Eddie paced around the room, pointing to the screen with alarm as they entered. Since he was no longer sitting directly in front of the laptop or its camera, he could not be seen by anyone watching. "Someone just shot fake Einstein!" Eddie exclaimed. "I think he's dead! I think he's dead!" Skylar remained on the screen, bound and gagged, but her captor was no longer visible.

"Pack up your things. We're leaving." Packard's voice was firm and left no room for equivocation.

Eddie stood his ground. "I am not going anywhere until Dr. Drummond is released. Fake Einstein promised me he would let her go, and a promise is a promise. Although I don't know if someone can be expected to keep a promise if he is now dead. My mother died giving birth to me, so she could not raise me. I do not think that was her fault. Is fake Einstein dead?"

Turning back to the second laptop, Eddie now recognized Butler, whose face was visible on-screen momentarily just before he disconnected the camera. "Detective McHenry, what are you doing there?"

Butler did not respond because he couldn't hear Eddie, due to Skylar's abductor having muted the volume on their end. Eddie turned to the two security guards who had entered his room. "That was Detective Butler McHenry. He got in trouble for helping me last week. I think he's going to be in even more trouble now."

Packard stepped right in front of Eddie and leaned down in his face. "Do I look like I care?"

Eddie stared at the man's polished shoes. "I am not very good at reading other people's expressions. Please tell me if you do care so I will know what your expression means the next time I see someone else make it."

Packard had already exceeded his patience threshold. "You will go anywhere I goddamn tell you to." He grabbed Eddie by the shoulders.

"Ow! Don't touch me!" Eddie jumped out of his chair, flinching at the physical contact. He backed away from Packard until he was against the window. "No, I won't go anywhere you goddamn tell me to." His delivery was a robotic imitation of the security head's voice. Accurate, but flat. And then for good measure, Eddie added, "I won't! I won't! I won't! And you can't make me!"

The head of security stared at him intensely. "No? Well, about that, you're wrong." He glanced at Clementine, who revealed a twelve-million-volt tactical stun baton. Packard asked, "Do you know what that is?"

"It looks like some type of baton."

"That's correct. Can you guess what kind?"

"A metal one."

"Also correct. This particular type is called a stun baton."

"Why is it called a stun baton?"

"My associate is about to show you."

Clementine stepped forward and pressed the end of the baton to Eddie's sternum. *ZZZTT!* The human body normally generates less than one hundred millivolts of electricity, which meant that Eddie's nervous system was suddenly overwhelmed with over one hundred million times the amount of electrical energy it was used to managing. His brain couldn't process the overload, and his muscles seized. He collapsed, convulsing involuntarily, just as he was supposed to.

Demonstrating his incredible strength, Clementine used only one hand to grab Eddie by the shirt and prevent him from hitting the floor. "Where do you want him?"

"Back of the van. We're taking a road trip."

Clementine put Eddie over his shoulder like a rag doll and carried him out of the room. Packard moved to the computer screen still transmitting his live image. He spoke to his superior. "Traffic permitting, we'll be there by four o'clock." He then closed both laptops and the echo box, taking all three devices with him.

CHAPTER 16

June 1, 3:18 p.m.

Bob Stenson watched the action in split screen with rising concern. On the left side of the monitor, Eddie and his revolutionary device had been carried out of Harmony House by a member of their security staff. They had confirmed the echo box was in working order and was now on its way to him. At least part of his plan was proceeding as intended.

However, on the right side of the screen, things had gone awry. Dr. Skylar Drummond should have been similarly carried out of the temporary office they had set up in Philadelphia and on her way to him as well. However, a man Skylar knew by name had unexpectedly intervened. She had called him "Butler." Stenson surmised this could only be Butler McHenry, the detective who had recently given her aid in New York. Observing her rescue, Stenson was surprised by the level of the man's abilities, which far exceeded civilian police standards. He had clearly received training from another source, almost certainly military. The man was formidable. But the most troubling part, in Stenson's mind, was that this Butler McHenry knew exactly where to find her.

Stenson had two questions he wanted answered immediately: Who was Butler working for, and where was he getting his intel?

The director of the American Heritage Foundation recognized the footsteps of his heir apparent as soon as he heard them running down the hallway toward his office. "Slow down, Jason."

Jason Greers slowed to a walk as he entered the office, carrying a small stack of papers. He handed the first document to Stenson. It was a printout of a screen grab from the video footage of Skylar's rescue. The image gave a clear view of Butler the moment he first noticed the camera after killing their contractor. Butler had unintentionally looked directly into the lens, making him easy to identify.

"Facial recognition got a ninety-six-percent hit. His name is Butler McHenry. He's—"

"I know who the detective is, Jason. Tell me what I don't know. What's his motive? Why would he risk his career for someone he only met last week?"

Greers handed him several more sheets of paper, allowing Stenson to read along as he continued, "I believe his background gives us a likely explanation. Before he was a cop, he was a Ranger."

Stenson nodded. "That explains his skill set."

"Note the black ops he was part of."

Stenson read them, recognizing a majority of the missions. "Most of them were ours."

"Seems like quite a coincidence, doesn't it?"

The director stared at his protégé. "I don't believe in coincidence. You know that."

Greers attempted to recover. "It's possible that he's trying to get back at us."

"Which means he knows about us, leading to the most important question we must answer: Where is he getting his information?"

The protégé stared at his mentor. His expression made it clear he thought the answer should be obvious.

Stenson knew the answer as well. He just didn't want to accept it. Wishfully, he said, "She didn't." He quickly worked his computer, calling up the tracking device hidden in the undercarriage of Caitlin McCloskey's Subaru. He glanced at Greers as a map appeared on one of his screens. "Every employee's vehicle is tracked. Including mine."

Greers shrugged as if to say, *Of course it is.* The map showed Caitlin's Subaru in the lot outside the Kelman Nursing and Rehab Center.

"Get the mess in Philadelphia cleaned up. I'm going to visit an old friend." Stenson exited abruptly.

CHAPTER 17

June 1, 3:21 p.m.

Butler gripped Skylar's arm as he helped her out of the office where she had been held hostage for the last two hours. Her eyes still couldn't focus due to the effects of the flash bang. Her equilibrium also remained off. She walked like she was drunk. He maneuvered her around the unconscious female zip-tied in the middle of the lobby floor.

Skylar couldn't identify the lump they skirted. "Is that a person?" She asked more loudly than was necessary because of the ringing in her ears.

"Yes." He gave an exaggerated nod and kept her moving toward the front door.

She stared at the body. "The receptionist?"

"Yes. Lower your voice. You're yelling."

"Sorry, I didn't realize I was," she responded, still a bit too loudly. She continued in a more hushed tone. "Is she dead?"

"No."

Skylar's brain was still scrambled. It took her a moment to come up with a response. "That was decent of you."

"It won't matter. She'll be dead before nightfall. The kind of people she works for don't tolerate loose ends."

"What?" She didn't hear a word he said.

"Never mind."

On the sidewalk, Butler kept his head down as he led Skylar in the direction of his Tahoe. She still couldn't focus. Everything remained a blur. "My car. It's in the other direction. At least, I think it is."

"We're not taking your car."

She seemed confused but didn't ask any questions. "Okay. I hope I don't get any tickets."

"Where's your phone?"

She reached into her pocket and handed it to him. He smashed it against a lamppost, then tossed it in a trash can. "What did you do that for?"

"Easiest way to find someone is through their phone." He took out his own phone, memorized the number of the most recent call, and disposed of it as well.

"We have to find Eddie." She sounded both determined and desperate.

He held her tightly as she continued to stagger. "Any idea where they might have taken him?"

"If he's not at Harmony House, I have no idea."

"He's not at Harmony House." Butler glanced at several security cameras focused in their direction. "Keep your head down."

She ducked as they rounded a corner. He put his cap on her head and pulled up his hood so that his face could only be seen directly from the front. "How do you know he's not at Harmony House?"

"If I had gone through all this trouble for his box, I'd bring him and the device to the most secure location I had access to."

"Where would that be?" Skylar asked.

"No idea. But I know someone who might. First I need to get a new phone." He led her down the block and across the street to a small

67

shop—Adolfo's Electronics & Phone Repair. It was crammed full of a variety of technology and gadgets, everything from used televisions to computers to phones. Their signs claimed they could repair them all with "100 Percent Reliability or Your Money Back."

The store sold only one type of burner phone, the Alcatel A206, so the choice was easy. No internet. No camera. But the battery had seventeen hours of standby time and five hours of talk time, so it was perfect—even if it was a flip phone that looked like it was from 2003. Butler also grabbed a charging cable and paid $34.95 in cash for the two items.

He powered up the device to discover the phone only came with a 20 percent charge. It would be enough for now. As soon as they left the store, he dialed the number he had memorized for the woman he knew only as Eleanor.

((•))

Caitlin heard an unfamiliar ring as she approached the Wells Fargo branch on Franconia Road in Alexandria. The sound was coming from her purse. She needed a moment to remember she'd gotten rid of her iPhone and had started using a burner. She took out the phone and did not recognize the number calling. There was only one other person who knew this number. *It has to be Butler.* "How'd it go?"

"I have Skylar, but they've taken Eddie."

Caitlin paused outside the bank, now certain that she had recruited the right guy. "You sound like a man who has unfinished business."

He paused in frustration. Not at her, but at himself. Because she was right. With surprising calm, he asked, "Where would they take him?"

"Was the box working?"

Butler asked Skylar the same question. He then replied to Eleanor, "That's affirmative."

"He and the device will be taken to a location outside Alexandria, Virginia. I'll give you more details when you get closer. You must reach them before they get there. They will be traveling in a white package van."

He responded with an understandable level of sarcasm. "Well, that'll really narrow it down, won't it?"

"They'll be looking for your vehicle. Find another. I'll be in touch with more details as soon as I have them." Ending the call, Caitlin placed the phone back in her purse and entered the bank. She paused to look around, remembering the last time she was inside this building, several years ago. For as long as she could remember, her father had done his banking here. She had been made a cosigner on all his accounts when she'd started managing his money. Until today, however, she hadn't known he had a safety-deposit box.

She presented her identification to a young male teller with a bow tie. He read the box number off the key: *1637*. He went to the bank's files to check the list of authorized users. There were two: Lawrence Walters and Caitlin Walters McCloskey. She signed a form and was buzzed through a security gate that permitted her access to the vault.

The teller led her to the box, one of the hundreds of the smallest boxes offered: two by five inches. Only enough room to store some papers and a small amount of cash. Like all the other boxes, it required two keys to open. The teller removed a key ring from his pocket and searched for the proper one. After a minute, he became flustered.

Caitlin studied him. "Is there a problem?"

Relieved, he finally found the key he was looking for. "No, no problem. I just couldn't find it there for a minute." He inserted the key into the left lock, turning it clockwise. He then inserted Caitlin's key into the right lock and did the same. The small stainless-steel door opened. He pulled out the box, which was twenty-four inches deep, and carried it into a small, brightly lit room the size of a closet. "Take as much time as you need. When you're finished, you may place your box back into the slot, or just leave it here and I'll be happy to do it for you."

He closed the door behind him, leaving Caitlin alone with her father's secret safety-deposit box. She opened the box without hesitation but was surprised by what she found. Or rather, what she didn't find. The box was empty except for a single scrap of paper. On one side was a handwritten phone number. On the other side were GPS coordinates, also handwritten. She plugged the longitude and latitude into her phone, which returned an address forty-four miles west of her current location, in Gilberts Corner, Virginia. It would take her about an hour to get there.

Caitlin returned to the Cutlass, dialing the handwritten number before starting the engine. After several rings, an unfamiliar male voice answered. "Hello, Caitlin."

She was concerned at being identified. *Am I being watched? Tracked? Bugged?* She looked around the car nervously. "Who is this?"

"There's no need for alarm. I'm an old friend of your father's." His voice was rugged and gravelly, a lot like Clint Eastwood sounded in *Unforgiven,* she thought.

Her fears were not allayed. "How were you able to identify me?"

"You are the only one who has this number. On the day he retired, your father gave me this phone. This is the first call I've ever received on it."

His explanation sounded not only plausible but exactly like something her father would have done. She breathed a little easier. "What should I call you?"

"Hogan."

She tried to remember if her father had ever introduced her to someone with that name, but couldn't remember anyone. "Okay, Hogan, what now?"

He paused to make sure the significance of what he was about to say came through clearly. "Once the Alpha Reset Protocol is initiated, there is no turning back. Is that clear?"

She was relieved to hear him use the phrase *Alpha Reset Protocol* and responded without hesitation. "Yes, it's clear."

He spoke with absolute clarity. "Intending no offense, let me make sure you understand the gravity of the situation. Right now, it's like you have entered the launch codes and your finger is on the button, but you have not pressed it yet. The only person who knows any of this is me. You can still turn back and go about your life as you have been, as will I. But once you press that button, there is no going back. Forces will be marshaled, and a battle will commence, which will become all-out war. So please, for both our sakes, take a moment before you confirm that you want to proceed."

Caitlin did as he requested. She then responded with conviction, "I confirm I want to proceed."

He hesitated briefly, as if this was not the reply he was hoping for and he was only reluctantly willing to accept. "Make your way to the address your father left for you. Call me when you get there." He hung up.

She started to drive, following the directions Google Maps was providing on her burner phone toward I-495 West, then texted a message to a number she had committed to memory long ago. The message read: *It's raining elephants in Tucson.*

CHAPTER 18

I-495 West

Outside Fairfax, Virginia

June 1, 3:47 p.m.

Caitlin was proud of her husband. Peter McCloskey had risen steadily through the financial ranks over a twenty-year career. After graduating from George Washington with a degree in accounting, he started off professional life as a CPA, then moved into purchasing, debt management, and accounts receivable before becoming controller of the grinding-wheel concern he was still employed by. When the CFO who'd hired him was forced to retire for health reasons several years later, Peter was handed the job, and he had been shining in the position ever since.

Caitlin knew that today was an important day for him. He was presenting the annual financial report to the company's board of directors. Peter used to get so nervous before such meetings that he wouldn't eat the entire day until coming home afterward, but that hadn't happened in almost a decade. He'd been through great years with the company, as well as outright terrible ones. This year was somewhere in the middle, as most of them were.

Caitlin tried to imagine how far he'd gotten into his presentation to the board when her text was received. She couldn't decide which would be better for him: if he hadn't started yet, or had already finished. Worst would be if he was right in the middle of his PowerPoint presentation, which included several dozen slides. She tried to picture the faces on his board of directors as he marched out without warning. And then a horrible thought occurred to her: What if the text hadn't gone through? No, she thought, they had already ruled out that possibility. He had tested his phone reception along his entire route to work, and in every room of the company's offices.

What if he didn't read the text? Or even worse, ignored it? No, she told herself, Peter wouldn't do that. Her contact information in his phone included not only a unique ringtone (courtesy of John Mayer), but a distinctive vibration pattern for her texts. It was a heartbeat. He would be able to feel when she was trying to reach him. And because of a conversation they'd had several months ago, he understood the potential urgency a text from her could represent.

Initially, Peter had thought she was playing a practical joke on him. *You want me to what?* But she had made certain he understood the seriousness of her instructions. She had stated in no uncertain terms that if she ever sent him a message that included the phrase *raining elephants in Tucson*, Peter was to immediately stop whatever he was doing, pick up their children, and take them to Potomac Airfield, where she would have a private aircraft waiting for them.

She made him promise that he would follow her instructions exactly and without hesitation. It was a moment that had fundamentally altered their relationship. Although he had given his word, his trust in her was rattled. The fear she saw in his face was something that Caitlin would never forget. It was the first time she could remember Peter ever looking afraid of her. Over the years, he had shared his suspicions about the foundation she worked for, but she had always assuaged his concerns convincingly.

The problem with getting caught in one lie is that it sets up a line of further questions like a row of dominoes. Peter had demanded to know what else she had lied to him about. *Was everything a lie?* No, she had assured him, it wasn't. She loved him dearly and told him she was probably just being overly cautious.

As it turned out, she wasn't.

Caitlin glanced down at her phone as it started to ring. She placed it in a cradle mounted on the dashboard. It was Peter calling. He was Skyping her—whenever possible, they preferred to see each other when talking on the phone. She clicked the button to answer the call, and his face appeared on her phone. It was clear that he was also driving, which gave her a sense of relief. "You're on the road. Good."

"What number is this?"

"It's a backup," she answered, eyeballing him that he should have known it was a burner phone.

"You want to tell me what's going on?" He conveyed grave concern on the verge of panic.

Reminded that Peter was unpracticed in this type of situation, she responded with unnatural calm and reassurance. "Peter, I can't talk right now. But I'll call you as soon as I can. I promise." She glanced toward the screen so that he could see her eyes. She was trying to communicate that phone conversations weren't a good idea right now, but she had no idea if he understood. In any event, she now knew that he had received her text and was making good on his promise. For the moment, that was all she needed to know.

She ended the call and continued toward the address her father had left for her.

CHAPTER 19

Back of a Delivery Van

Location Unknown

June 1, 3:51 p.m.

Eddie's eyes blinked open. He did not know where he was. Which scared him. Without moving his head, he glanced around. He was lying on his side in the back of a van. It was white inside and seemed to be fairly new. He could hear the road passing beneath the vehicle. They were traveling fast—faster than the cars around them moving in the same direction. Eddie guessed this meant they were on a freeway. But he didn't know which one. Or where they were going. Which was upsetting. His hands flinched. If they hadn't been handcuffed behind his back, he would have probably started slapping himself.

His cheek hurt where he had hit himself so many times earlier. It was far more than his daily average, and more than he knew he should have. He wasn't supposed to slap himself, both because his doctors had always told him, his whole life, that this was a behavior they wanted to help him curtail and because it was painful.

His wrists also throbbed because they were cuffed tightly behind his back. He did not like the feeling of the metal digging into his wrists. He could not see the cuffs, but he imagined what they looked like from the television shows he had seen over the years in Harmony House.

Policemen handcuff criminals. Criminals are bad people. Does that mean I have become a bad person?

The pain made him temporarily more angry than scared. "Where am I?" The two men in the front of the van did not answer him. They were separated from Eddie by metal mesh. He spoke louder. "I know you can hear me! Where are you taking me?"

The driver glanced over his shoulder. "You'll find out when we get there."

"How will I find out?"

"There will be a big sign that says, 'Welcome, Eddie!'" he answered sarcastically.

Eddie made his BUZZER sound. "Not true. There will not be a big sign."

"How do you know that?" the driver asked.

"I know because I can tell when people lie, and you just did."

"Tell me if I'm lying now." He glanced at his associate. "If you don't shut up, my friend is going to zap you with his baton again."

Eddie was confused. On one hand, the man had told him to say something, which required Eddie to speak. But then he said if he spoke, the other man was going to hurt him again, and he didn't want that. Eddie opened his mouth to respond, then decided not to say anything at all. He shook his head as if to answer, *No, you are not lying now.*

The associate held up the stun baton he'd previously used on Eddie. "You sure you don't want some more of this?"

"No, I do not! I never wanted any of that in the first place."

"Then shut your mouth." He said it sharply, in a tone that reminded Eddie of his father when he would get angry at him as a child. Eddie now responded the way he used to back then: he opened his mouth as widely as he could, but did not make a sound. It was an act of silent rebellion. Which meant they hadn't broken him yet. But he was sure scared.

His mind began to flit about at rocket speed in an unconscious attempt to hide from that fear. *What time is it? What highway are we on? What direction are we going? How much longer will we be driving? Are we driving the speed limit? Would a police officer notice if we were driving too fast? Does the driver have a proper license? When will they take me back to Harmony House? Where is Skylar? Does she know I am no longer at Harmony House? Is she okay? When will my next meal be? Will that meal be served by strangers? Will that meal include purple food? Will the strangers force me to eat the purple food if there is any being served?*

He certainly hoped not, because he found food the color of bruises disturbing. Just the thought of it was unsettling, and he was already unsettled enough. Fortunately, most meals at Harmony House didn't include any grapes or plums or blueberries or eggplant or cabbage, so Eddie had not had to confront purple foods with much frequency over the last decade.

He didn't like the feeling he got in the pit of his stomach when thinking about purple foods, so he decided to think about something that gave him a better feeling. And the first thing that came to his mind was Skylar. He closed his eyes to help him picture her. In the short time he had known her, he had studied her face more closely than that of any other person he'd ever known. Just looking at her made him feel good, which most observers would have found curious, because during his conversations with Skylar, he spent most of the time looking elsewhere. Eye contact, even with his favorite person in the world, was an incredible challenge for him.

As a child, Eddie had wondered why it was so much harder for him to look at people than it was for most others. He remembered reading that eyes were considered windows to the soul, and because he wasn't clear on what the soul was, or if he even had one, he didn't like people seeing what was inside him. It made him feel exposed, and that made him feel uncomfortable, which was never a good thing. He didn't understand how those not on the autism spectrum could feel comfortable enough with this sensation of looking others directly in the eye. Perhaps it was because they each had some invisible shield that protected their soul from inspection. He had asked where he could get one of those shields, but none of his doctors or nurses had ever given him a remotely satisfactory answer.

Eddie then thought about the time he had studied Skylar's face most closely. It was during their train ride from Secaucus to Philadelphia, only a week ago. She had fallen asleep right next to him. When Skylar's eyes were closed, Eddie had taken the opportunity to inspect her every pore—or, at least, most of them. He wanted to memorize her features because she was the mother figure he had always hoped for. Skylar looked quite like the only image Eddie had of his birth mother. He imagined that his mother would have made him feel just like Skylar did. Warm. And safe. And cared for.

Skylar's interest in him had piqued his curiosity about her. He couldn't read about Skylar the way she had about him, what with the boxes upon boxes of notes kept by his many doctors over the years, which she had pored over. So his study of her had to be visual, at least for now. The color of her skin (lightly tanned but fair). The number of freckles she had on both cheeks (they were asymmetrical; the left side had three more). The length of her eyelashes (approximately one-half inch, on average). He was quite certain her lashes were longer than his own. They were also not covered in as much makeup as those of the other female doctors he had encountered over the years in Harmony House, which was something he liked. Eddie found makeup confusing; he didn't understand why anyone, but mostly women, would wear it. The synthetic colors seemed to exaggerate certain features, but exaggerating was very close to lying, and lying was bad except in certain circumstances which Skylar had only recently helped him to understand.

On that train ride to Philadelphia, Eddie also discovered that Skylar had several different colors of hair: while most of it was blonde, some of her hairs were darker than others, and an even smaller number were gray. He knew that people started getting gray hairs as they got older. Nurse Gloria had told him years ago that he should never mention them to any woman, nor increasing baldness to any man. Eddie didn't understand why this was so important—it was only hair, after all—but the veteran nurse seemed to command the respect of her peers and the entire medical staff, so he had accepted her statement as fact.

Eddie had noted several other features about Skylar: She had a small scar on the left side of her chin. Her hands were small compared to those of most of the other women he had known, but her fingers were long. Her nails were short and always had white painted on the ends. Years ago, he had learned that this style of manicure was called French tips, but nobody he asked could explain to him why, so it was added to his Book of Questions, among the thousands of other puzzles Eddie hoped to have answered one day.

Lying in the back of the van, Eddie realized how much more comfortable he now felt as he thought about Skylar. He felt warmer, like he was wrapped in an imaginary blanket. And it wasn't just a sensation of heightened temperature; he no longer felt so alone or scared. Just the thought of her reassured him. He was now breathing more slowly and deeply, which were meditation techniques he had read about. And while he did not know how to meditate, he did know how to think about Skylar, so that was what he continued to do.

CHAPTER 20

Kelman Nursing and Rehab Center

Alexandria, Virginia

June 1, 3:53 p.m.

Stenson parked his Chrysler 300C next to Caitlin's Subaru in the nursing home parking lot. He placed his hand on the hood of her car, checking to see how long it had been there. The metal was cool. He glanced in the window. Her iPhone was visible next to the gear selector. *That isn't a good sign,* he thought. But he had to make sure.

He approached Quentin, the front desk clerk, who seemed to recognize him from his previous handful of visits. Quentin greeted him with "Well, isn't Lawrence the popular one today?"

"Excuse me?"

"Our residents don't get many visitors. Just one in a day is a big deal for them, but two is something they'll be talking about all week."

Stenson smiled politely. "Do you know if his daughter is still here?"

"I'm afraid I don't. But go ahead to his room. I'm sure he'll be glad to see you."

Stenson walked down the hall and poked his head into his former mentor's room. "Lawrence, may I come in?" There was no response. "Caitlin, are you still here?" He entered quietly to find Lawrence asleep in his easy chair, which faced toward the windows. There was no sign of his daughter. Stenson sat on the footstool, tapping Lawrence lightly on the shoulder. He spoke softly, just above a whisper. "Lawrence. Hey, old friend, I'm sorry to wake you."

Caitlin's father opened his eyes, smiling when he saw who had awakened him. "I know you, don't I?"

"You do. My name is Robert Stenson, but my friends call me Bob."

"I am your friend, aren't I?"

"Yes, you are." It had become increasingly difficult for Stenson to see his former mentor in this condition, but given the circumstances, particularly so today.

"I suppose that is why you are here. Because we are friends."

"It is," Stenson lied. He moved closer so he could look Lawrence squarely in the eyes. "I need to ask you something."

"This sounds serious." The old man clasped his hands in his lap to stop them from shaking.

"I need to know what you and Caitlin discussed."

"She's my daughter, you know. Caitlin. Such a sweet girl. She just came to visit."

"I do know. What did you two talk about?" His words were becoming more abrupt, which wasn't lost on Lawrence.

The old man seemed to be considering his response carefully. "Well, Bob, that is none of your damn business," he replied with a smile. "That is between a father and his daughter."

Stenson could no longer restrain himself. "Tell me!" He immediately regretted losing his temper, especially when he saw his former mentor's confused response.

Lawrence struggled to find the words to respond. He seemed frightened. And then frustrated. One of the orderlies poked his head in, asking if everything was all right. Lawrence barked, "Get out!" with surprising intensity. As the orderly backed out of the room, Lawrence turned to his visitor and said nothing. He just stared.

Stenson couldn't tell if Lawrence was baiting him or simply not present. The younger Lawrence, when he was in his prime and in command of the American Heritage Foundation, had used silence in conversation better than anyone Stenson had ever known. The former director used to wield it like a weapon and had broken several people with it in Stenson's presence.

((•))

In 1988, Ronald Reagan was in the third year of his second term in the Oval Office. The American Heritage Foundation considered the decision to facilitate the former actor's ascent to the presidency the single best move it had made during its first thirteen years of existence. Every policy it had acted to implement had been put into place. Likewise every judge and every appointee. The AHF now had measures of control in every area of the federal government, and in a growing number of state and local ones as well.

Things couldn't have been going better, which was what concerned the new director of the foundation—at least, that was what he told his most recent hire, a young Princeton graduate named Robert Stenson. Lawrence Walters was one of the seven original founders. It was understood back in 1975, when the foundation first opened its doors, that Lawrence would succeed the original director, Tobias Ritter, upon his retirement. That event occurred considerably sooner than anyone inside the American Heritage Foundation had anticipated, due to the discovery of Tobias's stage III pancreatic cancer. Sadly, the one factor the foundation's elder statesman couldn't manipulate to his liking was his own health.

After making sure Reagan was reelected, Tobias turned over the foundation director's chair to Lawrence with a quiet admonition: "Stay true. To our mission. To our principles. And our values. If you ever find yourself wondering if you've lost your way, you already have. You must be certain you can trust that all who join the effort have the strength of character to bring down the house if you, or anyone else, leads us astray. Everyone must have their own Alpha Reset Protocol."

Lawrence knew exactly what he meant. In the construction business, if a foundation wasn't rock-solid, the rest of a building could never be. The only way to fix such a problem was to tear the structure down to the ground and start over. The same was true within the intelligence community, particularly in black ops, where there was no reporting structure or oversight. Correction or repair had to come from within. Any member of a black-ops team had to be willing to demolish the enterprise and perform a master reboot.

Caitlin's father had explained this to Robert Stenson on his first day. The new hire, who came to be called Bob, seemed to take it to heart, although such a demolition never became even a remote consideration while Lawrence was in charge. His character was impeccable, and he never allowed his ego or other personal considerations to influence any decision he made while director.

When his eldest daughter, Caitlin, had proven herself worthy to the rest of the foundation's hiring committee, Lawrence made sure to privately impart the importance of developing an Alpha Reset Protocol. She said she understood the value of such a plan but admitted to having no practical idea of how to execute one, should the time ever come. That was when her father put his arm around her and said, "If that day ever does arrive, you can use mine."

((•))

Stenson, studying the face of his now-feeble mentor, was distracted by the antiseptic smell that permeated Lawrence's retirement home. It wasn't quite as bad as the inside of a hospital, but it was close. Stenson regretted that he, too, would most likely live out his final days in a facility like this. He spoke on a completely even keel. "Tell me what you discussed."

Lawrence stared back with an expression that was difficult to read. It was either defiance, disdain, or a complete lack of comprehension. His hand shook as he unconsciously reached for the necklace that was no longer around his neck, but his voice didn't waver. "Alpha. Reset. Protocol."

Stenson stared back with both surprise and disbelief. "You didn't."

Lawrence repeated the three words exactly as he had spoken them the first time.

Stenson couldn't believe the old man was still capable of such a move. He was disappointed in himself that he hadn't considered that the enactment of an emergency plan might have been the reason for Caitlin's visit. "You son of a bitch."

Lawrence remained expressionless. His hands continued to shake as he spoke with slow determination. "You were never Churchill."

"Good day, Lawrence." Stenson got up and left.

((•))

Lawrence did not try to watch him leave. A slight smile spread across his face. After a moment, he closed his eyes and drifted off to sleep like nothing at all had happened.

CHAPTER 21

June 1, 4:08 p.m.

Butler McHenry hadn't stolen a car since he was fourteen years old. It had been a crime of opportunity when he and his closest childhood friend, Lamont, had come upon a Mercedes pulled to the side of the road. A couple was arguing inside it. They were yelling in a language he didn't understand—he guessed that they were speaking Russian, but it could have been German or Czech, for all he knew. Anger needed no translation.

The woman in the passenger seat suddenly jumped out of the car and ran down the block, kicking off her stiletto heels when they proved to be an impediment. The guy in the driver's seat immediately got out and went after her, picking up her shoes along the way. Butler often wondered why the man had remembered to do that, particularly in light of what he had forgotten: his keys. He had left the door open and the engine running.

The two fourteen-year-olds turned to each other, deciding this must be a sign from God that they were supposed to steal this car. *I mean, why would the guy leave a Mercedes unlocked and running right in front of us if the good Lord didn't want us to steal it?* Butler scrambled into the driver's seat and put the transmission into drive. The car accelerated so quickly that he almost instantly lost control of it.

"Look out!" Lamont screamed.

Butler barely managed to avoid sideswiping several parked cars and screeched to a halt. "Damn, this thing is fast!"

"You mind trying not to kill us?"

"Relax, Grandma." Butler resumed driving, gradually growing comfortable with the power of this machine. In fact, he would be spoiled for years by the performance of its engine. No car he would drive for another decade would come close to its level of horsepower or handling.

Lucky for them, the car had less than an eighth of a tank of gas and ran out before they could get into serious trouble. Thereafter, Lamont never let Butler forget that he didn't get a turn behind the wheel that night. He used it as an excuse to go first whenever the boys did anything together, including when they went down to the army recruitment center, in their senior year of high school, and enlisted. And he was still using that excuse six years later, when they were placed on the same black-ops team because of how well they collaborated.

Lamont always insisted on going first, and he did so in a Baghdad alley when their team was ambushed. Even after taking a fatal bullet, he still managed to kill four hostiles, probably saving Butler's life along with the other members of his team.

Butler would never again let anyone else he cared about go first in anything.

Now he and Skylar were in the back of a Philadelphia cab, which he had hailed after the phone call with Caitlin. Butler was never more thankful that Lyft and Uber hadn't entirely eliminated traditional taxi service, because those newer services required an account and payment by credit card. They did not accept cash, and that was bad for anyone who wanted their whereabouts to remain unknown.

He had instructed the cab driver to take them to the nearest shopping mall, which turned out to be only a few blocks away. Skylar didn't seem to understand why they would be going to a mall but had regained enough of her senses not to ask any questions until they had gotten out of the vehicle at One Liberty Place. The sidewalk was bustling. They moved with the crowd. "You mind telling me what we're doing here?"

"Getting a vehicle." He methodically scanned the area around them.

"What's wrong with yours?"

"They'll be looking for it."

She hesitated for a moment. "Who is 'they'?"

"The people who have Eddie and his box."

Skylar stopped, looking at him skeptically. "You're a police officer. You can't steal a car."

Butler paused, exasperated, and then asked sharply, "Do you want Eddie to live through the day?"

Her knees nearly buckled. She was clearly becoming overwhelmed. "I don't understand what's going on, Detective."

Butler felt bad. He had dealt with life-or-death situations more times than he would care to count, but these experiences had given him the ability to remain emotionally detached when such circumstances arose. Unfortunately, at least according to the NYPD's Sixth Precinct shrink, Butler reacted as if every situation were life or death. *You'd be great in a life raft,* she once told him. *But most days, you aren't in one.*

Today, however, he was. "Honestly, I don't know what's going on, either. All I know is I got a call from someone who said you were in danger. And she was right."

Skylar tried to collect herself. "Who called you?"

"I don't know. But she knew about you, and she knew about Eddie and the box. She also knew things about my military record that were supposed to be classified."

Skylar had the expression of someone whose suspicions had just been confirmed. *Once in the service, always in the service.* "When were you in the military?"

"Before I became a cop."

"Did she know where Eddie is?"

"She said he's being taken to Alexandria, Virginia, and that we need to intercept him before he gets there."

"So what are we standing here for?" After a moment, she cracked a smile. She might not have been completely back to normal, but she was getting there.

Butler surveyed the area. "Wait here, sunshine. I'll be right back." As he moved toward the parking garage, several car horns started blaring from the entrance of the adjacent Westin hotel. An unexpected rush of arriving guests had overwhelmed the valets on duty, who were scrambling from car to car to greet arrivals and unload their luggage. The valets had double-parked a number of cars in the entrance until they could clear up the logjam. Keys for these cars were left on the valet stand, where there was normally an attendant on duty. Butler reached the valet stand and quickly surveyed the keys. He yelled toward an attendant: "Excuse me."

The flustered attendant responded as politely as he could. "Sir, I'll be right with you."

Butler held up a set of keys. "I just need to get a bag from my car. I'll put the keys right back." He walked briskly toward the double-parked cars before the attendant could protest. Butler maneuvered around a Bentley and a Maserati, the kind of cars valets left closest to their stands, and pressed the "Unlock" button on the remote in his hand. The headlights of a Chevy Impala blinked. It was easily the oldest and least valuable car parked at the hotel's entrance.

He got in, started the engine, and sped away before the valets had time to notice. He pulled to the curb in front of Skylar and rolled down the passenger-side window. "Get in."

She got in the passenger seat and said, "You couldn't have found us a nicer ride?"

"New cars have tracking systems." He pulled into traffic.

Skylar shook her head. "I would make a terrible criminal."

CHAPTER 22

Real Estate Office

Rittenhouse Square

June 1, 4:21 p.m.

The yellow van with the Superior Cleaners logo parked abruptly in the alleyway next to 1731 Locust Street in Philadelphia, just off Rittenhouse Square. A crew of three in matching yellow coveralls quickly placed orange cones around the van and began unloading several large pieces of industrial cleaning equipment, including two empty fifty-five-gallon barrels, which they moved to the front of the building owned by the American Heritage Foundation.

Upon entering the foyer, all three were surprised to find someone still alive on the premises. In their line of work, this was almost never the case. Carla remained hog-tied in the middle of the front foyer and had only managed to move thirteen feet in the hour since Butler and Skylar had left her. Her wrists and ankles were badly bruised and bleeding from her struggles against her restraints. "Thank God you're here."

The cleanup men glanced at each other, not entirely sure how they were supposed to proceed. The leader motioned to the older of his guys to deal with the woman while he inspected the rest of the premises. In an office down the hall, he readily came upon Tristan's body, still wearing the rubber Einstein mask, which had a bullet hole through its forehead and was spattered with dried blood. The body was cold and lying in a pool of dark-red fluid. *At least one thing on this job is as it's supposed to be.* The leader took out his cell phone and called their employer.

((•))

In the front lobby, Carla pleaded with the older cleaner, promising to do anything he asked if he would only untie her. "I'll give you all the money I have."

"How much is that?" The older man glanced to his colleague, seeming amused.

"A little over thirty-seven thousand. I'll take you to my bank and have them write you a cashier's check." There was a desperate level of urgency to her voice.

"I'll tell you what, it's tempting. I could do a lot with thirty-seven grand." He glanced over to his younger associate. "What about him?"

"That's all I have. You'd have to split it."

"I think he'd be more interested in other services you might be able to provide."

"Whatever he wants," she replied convincingly.

The younger cleaner stepped closer, about to join the conversation, when their superior returned. "Let her go."

Carla visibly relaxed and breathed a sigh of relief. "Oh, thank God."

The older cleaner turned to his boss with genuine surprise. "Really?"

The leader smirked. "You know these people better than that." He quickly took out a plastic bag and wrapped it over Carla's head. She started to suffocate immediately. "Lay down some plastic before she creates more mess for us to clean up."

The other two men swiftly set down a large plastic sheet on the floor and moved Carla's thrashing body on top of it. Her eyes bulged wide while she screamed as loudly as she could. Outside the bag, however, little sound could be heard. As her body started to go limp, a yellow puddle formed on the plastic beneath her.

The older man nodded to his boss. "Good call."

"It wasn't me who was gonna be cleaning it up." As soon as Carla stopped twitching, they rolled up her body in the plastic sheet, then folded her in half at the waist so she would fit inside one of the fifty-five-gallon drums. There wasn't a drop of bodily fluid to be found anywhere on the floor. They were, after all, professionals. Satisfied with their work, they carried the second barrel down the hall to the other body, which was going to take them considerably longer to clean up due to the amount of dried blood and bullet holes.

$$((\bullet))$$

Caitlin McCloskey was surprised how much she liked driving her father's vintage Cutlass. It might have had 117,000 miles on the odometer, numerous cracks in the vinyl seating, and passenger-side windows that would no longer roll down, but it also brought back a lot of memories from her youth. This was the car she had first learned to drive in. It was the vehicle she'd been driving when she got her first speeding ticket. It was also the car her father took her to college in. She couldn't help but feel that this was the car she was supposed to be driving now as she headed to whatever was waiting for her.

The Google Maps directions to the location of the GPS coordinates her father had written down had taken her around the southern edge of Dulles Airport. It made sense to her that he had chosen a location close to a major international airport. Gilberts Corner was a small unincorporated area in Loudoun County, Virginia, that was about as rural as you got in this part of the country. There was no town, and not even a traffic light. Only three recently installed roundabouts that forced passersby to slow down when driving through the local residents' beloved hamlet.

Caitlin turned left onto a dirt road called Toad Hall Lane and continued driving until it dead-ended at a single overgrown driveway that was protected by a weathered metal gate. Google Maps informed her, *You have arrived at your destination.* She stepped out of the car to find that the gate was locked with a rusty combination lock that required four numbers to open. She rotated the tumblers to her birthday, *0-1-0-8*, but the lock wouldn't open. She then tried her father's birthday, *1-1-2-7*, but that didn't work, either. Caitlin grew momentarily concerned, when she realized what the combination had to be. She entered the numbers of her parents' wedding anniversary: *1-0-2-3*. Presto, the lock opened. Now certain that she was in the right place, she pushed open the old gate just enough to allow the Cutlass through.

Caitlin drove up a narrow driveway that wound through dense trees until it reached a small clearing, where a modest farmhouse stood on a knoll. A developer would have described it as a teardown, which meant it had a lot in common with the Cutlass she was driving. She parked the car and approached the front door, somewhat surprised to see no evidence of a security system. There was only a small lockbox attached to the door handle, the kind Realtors use when selling empty homes. The box required a combination of three entries—letters this time, not numbers. Caitlin knew the answer immediately: *A-H-F.* The initials of the American Heritage Foundation opened the box, revealing a key. She inserted the key into the front door and opened it.

CHAPTER 23

AMERICAN HERITAGE FOUNDATION

ALEXANDRIA, VIRGINIA

June 1, 4:40 p.m.

Returning from the nursing home, Bob Stenson was greeted by Jason Greers the moment he stepped out of his car in the parking lot. "Sir, we—"

Stenson shook his head in disbelief that his protégé would once again ignore protocol and interrupted him quickly. "Not until we're inside the building." He glanced upward at the sky, then continued briskly toward the front entrance.

Greers struggled to bite his tongue until they were safely inside the foundation's walls. "Sir, something's happened."

Stenson responded tersely. "I'm well aware that something has happened, Jason, but addressing it where others could become privy to our conversation might only make matters worse. Haven't I taught you anything?"

Greers nodded, his cheeks slightly flushed with embarrassment. "You have, sir. My apologies."

He remained alongside Stenson as he walked down the hallway to his office. "You get the mess in Philadelphia cleaned up yet?" Stenson asked.

"Cleanup is complete. Our office is as good as new. But I encountered a problem transmitting payment."

"What kind of problem?"

Greers stammered, as if not quite certain how to deliver awkward news. "Insufficient funds."

Stenson smirked. "Not possible."

"That's what I thought, too, until I tried to resend the payment from two other accounts at different institutions. Those wouldn't go through, either."

Arriving in his office, Stenson was determined to show his lieutenant just how incompetent he was. He entered the passwords to review the foundation's primary accounts with Citibank, along with the six-digit random code generated by the small device affixed to his key chain. His eyes went wide when he saw the zero balances. *This doesn't make any sense. What the hell is going on?* Collecting himself, he said, "Jason, will you excuse me for a second?"

Greers backed out of the office, clearly feeling vindicated.

Stenson dialed their Citi banker, Thomas Kincaid, who had occupied the role with the American Heritage Foundation for over a decade. He answered on the first ring, as he always did whenever his biggest client called. "How's my favorite tennis partner doing today?"

"Well, Thomas, I was wondering if you could tell me where my money is."

The banker chuckled, apparently thinking this must be some kind of practical joke. "Which money would that be?"

"The six hundred million and change I keep with you guys."

Kincaid could be heard typing through the phone. There was then an uncomfortable pause. "What the hell?"

"I gather you're now looking at the zero balances I'm looking at. Would you care to help me understand where it all went?"

Kincaid kept typing as he spoke. The words came out awkwardly. "It appears the money was transmitted by multiple wires to several different banks in the Bahamas, Cayman, and Bern."

"I thought any transfer larger than a million required my direct authorization?"

"It does. When I said multiple wires, I meant multiple hundreds. Six hundred, in fact."

Stenson snapped, "Who the hell authorized six hundred transfers?!"

It took the banker a moment to find the answer. "Your predecessor, Lawrence Walters."

Stenson slumped in his chair. The threat of an Alpha Reset Protocol was now real. But it made no sense. "That's not possible. He isn't capable of it. He's a goddamn vegetable in a nursing home."

"Well, if it wasn't him, somebody used his credentials to initiate the transfers."

"Over what time frame?"

Kincaid double-checked the time stamps of the first and last transfers. "All occurred within the last hour."

"That's over ten per minute! Why the hell didn't you stop it?"

"What our clients do with their money is strictly their business. As long as what they're doing is legal, of course."

Stenson was steaming. "Why the hell wasn't I told Lawrence was still on the account?"

"I just assumed you wanted him to have access."

"Why the hell would you assume that?!" Stenson exploded.

The banker answered calmly, "Because you could have had him removed at any time, but you didn't. You know, it isn't uncommon for accounts to have legacy owners remain as authorized users."

Stenson rested his forehead on the heel of his hand. Leaving Lawrence on the account was a mistake. His mistake. An oversight that should have been rectified years ago. "Until I get this sorted out on my end, I'm going to need you to extend us a line of credit."

"How much would you like?"

Stenson picked a number out of thin air. "A hundred million."

Kincaid had to clear his throat. "And what will you be using for collateral?"

"I'll send you a list of our real estate holdings. You can take your pick. Let me know when the funds are available." He hung up the phone, doing his best not to slam it.

CHAPTER 24

June 1, 4:49 p.m.

Stenson stormed out of his office and down the hall to their conference room, where a lone man sat at the large mahogany table. His name was Carter Harwood, and he was the only computer scientist Stenson trusted to work on advancing Eddie Parks's technology. Harwood had been employed in this capacity for over a decade, even though the American Heritage Foundation had little to show for his efforts. To date, his most significant contribution had been the discovery that Eddie had reverted his previous version of the device to nonworking status. It was this revelation that had led to today's proceedings.

Stenson had taken out some additional insurance to guarantee their success. In advance of "convincing" Eddie to restore his device, Stenson had Harwood install a keylogger program on Eddie's laptop supercomputer earlier that morning. Like most malware, it had been downloaded remotely. This type of software allowed access to a device, providing a record of every keystroke entered on its keyboard. That permitted Harwood to analyze every minute change Eddie had made to the control code of his echo box.

In the two hours since Eddie had demonstrated the restored functionality of his device, Harwood had carefully entered the same keystrokes into his duplicate supercomputer, which in turn controlled his duplicate echo box, which sat before him on the conference table.

"Well?" Stenson asked.

Harwood shook his head. "All I have to say is, I'll be damned."

Stenson did not attempt to hide his annoyance. "You'll be damned, what?"

Harwood paused smugly. "Take a listen." He then played a conversation the two of them had had earlier that day.

> STENSON: *Are you certain this program you downloaded into his machine will record every keystroke he makes?*
>
> HARWOOD: *Yes, sir, every single one. Keyloggers are usually used to grab people's passwords or credit card numbers, but it will work fine for this purpose as well. If you can get him to restore the device, I'll be able to duplicate it exactly.*

Stenson smiled. "It looks like you were correct. Well done, Harwood."

The programmer nodded, appreciating the compliment. "Thank you, sir."

"Now delete the file. If you can rebuild the echoes from earlier today, you could also rebuild them from last year or any date since this room was constructed decades ago. I'd hate for the wrong ears to hear some of those conversations."

"Copy that." Harwood dutifully deleted the files. He clearly understood the repercussions of deviating from any of Stenson's instructions. The expression on his face was a combination of respect and utter fear. He knew enough about the man to know what happened to those who disobeyed him.

"Teach Trotter and Greers how to use the device. I'm sending them on a little recon mission."

"I'd be happy to. The technology makes it surprisingly easy to record the echoes of a given space. Rebuilding the decayed energy waves into audible sound waves for proper playback gets quite a bit more complicated, but if all you need is for them to retrieve the raw files, I can teach them what they need to know in fifteen minutes."

Stenson walked down the hall to the office space that until today had been shared by his three lieutenants. As he poked his head in, one of the three desks inside the room was conspicuously empty: Caitlin McCloskey's. He stared at it for a moment, still not quite believing what she had done. Stenson then turned toward the desks that were occupied by his two remaining lieutenants, Trotter and Greers, both of whom looked up attentively. "What can we do for you, sir?" Greers asked readily.

"Transmit payment to the cleaners for the job in Philadelphia. Our accounting irregularity has been rectified."

"Will do, sir. Glad to hear it." Greers sent the money with a few keystrokes.

Stenson positioned himself in front of the two younger men so that he could address them equally. "Gentlemen, how would you like to be the first ones to use the echo box in the field?"

"God, yes," Trotter blurted out in disbelief. "You mean it's working?"

Stenson couldn't help but mock him. "How very astute of you."

Greers was too excited to care. "How soon will Parks and his device arrive?"

"We are already in possession of a working machine." Stenson grinned like a Cheshire cat.

Trotter could barely contain himself. "The duplicate works?"

Stenson nodded, still grinning. "It does."

Greers was not about to be left out of the conversation. "Where are we taking it?"

Their superior paused for dramatic effect. "Where do you think?"

"Knowing you, I'd say wherever it can give us the biggest and most immediate strategic advantage."

The director smiled. "And where would that be?"

"Well, I'd have to say the Oval Office," he answered rather casually. It took Greers a moment to realize he was correct. "My God, we're taking the echo box inside the Oval Office?"

"That's one hell of an opening move, sir," Trotter commented.

"I'm rather inclined to agree," Stenson replied smugly.

Greers studied his boss. "There's so much that we could use against him, but if I had to guess, I'd say first up will be proving the president made a deal to rig the next election."

Stenson smiled slyly, which was all the answer his heir apparent needed.

Trotter remained unemotional. He was already thinking about process. "How will we get the echo box through White House security?"

"With a little imagination." Stenson took out his phone and dialed the president of the United States. One of his three secretaries answered, "White House, Oval Office."

"Sarah, it's Bob Stenson. Is he in?"

"One moment, Mr. Stenson."

((•))

The call was routed to an encrypted line on Air Force One, which was currently flying at an altitude of thirty-five thousand feet toward Tempe, Arizona, where the president would be attending several $25,000-per-plate fund-raisers later that evening. He was in the middle of meeting with the two leaders of the House Freedom Caucus, which did not officially disclose its membership, when the incoming call was announced. One of the conservative torchbearers was from Arizona; the other was from South Carolina. The president apologized but explained that this was a call he needed to take. Both men nodded knowingly. It seemed that at the highest level of government, everyone in American politics either knew Bob Stenson or claimed that they did.

"Bob, it's been too long. How the hell are you?"

"Fine, Mr. President. I hope I'm not interrupting anything."

"Nothing that can't wait. What's up?" The president glanced briefly at his colleagues to make sure they weren't offended. They didn't appear to be. Not by a long shot. In fact, they looked eager to listen in.

"I'll get right to the point. You may have an undisclosed security issue at the White House."

There was a pause on the line as the president considered what type of issue he might be dealing with. "How could that be possible?"

"A new technology we've just become aware of. It's nothing that could have been prevented."

This made the president feel better about the team tasked with protecting him, but anxious about what type of new threat might have landed on his doorstep. "What's the technology?"

"The hostile's system is satellite-based."

Pressing the phone to his shoulder, the president held his palms up with absolute disbelief. "Somebody's been listening to me inside the goddamn West Wing from space?" The two members of Congress sitting with him glanced at each other with the same expression: *Holy shit!*

"The Oval Office would be my primary concern, sir." His understatement was chilling.

The president seemed to know exactly what Stenson was referring to. "Which hostiles are we talking about?"

"That's what we're trying to figure out. With your permission, I'd like to send a two-man team to scan the office with a new device we've developed that should be able to tell us what we're dealing with."

"Yes, by all means, you have my permission. Let me know what they find as soon as you hear anything."

"You'll be the first to know." Stenson paused briefly. "Rest assured, Mr. President, the matter will be handled."

"I have no doubt." The president clicked off the line.

((•))

Stenson pocketed his phone and turned to address Trotter. "That is how we get the echo box through White House security."

CHAPTER 25

I-95 SOUTH

OUTSIDE HAVRE DE GRACE, MARYLAND

June 1, 5:01 p.m.

Butler took advantage of the fact that southbound traffic on I-95 was moving at speeds well over eighty miles per hour. It made the ninety-three miles per hour he was driving in the stolen Chevy Impala seem like he was barely traveling above the limit.

The interstate, also known as the John F. Kennedy Memorial Highway in the state of Maryland, was the longest north–south interstate in the US. It was part of the Dwight D. Eisenhower National System of Interstate and Defense Highways. With the advent of the nuclear age, the general-turned-president needed some way to be able to move our intercontinental ballistic missiles in the event of an attack. It seemed that regular roadways weren't designed to handle loads in excess of seventy-five thousand pounds.

Butler glanced at the name of the bridge as they crossed over the Susquehanna River. "Who the hell was Millard E. Tydings?"

"Who?"

"Millard Tydings. This bridge was named after him."

"If you had to be stuck with the name Millard your whole life, don't you think it's only fair you get a bridge named after you?"

He glanced at her, glad to see that she had recovered from her recent ordeal. "I gather you're feeling better, then."

"I feel a bit like I did back in high school after the first time I threw up from drinking too much. My brain is rattled, my skin hurts, my bones ache, and I wish I could go back in time a few hours to do things differently, but other than that, I'm peachy." She paused to reflect, then added, "At least the ringing in my ears has stopped."

Butler nodded. "I'm surprised you don't wish you could go back a few weeks." He was referring to the murder of her boyfriend, which had occurred only a week ago.

"What good would that do?" she asked earnestly.

"Not a thing. But if you're telling me you haven't had the thought, I'm calling bullshit." His tone was both compassionate and direct.

"I didn't say I hadn't."

"Then say it so you can get it off your chest, like you did about going back a few hours."

She shook her head. "You're helping me understand why people hate therapists."

"Only right before they realize how much they've helped them."

"Sounds like you've spent a fair amount of time on the couch."

"I've single-handedly kept your profession in business."

She looked at him and then spoke with building intensity. "Yes, okay? I wish I'd never met Marcus Fenton and that I'd never gone to work at Harmony House, because Jacob would still be alive. You happy now?"

He glanced over at her. "It's not your fault that he's dead, you know." Before she could respond, her demeanor changed suddenly when she noticed a particular vehicle ahead of them. She pointed to it. "White van."

He had clocked it at almost the same time she had, and he accelerated alongside it, only to see the van was driven by an elderly Latino man in paint-spattered clothes. "Go fish."

"What are you, prejudiced? How can you be sure it's not them?"

Butler shook his head. "It's the driver's age, not his ethnicity. That guy look to you like he could carry Eddie?"

"Why would he have needed to carry him?"

"I don't think me describing any of the scenarios I'm imagining will help anything. Just trust me when I tell you that's not our guy, and that's not our van. Eddie is not in it."

She glanced at her watch. "How much longer until we get to Alexandria?"

"Twenty minutes less than the last time you asked me."

"What did you say then?"

"Twenty minutes less than the last time you asked."

"I didn't appreciate the answer then, either."

"So stop asking. I promise, I'll tell you when we're close."

Skylar paused, stewing. "What if she doesn't call?"

"She'll call."

"What if she doesn't?"

"The only reason she wouldn't is because she's dead or incapacitated. If either is the case, we'll deal with it then." He was reminded of the missions out of country that had gone completely FUBAR, where he and his team were left to improvise without any support whatsoever. He had managed to survive those, and he sure as hell was going to survive this.

"You sure your phone has enough battery left?"

"Yes." He did not bother to look at it. The phone was brand-new and they had used less than one minute of talk time.

"How about we call her?"

"Wasn't the plan."

"Why not?"

"She said she'd call us as soon as she had more details."

"So she didn't explicitly say not to call her."

"If she wanted us to call her, she would have said that. She didn't. The only reason we should call her is because we've encountered a problem she needs to know about. You becoming impatient isn't one of them."

She nodded, biting her tongue, then closed her eyes and started to slow her breathing. From the furrow in her brow, it was taking all the concentration she had. Inhaling through her nose, exhaling through her mouth, she gradually took longer and deeper breaths. Clearly, this was something she had practiced. In relatively short order, Skylar appeared noticeably calmer and more composed.

All Butler could think was, *Thank God.*

CHAPTER 26

SAFE HOUSE

GILBERTS CORNER, VIRGINIA

June 1, 5:12 p.m.

Caitlin had already walked through each room of the farmhouse. Every piece of furniture was coated in a light layer of dust. Clearly, no one had been here in over a decade, maybe two. The bar of Dial soap in the powder room had never been used. Neither had the full roll of toilet paper. The Sony television in the living room was connected to a VCR near a small stack of videos that included *Out of Africa*, *The Shawshank Redemption*, and *Schindler's List*. Each of the movies was one of her father's favorites, and the thought of them watching them together caused her to smile. Only she had never been here. This place was clearly some sort of crude approximation of the home she had grown up in.

The refrigerator in the kitchen was cold inside, but empty. The cupboards, on the other hand, were stocked with items that had long shelf lives: cans of soup, beans, fruit, tuna, and condensed milk; containers of instant coffee, boxes of tea, and a case of Bushmills, another of her father's favorites. She opened one of the bottles and smelled the Irish whiskey within. While she had never developed a taste for it, there was something comforting to her about its scent. It reminded her of her father when he'd been at the top of his game.

There was a twenty-year-old Dell desktop computer in the den connected to a floppy disk drive and a dot matrix printer. All were items that reminded her of her childhood home. She sat down at the computer and pressed the power button, but nothing happened. The screen remained black. All she could see was her own reflection, as well as a piece of art that hung on the wall behind her. Which caught her attention.

The painting was a cheap reproduction of Gustav Klimt's *Portrait of Adele Bloch-Bauer I*, which sold in 2006 for a then-record $135 million. More than a few family friends had commented in Caitlin's youth how much the woman in the portrait reminded them of her mother—which was why her father would have never displayed such a cheap imitation. Caitlin stood up to study the painting more closely. Shaking her head at the poor quality of the wretched thing, she took it off the wall—which was, apparently, exactly what she was supposed to do.

A state-of-the-art retinal scanner was revealed. While the rest of the technology in the house was at least twenty years old, this device was quite new. There was no dust on it. Whoever had installed it had done so recently.

With caution, Caitlin placed her chin on a small pad and looked directly in the scanner. The device instantly came to life, simultaneously scanning both her retinas. In the wall next to the scanner, several metal clicks were heard. Large tumblers rotated. A previously concealed door opened, revealing a staircase leading down. As if to her father, she commented, "A little dramatic, wouldn't you say?"

As she made her way down the stairs, the hydraulic door closed itself. The large tumblers rotated again, this time locking her in. But Caitlin did not appear concerned. To the contrary, she seemed suddenly at ease. "I knew all that up there was bullshit," she said as if Lawrence could hear her.

At the bottom of the stairs, she found herself staring at an incredibly high-tech control center. All the technology in this room was brand-new and state-of-the-art. A variety of flat screens showed a dozen security views in and around the house. Several more were connected to various news feeds.

Another screen showed a webcam view of a man who looked vaguely familiar to her. His military-short hair was completely gray, but full. His skin was weathered from too much time in the sun. Caitlin guessed he was in his sixties, but his musculature was that of a man half his age. "What the hell took you so long?" It was the same rugged and gravelly voice she had spoken to earlier.

"Hogan?"

"Well, I ain't Cinderella."

His name was Aloysius Hogan, but nobody had ever called him by his first name in the twenty years she had known him. Caitlin studied his face, which was worn but comforting in its familiarity. "It's been a long time."

"The last time I saw you, you were still in elementary school. Sixth grade, I think. I'm glad to see you never lost your freckles."

"Why is that?"

"I like a girl with freckles. My wife has them, too, God bless her."

"To ask the obvious, how did you get involved in this?"

"Your father—how do you think?" He smiled wryly.

Caitlin paused briefly, then asked, "What did you owe him?"

"More than I could ever repay."

She recalled that was one of her father's gifts—to make people feel so indebted to him, so grateful, that when it came time to return the favor, there was nothing they wouldn't do. No matter what the personal cost. No matter how much time had elapsed. He could engender a level of personal obligation that bordered on the religious. Caitlin looked around at her surroundings in marvel. "What is this place?"

"Your father originally built it for himself in the event he ever needed to initiate an Alpha Reset Protocol. When he retired, it became yours by default."

"But this technology, it all looks recent. How?"

"He set aside enough funds for me to keep it updated every six months in perpetuity. He knew that a successful reset would require three things: the best technology available, the best personnel available, and enough money to afford both."

"How much are we talking about?"

"Well, the amount just grew considerably. Check the offshore accounts on the screen to your left."

Caitlin did so but didn't believe her eyes. She quickly added the very large numbers together and gasped. "This is six hundred million dollars."

"A bit over it, actually." Hogan sounded like he was talking about counting the correct change from a Starbucks order.

She still couldn't wrap her head around it. "Where the hell did my father get six hundred million dollars?"

"He transferred it out of the American Heritage Foundation accounts earlier today."

Now she was stupefied. "He . . . what?"

"Well, I executed the transfers, but the credentials were his. I was only following his instructions from a script he prepared years ago that started with your phone call to me. Now you can appreciate why I asked you to confirm that you wanted to proceed with the Alpha Reset Protocol."

This was a lot for her to take in. Caitlin's mind was reeling. "Wow." She was imagining what Bob Stenson's reaction would be upon learning that the American Heritage Foundation accounts had just been drained of over half a billion dollars.

Hogan nodded. "I get it, believe me. I was praying you'd change your mind when I asked you to confirm that you wanted to proceed. Make no mistake, Mrs. McCloskey, you have gone to war with your former employer. Only one of you can win. My job is to make sure it's you."

She started thinking clearly again. "I'm going to call you right back."

He nodded again, knowing exactly what she was going to do.

CHAPTER 27

SUBTERRANEAN BUNKER

SAFE HOUSE

June 1, 5:17 p.m.

Caitlin worked her keyboard rapidly, gaining access to the restricted portion of the Potomac Airfield in Friendly, Maryland. Specifically, the views from its security cameras, which now appeared on several monitors. She had received a username and password by the same person she had made other arrangements with. Given what she had already paid this individual, there was no additional cost for the access.

She watched as her husband's Audi A6 approached the main security gate, passing a large wooden sign that read: "Potomac Airfield—The Preferred Airport for the Intelligence Professional." She could see that two other people were in the car—one in the front seat, one in the back. These were her children, Marissa and Mikey. Marissa was thirteen and tall for her age. Through the windows, she looked like an adult. Mikey, on the other hand, was eleven but could have passed for younger. Caitlin could not hear what they were saying, but they seemed to be arguing with their father. She had no trouble imagining what the subject might be. Her kids had every right to want to know what was going on. Unfortunately for them, their father didn't know any more than they did.

Peter presented his identification to the front-gate guard, who found his name on a list and allowed him to pass after giving him some instructions.

Caitlin followed her husband's Audi on several different views until he arrived in front of hangar thirty-seven, where a man in a pilot's uniform approached the car. He was barely in his thirties. Caitlin couldn't hear him, but by reading his lips, it was clear that he had asked, "Mr. McCloskey?"

Peter rolled down his window and nodded.

Caitlin watched the two men have a brief exchange. After a moment, Peter handed the man his phone. The pilot, whose name was Kent, popped out the SIM card, then twisted the phone in his hands until it broke. He then handed Peter another phone, which was larger and looked more like a phone from the 1990s. It was a satellite phone made by Iridium called the Extreme, and it was widely considered the most secure commercially available phone in the world. While certainly impressive, the device was over a generation behind the technology in the phones used by Bob Stenson and the American Heritage Foundation. Kent explained the phone's basic functions and showed Peter the number on the back to help him memorize it.

"Tell him it works anywhere in the world," Caitlin said to the screen, as if to the pilot. "Tell him it's the most secure communications device there is." Alas, Kent could not hear her and did not do as she requested.

She watched Peter say, "Thank you."

The pilot pointed to the side of the building, instructing Peter to park there. Kent then pointed to the aircraft he and the children were to board. It was an Embraer Phenom.

Peter parked his car and led the children toward the craft. He walked briskly, catching up to the pilot. He leaned toward Kent and asked him something quietly, but Caitlin could only see him from behind and didn't know what was asked. It didn't matter; the pilot shook his head, refusing to provide any answers. Because those were his instructions. The ones Caitlin had given him. She quickly dialed the number for her husband's new satellite phone, which she had already committed to memory.

Caitlin watched him as he heard the phone ring. He turned to the pilot, obviously asking if he should answer it. The man nodded, so Peter clicked the appropriate button. "Hello."

Caitlin could hear him clearly and spoke through her headset. "How are the kids?"

"A little unsettled. How do you think?" There was an edge in his voice. One that she couldn't blame him for.

"You can trust the pilot, Kent. He is someone I've known for years."

On-screen, Peter paused, realizing she could see him. He looked around for security cameras but couldn't see any. He held up three fingers. "How many fingers am I holding up?"

"Three. Don't you dare hold up one." She smiled, hoping he would appreciate her joke.

He smiled briefly, then quickly stifled it as the children moved toward him. Caitlin could hear them clearly through the phone. "Is that Mom?" asked Mikey.

Before Peter could answer, Marissa chimed in. "Where is she? How come she isn't coming with us?"

Caitlin replied, "Tell them I'll be joining you as soon as I can."

"When exactly will that be?" he asked.

"I can't quite answer that yet. What I can tell you is that your flight plan is for Minot International Airport."

"Never heard of it."

"It's in North Dakota. About fifty miles south of the Canadian border."

Peter paused to digest the information. "Sounds cold."

Caitlin answered, "I've never been. I'm told it's nice."

After a moment, Peter asked, "Is there anything you can tell me?"

"I will tell you everything just as soon as I can. Right now, just know that I'm only having you do this out of an abundance of caution, but I didn't want to take any chances. I promise I'll answer every question you ask, but right now, I can't. Call me when you arrive." She hung up quickly.

Caitlin watched Peter on-screen as he hung up the phone. Kent approached him with a leather briefcase, which he handed to Peter. Caitlin lip-read the pilot's words: "My instructions are to give you this. You are not to open it until we are airborne." He then turned to the children, apparently welcoming them aboard the aircraft.

Whatever he said seemed to excite the kids, because they both charged up the stairs. Caitlin imagined that they'd been told they could sit wherever they like. Knowing Mikey, she figured he'd try to sit in the captain's seat—which was exactly what he did. Caitlin switched her view to the three cameras she'd had mounted inside the craft: one in the cockpit, and two in the main cabin. She might not be able to physically be with her family on this journey, but she was going to keep an eye on them every step of the way.

Kent appeared on the cockpit camera, shooing Mikey out of his seat. After a failed attempt at negotiation, her son moved into the main seating area with Peter and Marissa.

As her kids hopped around from seat to seat in the main cabin, Caitlin felt guilty for spying on them. They had no idea she could see them. She told herself she was only doing it for their own good, but she knew it was a lie. She was keeping an eye on them to assuage her guilt—and because she could. It was her training. It was what she would do if they were part of her professional world, and never before had the line between church and state been so blurred.

Caitlin tracked the Embraer's progress as they took off. Inside the craft, she could see Mikey and Marissa staring out of their respective windows, watching the world below them disappear. Peter's gaze, however, was not out the windows, but fixed on the briefcase in his lap, which he tried unsuccessfully to open. The case was locked. There were two locks, each with three tumblers. He rotated the numbers to his birthday and hers, but that didn't work. Then he switched the order, putting her birthday on the left and his on the right, but that didn't work either.

"It's not our birthdays," Caitlin commented as if he could hear her.

On-screen, after pausing for a moment, Peter set both combinations to their anniversary: *3-1-4. Click, click.* Both locks opened readily.

Caitlin smiled. She'd known it wouldn't take him long.

Inside the briefcase, Peter first saw several stacks of freshly printed cash. Six, in fact: a stack each of ones, fives, tens, twenties, fifties, and hundreds. He hadn't realized that his son could also see inside the case.

Mikey pointed to the cash. Caitlin lip-read as he exclaimed, "We're rich!"

Peter lowered the briefcase lid so that the contents could no longer be seen and told their son to be quiet. He rotated the case to block his son's view of the inside, then opened it once again. Next he picked up a set of house keys with a card attached. The card read: *48 Pleasant Street, Harvey, ND.*

He then flipped through three brand-new passports: one for each of them. But these were not the same passports they had used recently to travel to Grand Cayman for their Christmas vacation. Their photos were the same, and so were their first names, but these had no travel stamps, and their last name was different: *Montgomery.* They were no longer the McCloskey family; they were the Montgomery family.

Caitlin touched the screen with her finger as she watched Peter swallow hard. His family name was gone, just like that. Caitlin understood what this meant. He had only sisters. It was his duty to carry on the family name, and he took great pride in continuing the legacy. Peter had been relieved when their son was born because it meant he had fulfilled his familial duty. The name would continue. At least, it would have. But now, because of whom he had married, and his wife's secret life, it wouldn't.

Caitlin was riddled with guilt as she watched him slump in his otherwise comfortable seat. He was clearly feeling the weight of the world on his shoulders. He closed his eyes, seemingly in prayer. She couldn't help but wonder if he was asking God for relief, or for answers, or for all this to be an awful nightmare that he would soon wake up from. Her only hope was that one day, he could forgive her.

CHAPTER 28

I-495 SOUTH

OUTSIDE ADELPHI, MARYLAND

June 1, 5:33 p.m.

Butler had slowed his driving speed to accommodate the increasingly dense traffic. He was now traveling only eighty miles per hour. Sitting next to him, Skylar kept her eyes focused ahead of them, scanning for white vans. She pointed. "There's another one."

"That's tan, not white."

"You sure?" As they got closer to the van in question, she could see that he was correct. The van had Maine plates and appeared to be transporting a group of senior citizens. "Never mind." She practically jumped out of her seat as Butler's burner phone started to ring. She glanced at the caller ID. "Is that her?"

Butler did not recognize the number. "Don't know who else it would be." He answered the call, hitting the speakerphone button. "Yeah."

Eleanor's familiar voice came over the phone's speaker. "Where are you?"

"In Maryland. Just passed a town called Adelphi. About thirty minutes north of Alexandria."

"You should be coming up on them any minute. New Jersey license plate Bravo-one-seven-Delta-Charlie-Mike."

((•))

Inside her safe house basement operations center, Caitlin had a real-time satellite view of the van, which Hogan had given her access to. The American Heritage Foundation tracked every one of its vehicles via satellite, not unlike FedEx or the US Postal Service. What would become clear to her shortly was that any technology the foundation had at their disposal, she now had, too.

((•))

Butler glanced at Skylar: "Eleanor, I'd like to introduce you to Skylar, who's in the car with me."

"Hello, Skylar, how are you feeling?"

"Better, thanks. Uh, how are you?"

"I want you to know how sorry I am about what happened to you and Eddie Parks. It's inexcusable. I'm determined to prevent it from ever happening again."

Skylar's eyes widened. "Thank you. That's very decent of you. I hope I get to meet you someday so that I can thank you in person."

"I hope so, too." There was a hint of guilt in her voice.

Butler knew what Eleanor was saying. She meant if they both lived through this, that is. He had been in her position in his previous life as a Ranger, where operations he was part of had placed innocents at risk. It happened regularly back then. He remembered carrying a tremendous sense of responsibility during each event and a heavy burden afterward when collateral damage was left behind. It had a lot to do with why he had retired from that life to become a cop.

He spotted another white van seven vehicles ahead of them in the fast lane. He sped up slightly to get close enough to make out the license plate. He squinted, turning his eyes into zoom lenses as best he could. He read the plate twice to confirm that it was the one they were looking for. "Eleanor, I have eyes on Jersey plate Bravo-one-seven-Delta-Charlie-Mike. I'll call you back after we have Parks and the device in our custody."

"Good luck." She hung up.

He pointed to his bad-day bag, on the floor between Skylar's feet. "There are two handguns in the bag between your legs. I need you to hand them to me."

"Are they loaded?"

"Yes. Have you ever handled a firearm before?"

"No."

"Don't touch the triggers and you'll be fine."

"Don't touch the triggers. Got it." She reached into his bad-day bag and withdrew two handguns. She held them upside down, her thumbs and forefingers on the handles, well away from the triggers, as she passed them to Butler.

He tucked one between his legs and placed the other in his lap. They were now five cars behind the van. "What are the odds the driver of the van knows what you look like?"

"If I had to guess, it's a member of the Harmony House security staff, so the odds are good."

"Whoever it is, they won't be alone." Butler was rapidly running through several tactical scenarios that would accomplish their goal with the least risk. He could be patient and simply follow them, but if they had any of the training he had, they'd eventually spot him. In that case, they would run. A high-speed chase would only put Eddie in even greater danger. They might also just put a gun to Eddie's head, and that wouldn't be any better.

Right now, he had the element of surprise, which was never to be underestimated. It was a tactical advantage he intended to capitalize on, so the question then became one of approach. How could he get close enough to the van without drawing attention to himself, incapacitate the bad guys holding Eddie captive, stop their vehicle, rescue Eddie, and do it all without harming any innocent civilians by causing a massive pileup? "We can't let them see you."

"Should I duck down?"

"When I say so." They were now three cars behind the van. Butler was focused on the rearview mirror, looking for something. "Here's what's going to happen. Look in the side-view mirror. You see that big rig in the outside lane passing everyone?"

She did as he instructed, and had no trouble seeing it in the right lane. "Yes."

"He's going to be our blocker."

"You mean like in football?"

"Exactly."

"Does he know that?"

"He will soon enough." Butler changed lanes into the rightmost of the three, directly in the path of the speeding yellow big rig. The trucker didn't seem to appreciate Butler's maneuver and tailgated him by only a few feet until finally swerving around him to the left, into the middle lane. As the big rig accelerated, so did Butler, who kept right alongside him at seventy-five miles per hour. Then eighty. And eighty-five.

The truck driver could see Butler in his side view and gave him the finger. Butler waved back, as if he didn't understand the gesture. The truck accelerated to ninety. So did Butler.

He glanced to his left but couldn't see beyond the truck. "Tell me when you can see the van."

Skylar kept her eyes peeled on the inside lane behind them. "I can see it."

"Duck down." She did. Butler punched the gas, accelerating rapidly. The Impala was now going over one hundred miles per hour as it swerved in front of the big rig in the middle lane, and immediately proceeded to slow down again. Anyone who's ever witnessed unadulterated road rage on the freeways of Southern California would recognize the dangerous game these two vehicles were playing. Usually, the combatants were of more comparable size; civilian drivers rarely chose to take on big rigs, for the same reason that lone velociraptors never battled a tyrannosaurus back when dinosaurs were the planet's dominant species. Size matters.

The big rig came ever so close to rear-ending the Impala before swerving right to pass him for a second time. The trucker clearly expected their game to continue and almost seemed disappointed as the Impala continued decelerating. The trucker blared his air horn as a pronouncement of victory.

Butler's eyes were now focused on the van in his side-view mirror. The white vehicle was several car lengths behind them. He rolled down his window. "Push down with your feet to brace yourself against the seat."

Skylar did so, clearly scared. "Please make sure Eddie doesn't get hurt."

"I'm doing everything I can." He continued slowing down. The van was now only one car length behind them. Neither of the two men in the front seats seemed to be paying any attention to them. *So far, so good.* "After we stop, slide over and drive."

"What?" she replied with alarm. "When are we stopping? In the middle of the highway? Where are you going to be?"

Focused on the job at hand, he did not answer. He gripped the gun firmly in his right hand and held the steering wheel with his left. He allowed the van to pull alongside them. Butler kept his eyes directed ahead until he suddenly turned to his left and aimed his gun through the open window.

CHAPTER 29

INSIDE THE WHITE PACKAGE VAN

I-495 SOUTH

June 1, 5:36 p.m.

Packard and Clementine had briefly noticed the Impala playing chicken with the big rig ahead of them. It was hard not to notice, but neither paid much attention to it. Civilian drivers were stupid. Whoever was driving the old Chevy was an idiot to be messing with an eighteen-wheeler. As they pulled up alongside the Impala, both glanced over to get a look at the driver with bigger balls than brains.

Unfortunately for them, that was exactly what this other driver had wanted them to think. To underestimate him. Right until they were both looking down the barrel of his weapon.

(((•)))

In the back of the van, Eddie had no idea what was about to occur. He was lost in his own world of happy memories. In particular, the sound of his mother's voice, which he'd only recently heard for the first time, thanks to his echo box. He remembered every syllable of every word of the beloved hymn she had sung that day in church just over three decades ago. Few people knew that "Amazing Grace" had been written by a reformed slave trader, John Newton, who then took up the abolitionist cause.

Eddie remembered how happy he felt to see his grandparents in the church as they listened to the beautiful echoes of his mother's voice, and how they had cried happy tears together. He had never cried together with anyone before, especially not happy tears. It was a feeling that gave him a warm sensation all over, which he didn't fully understand, but the memory of it was reassuring.

Eddie's happy memories were suddenly cut short by the sound of four gunshots in quick succession. BOOM-BOOM-BOOM-BOOM! Other than on television, he had never heard a weapon being fired. Real ones were much louder. And piercing. And frightening. They hurt his ears tremendously. So did the SHATTERING glass and the SCREECHING metal.

However, that was nothing compared to the other types of physical pain he was about to endure.

((•))

Butler's first bullet had punctured the torsos of both his targets and was the only one he really needed to have fired. The passenger, the closer of the two, was hit squarely in the chest. Two valves of his heart were shredded. He died instantly. The bullet must have changed angles as it exited his body, because the driver was hit in the hip, where the bullet lodged. He could no longer operate his right leg, which explained why the van slowed down so rapidly. Well, that and Butler had swerved into them, wedging the van between a guardrail and the Impala.

His second bullet ripped through the passenger's neck and would have killed him if the first one hadn't. This bullet then hit the driver in the jaw, creating a truly hideous profile. The third bullet missed both men entirely, probably due to the side impact of the vehicles causing Butler's shooting hand to jolt. He knew his objective had already been accomplished, but he had told himself he was going to fire four times in rapid succession, and that's what he did. He pulled the trigger a fourth time, making a further mess of the targets' skulls.

Butler returned his focus to the road ahead, putting both hands back on the steering wheel. After all, distracted driving was just as dangerous as drunk driving, according to the most recent Federal Highway Administration statistics. The screeching metal was almost as piercing as the gunfire when he forced the van into the guardrail, rapidly slowing down both vehicles.

((•))

Skylar worried about Eddie's hearing, but she knew there was nothing she could do. She flashed back to the grenade that had temporarily blinded her and caused her momentary deafness. It was frightening and painful, and would be only more so for Eddie, but she had faith that he, too, would survive.

To her amazement, Butler's strategy seemed to be going according to plan. They and the van continued slowing down amid a hail of sparks from the metal-on-metal contact of the van with the guardrail, on the left side, and the Impala, on the right. Both vehicles came to a stop a quarter mile later. Butler's door was wedged against the side of the van, and his handle would not open it. He quickly pulled ahead of the van one car length so that he could get out of the car. He slammed the transmission into park and stepped out of the car. "Your turn to drive."

"Where am I going?" she asked with panic as she climbed over the gearshift into the driver's seat.

"Just follow me when I start to drive." He ran back toward the passenger side of the van since the driver's side was wedged against the guardrail. There was no way to open the doors on that side. He would have to use the ones closer to oncoming traffic.

((•))

In the back of the van, Eddie's ears were throbbing; he was crying in pain from the aural damage caused by the gunshots. He estimated the decibel level of each at over 150. Noises of 140 decibels could permanently damage a person's hearing, and Eddie was afraid that the terrible ringing in his ears would never stop, that his hearing might forever be impaired. He had no idea what he would do if he couldn't hear clearly—if he had lost his "golden ears." While it was scary to think that Packard and the other man had been shot and killed, and that their blood was now spattered all over the van, including some that had gotten on him, it was scarier for Eddie to consider the possibility that he would no longer hear the world in the same way.

Besides, the two men in the front of the van had not been nice to him, so Eddie didn't feel bad for them that they now seemed to be dead. He knew that kidnapping was a serious crime, and he was quite sure that they had kidnapped him. People who did bad things deserved to be arrested and sent to jail, at least if they were not killed first.

Eddie also hadn't liked when they had refused to tell him where they were, or where they were taking him. That just wasn't right, not telling somebody those things. He would never do that to another person, and he felt a degree of satisfaction that the bad men could no longer be mean to him. They had gotten what they deserved.

The gunshots were immediately followed by tires SCREECHING and metal SCRAPING and glass SHATTERING, which only added to Eddie's terror. As the van slowed rapidly and finally came to a stop, he was thrown forward against the metal mesh that separated him from the two dead men in the front. The bloody mesh created a kind of graphic artwork across his back and right cheek—the same one that had already borne the brunt of his self-inflicted wounds. It was hard to tell whose blood it was, his or theirs. Eddie had numerous cuts around his body, including a gash in his forehead, but none were terribly severe. A stitch here, and a stitch there, and he would be back to normal in short order.

That was, until the driver of a brand-spanking-new Mercedes S550, who had been a number of car lengths behind the white package van when it finally stopped along the guardrail, was currently so busy texting a response to his divorce lawyer that he didn't notice the right rear bumper of the van sticking into his lane until it was too late.

CHAPTER 30

I-495 SOUTH

SCENE OF THE ACCIDENT

June 1, 5:38 p.m.

The German-made luxury sedan had a gross weight of 4,729 pounds. Traveling at eighty-three miles per hour, the vehicle had kinetic energy of almost 1.5 million joules. In nonscientific terms, that was enough to do major damage to anything it hit, particularly an object that was standing still. WHAM!

Inside the Mercedes, the driver's toupee flew off into the windshield as his head was jolted forward from impact with the van. The collision crumpled the right rear of the van, causing the tire to explode instantly.

The impact triggered the release of the driver's airbag, which only took 0.01 seconds to inflate. This happens to be the same length of time as the average blink of a human eyelid, which means that many people who witness airbags deploying don't actually see it happen. That was the case now. The driver did not see the bag deploy, but he certainly felt it hit him in the face. It knocked him unconscious and broke his nose. It also caused several blood vessels in both eyes to burst, making him look hideous for weeks to come.

The pursuit of wife number four was going to have to wait.

((•))

Butler saw the expensive German car barreling toward them and barely had time to react. He knew the impact was going to throw the white van forward, possibly pinning him between it and the rear of the Impala. Diving over the guardrail would send him into oncoming traffic traveling in the opposite direction, which would have been just as bad as diving into traffic on his side of the interstate. His only option was to jump onto the Impala's trunk, which he did just before the van slammed into its bumper. It missed Butler's legs by a matter of inches. When the car finally came to rest, he yelled to Skylar, who had just climbed into the driver's seat. "You okay?"

She grimaced as she rubbed her neck. "Fine. You?"

"Barely."

"Check on Eddie!"

Butler quickly scrambled off the car and went to find Eddie. The rear doors of the van had slammed open during the violent collision. Eddie lay on the floor of the van, unconscious. His hands remained cuffed behind his back. The impact had thrown him around the back of the van. He was bleeding through his pants from a gash in his calf, as well as from his head. He was lucky it hadn't killed him.

Skylar quickly joined Butler at the back of the van. "He needs a doctor."

Butler moved to the front of the van, looking for the handcuff key. He reached into several of the dead driver's pockets until he found it. Butler took the key and then uncuffed Eddie's wrists, picking him up in his arms. "Get his devices. They're in front." He motioned through the mesh, where the two dead bodies were sprawled. The echo box and Eddie's computer were both covered in blood.

Skylar walked around to the front passenger door and opened it. She recognized the driver—Packard, Harmony House's newly hired head of security. She reached over the other body in the passenger seat, trying hard not to touch the bloody corpse as she grabbed Eddie's equipment and quickly carried it to the Impala, where she joined Eddie in the back seat. Butler had laid him across it before getting in the driver's seat. Blood was now streaming down Eddie's leg. "Give me your hoodie," Skylar said.

Butler took off his sweatshirt and handed it to her. She created a tourniquet by wrapping it around Eddie's leg just above the knee, then tying it as tightly as she could. Skylar elevated his leg above his heart to reduce the amount of blood being pumped to the wound. She pressed her hand against his head wound to stem the flow of blood and couldn't stop staring at the lacerations on his face that he'd inflicted on himself earlier. "Oh, Eddie . . ."

Behind them, Butler could see that a number of motorists had gotten out of their vehicles to offer assistance, or just because they were curious. Several were talking into their phones, most likely to 911 dispatchers. Several more filmed the scene to sell it to the highest bidder, or just to post the day's excitement on their social media accounts.

Butler punched the Impala's accelerator to the floor, hoping they might get lucky and avoid anyone recording their license plate. Skylar turned to him urgently. "We need to find the nearest medical facility."

"I'm getting off at the next exit." He swerved across the three lanes and took the off-ramp, heading west as he hit "Redial" on his burner phone.

CHAPTER 31

SAFE HOUSE

GILBERTS CORNER, VIRGINIA

June 1, 5:42 p.m.

Caitlin had been following the action from the GeoEye-1 Reconnaissance Satellite operated by the National Geospatial-Intelligence Agency. It was the most advanced imaging satellite in orbit around Earth. The American Heritage Foundation had a unique relationship with the agency that afforded it complete access to the classified abilities of this satellite. And if the foundation had access to it, that meant Caitlin did as well.

She had become thoroughly impressed with Butler, watching him maneuver into position to take down the white van. *It was just how I would have drawn it up.* He had executed his plan perfectly, and they should have gotten away cleanly. But even with the best plan and deft execution, things go wrong as often as they don't. Those who can improvise at critical moments are the ones who become the most renowned in their chosen fields. Just ask Ben Roethlisberger or Jordan Peele.

When she saw him carry Eddie from the van to their vehicle, Caitlin knew Eddie needed medical treatment, and she was already researching facilities in their vicinity by the time Butler called. She answered on the first ring. "You're good."

"Not good enough." He was clearly blaming himself for Eddie's injuries.

"Shit happens."

"Always does."

"If you're calling to tell me you need medical, I've got a couple options for you. What level facility do you need?"

Skylar answered for him. "Eddie has two wounds that require stitches, and a possible fracture. He's lost a fair amount of blood. I'd also like to get him a head CT and an MRI, but those aren't as urgent."

Caitlin asked, "If I get you the supplies, can you do the work?"

"If I had to, I suppose," Skylar reluctantly offered up. "But I'd really prefer someone who's used to performing emergency medicine."

"Traditional facilities aren't an option for us," Butler interjected.

"Why not?"

"The personnel will ask questions that you won't have good answers for," Caitlin answered.

Butler added, "We can't risk having the authorities notified."

"Because we stole a car?" Skylar asked incredulously.

"Because the people who had you kidnapped have access to law enforcement communication," Caitlin answered. "If anyone notifies the police about Eddie, he's done."

"Usually when people say it feels like they have the whole world against them, it's a metaphor."

"We'll get you through this," Caitlin said with certainty. "While I work on the supplies, find yourselves a new vehicle. Odds are good one of the Samaritans on the interstate captured your plates."

"Copy that," Butler replied, and then hung up.

(((•)))

Skylar was reeling. This was all too much for her. In just one day, she had been kidnapped, then rescued; she'd ridden in her first stolen car,

131

witnessed three people being shot to death, and was now trying to keep her most important patient from bleeding to death while fleeing the scene of a three-vehicle highway accident.

And happy hour wasn't even over yet.

Butler glanced back at her in the rearview mirror. "You're hyperventilating."

"I'm what?" She was so lost in thought, she didn't hear what he said.

"Your breathing. Slow it down."

She only now realized that she was breathing rapidly, as if she was in the middle of a spin class. After taking several long, deep breaths, she looked at Butler with curiosity. "How the hell are you so calm?"

"I'm not."

"Well, you look it."

"I'm faking it because if I let you see how nervous I really am, you'll start hyperventilating again and pass out on me. Then I'll have to stitch up Eddie with a sewing needle, and he'll have such terrible scars that neither of you will ever forgive me, and I'm living with enough guilt as it is."

She couldn't stop herself from cracking a smile. If she had to be having the worst day of her life, she was certainly glad Butler McHenry was the one to help her get through it.

CHAPTER 32

EN ROUTE TO THE WHITE HOUSE

WASHINGTON, DC

June 1, 5:50 p.m.

The drive from the American Heritage Foundation to the White House took only eighteen minutes, if you excluded the thirty to sixty minutes it took to get through the many security checkpoints protecting the home of the president. It was no accident the AHF's base of operations was close, but not too close, to the Oval Office. When Lawrence Walters and the other founders wanted access, they wanted it readily; but when they didn't, they preferred not to see any sign of the squalor they associated with our nation's capital.

Jason Greers drove along the Potomac River, which Lyndon Johnson had declared "a national disgrace" in 1965 due to the pollution levels caused by unchecked sewage flowing into it. Looking out through the windows, Greers admired the view of democracy's epicenter. "Every time I approach DC, I get this feeling, you know?"

Daryl Trotter sat next to him, fidgeting. He nodded. "I've never been inside the White House as an invited guest. Have you?"

Greers shook his head. "Nope. My first time, too. Looks like we're popping our cherries together."

Daryl smiled politely, secretly hating when his counterpart used sexual metaphors. He was never much for locker-room talk; the subject never interested him that much. In a world where identities of sexual preference were ever-expanding, Daryl was in the rarest category. He was asexual; he just wasn't very interested in the whole deal. The few times in his life when he had engaged in some form of sex with another person, he couldn't help but feel during the act that a good game of chess would have been much more enjoyable.

"I'm glad the president isn't going to be there," he commented. "I think I'd have a hard time concentrating if he was in the office with us."

Greers shook his head. "It's not like we're going there to dust the drapes. He wouldn't just conduct business as usual."

"No, I suppose not." Daryl wiped his sweaty palms on his pant legs.

"What are you so nervous for? I mean, just because we're about to come into possession of probably the biggest cache of government secrets in the last hundred years or so, what's the big deal?" Jason smiled wryly.

Daryl cleared his throat. "I sweat when I get nervous. You get sarcastic. Two different reactions to the same stimulus."

"The difference is, I can bite my tongue, and nobody knows the difference. But if someone shakes your hand . . . yikes."

"I'll do my very best to be more like you," Daryl retorted sarcastically.

((•))

Jason smiled. He liked Daryl for two reasons: their skill sets were complimentary, and he'd pose no threat in terms of succession when the time came.

Jason admired the Lincoln Memorial as they drove around it, finally deciding to ask something that had been on his mind ever since they had left Alexandria. "What do you think Caitlin's up to?"

Daryl answered flatly. "I think it's pretty obvious."

"When don't you think something is obvious?"

"It happens, on occasion," he replied smugly. "What do you think she's up to?"

"I think she's lost her mind."

"I would agree."

"The question is to what extent."

"It seems to me that was answered when you had difficulty transferring payment to the cleaners in Philadelphia."

Jason paused to make sure he understood what Daryl was implying. "You think that was her?"

"Who else?"

"I figured it was an accounting issue, or something technical with the bank." Jason was embarrassed. He had not considered the possibility that Caitlin was behind it.

"Think probabilistically. Have you ever been aware of an accounting issue, or something technical with a bank, occurring with the foundation's finances in the entire time you've worked there?"

"No."

"Me either. So the probability is nil. Coincidence can be ruled out."

Jason paused to consider the ramifications. "Do you think she merely blocked the funds or stole them?"

Daryl studied Jason closely, clearly relishing his intellectual superiority. "You really do need me for this, don't you?"

"In the end, you should be glad." He said it with just the right amount of confidence to let Daryl know he would only tolerate so much mental preening. If he didn't stop, Jason would make him pay somewhere down the road.

"I think you underestimate her."

"Why do you think that?"

"Because she's not you."

The hairs on the back of Jason's neck started to stand up. "I gather you think I'm pretty arrogant?"

Daryl tried to assuage whatever feathers he had ruffled. "No more than an heir apparent should be. Though considering the pedigree Caitlin comes from, it should be her, not you, who's next in line. But she's not. There's no question, and there hasn't been for some time now."

Jason paused, appreciating the compliment. "Do you think that's what this is about? Jealousy?"

"No, I think it's a matter of principle."

"Because of how we've treated Eddie Parks?"

"No. She did this because of how we've treated Skylar Drummond."

Of course! Caitlin identified with the ambitious young doctor struggling to make her way in a male-dominated field, just like Caitlin had been doing her entire career. Skylar's only crime had been to have a boyfriend who stuck his nose into her business where it didn't belong. Her employer had had him killed for it, leaving her ridden with blame for the rest of her life. Instead of using her patient's technology to prove her former boss's guilt, she had helped Eddie accomplish the only thing he ever wanted in his life: to hear his mother's voice. And what did she get for it? To be kidnapped and tortured. "It is shameful, isn't it?"

"Yes. In our business, there's always collateral damage that's difficult to stomach. I choose not to."

Jason nodded, realizing that Daryl was describing his own approach. "We're better at shutting off our feelings, aren't we? Guys, I mean."

"Shutting them off implies you know what you're feeling. I can honestly say I have the emotional maturity of a newt."

"That's because you spend too much time thinking."

"I don't know how not to."

Jason nodded again. "If Caitlin really is going against Stenson, it's suicide."

Daryl responded thoughtfully, "She may be many things, but she's not suicidal."

"What, then?"

"You're assuming she's doing this alone."

"From what I understand, her father is practically a vegetable."

"Do you know the real benefit of coming from a rich and powerful family? Sure, the money and education are both great, but the thing that gives rich kids the most help over commoners like us is connections. The relationships their birthright affords them. It could be a relative, or a business associate, or just an old family friend, but where we have to scratch and claw on our own, sometimes for years, they make one phone call and it's done."

Jason paused. "You're right. There is no way she could have drained the accounts without help."

Daryl nodded. "Exactly."

"So who do you think she's got working with her?"

"Whoever it is has got Stenson nervous."

"Why do you say that?"

"Because he sent us to go to the White House instead of doing it himself. Think about what he's trusting us with. It's one of the reasons he's been so focused on acquiring the echo box from the first time he heard about it. Knowing everything that's ever been said inside the Oval Office will give him the highest-value trump card he's ever had to play."

Jason nodded in agreement. "It's an unbeatable one."

"The only possible reason he's not doing this himself is because there is something more urgent that requires his attention."

Jason now fully understood. "You mean, he's playing defense while we play offense."

"Exactly."

"I would sure like to know who the hell she managed to recruit and how she got them on board so fast."

Trotter studied Greers as he inched their car toward an armed guard at the first White House security checkpoint. "There was nothing fast about it. To get somebody good enough to create such a serious and immediate threat to Stenson, that doesn't happen in minutes or hours or even days. She had to have laid the groundwork a long time ago. The only thing she did quickly was initiate the plan."

Greers did his best to hide his surprise. He had completely underestimated his female colleague. *God, I am such a chauvinist! My mother would be so disappointed if she ever found out.* His concerns then quickly turned practical—namely, his own survival. While he did not expect Caitlin to win this battle, he had to consider the possibility. And if she did, how would she view him—as an ally or an adversary? And if it was the latter, would he be given the opportunity to persuade her that he was on her side?

He put his strategic considerations aside as he rolled down the window to present their identification to the checkpoint guard. "Jason Greers and Daryl Trotter. We're expected."

CHAPTER 33

AMERICAN HERITAGE FOUNDATION

ALEXANDRIA, VIRGINIA

June 1, 6:11 p.m.

Bob Stenson was working on locating the nearest team of contract killers when he first received notice of the accident in Maryland involving the two independent contractors he'd recently placed in Harmony House. The van was owned by a shell corporation that had a special designation within most police departments and US law enforcement agencies. This designation meant that Stenson was notified whenever one of its vehicles was involved in an accident or any other type of incident that required police involvement, particularly one that included a double homicide.

Stenson only now realized how formidable an opponent he was facing. Whoever had taken out his team had also grabbed Eddie Parks and his box. Current whereabouts were unknown, but based on blood discovered in the back of the van, it was believed that Eddie was injured and in need of medical treatment. Which meant he couldn't have gone far.

Witnesses at the scene described a man and a woman who had removed an unconscious male from the rear of the van, along with some equipment or suitcases, and fled the scene. The descriptions matched those of Skylar Drummond and Butler McHenry, so apparently they had driven down from Philadelphia and intercepted Parks. But how? It could only be possible if two things were true: they were in communication with Caitlin, and she had access to the foundation's tracking system—or worse, to the same real-time satellite surveillance they had. *My God, how long had she been planning this? And who the hell is helping her?*

It was at this moment that Caitlin stopped being his former employee and the daughter of his mentor and became the single biggest threat he had ever faced. He was willing to go to absolutely any lengths to stop her.

This was about to get very ugly.

CHAPTER 34

Safe House

Gilberts Corner, Virginia

June 1, 6:13 p.m.

Caitlin tracked the Embraer Phenom, which was currently somewhere over western Pennsylvania. The aircraft was flying at an altitude of twenty-eight thousand feet. Its Pratt & Whitney turbofan engines could maintain a cruising speed of five hundred miles per hour, so the 1,400-mile flight to North Dakota would take approximately three hours. There was still quite a bit of flying time left.

On another screen that showed the inside of the aircraft, Peter McCloskey stepped out of the cramped lavatory for the third time since the plane took off. Caitlin recognized the look on his face. It was the same one he used to get before his board meetings years ago. His stomach was in turmoil. Given the circumstances, she supposed it was to be expected.

Peter glanced at their two children, who were now both sound asleep. Marissa was curled into a little ball, with her clenched hands tucked beneath her cheek, making her look almost as if she'd been posed that way. Mikey was stretched out on his back with his mouth wide open. Caitlin was certain he was snoring up a storm, as usual. All she could think was that as long as they were safe, nothing else mattered.

Now back in his seat, Peter, on the other hand, looked like he was stewing. His face was full of frustration. Then anger. Then doubt and disbelief. Caitlin could imagine the thoughts running through her husband's mind—because she knew how it worked, and she knew what she'd be thinking if the shoe were on the other foot.

Apparently deciding he needed to occupy himself, Peter reviewed the contents of the briefcase once again. He flipped through the passports, recounted the cash, and studied the house keys. He then noticed a compartment in the briefcase lid he hadn't seen before. It contained a manila folder with two years of joint tax returns for Peter and Caitlin Montgomery, a certified copy of their marriage license, and copies of their social security numbers, along with the children's. He shook his head, apparently at his wife's thoroughness.

Watching her screens, Caitlin spoke as if he could hear her: "Would you find it, already?" On-screen, Peter then saw a handwritten envelope addressed to him. He recognized the writing. It was Caitlin's. The envelope was not sealed, but he still opened it carefully and took out the one-page letter. Caitlin smiled slightly, remembering every word of the letter she had written. She repeated them as he read: "Dear Peter, please know how sorry I am that you are having to read this letter. This was never supposed to happen. I'm sure you must have a great many questions, which I will do my best to answer as soon as I am able to join you. The most important thing I want you to know is how much I love you and the children. You are my heart and soul. I have only taken this precaution to protect you, given circumstances that are beyond my control. Your safety is my paramount concern. I hope to see you soon. All my love, Caitlin."

She saw him touch the ink where she had signed her name and rub some of it onto his finger, staining it blue. This was all Caitlin needed to see. She knew that as mad and confused as he must be feeling, he was doing his best to carry on. For the time being, that was all she could ask.

CHAPTER 35

David's Place

Woodsdale, Maryland

June 1, 7:32 p.m.

Skylar stood over Eddie, admiring her surgical handiwork. She hadn't stitched up a patient since medical school, and she had done it then only because it was a course requirement. She had always been much more interested in the workings of the mind than the body, but Harvard Medical School seemed to think it was important that all their doctors-to-be were capable of basic emergency medicine.

Until now, she had never seen the point.

Eleanor had located the supplies Skylar had requested from a nearby urgent care facility. The young nurse who answered the phone was willing to make a cash deal for certain items, as if she'd done it before, but was unwilling to approach the doctor on duty out of fear it would expose her proclivity for extracurricular income. Apparently, he was her father. For a $1,700 Venmo transfer, Eleanor purchased dissolvable catgut sutures (which, curiously, were made from the intestines of sheep or goats instead of cats); Betadine, an antiseptic; lidocaine, a topical anesthetic; propofol, a sedative; an IV bag and tube; several bags of saline; and rolls of gauze and tape for wrapping the sutured wounds afterward.

They had met the young nurse at the rear of the facility, where the items were exchanged and the money transfer received. Butler asked how long it would be until her shift ended. Apparently misinterpreting his intentions, she answered that she got off at ten o'clock, which would be in four hours. Butler pointed his gun in her face and asked for the keys to her car. He told her not to report it stolen until her shift ended. Otherwise, the authorities would also find out about her supplemental income.

After they put Eddie in the back seat and drove away in the nurse's thirty-year-old Jeep Wagoneer, Skylar commented, "I bet that's the last time she sells any more drugs off the books."

Butler shook his head. "Don't try to make me feel better. What I did was wrong."

"What you did was necessary."

"It's a slippery slope. Trust me."

He then realized Eleanor must be following them in real time, because she called them immediately. "I found a facility where you can do the surgery—it's called David's Place. It's a residential facility for adults with special needs. Eddie should feel right at home."

"That's a hell of a coincidence," Skylar chimed in, a bit suspicious.

"It's intentional," Eleanor corrected her. "You will need a place for him to recover. I figured it would be best if you didn't have to move him."

Butler grinned, clearly appreciating the number of moves his counterpart was thinking ahead. "Eleanor, I want you to know I'm really starting to like you."

Skylar regretted having any doubt. "Me too."

"The feeling's mutual." There was a pause on the line. "By the way, my real name is Caitlin."

Butler glanced at Skylar, eyeballing her to make sure she appreciated what a big deal it was that Caitlin had revealed her identity. Skylar nodded. She understood.

When they arrived at David's Place, it was obvious the building had seen better days. Or, more accurately, better decades. The facility was ripe to be leveled. Butler and Skylar were greeted by two orderlies. One appeared to be at least seventy years old and walked slightly hunched over. His name, Roberto, was stitched on the lapel of his shirt to help the residents remember it. The other man was half his age and walked with a limp. His name, Zeke, also appeared on his uniform. "You all friends of Eleanor?"

Butler nodded. "That's us." Whatever financial arrangements Caitlin had made with them, the two men were clearly motivated to help and moved with all the vim and vigor they could muster.

They opened the doors for Butler, who carried Eddie. Roberto and Zeke led them down a hallway to an empty room with a bed and not much else. "You let us know if there's anything we can get for you," Roberto said. "We'll be right down the hall."

They shut the door to give the new arrivals some privacy. Apparently, this facility had several empty rooms—which, given its appearance, wasn't much of a surprise.

Butler laid Eddie down gently and assisted Skylar as she prepared to stitch up his wounds. She ran his IV, adding propofol to the saline, then sterilized his leg wound, which was the more serious of the two. After injecting the area with local anesthetic, she began to stitch him up. Her hands moved with careful precision.

Looking on, Butler couldn't help but be impressed. "When did you say was the last time you did this?"

She maintained complete concentration on the wound. "Medical school."

"If this is what you're bad at, I'd like to see what you're good at."

"If you ever want some therapy, just let me know. It would seem like the least I could do." Her focus never deviated. In fact, the chitchat seemed to help her relax, much like doodling in the margins does for students during a long lecture.

Given the number of stitches Eddie was going to need, that was a good thing.

CHAPTER 36

115 NORTH PENNSYLVANIA PLACE

INDIANAPOLIS, INDIANA

June 1, 8:17 p.m.

Indiana senator Corbin Davis had been meeting for seventeen minutes with the director of the state's Department of Natural Resources, who oversaw the thirty-five thousand miles of rivers that flowed through Hoosier terrain, as well as its nine hundred lakes. Today, the priority item on the agenda was the rising level of toxins being dumped into the Wabash River by residents of Ohio, where the waterway originated. It seemed that Buckeyes were increasingly viewing Indiana's state river—the longest free-flowing one east of the Mississippi—as nothing more than a mechanism for removing their waste.

Senator Davis flipped through the dozens of charts and graphs the director had brought with him to support his claims. "It's too bad we can't just reverse the direction the river flows in. Give them a taste of their own putrid medicine."

"That would require the good Lord jumping in to our little spat, and I'm not quite sure He'd abide."

The senator smiled, thinking that it all depended on what you offered up in exchange for the request. He saw the world through more of an Old Testament prism, which meant "an eye for an eye" was completely justified. "What about carrying the garbage back across the state line in dump trucks?"

Now it was the director's turn to smile. "I've already had my people price out what a convoy would cost." He shook his head. "You don't even want to know."

"Would be a hell of a visual, though, wouldn't it? Especially if we dumped the shit right in downtown Columbus." Davis enjoyed the thought of all the news coverage it would receive.

"Problem is, it might not look all that different than it does now." The director chuckled.

Senator Davis joined in the laugh as his chief of staff, Bob Welker, entered quietly and stood by the door. He was holding two sheets of paper. He gave his boss a slight nod, which was their signal for "I need you privately." Davis stood, signaling that his meeting with the state's chief environmentalist was coming to an end. "I'll give my counterpart in Ohio a call and see if he'll take responsibility for this mess. If not, you know what we're going to do?"

"What, sir?" The director honestly had no idea as he shook the senator's hand.

"We'll send one truck, just one, with the nastiest crap that's flowing into our beautiful state and dump it right in front of their capitol building."

"In that case, I hope he hangs up on you." He nodded to Welker as he exited.

Davis's chief of staff shook his head with admiration as he joined his boss on the couch. "It's no wonder people love you. Your knack for lighting a fire in everyone who works for you never ceases to astound me."

"Wait until I get the big job," the senator said, referring to the presidency.

Welker shook his head. "No need to gild the lily, sir."

Davis paused. "You've got that look you get when you're about to share big news or tell me a big secret. Which is it?"

"I can't say with certainty yet, but I actually think it's both," Welker answered. "I just spoke to Walt Connell's chief of staff, who said his boss had a curious ride in Air Force One."

"Curious how? They didn't decide to disband the Freedom Caucus, did they?"

"That'll be the day. But his little tête-à-tête with the president was briefly interrupted by a call from your new benefactor, Bob Stenson."

Now Welker had the senator's attention. "Was it, now?"

"Seems that Stenson was calling to inform our chief executive that he may have a security problem at the White House."

"What kind of security problem?"

"Some new type of threat—from space, if you can believe it. Stenson is sending a team to the Oval Office to scan it with some new device they've developed."

The senator processed the information. "Sounds like complete bullshit to me."

"To me as well. Seems like more of a ploy on Stenson's part to get his men and this new device into the office."

It now hit Davis what his number one was suggesting. "Holy shit."

"I have a contact in White House security. When Stenson's team passes through their system, he's going to send me screen grabs of the team and this device."

"If it's what I think it is—"

His chief of staff finished the thought for him. "Something very big is being set in motion."

CHAPTER 37

David's Place

Woodsdale, Maryland

June 1, 9:01 p.m.

Eddie's leg wound required thirty-six stitches: eighteen internal and eighteen external. His head wound only needed twelve. By the time Skylar had finished tying off the last of them, ninety-two minutes had passed. "As long as we can keep him calm, I think those will hold."

Butler was impressed. "There were a number of times I could have used you back when I was in the military."

She nodded, appreciating the compliment, and breathed a sigh of relief. "I am absolutely starving."

"I'll go see what our options are." He left the room, practically knocking over the person who'd been standing on the other side of the door, listening to their every word.

Butler instinctively adopted a defensive pose, then recognized that she didn't represent a threat. "Can I help you?"

The young lady seemed flustered. And embarrassed. She was in her twenties and wore a University of Maryland sweat suit with fuzzy pink slippers. She wore no makeup. Her hair was shoulder length, but not styled in any fashion Butler could discern. "That was Helena's room." Her voice was soft, not much above a whisper.

"Who's Helena?"

"Helena was my friend. Very special, Helena. She was nice and kind and clean because she showered every day, sometimes twice." Her cadence was inconsistent, almost like she momentarily forgot what she was about to say and then, upon remembering the words, pronounced them as rapidly as she could before forgetting them again. "But she died. Very sad. Did you know her, Helena?"

Butler realized she must be a resident of the facility. He didn't know if she was on the autism spectrum, like Eddie, or what kind of neurological issue she had, but it was clear to him that she was not what clinicians would describe as being in the neurological mainstream. "No, I didn't."

"That's too bad for you. Sorry. Maybe you already know someone like Helena, but I didn't. I had only her. One Helena. So sad. Feels empty, you know, on my insides. Do you know that feeling?"

He nodded. "I do." *Boy,* he thought, *do I ever.*

"You live here now, in Helena's room?" the young lady asked expectantly.

Butler smiled, utterly disarmed. There was something so gentle about her, so trusting, so delicate, but, at the same time, incredibly sad. "No, I'm just visiting."

"We don't get many visitors, not here. No, not many. Very exciting, having a visitor. Dr. Davenport should make an announcement over the loudspeakers so that everybody knows." She quickly turned to leave.

Butler nearly grabbed her, when he remembered what happened the first time he touched Eddie—so he stepped around her instead to block her path. "My name is Butler. What's yours?"

"My name is Lolo. Well, it's not my real name, but it's what my mother called me when I was young because I had little brothers and sisters—two brothers and three sisters: Jake, Charlie, Marla, Francine, and Beatrice—and they couldn't pronounce my real name, which is

Lorraine, so they started calling me Lolo. That's what everybody's called me ever since. Lolo. Do you think it's a funny name?"

"No, I think it's a nice name."

"Are you sure? Sometimes people say nice things when they don't really mean them."

"Yes, I'm sure. I like it because it's easy to remember. I also think it suits you."

"Well, thank you very kindly." She delivered the response with a slight southern accent, like she was repeating a line she had heard in an old movie. She then curtsied, holding the bottom of an imaginary dress.

"Lolo, I would like to ask you a small favor," he said with surprising tenderness. "Would that be all right?"

"That's hard to answer until you ask the favor, because what you think is a small favor might be a super, giant, big one to me. What's-what's-what's the favor?" Butler took note of her nervous stutter.

"Would you mind not telling Dr. Davenport, or anyone else, that I'm visiting, just yet?"

She looked flabbergasted, like he must be joking. "Well, why not? I mean, it is kind of a big deal, you being a visitor."

"Because I'm not ready to meet anyone else just yet."

Lolo immediately nodded. "Oh. Okay. I understand. Meeting people can take a great deal of energy. In fact, meeting you is making me feel a little bit tired, I think. Right?"

"Would it be possible for you to wait a little while before you tell anyone?"

She gave the question time for serious consideration. "Yes, I think so. But don't expect me to keep a secret like this for too long, because my head might explode. And you wouldn't want that. I know I wouldn't. Let me know as soon as you are ready to meet some of the other residents, Butler."

"I appreciate your understanding," he responded sincerely.

"Well, I appreciate your visiting," she answered, clearly not about to let him have the last word. "Like I told you, this is very exciting." She turned to go, this time heading in the other direction.

"Hey, Lolo, would you happen to know where I might be able to get some food?"

She whirled around with a look of absolute certainty. Of all the questions he could have asked, this was the one she felt most confident in answering. "Would I!"

CHAPTER 38

AMERICAN HERITAGE FOUNDATION

ALEXANDRIA, VIRGINIA

June 1, 9:14 p.m.

Stenson felt that his two most recent hires were two of the best he'd ever made. Enola Meyers was a small-town girl from Ohio who'd managed to get Georgetown University to pay for her education, both her bachelor of arts in economics and her law degree. Having a perfect sixteen hundred on her SAT and just under 67 percent of her DNA from Native American roots went a long way toward explaining why.

That, and she was a national debate champion.

Charlie Johnson had intelligence in his blood. Both his father and grandfather had worked for the CIA. The father had only recently retired from the agency after a stellar thirty-year career. Back in the early days of the AHF, he had applied for a position and been seriously considered until his ongoing marital infidelities were revealed. It seemed that the man couldn't even be faithful to his mistress.

The son, on the other hand, was the picture of a devoted husband and new father. He and his wife had just had their first child, a daughter named Dorothy. Stenson had never seen a more dedicated husband and father, except perhaps when he looked in the mirror.

As good as Enola and Charlie were separately, their real strength lay in their complementarity. Each was good at what the other wasn't. They never fought over responsibilities. When a task was a toss-up, they literally took turns, much the way college basketball uses the possession arrow. They passed a dollar coin back and forth, designating whose turn it was.

What made this coin unique was that it was a "Cheerios dollar," a Sacagawea dollar from 2000 that had been inserted into a Cheerios box as part of a US Mint promotion to raise awareness of the new coin. Of the ten million Sacagawea dollars distributed over the next several years, only 5,500 were part of the Cheerios promotion. Enola still remembered the day she discovered it at breakfast and had considered it her good luck charm ever since.

With Daryl Trotter and Jason Greers currently "off campus"—that was how American Heritage Foundation staffers referred to being outside the office, due to the sheer number of hours each of them spent inside the building—Bob Stenson decided to give his promising new hires their first operational responsibility. He wanted Edward Parks and his device located and acquired. Not by any public agency, but by private hands. Bounty hunters and the like. Ones they trusted.

The director suggested they hire at least three teams to scour the vicinity of the interstate accident Parks had been taken from. The details were left entirely up to them. Stenson only wanted to hear from his newest dynamic duo when their mission had been completed. "Do not disappoint me."

((•))

After their boss had left the small office, Charlie turned to Enola. "This is big for us."

"You think?" she said sarcastically.

"Just to be clear, he said *at least* three."

"Which means four," she replied with a nod.

"It also means he wouldn't mind five."

Enola nodded again. "I'd hire a dozen if I thought it would help."

Charlie shook his head. "Would be too obvious. We don't want the attention."

She couldn't help but smirk. "No shit." On her computer, she pulled up several databases used by the AHF for such hires. In total, the lists included 150 individuals and teams. An incredible amount of information was known about each one: a complete list of the work they'd performed for the AHF over the years, their rates, their career highlights outside their AHF work, and personal details no employer had the right to possess, along with multiple photographs. "Aren't you glad we spent the last month refreshing all this data?" she asked cheerfully.

"Best time of my life," he responded dryly.

"Will be when we deliver the goods."

"You're right. *When* being the operative word."

Enola reviewed the list of candidates. "You want to start with who's available?"

He shook his head, already clicking away at his keyboard to narrow down who they were going to approach first. "If they're in the area, we'll make them available."

"Aren't we feeling all badass today?"

"If we tell any one of these guys that Bob Stenson would consider it a personal favor if they drop what they're doing to take a job for the American Heritage Foundation, how long do you think it will take them to get on it?"

She also started working her keyboard. "Less time than it's taking us to chat about it. Start with the most expensive."

"Most expensive doesn't always mean best."

"In this case, it does. If our predecessors paid some of these guys more, there was a reason, which we don't have time to research now. They wouldn't still be on this list if they had ever failed."

He nodded his agreement, looking at the same narrowed-down list she was scanning. There were a dozen names on it. "I'll start with the O'Briens." Those were two brothers, Shamus and Sean, who were legendary East Coast private investigators. Charlie dialed his phone.

Enola dialed the next number on the list, which happened to be for a tatted-up female bounty hunter who competed in mixed martial arts for fun. "I'll take Cobra Kelly."

In short order, Enola and Charlie had their five teams—some individuals and some pairs of contractors. Each team they asked had said yes without hesitation. One was already in the area. Two were less than an hour away. The other two were between ninety minutes and three hours out but were already en route. The two new AHF hires studied a shared map on their screens that showed the location of each team; each one was assigned a number. "The game is afoot," Charlie said, more to himself than his partner.

Enola picked up the Cheerios dollar and clutched it tightly in her hand. She closed her eyes briefly and said a quick prayer.

"Does it work?" He nodded toward her coin.

"What?" She wasn't being coy; she wanted him to be more specific.

"When you pray like that?"

"I'm a Native American half-blood from the wrong side of the tracks in a small Ohio town, sitting next to a third-generation intelligence man born and bred for this life. What do you think?"

"I think you'll do whatever it takes."

She looked him directly in the eyes. "And then some."

CHAPTER 39

David's Place

Woodsdale, Maryland

June 1, 9:29 p.m.

The facility's kitchen was disgusting. It looked like it hadn't been properly cleaned in years. There were cobwebs on top of the commercial refrigerators, only one of which appeared to be working. On the walls were stains of various colors; several seemed to be either ketchup or blood. Butler noticed large, dark crumbs on the floor—probably rat droppings, but he opted not to look too closely.

He had required some convincing that Lolo was allowed in the kitchen, much less permitted to cook anything. Butler was certain she was exaggerating when she told him she cooked every day for herself, the orderlies, and even Dr. Davenport, who apparently ran the facility. She apologized for the limited number of meal choices she could offer him, but their food was delivered at five in the morning, and they didn't keep much extra around, given their lack of regular visitors and all.

Finding some eggs and butter and a few other perishables, she offered him an omelet, which he said would be fine. He asked for two omelets, in fact—one for him and one for Skylar. From the moment Lolo started to cook, Butler felt like he was watching a completely different person. Her hands moved with precision as she swirled a slice of butter around in a pan and delicately sliced mushrooms and tomatoes. She handled the knives and other implements with seasoned dexterity. It reminded him of the way he handled a gun.

As it turned out, Lolo couldn't just cook—she was a chef, and an incredible one. She prepared two plates with a garnish each of parsley and an orange wedge, then served him one with a confident flair. She studied him closely as he took his first bite. "Well, what do you think?"

Butler gasped. He couldn't remember ever tasting anything so delicious. On a diet that primarily came from Chipotle, Panda Express, Subway, and Starbucks, it was easy to forget just how good food could taste. He quickly took another bite and spoke with his mouth full. "This is absolutely incredible."

She smiled sweetly. "You are not the first person to tell me that. Or the second. Or even the third."

He took another bite, and then another, only now realizing how hungry he was. He hadn't eaten all day, nor had Skylar. "How did you learn to cook like this?"

"The meals were bad, very bad, at first. When my parents first dropped me off here. I did not like them. Not at all. The meals. Long time ago. I was sixteen years old. Much younger than now. They did not want to take care of me anymore, so I live here now. I lost weight. Too much. Dr. Davenport said it was no good. But the food, I couldn't. It was bad leftovers you give to smelly old dogs. They sleep outside even though rain is freezing. Mom and Dad don't want them inside. Too smelly. Dr. Davenport told me to eat more. I asked him if I could cook for me. Peanut butter and jelly, I started with. Other kinds of sandwiches, too. Roast beef. Turkey. Tuna. I like making tuna. Funny. Maybe because tuna is a fish. I like fish. All kinds. Pretty soon, Dr. Davenport said I could cook more. Then he said more, okay. What I want. Other people, they ask. Doctors, too. I say yes, always. I like to cook."

It made complete sense to him. If necessity was the mother of invention, it was also the wellspring of talent. "Do you cook for everyone here?"

She smiled with satisfaction as he devoured the remainder of his omelet. "No, not everyone. Some of the residents, no. Restricted diets. They only eat bland. Protein shakes. Fruit cups. Corn. Other people make those." She paused for a second, looking at his empty plate and the other plate she had prepared. "The other omelet—you eat that, too?"

$$((\cdot))$$

Lolo followed him back toward the room where Skylar and Eddie had remained. They passed another resident of the facility, a middle-aged man with a misshapen head and swollen features. Leaning on his walker, which he used to steady himself, he stared aggressively at Butler and mumbled something unintelligible.

"Don't you worry now, Edgar. Seriously. Everything's fine," Lolo said reassuringly.

He mumbled again, clearly concerned about the presence of a stranger in their midst.

"You just go back in your room now." She pointed into his room.

Edgar didn't move. He stared vacantly, not blinking.

"He's got a pause button that sometimes gets pressed," Lolo said to Butler. She snapped her fingers in front of Edgar's face, which seemed to break him out of his trance. He nodded and shuffled back inside his room.

She and Butler continued to the room where Skylar had stitched up Eddie. His head and leg were now bandaged, and he was sleeping soundly. He was still connected to the IV. Skylar was sitting next to the bed, keeping an eye on him like a protective mother. She looked up as Butler entered. "Any luck?"

"Trust me when I tell you, you're in for a real treat." He led in Lolo, who carried the omelet and some utensils. "Skylar, this is Lolo. Lolo, this is Skylar."

Skylar smiled warmly and stood to shake her hand. "It's very nice to meet you, Lolo."

Lolo nodded and shook hands weakly, but didn't say anything. She was too busy staring at Eddie, who remained sound asleep. "Who is he?"

"That is Eddie," Skylar replied.

"Is he dead?"

"No, don't worry, he's just resting. Eddie's going to be fine."

"I am glad. Helena died in this room. Last week, I think. Yes, pretty sure. Very sad when people die. We were friends. Good friends. Helena."

"I'm sorry to hear about your friend Helena."

"Skylar, Lolo made you an omelet. Get ready to taste some of the best food you've ever eaten."

Lolo placed the plate on a tray with wheels, which she moved to Skylar, and handed her a fork. "I hope you like it. I really do. Really-really." She bounced on her toes, clearly nervous.

"Thank you so much. I'm starving." Skylar hungrily shoveled the first bite of food into her mouth, when she suddenly stopped chewing to savor the incredible taste. "Oh my God."

Butler smiled. "Told you."

Skylar quickly tasted another bite, then repeated herself more emphatically. "Oh. My. God."

Lolo smiled sheepishly. "Do you like it? I think."

"Like it? This may be the best omelet I've ever tasted." She continued scarfing down the meal.

"I can do better. More ingredients. I didn't have them right now. My spices. I thought, no more cooking tonight. I was wrong. Funny. I didn't know we were getting visitors. It is a big deal, I mean. Visitors. Not many."

Skylar studied her. "Do you live here, Lolo?"

"Yes, yes I do. Long time. Over ten years, I think. Yes?" Lolo glanced toward Butler, as if he could confirm what she had said, then turned back to Eddie. "What happened to him?"

"Eddie was in a car accident, but he's going to be just fine."

"Car accidents are scary."

"Yes, they are."

"I have seen them on television. Many times I have seen them. Very scary." She turned to Skylar. "Are you a doctor?"

"I am."

"My elbow. It itches. Do you know why?" She lifted the sleeve of her sweater to reveal her elbow, which was white with dry skin.

"Well, it could be for any number of reasons." Skylar was about to start listing possible causes of eczema when Eddie began to stir.

CHAPTER 40

Eddie's Room

David's Place

June 1, 9:37 p.m.

Lolo peered at Eddie as his eyes started to blink. "You were right, Skylar. He's not dead."

Eddie was clearly groggy, struggling to open his eyes. He looked around the room but seemed to be having trouble focusing. "Where . . . am I?" He slurred his words due to the lingering effects of the propofol.

"Eddie, it's Skylar. You're with Butler and me. You're safe now."

"Skylar? Is that really you?" He turned toward the sound of her voice.

"Yes, it's me." She instinctively reached for his hand to comfort him, forgetting that the gesture would probably have the opposite effect. But it didn't. He gripped her hand firmly, as if holding on for dear life.

"Are you okay?" he asked with genuine concern. "I was worried."

"I'm fine." She smiled warmly.

"Is fake Einstein dead?"

"Yes, he is." The warmth in her face faded.

"He was a bad, mean man. He was hurting you."

She nodded. "How are you feeling?"

He grimaced. "My leg hurts. So does my head. But it's fuzzy, kind of."

"I understand." She paused, asking gently, "Can you hear me okay?"

He nodded. "Yes. My hearing has not changed. At least, I do not think so." He struggled to sit up. "Could you . . . help me sit up . . . please?"

She did so carefully. Eddie sat up enough so that he could pull his head off the pillow and rotate it back and forth, allowing him to acoustically familiarize himself with the unfamiliar space. "Where am I?"

"You are safe. Right now, that's all you need to know."

Believing her, he nodded. He closed his eyes to focus on his hearing. "No birds. I don't like it here." He dropped his head back down to the pillow.

Lolo looked on with curiosity. "What was he doing?"

"That is something he does to make himself more comfortable in new places," Skylar answered. "It helps him become familiar with the acoustics of a room."

Lolo imitated the action, rotating her head back and forth.

Eddie remained in a fog. "Why is Detective McHenry here?"

"He's helping us."

"I don't think that is such a good idea, Skylar. He got in trouble the last time he helped us."

"Yes, he did."

"I don't want him to get in any more trouble because of me. He gave me graham crackers and milk in his mother's house where his stepfather used to hit him when he was a little boy."

"Don't worry, Eddie," Butler interjected. "I can take care of myself." He leaned over so Eddie could see him. "The question is, how are you feeling?"

"Why is that the question, Detective?"

"Because I've been concerned about you. We both have."

"You express your concern very differently from Skylar," he slurred. Eddie then turned briefly toward Lolo, realizing someone unfamiliar was in the room but not knowing what to make of it. He turned back to Butler, remembering he hadn't answered the question. "I am not sure how I'm feeling. It's strange, and not a kind of strange I have felt before. Like I'm not really here. Have you ever felt that way before?"

"Yup." Butler nodded.

Skylar responded with a careful bedside manner. "You were in a car accident earlier today."

"I was?" After a moment, he remembered what had happened. "No, I was not in a car accident. I was in a van accident."

"You're right, that's more accurate." She was relieved to know he had some memory of the day's events.

"The nasty man with the cattle prod isn't going to hurt me again, is he?"

Butler responded with certainty. "I can promise you that he will never hurt you again."

"A promise is a promise, Detective."

"Yes, it is." He looked Eddie in the eyes.

Eddie turned toward Skylar—or, at least, what he was fairly certain was Skylar. "It feels like there is a pillow inside my head."

Skylar smiled. "That's the effect of the sedative I gave you, so I could stitch up your wounds."

"I have wounds?" He tried to sit up farther, wanting to see his injuries, but quickly fell back down on the bed. "Ow. I forgot."

"Just rest. You'll feel better in the morning. I'll show them to you then."

"How many stitches do I have?"

"Thirty-six in your leg and twelve in your head."

"Thirty-six plus twelve is forty-eight. Forty-eight stitches: that's two to the fourth times three stitches, or two times two times two times two times three stitches, which is a good number for stitches—or anything else."

Skylar added some more propofol to his IV, which immediately started to take effect. "Just try to relax, Eddie. What you need most right now is sleep."

A blissful smile crept across his face. His eyes glazed over and rolled back a little. "Skylar, can I tell you a secret?" he asked conspiratorially.

"You can always tell me anything." She leaned down, putting her ear right next to his mouth.

He whispered, but loudly enough so that Butler and Lolo could also hear him. "I think I might be dying." There wasn't a hint of concern in his voice.

"I don't think so," she responded reassuringly.

"Well, I may not have gone to Harvard Medical School like you did, but I am pretty sure I am dying."

"Why do you think that?"

"Because I can see an angel. Standing right there." He pointed directly at Lolo. Eddie's arm wavered from the effect of the sedative. "She is the most beautiful thing I have ever seen."

Lolo blushed sheepishly. She took a step toward the door, then stopped herself. It was clear that she didn't know how to respond.

Eddie continued, "I have always heard people talk about angels, but I was not sure what they meant. I think I understand now." He continued staring vacantly at Lolo, who looked at him, then away. He turned to Skylar. "Is she real or imaginary?"

"She's real, Eddie."

"Can you see her, too?"

"I can."

"Are you dying, too?" he asked with grave concern.

"No, Eddie, I'm just fine. And so are you, I promise. And you would know if I wasn't telling you the truth."

"Yes, I would. I always know if someone is lying. I am the best walking lie detector the government has ever tested. At least, that is what Dr. Fenton used to say. But he is dead now." He continued staring in Lolo's direction.

After a moment, Skylar said, "Your angel's name is Lolo."

He looked flabbergasted. "How do you know my angel's name?"

"She told me."

"You talked to her?!" He seemed genuinely shocked. "I did not think it was possible to talk to angels. Do you think she will talk to me?"

"Yes, I'm pretty sure she will." She glanced at Lolo, who nodded slightly. Skylar turned back to Eddie, who no longer looked at Lolo. He seemed to be at a loss for words. He was blushing, but she couldn't be sure if that was due to embarrassment or the sedative.

Eddie smiled as he started to drift off. "I have never talked to an angel before. I don't know what I should say."

"Allow me to introduce you, then. Eddie, this is Lolo. Lolo, this is Eddie." Before she could complete her introduction, his eyes closed. He had already fallen asleep, but the blissful smile remained across his face.

Lolo stared at him. "He's sleeping again. Like a baby. They sleep like that, you know? Babies." She paused, then added, "I'm glad he isn't dead."

Skylar nodded. "We'll try that again when he's awake."

"When do you think that will be?"

"Probably morning. I'm going to give him enough sedative to sleep through the night."

Lolo then had a thought that seemed to energize her. "I will bet he's going to be very hungry when he wakes up."

Butler seemed to realize what she was thinking. "I have a distinct feeling he's going to be absolutely starving."

"Do you know what Eddie likes to eat in the morning?"

He answered quickly. "Pancakes and bacon and hash browns, bacon not too crispy." He ignored Skylar's glare.

Lolo nodded, heading for the door. "Does he like egg soufflé?"

"Can't hurt."

"I like making egg soufflé. Dr. Davenport says it's one of my better dishes."

"It's hard to imagine anything you cook not being fantastic," Butler commented.

"Just nothing purple," Skylar added. "Eddie doesn't like purple foods."

"No purple food. Right. That's good to know." And with that, she was out the door.

CHAPTER 41

THE WHITE HOUSE

WASHINGTON, DC

June 1, 9:46 p.m.

The first time someone walks into the Oval Office, they immediately pause to take in their surroundings. Because it's so iconic. Because they've seen it so often in the news and photographs and movies, from the time they were born. Because they can't really believe they are actually in the office of the president of the United States.

The first thing Daryl Trotter noticed as he carried in the echo box was not the impressive collection of photographs, nor the two-hundred-year-old Seymour clock, known as the Oval Office grandfather clock. What caught Trotter's attention was the plushness of the rug. His shoes seemed to sink a full inch into the perfectly groomed fibers as he cautiously stepped into the room. It was the softest carpeting he'd ever walked on. He had to stop himself from audibly saying, "Ahhh."

He looked up to admire the domed ceiling, another thing most first-time visitors do. It is adorned with the presidential seal. The ceiling, over eighteen feet high, is legendary for supposedly allowing the president when seated at his desk to hear any conversation in the room, even when whispered. Kennedy had famously attempted to use this to his advantage during several critical negotiations during the Cuban missile crisis.

Jason Greers, on the other hand, acted like his first visit to the Oval Office was no big deal. Like he belonged here. Because that's what he seemed to want the two Secret Service agents who had escorted them in to think. These two stone-faced men had greeted them as they passed through the metal detector that all West Wing visitors were required to go through. Both the echo box and laptop were scanned for residue of explosives, toxins, and any other type of substance that might bring harm to the president's work space.

Greers and Trotter were also full-body scanned. Both, of course, were clean. Given the nature of their work, and that their presence had been requested by the president himself, the process should have been expedited. However, the White House had been suddenly placed on lockdown when a protestor of the current administration had decided to climb the perimeter fence, resulting in a three-hour delay. Gaining entrance to the White House, it seemed, had a lot in common with getting through airport security during Thanksgiving weekend. The taller of the Secret Service agents had closely inspected the echo box after it passed through the scanners. "What type of equipment is this?"

Before Trotter could answer, Greers jumped in. "It's classified."

The agent received some information through his headset that seemed to confirm this. "Follow me."

Greers slowly walked the perimeter of the Oval Office, stepping softly while closely inspecting the walls and windows, in particular. He turned to the agents and asked, "Would you mind giving us the room?"

The agent repeated the request into the microphone on his wrist. The response was immediate. "Can't do that. If you're in here, we're in here."

Pretending to be annoyed, Trotter shook his head with exasperation. "Then don't move until we conclude our business." He kneeled next to one of the windows as part of the performance and looked up into the sky.

Piecing together what little information they had gleaned, the agents would later surmise that Trotter was imagining the spy satellites supposedly looking down upon them, listening to the president's every word.

Greers turned to Trotter. "What kind of wave refraction do you think we're dealing with?"

Trotter responded with a nonsense answer to the nonsense question as he connected the laptop to the echo box. "Depends on the satellite's orbit. Seventy-one to eighty-seven if it's geosynchronous; thirty-two to forty-nine if it's not." His tone was clinical, just like it always was. It was hard for him to keep a straight face; he would later admit to enjoying his part of the ruse.

Stenson was counting on the fact that, somewhere between his earlier conversation with the president and the tidbits these two Secret Service agents would pick up, word would get out about the spy satellites that had apparently been listening to Washington elites for who knows how long. *Oh, the havoc it will wreak!* Those with the most to hide would be the first to ask the president whom he had hired to check his acoustic security. After procuring a favor from the worried party, he would forward their concerns to the American Heritage Foundation for consideration. Stenson was counting on them lining up in droves.

((•))

Greers was once again in awe of how deftly his superior could leverage an already impressive advantage into an overwhelming one. For years, the director-in-training had privately wondered, should they ever get the echo box to work, how they would manage to physically get the device inside the most sensitive spaces, which were always the most secure. It had never occurred to him to fabricate an espionage campfire tale, such as the threat of bad actors spying on Americans from outer space. It seemed preposterous to him—but then again, so did the ability to re-create never-before-recorded sounds; and yet, here he was, echoing the Oval Office with the explicit permission of the president.

Greers had a lot to learn from Bob Stenson.

Trotter looked up from the laptop. "Ready when you are."

Greers glared at the agents. "You can breathe normally, but otherwise, remain absolutely still." They nodded their understanding. Greers turned to his counterpart. "Commence."

Trotter activated the process. The protective doors of the echo box popped open, revealing eight microsatellites. Their synchronized movements were mesmerizing. These extraordinary devices had the ability to record the decayed remains of partial energy fragments, which were once-audible sound waves, still bouncing around the room. And as any physics student knows, matter can neither be created nor destroyed—it can only change form. Much like water can be frozen into a solid and also warmed back into liquid, similarly, once properly recorded with Eddie's device, his recently revised algorithms could take these decayed acoustic remains and re-create the original sounds.

Anything that was ever spoken in this or any other room could now be heard. Any lie. Threat. Promise. Deal. Plea. Seduction. Scream. Manipulation. Negotiation. Debauchery. Or crime.

There would be no more secrets.

Greers and Trotter both had goose bumps. They felt like they alone were in on the most amazing secret in the modern world as they watched the three-dimensional acoustic map of the space appear on the laptop screen. A progress counter appeared below it: *9 percent complete . . . 17 percent . . . 28 percent.* It continued rising steadily.

One of the agents could see the screen as well, and he became concerned. When he lifted his wrist to communicate with his superior, Greers quickly raised his hand with one finger extended. His meaning was clear: *Don't you dare speak a word.*

The agent quickly considered his options and acquiesced, lowering his arm back to his side. The progress continued: *45 percent . . . 61 percent.* It took less than three minutes for the entire process to complete. The counter read: *100 percent.* Trotter looked up at the agents and couldn't resist the opportunity to perform an encore. "Our work here is complete. We will now process the data for analysis. You can tell the president he will have our results shortly." He started shutting down the technology and began to pack it up.

Greers was tempted to roll his eyes as he watched the two agents closely. Both were obviously curious about what had just occurred, but neither was about to ask. "Gentlemen, thank you for your cooperation. Would you be so kind as to escort us out?"

And with that, Trotter and Greers were led out of the White House in possession of the greatest trove of national secrets in the history of the United States.

CHAPTER 42

American Heritage Foundation

Alexandria, Virginia

June 1, 10:22 p.m.

Very few people scared Bob Stenson. After all, he'd hired dozens of different assassins and teams of killers over the last twenty years to ply their trade on behalf of the American Heritage Foundation. These people were the best in the world at what they did. Most were former military turned mercenary. Some used guns, some used knives, and others preferred garrotes or poison or plastic explosives. Each had a specialty. But Mr. Elliott was different. His signature was not defined by method, but by style.

He was brutal. Intentionally, cruelly, unspeakably brutal. A genuine sadist. The man enjoyed inflicting pain upon others, and the more, the better. He rarely killed a target quickly, because it denied him the pleasure of witnessing the fear and pain that preceded an imminent death. This was known because his methodology included documenting his efforts whenever possible.

For those who had cleared his complex security-screening process and been granted access to his ultraexclusive dark-web site, a collection of the most horrific videos ever made was available for viewing. These showed Mr. Elliott killing heads of state in front of their wives and military leaders along with their children; he had even videotaped himself decapitating foreign journalists and their entire families. Several of his torture methods could only be described as barbaric, if not medieval.

He was believed to be American but had conducted his business exclusively outside the United States. Most of his clientele lived in South America or territories in or around Russia, because they seemed more attracted to his approach. That also explained why he had never been caught. The few times Interpol or other international agencies had sent men after him, they'd ended up playing the lead roles in Mr. Elliott's snuff films, which he had made available as free downloads on his site.

Bob Stenson was repulsed by Mr. Elliott—both by what he had already done and by what he was capable of doing. Stenson was genuinely scared of him, which explained why he had never hired him. But every now and then, circumstances have a way of conspiring against someone to act in opposition to their established principles.

The director of the American Heritage Foundation had reached out to the nine teams and individuals he trusted who were believed to be currently active in the field. One team's members were recovering from injuries sustained during a recent mission for Stenson and wouldn't be operational for several months, if ever. Two simply didn't respond, which meant they were dead or off-grid. And the other six were already on assignment and wouldn't be available for weeks. That left him one choice.

Stenson took a moment before he placed the call, making sure this was something he was comfortable doing. The answer was no, but he didn't have any other options. *Fuck it. This is her fault. She forced me into this situation.* He needed a job done, so he took a deep breath and dialed the number listed on the man's website.

It was answered on the second ring. "To whom do I have the pleasure of speaking?" the killer asked with surprising eloquence.

"Bob Stenson."

There was a slight pause on the line. "Well, isn't this an honor! Mr. Stenson, your reputation precedes you, sir. How nice to receive your call."

Stenson had trouble reconciling Mr. Elliott's elegant voice and educated manner of speaking with what he had just glimpsed on the man's website. Stenson had expected someone brutish, even beastly. A talking gorilla, or a Cro-Magnon man. Something less than human.

Of course Mr. Elliott was educated. And literate. And intelligent. The only way anyone got away with what he had for so long was by being a diabolically clever actor playing a role. The man had found a marketing angle, a truly unique niche, and he exploited the hell out of it. While he wasn't the first to do so, he had certainly taken the act to an unprecedented level of depravity. What David Blaine was to magicians, Mr. Elliott was to assassins.

"I have a job."

"I had already assumed this wasn't a social call." He said it with a charm that even Tom Wolfe would have admired.

"The task needs to be completed immediately."

"In my line of work, it's rare when one doesn't."

"The job is in the States."

There was now a considerable pause on the other end of the line. Mr. Elliott could be heard taking a long, deep breath as he considered the proposition. "You do know I prefer to perform my services elsewhere."

"I'm prepared to compensate you for the inconvenience."

"Mr. Stenson, what we are discussing is not inconvenience—"

"One," he said abruptly. Stenson meant one million dollars.

There was no misunderstanding. It was more money than Mr. Elliott had ever been offered, by a factor of two. Mr. Elliott continued, "This would involve a level of risk I have never previously been willing to take on."

"Two." The offer was doubled. Two million.

The killer paused briefly. "I sincerely don't want to decline your offer, for a number of reasons, not the least of which is that I am well aware that once rebuffed, you will never—"

"Three." Stenson's voice didn't waver. He clearly wasn't going to take no for an answer.

There was another pause on the line.

"Five," Mr. Elliott countered.

If there had been an audience for this negotiation, as in an auction house during bidding over fine art, a hush would have fallen over the crowd, like the one that followed the $450 million bid for Da Vinci's *Salvator Mundi*.

"Done," Stenson replied almost immediately. To his knowledge, this was now the most expensive hit ever contracted. It was certainly the most expensive one he'd ever paid for. Half of the payment would be expected now, half upon completion.

"I will transmit my banking details momentarily." Mr. Elliott tried to conceal his own astonishment, but imperfectly. He clearly couldn't believe that Stenson had called his bluff. The sadist was atwitter.

"I will send the first payment, along with all pertinent information about the target."

"Forward everything you have, pertinent or otherwise. It is not uncommon for a seemingly trivial detail to be of great significance." Mr. Elliott paused. "I can't believe I haven't asked this yet. What's the target's name?"

Stenson paused briefly, knowing he was about to seal the fate of someone he had considered family for many years. And it wasn't simply that she was going to die. She was going to die horribly. There was a high likelihood that she would be tortured first. In ways that were unthinkable. And worse, the hit might include members of her family. Her husband. Her children. And her father, whom Stenson considered to be his father figure and mentor.

This is her fault. She brought this upon herself. There is no mistaking her intentions. She means to burn the house down to the very ground. It was she who declared war first, not I. So I am entitled to use whatever means necessary to protect all that I have built, which includes her father's legacy. I'm not going to let her get away with this, for his sake as well as mine.

He knew that once he spoke her name, there would be no going back. Once you jumped off this cliff, you could not unjump. "Caitlin McCloskey."

CHAPTER 43

Safe House

Gilberts Corner, Virginia

June 1, 10:33 p.m.

Caitlin tracked the Embraer Phenom as it descended toward Minot, North Dakota, home of the worst anhydrous ammonia spill in US history, which sickened most of its citizens when a train derailed in 2002, resulting in a gigantic cloud of gas enveloping the city of thirty-seven thousand.

She was relieved as the plane touched down safely. Part one of her family's journey to their new lives, the air-travel portion, was now complete.

Part two was the driving portion. A car was waiting on the tarmac for them. Well, a truck, actually. A Ford F-150 with seventy-six thousand miles on the odometer. The vehicle wasn't much to look at, but that was the point. It looked like most of the other trucks in the area, and that meant they wouldn't stick out. They would look like they belonged here. And that was important, especially in these first few days and weeks.

Minot was only fifty miles south of the Canadian border. Anyone trying to follow them would assume that their final destination was somewhere in Manitoba or Saskatchewan. But crossing the border would mean presenting their new identification to the border guards.

While Caitlin had every confidence in the document forger who'd created the passports for her, she didn't want to press her luck unless it became absolutely necessary. Besides, she wanted her kids to grow up in this country. She'd already devoted too much of her life to propping up the American dream to completely abandon it now.

If things went according to plan, she would be able to bring them back in relatively short order. A cover story involving national security would be created, allowing Peter to return to his position as chief financial officer, and her children could resume their studies at their elite private school. If, however, things went awry, Caitlin wanted her progeny to live out their lives without her while still cheering for the red, white, and blue when it came time for the Olympics.

Besides, heading south was a good strategic move because it wouldn't be expected.

Her phone rang. It was Peter. He was not using video. "Just wanted you to know we landed safely."

"Don't I get to see your face?" she asked expectantly.

"Let's just talk. I'm still struggling to get my head around all this."

She nodded. "How was the flight?"

"The kids think we're rich now that they got to fly private."

"Tell them not to get used to it."

"At least now they're not the only ones in their class who haven't."

She smiled briefly, then asked a question she already knew the answer to. "Did you read my letter?"

"How long ago did you write it?"

"A few months ago. I can't explain in detail right now, but some things started happening that gave me cause for concern. I thought it was prudent to be more safe than sorry."

"You're being vague as hell. You know that, right?"

"One day, I'll explain everything."

"Be careful not to make any promises you can't keep." He tried to say it with some degree of understanding, but it came out sharply.

"I really am sorry about all this, Peter."

"You said that in your letter." The statement was not just sharp, but terse. He clearly could no longer hide his anger.

Caitlin didn't blame him. In his shoes, she would have been even more upset. "How cold is it there?"

"If I breathe in through my nose, it feels like the hair in my nostrils freezes."

"Then I suggest you breathe through your mouth."

He paused to laugh, which broke the mounting tension. "God, I hate you."

"Right now, I hate me, too." And she meant it. "I'm only doing this because I had no other choice."

"I believe you." It was clear from his tone that he did.

Caitlin breathed a sigh of relief. "Are the kids okay?"

"Seem to be, for now. But we'll have to see." He was obviously just barely holding it together. "Where the hell is Harvey, anyway?"

"It's about seventy-five miles southeast of where you are now. I'll send directions to your phone."

"That's very kind of you," he replied sarcastically. "So, to ask something obvious, are you sure it's safe for us to even be talking right now? I mean, couldn't somebody be tracing this call, or something?"

"The phone I gave you is completely secure. Any call made to or from it is untraceable."

He exhaled briefly. "God, I hope you're right. What about on your end?"

"I've taken every possible precaution." She appreciated that even in a situation he didn't understand at all, he was still trying to protect her—or, at least, help her to protect herself.

"One last question." He paused to emphasize the great import of what he was about to ask. "Did it have to be a truck?"

She burst out laughing. "Yes, as a matter of fact, it did."

"You couldn't have at least gotten me an Audi, or a BMW, or maybe an Aston Martin, for what you're putting me through?"

"Do you have any idea how many Audis or BMWs or Aston Martins there are within five hundred square miles of you? The idea is to blend in, knucklehead, not to stick out."

"Oh, fine. Now I suppose you're going to tell me I need to get used to waking up at four o'clock in the morning to milk the cows."

"It's goats, not cows."

He paused. "I'm waiting for you to say that you're kidding."

"Who said I am?" she asked playfully.

"Please don't say you stuck us on a farm."

"Of course not," she answered. "It's actually more of a gentleman's ranch."

Peter garbled his voice, producing the sound effect of static. "You're breaking up, honey, I couldn't hear you. What was that?"

"These kinds of phones don't get static, honey." She closed her eyes, desperately wishing she could hold him for just a moment. She imagined the warmth of his embrace, and the comforting scent of his cologne.

"Oh, right. I knew that. Just please tell me I won't have to muck any stalls."

She paused briefly. "There will be no mucking of stalls."

Now it was his turn to pause. "You know, when this is all over, you are buying me an Aston Martin."

"Any color you want."

"I'll call you when we get to Harvey."

She paused to emphasize the following. "I love you, Peter McCloskey."

"I know." And with that he hung up.

Peter had no idea that a man who'd already been there for an hour was watching him from the shadows. This man also drove a truck, which he kept at a safe distance behind Peter's as the family began the drive to their new home.

CHAPTER 44

Safe House

Gilberts Corner, Virginia

June 1, 10:50 p.m.

Caitlin turned her attention to another screen, which was tapped into the American Heritage Foundation vehicle-tracking system. She watched as Daryl Trotter's vehicle headed toward their offices, returning from the White House. "My God, they did it." Speaking to no one in particular, she had forgotten that her connection to Hogan remained open.

"Who did what?" he asked from his dedicated screen. He was not visible until he adjusted his camera.

"My counterparts at the foundation just paid a visit to the White House. There's only one reason Bob Stenson would have arranged it."

"What reason is that?"

"I believe they are returning to our offices with the greatest cache of intelligence ever gathered."

"With all due respect, you're being a little overly dramatic, don't you think?"

"If I'm right, they now have a record of every single conversation ever held inside the Oval Office."

"Ever?" He leaned in toward his screen so that he now appeared in close-up.

"Ever." She left no doubt.

"I stand corrected." He paused, then asked, "You mind telling me how this is possible?"

"We acquired a device that can re-create never-recorded sounds using acoustic archeology. It's called the echo box."

Hogan's eyes went wide. "Seriously? There will be no more secrets. Stenson will know everything."

"That's correct." She locked her gaze on the camera to emphasize the gravity of what had occurred.

"Holy shit." It took him a moment to process. "May I ask how he acquired it?"

"The guy who created it lives in a facility for high-functioning savants. He's autistic. Stenson tortured his doctor until he gave up the code." Her tone revealed her disdain for what had occurred.

He nodded. "No wonder you initiated an Alpha Reset Protocol."

"We don't touch innocents. My father taught me that."

"Was there something specific Stenson was after in the Oval Office?"

"The president cut a deal with the Fields brothers to rig their voting machines in certain districts in the upcoming election, which will swing things in his favor. Stenson is going to bring him down."

"Why would he do that? I thought the president was one of your guys?"

"He was. Until he wasn't. The president went to outside help instead of using the AHF. Stenson didn't care for that very much."

"Seems disloyal to me, too," he commented. "If you leave a dance with a different date than the one you brought, somebody's going to get bent out of shape."

"Stenson became obsessed. His priority for months has been to make an example of the president so that no one ever tries it again."

"With this device, the echo box, Stenson will be incredibly dangerous."

"I agree. That's why we're here." She paused, then asked, "Where are you, by the way?"

He smiled directly into the camera. "I am everywhere, and I am nowhere."

She rolled her eyes. "Now who's the one being overly dramatic?"

"Hey, if you can't have some fun with this shit, we might as well pack it in and go home."

"Some of us can't do that, remember?" she responded sharply.

"Oh, give me a break. This will be over soon enough," he tried to reassure her. "Do you want to know why our connection cannot be terminated?"

She slammed down her fist in mock exasperation. "Wait a minute. You mean I can't even hang up on you?"

He smiled with genuine affection. "Your father wanted you to know you would never be alone," he answered seriously. "What you've done is brave. Most people couldn't or wouldn't take the risk. I gather you didn't see yourself having much of a choice."

She nodded. "I'm pretty stubborn that way."

"You are your father's daughter." He then cited the famous quote often attributed to the Irish statesman Edmund Burke: "The only thing necessary for the triumph of evil is that good men should do nothing."

"That goes for women, too, pal."

He paused for a moment. "If you're right about the trove of intelligence your counterparts are bringing back to the American Heritage Foundation, I can tell you how we're going to win this thing."

If anyone else had said that, she would have rolled her eyes. But this was Hogan, and Caitlin was eager to hear what he was thinking. "Do tell . . ."

CHAPTER 45

115 North Pennsylvania Place

Indianapolis, Indiana

June 1, 10:55 p.m.

Senator Corbin Davis was working at his desk on the speech he was to give the following day, at a banquet for the newly elected leadership of the American Federation of State, County and Municipal Employees, when he heard a knock on the door. "Elaine, I told you I don't want to be disturbed."

Davis's chief of staff, Bob Welker, poked his head in. "And I told her I thought you'd want to see these." He waved several printouts of grainy surveillance photos.

Davis waved him in. "Those from your friend in White House security?"

"They are," he answered smugly. Welker approached the senator and placed the screen grabs neatly in front of him, one at a time for dramatic effect.

"Well, I'll be damned." The senator picked up one of the images and studied it closely.

"Is that it?" Welker asked.

Davis nodded. "That is the echo box."

"You're sure?"

"No question. This is the device I told you about last week. The top of it pops open right there at the hinges. Inside are eight one-inch satellite microphones that move together in this weird kind of dance."

His chief of staff sounded dubious because it was his job to be. "This is also the thing you said didn't work and led Homeland Security all around New York on a wild-goose chase, wasting lots of valuable time and resources."

"It didn't work. I had two world-class experts who proved it didn't." The senator paused to think it through. "Which means one of two things happened. Either they put on a show for me last week to lead me to think it didn't work when it actually did, or somebody fixed it in the last eight days and just took the thing out on its maiden voyage."

Welker nodded. "So the space-based surveillance nonsense was just a cover for them to get the box into the Oval Office. What we need to understand is, to what end?"

Davis stared at his chief of staff like it was the dumbest question anyone had ever asked him. "I can think of a thousand reasons—my God, ten thousand—but only one is a clear favorite."

The chief of staff struggled to hide his annoyance. "Which one would that be?"

The Indiana senator smiled. "The rumor is true."

"Which rumor?"

Davis paused for emphasis, stating what he thought should be obvious. "The one involving the Fields brothers and their voting machines."

Now it was Welker's turn to pause. His tone of voice sounded like that of a man who could see the future and liked what he saw very much. "Stenson is going to bring him down."

Davis nodded, staring out the window, imagining what his future might hold. He took out the special phone that the American Heritage Foundation director had recently given him and stared at it. "When he asked me if I wanted to be president, I assumed he meant following the president's reelection."

"Looks like we may be in the Oval Office sooner than either of us had thought possible."

CHAPTER 46

AMERICAN HERITAGE FOUNDATION

ALEXANDRIA, VIRGINIA

June 1, 11:11 p.m.

Bob Stenson imagined the giddiness his two lieutenants must have felt during their drive back from the White House. In possession of every conversation ever held inside the Oval Office, they had an absolute treasure trove of intelligence. They had Bill Clinton's little chitchats with Monica Lewinsky that had preceded the blue-dress incident; the Richard Nixon temper tantrums before he started the tapes rolling during Watergate; the brotherly confidences shared between Jack and Bobby Kennedy; and the legendary thumpings of Lyndon Johnson's reportedly oversized member on his desk, just to name a few.

In other words, they had a gold mine. Now the only question was how much Stenson was going to let them hear. Trotter and Greers sat in the foundation's conference room across from their boss as their chief technician and resident acoustic archeologist, Carter Harwood, analyzed the files of echoes they had retrieved from the Oval Office.

Trotter and Greers knew the years of research and frustration that had gone into the development and acquisition of the echo box, including Stenson's most recent embarrassment involving Homeland Security and the New York City Police Department. And now, it was all about to have been worth it. Their superior was going to share his moment of glory with them, and they were grateful to be present. Trotter commented anxiously, "I imagine this is what it felt like to be in Alamogordo, New Mexico, the morning of July 16, 1945."

Greers had no idea what he was talking about. "Why is that?"

Harwood responded without looking up from the laptop screen. "Trinity."

"What's Trinity?"

Stenson answered, "It was the code name for the first successful detonation of a nuclear weapon."

"It occurred at five twenty-nine a.m.," Trotter interrupted.

"And forty-five seconds," Stenson added.

"And forty-five seconds," Trotter repeated, impressed. "Touché."

Stenson addressed Greers, who was clearly not a nuclear-history buff as they were. "Trinity marked the end of the Manhattan Project and the beginning of the nuclear age." He turned to Trotter. "Yes, this is a lot like that."

Greers thought quickly, trying to play catch-up. "Except that was a technology they wanted everyone to know about."

Stenson nodded in agreement. "Awareness amplified its effectiveness. The threat of its use has proven to be even more effective than its actual use. In the case of the echo box, however, the opposite is true. The longer we can keep it a secret, the more effective it will be."

Greers continued gaining momentum. "And thanks to the newly discovered threat of satellite-based eavesdropping, every major politician in the country will want the same reassurance you'll soon be giving the president."

Stenson nodded some more. "And we have just the technology to give them that reassurance."

Trotter looked a bit puzzled. "What are we going to tell people this device actually does? I mean, if the supposed threat is space-based, we have to come up with something we can sell to the tech guys."

Greers smiled. "I guess we know what you're going to be focused on for the next couple days."

Harwood mumbled under his breath, "It never ceases to amaze me how dumb some politicians can be." He clearly hadn't meant to verbalize the thought, because he quickly looked up nervously. "Sorry."

Stenson stared at him coldly. "It's not just some of them. It's all of them." He then cracked a smile.

"Our goal should be simple," chimed in Greers. "Get them to invite us into every space where they know they communicated something that could hurt them."

Trotter interjected, "That would be every room they have ever entered."

Greers continued without noticing that Stenson was now glaring at him. "The more urgently they want us to analyze a space, the more serious we know their indiscretion was."

All Harwood could say was "Wow." Both because of the diabolical genius of the plan and because such a strategy was being mentioned in front of him. He was usually excluded from this kind of discussion.

Which was why Stenson stared daggers at Greers, who only now realized his transgression. He looked down at the tabletop quickly.

Trotter was oblivious. He was too busy thinking about ramifications. "Eventually, the cat's going to get out of the bag. There's no way around it. A secret like this can't be contained forever."

Stenson didn't disagree. "It's too bad, really."

"A sure sign will be when there's a sudden rash of unexplained explosions in high-powered homes and offices around DC," Trotter commented. "People will start destroying all the evidence they can."

Harwood chimed in casually, "I would imagine that's right around when we'll be introducing the echo box 2.0."

The others in the room went silent. It was Greers who spoke first. "We'll be introducing what?"

The technical whiz looked pleased that he was ahead of the others. "Oh, I thought we'd discussed this. Now that we have the algorithms to rebuild the decayed sound waves produced in enclosed spaces, it's only a matter of time before we can refine the process to where we can re-create waves produced anywhere."

"Even outside?" Greers asked.

"Yes, even outdoors."

Greers practically gripped the table. "No. Way."

Trotter nodded. "Well, technically speaking, it makes sense."

"There are plenty of molecules in the air for the decaying energy waves to bounce off of, whether there are walls or no walls," Harwood explained. He was clearly intent on demonstrating his value beyond technical forgery.

Greers grinned slyly. "In other words, we will know everything. I mean, absolutely everything."

The computer scientist nodded. "That is precisely what I'm saying."

"Enough conjecture," Stenson said. "It's time to focus on the here and now."

Harwood took a deep breath. "Well, sir, I think I'm just about ready. What echoes from the Oval Office would you like to hear first?"

CHAPTER 47

David's Place

Woodsdale, Maryland

June 1, 11:16 p.m.

The lights in the room were dim. Butler and Skylar sat quietly as Eddie slept soundly. "You really care about him a lot, don't you?"

"No, I do this kind of thing for all my patients." She smiled warmly.

"The way you look at him, if he was younger, I swear I'd think he was your son."

"You mean if he was a lot younger, right? Like an infant?"

"Yes, exactly. A newborn."

She paused, answering sincerely. "Eddie reminds me of my little brother, Christopher. He was also on the spectrum. A really special kid. He had the most wonderful laugh."

"What happened to him?" Butler asked.

((•))

It was the last week of March during her senior year of high school. Most of Skylar's friends were on pins and needles, waiting to see whether the college envelopes they received were thick or thin. Thick was good, thin bad. Skylar, however, had been spared the anxiety courtesy of the lacrosse scholarship she had already accepted from the University of Virginia. Combined with the academic grants she had also been awarded, she would be attending that fine institution of higher learning without paying a dime.

This explained her carefree attitude as she arrived home after practice and yelled down their basement stairs. "Christopher?"

"Who else would I be?" He laughed at his own joke as she made her way down the wooden stairs toward him. It was an infectious laugh and never failed to make Skylar smile. Christopher was fifteen but had the face of a child. He was sitting at a workbench, surrounded by hundreds of drawings he had made with crayons and colored paper.

"How was school today?"

"I need more physics. Especially quantum physics. I can't finish designing my time-travel machine until I understand more about black holes."

"You will soon enough. I know you will." She glanced at his drawings, particularly the newest ones. "I bet you could sell some of these as art if you wanted to."

"I don't want to, Skylar. They are not art. They are technical drawings of a machine that is going to revolutionize the travel industry."

"Okay, okay, I was just saying."

"I don't like when you say things like that."

"I promise, I will never say that again." She realized he was staring down at her Tretorns. "Hey, what's going on? Is something wrong?"

"No, nothing is wrong."

"I know you, peckerhead. Something's bugging you."

He fumbled with his crayons. "Are you really leaving next September, for college, I mean?"

She answered softly. "We've already talked about this. September is a long way off."

"No, it's not. It's 157 days away. That's less than half a year."

"Then I think we should make this the best 157 days either one of us has ever had. What do you say?"

"I don't want you to go away to college, Skylar. I want you to stay here with me."

She sat down next to him. "You know how you've told me that working on your invention is something you have to do? I would never ask you not to do it. Well, going to college is like that for me. It's something I have to do."

"But why? Why do you have to do it?"

"So I can become a doctor and help people like you."

He nodded, but not with understanding. With profound, heartbreaking sadness.

((•))

Butler waved his hand in front of Skylar's face, prompting her to snap out of her reverie. "I was the only person in the world Christopher would talk to. My dad never had any interest. When I left for UVA, Christopher couldn't handle it. Before my dad could put him in a home, he hanged himself in our basement."

He didn't say anything for a long moment. "I'm sorry."

"Me too." Changing the subject, she asked, "You mentioned that Caitlin knew things about you that were supposed to be classified. What kind of things?"

"When I was a Ranger, I developed a reputation for being the guy who would do things the other guys wouldn't. You know, dumb shit. Dangerous shit. Off-book shit. Which is how I got involved with black ops toward the end. Looking back on it, some very questionable stuff. But at the time, you know, I thought I was just being a good little soldier, doing whatever was asked of me. As it turns out, it wasn't even the government who was asking me. It was the same people who kidnapped you and Eddie. And you know what the most fucked-up thing is? I still have no idea who these bastards are."

Gently, she asked, "Is that why you're doing this? To get some answers?"

"Hell yes. After all this time, what I would like is some clarity. I want to know if the things I did that still haunt me were at least done for the right reasons, or if I was just a pawn in a much bigger game where everyone was dirty."

She nodded. "You know, even if you get the answers you want, it won't be enough."

"Why not?"

"What I think you want more than clarity is relief."

"Is that your professional opinion, Doctor?"

"Yes, as a matter of fact, it is. Whatever you did, you did. That won't change. What can change is how you live with it. What you need to do more than anything is forgive yourself."

"Can I kill them all first?" he said with a smirk.

"As long as you take ownership of whatever actions you take, and can live with the consequences, you do what you need to do."

"So you give me permission to kill them all."

"That's not what I said."

"Oh, I think you did."

"Good night, Butler."

"What, is our time up already? But this was turning out to be such a productive session. I think I was really making some progress."

She leaned back in her chair, preparing to go to sleep. "You know why I prefer to work with patients on the spectrum? They're not so full of shit."

He smiled. "Good night, Skylar."

CHAPTER 48

AMERICAN HERITAGE FOUNDATION

ALEXANDRIA, VIRGINIA

June 1, 11:23 p.m.

Stenson looked across the conference table to Harwood. "Let's not get ahead of ourselves. Start with this morning. I want to hear the president's voice loud and clear before I start believing the damn thing truly works."

Harwood studied the timeline of wave history for the Oval Office. He moved the designator to the end of the timeline: the present, specifically this morning. The timeline could be expanded and contracted in the same way video editors can look at an entire movie in overview or zoom into one shot of one scene to study a particular sequence frame by frame. In a two-hour movie filmed at twenty-four frames per second, there are 172,800 frames; at sixty frames per second, there are 432,000 frames. It's no wonder postproduction on films can take months or even years.

In the Oval Office earlier that morning, there were only a few thousand sound waves produced, all of which occurred between 7:03 a.m. and 9:34 a.m., which was the time the president had embarked on his current fund-raising trip to Arizona. The first waves were a single set of footsteps. Whoever it was moved quickly, as if scurrying about from the hardwood floor around the perimeter of the room to the thick carpeting in the main area, and back again. The footsteps sounded light. Probably female. It definitely wasn't the president. Most likely, it was one of the nine maids who maintained the Oval Office and the other rooms in the West Wing, part of the ninety-six-person staff that maintained the 132-room White House.

These footsteps were followed by repeated brushing sounds—the kind of light "swooshing" sounds produced by a feather duster. Yes, it was definitely one of the maids. She was prepping the office for the president's arrival. Upon completing her duties, she exited quickly.

Another single set of footsteps followed a moment later, this one accompanied by the tinkling of china being carried on a silver serving tray, which was then carefully placed on either a coffee table or the president's desk.

Stenson grew impatient. "Fast-forward until he enters." Harwood slid the time designator several minutes later, when a number of new waves first appeared.

PRESIDENT: *Is this trip really necessary?*

CHIEF OF STAFF: *You haven't been to Nebraska in almost a year.*

PRESIDENT: *There's a reason for that.*

CHIEF OF STAFF: *Some of our most important friends live there. It's home to an electronics manufacturer you are going to owe quite a debt of gratitude come next election.*

There was a slight pause, indicating the president now realized whom he was talking about.

PRESIDENT: *EVS?*

CHIEF OF STAFF: *In fact, the two brothers who own it are underwriting tonight's event, although not officially, of course.*

"You can stop now," Stenson instructed Harwood, who paused the echo playback.

Trotter had listened with his mouth agape. "I can't believe how clear these echoes are. It's like they're having the conversation right in front of us."

"That is what impresses you most about what you just heard?" Greers asked.

"Well, it's not that the owners of Electronic Voting Systems are rigging the next election. They own and operate seventy-eight percent of the machines used in the last presidential election. They'll control even more in the next one. Given their increasing ties with the president, I took it as a given that they'll be at least part of predetermining the outcome."

Greers turned to their superior. "Did you know?"

Stenson paused, clearly offended by the question. "I'm still surprised when you ask me a really dumb question."

Harwood was curious. "Do you think the vote count has already been determined?" For all he knew about computers, he knew surprisingly little about game theory.

"Of course not," Trotter replied abruptly. "If you want a basketball team to throw a game, you don't want them to miss every shot. You only want them to miss one. The one you need them to. In politics, it's the same thing. For the outcome to look legitimate, you change as little as possible. You wait until the day before the election, analyze the polling data, then modify as few precincts as necessary to achieve the desired result."

Stenson flipped through a small leather-bound notepad he kept in his pocket. Without looking up, he said, "The revelation here is not that the upcoming election is going to be manipulated. What's important is who this administration is trusting to do it for them. Namely, not us." The other three looked around at each other as Stenson continued perusing his notepad. Finding what he was searching for, he turned to Harwood. "I want to hear July twenty-third of last year. Eleven thirty in the morning."

Harwood scrolled through the echo timeline of the Oval Office, focusing on the requested day. The three-dimensional rendering of the audible sound waves bouncing around the space that day was dense. There were dozens of overlapping waves. "Looks like it was a busy morning. I'm going to need some time to clean up all the harmonic distortion and sort through all the voices before I can play you anything useful."

"How much time?"

"Hard to say, sir, but it could be a while. If you could give me a clue about who you want to hear, or the subject matter they discussed, it would make the search go more quickly."

Stenson stood up, preparing to exit. "It was the first meeting between the brothers who own Electronic Voting Systems and the president. I want to hear what kind of deal they made and who was responsible for bringing them together."

"I'll let you know as soon as I have something worth listening to."

Before his boss could exit, Greers quickly asked, "Sir, where would you like our focus?"

Stenson paused in the doorway. "Help the newbies track down Edward Parks. I want him found."

"What parameters did you give them?"

"By any means necessary. This is their baptism. I threw them in the deep end. I'm still waiting to find out if they're going to sink or swim." And then he left.

Trotter turned to Greers. "I'm confused."

"By what?" asked Greers.

"His instructions. He wants us to help them do their job, but not help them at the same time."

Greers shook his head. "Watch and learn." And he turned to go.

CHAPTER 49

June 1, 11:28 p.m.

Enola Meyers and Charlie Johnson each studied their screens, monitoring the five teams they had hired. The two youngest employees had figured it best to be redundant, so both were following all five teams. This way, in case one of them missed something, the other might catch it.

Greers and Trotter entered a moment later. Greers leaned over Enola's workstation, somewhat encroachingly. "How's it going?"

She blinked a few times, struggling to be neither intimidated nor annoyed. She recognized the violation of her personal space as a test. He wanted to see how she'd respond, so she answered succinctly and without hesitation. "Five teams have been hired. All are among the best the foundation has ever used." She handed him a list of the personnel.

"You mean the most expensive," he corrected her, reviewing the teams.

"We do better due diligence than any firm in the world," she answered flatly, keeping her eyes on her screen. "We wouldn't have paid them more if they weren't better."

Behind her, where Enola couldn't see his face, Greers smiled slightly. She had passed the first test. What he didn't notice was that she could see his expression in the reflection of her screen. She revealed nothing as he leaned back slightly, allowing for a little more breathing room between them.

All the while, Trotter watched with bemused silence. He looked like a business-school student in a leadership-training seminar.

"How have you divided up your supervision?" Greers continued, referring to her partner.

She looked over to Charlie, deferring to him, both to seem less spotlight-grabbing and because she wasn't entirely confident in her answer.

Charlie seemed to appreciate her giving him a turn. "We've divided the search area into sections," he answered, passing a copy of the search grid that showed five different color-coded regions surrounding the accident location Eddie Parks had been taken from. Their plan was well thought out and logical. "We're both monitoring all five teams to make sure nothing gets missed."

Greers nodded. "That would be perfect if this was a casual exercise. Is that what you thought this was?" He waited for a reply, but Charlie knew better and waited for Greers to continue. "Mr. Stenson did explain this was an all-hands-on-deck situation, didn't he?"

Charlie made the mistake of trying to answer quickly. "He did, but with five teams—"

Greers cut him off: "With five teams, you could have turned it into seven by both of you operating as independent agents. But you didn't." He paused to let their error hang in the air above him like a dangling noose. "You said you hired the best, didn't you?" He glanced at Enola, who turned her eyes back to her own screen to avoid his glare.

Greers continued, "If you hired the best in their field, what can either of you do to assist them? Sounds kind of arrogant to me. The answer as to what you can offer them is simple: nothing. And by even attempting to, you wasted your own valuable time, and possibly slowed them down in the process, working in direct opposition to the very reason you hired them."

Charlie immediately took responsibility. "You're right. It was my oversight."

Enola knew better than to let him take the responsibility alone. "It was both of ours."

"That's a given," Greers snapped. "Here's what's going to happen. You are both going to remain apprised of each team's whereabouts and progress, but your main effort should be spent working independently. In parallel. Play out the scene of Parks's departure from the accident. Proceed step-by-step, imagining where you'd take him and why. Take note of every choice you make. When a particular path leads nowhere conclusive, go back to the spot of that initial decision and take a different route, again making note of each new subsequent choice. When you've exhausted your options, then and only then should you confer with each other and discuss your conclusions. At that point, if you've got anything worth sharing, we'll be just down the hall."

"Thank you for the help and guidance," Charlie said sincerely. He seemed genuinely motivated. "It's much appreciated."

Greers and Trotter headed for the door and then paused. "By the way, Daryl and I will be doing the same thing you are. We will be teams eight and nine. It would be rather embarrassing for you if either one of us finds them first after both of you had such a head start, so I'd get cracking."

Enola nodded her understanding as they left, then turned back to Charlie. "Fuck them. Let's go."

$$((\bullet))$$

Neither Greers nor Trotter spoke until they reached their office. Trotter's face was full of admiration. "That was genius."

"We all have our strengths," Greers responded humbly.

Trotter paused. "You know we're going to find them first, don't you?"

"We'd better." Greers eyeballed him for a moment, then they both went to work.

CHAPTER 50

SAFE HOUSE

GILBERTS CORNER, VIRGINIA

June 1, 11:35 p.m.

Caitlin answered the video call on the first ring. It was, of course, Peter. The interior of the truck he was driving was dark. His face was dimly lit, yet she couldn't help but think how handsome he looked. "Where are you?" She knew, from tracking his progress via the GPS transmitter in his phone, but she didn't want him to know that.

He held his finger up to his lips, motioning her to lower her voice, then panned his phone toward their sleeping children. Turning the phone back toward himself, he whispered, "So far, so good. We just pulled in to Harvey."

She paused knowingly. "I should warn you, the house is modest."

"If it's not a Four Seasons, we're coming home," he answered sarcastically, and perhaps a little too loudly, because Marissa stirred.

"Is that Mom?" she asked in a sleepy voice.

"It is," Peter said.

"Is she okay?"

"Why don't you ask her yourself?" He handed her the phone as he checked the street number of the house he was looking for.

Marissa stared at her mother's face on the phone. "Mom, are you okay?"

Caitlin's eyes softened. "Of course I am."

"Then why aren't you here with us?"

"I've got a few things I need to take care of first."

Her daughter shook her head. "I know when you're lying, you know."

"I'm not lying. That's the truth."

Marissa looked up from the phone as they pulled into the driveway of a home that was modest even by local standards. About the only kind thing that could be said about the place was that it wasn't a double-wide.

"You have got to be kidding me."

Peter shut off the engine and turned back to face her. "Kidding about what?"

She was staring out the window at their new house. "Tell me this is some kind of bad joke. We're not honestly going to live here, are we?"

"Don't worry, it's only temporary," Caitlin chimed in.

"What's so wrong with it?" Peter asked from off-screen.

"For real? Where should I start?" Marissa didn't realize how near to her face she was holding the camera. Caitlin watched her disdain in extreme close-up.

Peter reacted with as much sincere offense as he could muster. "Do you have any idea what kind of snob you sound like?"

"I don't know, Dad, how many kinds are there?"

"That's quite enough out of you, young lady. I strongly suggest you zip your mouth before I lose my temper." Caitlin could hear him open the truck door. "Wake up your brother while I open up the house." He slammed the door as he exited.

Marissa watched her father unlock the front door and enter the house, then quickly nudged her brother awake. "Hey, get up."

Caitlin shook her head. "Is that really as nice as you can be?"

Marissa stared into the phone at her mother. "Under the circumstances, yes."

Mikey struggled to get his bearings. "Where are we?"

"In hell."

He then saw his mother on the phone. "Hey, is that Mom?"

Caitlin waved at him on-screen. "Hi, baby."

Mikey grabbed the phone from his sister's hand. "Where are you?"

"I'm at work," she lied.

"Let's go," Marissa said impatiently, motioning toward the clapboard house. Mikey kept the call going as Marissa led her little brother out of the truck.

Inside the house, the kids couldn't believe their eyes. The home was even more modest on the inside. The stove was an old electric. There was no dishwasher. The washer and dryer were in one of the bathrooms. There were cracks in the ceiling in almost every room. For his mother's benefit, Mikey pointed the phone at the various highlights. "Mom, all I can tell you is you should be glad you're not here."

Marissa grabbed the phone and looked at her mother. "It stinks like those nasty porta-potties at my soccer tournaments."

"I think something died in here," Mikey added as he pointed to several stains in the living room carpet. "We flew halfway across the country in a private plane to live in this dump?"

"I cannot believe what little snobs you two are." Peter threw up his hands. "When did you become like this?"

"Since the first day you sent us to private school."

"Well, then this is long overdue. And you better get used to it, because this is where we live now."

Marissa stared angrily into the phone. "Well, gee, Mom, thanks a lot for ruining my life!" She clicked "End" and the screen went black.

((•))

Across the street from the house in Harvey, the man sitting in the dark, watching them through binoculars, dialed his phone. His name was Coogan, and he had followed them from the Minot International Airport. "They've arrived."

"Have they seen you?" asked Bob Stenson.

"Negative, sir. And they will not unless you want them to."

"I do not want them to. Not yet. For now, just don't let them out of your sight."

"Copy that," replied Coogan.

"Where are you, by the way?"

"A shithole town called Harvey. And they're in the armpit of it."

"In the armpit of Harvey," Stenson said smugly. "It's too bad, really. Her plan was a good one. She just shouldn't have used the same airport I would have used in the same situation."

CHAPTER 51

Bob Stenson's Home

Falls Church, Virginia

June 1, 11:56 p.m.

Bob Stenson enjoyed his evening commutes home. It had been the same drive for nearly thirty years, because he hadn't changed jobs or houses or wives during all that time—a trifecta few men these days could claim. The trip was exactly twenty-four minutes, door to door. He could practically navigate it blindfolded. The soundtrack was always the same: jazz. Sometimes it was vintage Miles Davis or John Coltrane; other times, it was one of the more current masters like John McLaughlin or Ahmad Jamal. But the music was always soothing, which helped Stenson unwind from whatever challenges he had faced that day.

What made today different was the phone call he had placed upon leaving the Kelman Nursing and Rehab Center. From the moment Lawrence Walters had uttered the words *Alpha Reset Protocol*, Bob knew he was facing a serious potential security threat, both at the office and at home. In all his years of directing operations at the foundation, he had never once felt the need to add additional security measures at either location. While he had initiated and orchestrated a great many efforts involving threats to the physical safety of others located elsewhere, they had never involved him directly.

This time was different.

Bob had reached out to an exclusive private security firm called Oak Ridge, whose staff were among the most well trained in the world. All had previously been part of an elite fighting force: either Special Forces, Delta Force, Navy SEALS, Green Berets, Night Stalkers, or Rangers. Soldiers retiring with such high levels of lethal expertise needed somewhere to put their skills to use in the civilian world, and Oak Ridge was one of their primary employers.

Bob felt safe knowing that, as of two thirty this afternoon, his home was being protected by a team of four of these men. He had done so much business with Oak Ridge for the last two decades that he knew he would be getting their best. Which was why he found what happened that evening so surprising.

((•))

As the car pulled into the driveway, a shadow moved quickly toward it. A professional shadow with decades of experience.

He was large, at least six feet four inches tall and a good 240 pounds. He was clad in black from head to toe. Black boots. Black pants. Black jacket. Black balaclava tactical hood. It was Hogan. The only visible part of him was his eyes, which were cold-blooded, intense, and alert. A hunter's eyes.

Outside the vehicle, the last glorious notes of Coltrane's "Blue Train" could be heard before the engine was shut off. The driver stepped out and walked toward the kitchen door.

Hogan pointed a gun at the back of his head and clicked back the hammer. "Don't move, Stenson." His voice was emotionless and direct, like he'd done this a thousand times.

The driver turned around slowly. He was not Bob Stenson. He was an Oak Ridge employee who had the same basic features as the American Heritage Foundation director. A stunt double, if you will. "And who might you be?"

If Hogan was surprised, he didn't show it. "I'm wondering the same thing about you."

"I'm the last person you are ever going to see." He stared defiantly in Hogan's eyes, waiting expectantly.

Hogan stared back, continuing to point his suppressed Glock 17, the only handgun he ever carried. The weapon was named for the seventeen nine-millimeter bullets it carried, which made reloading a less frequent necessity. But what Hogan really liked about the weapon was its simplicity and reliability. To clean it, you only needed to press one button to remove the slide. Few other handguns could make that claim. "Tick. Tick. Tick."

"What's that supposed to mean?" the Stenson look-alike asked.

"The men you're waiting for, the ones who are supposed to take me out, have made other plans." He motioned to the side of the driveway, where four bodies were lined up neatly in a row. Each one showed evidence of having been taken down with a double tap: one bullet to the forehead, one to center mass. The heart shot usually killed the target, but just in case, a second bullet was fired through the brain to confirm that all function had ceased. Hearts could be revived, but brains could not.

The bullets were usually fired in rapid succession; it was common practice among most of the world's elite fighting forces in the world. "I highly doubt you will be the last person I ever see."

The decoy couldn't help but be impressed. "Were you SEAL, Green Beret, Delta Force, or what?"

"Something like that." Hogan remained perfectly calm.

The stunt double took a moment to gather himself. "Get it over with."

"You're in no position to dictate anything." The other man's phone began to vibrate inside his pants pocket. Neither man moved. "Aren't you going to answer that?"

CHAPTER 52

Backyard

Bob Stenson's Home

June 1, 11:59 p.m.

The man reached carefully inside his pocket and answered his buzzing phone. "Hello."

"Now say goodbye." Hogan fired two quick shots: one center mass, and one through his forehead. A double tap, just like the others. Stenson's alternate went down like a dropped sack of potatoes. His phone fell next to him, which was what Hogan wanted. He didn't want to have to reach inside another man's pants pocket. He picked up the phone and put it to his ear. "Sorry about that. With whom am I speaking?"

"The man you came there to kill," answered Stenson.

((•))

He was sitting at a modest table in the outdated kitchen of a house that was unremarkable except that it was located within the confines of Joint Base Anacostia-Bolling, fourteen miles away. It was one of several safe houses he had established over the years. Given that it was located on a military base, it was a very safe house.

Stenson's wife, Millie, had arrived earlier that evening. After his regrettable meeting with Lawrence Walters, Stenson had called his wife and calmly asked her to pack their bags and meet him on the base. She had surprised him with her lack of concern or worry. It seemed to have been a call she had been expecting for a very long time, and therefore she knew exactly how to proceed. She had even stopped at a market along the way so she could have dinner waiting for him upon arrival.

Holding the phone to his ear, Stenson watched four different surveillance-camera views of his backyard that appeared on his laptop. The man there clearly knew where the cameras were located and stared directly into one. The balaclava tactical hood concealed his identity. "You were smart not to come here."

"You're not as clever as you think."

The man paused briefly. "You and the wife like to travel?"

"No, not much."

"That's too bad."

Stenson studied the man standing in his backyard next to five dead bodies. "Do we know each other?"

The assassin shook his head. "I don't think so."

"What's your stake in this?"

"Keeping a promise to an old friend."

"You know, Lawrence was my mentor."

The man nodded. "He would be very disappointed. But not terribly surprised. He had planned for this a long time ago."

The words hung there a moment. Stenson gritted his teeth, then glanced at the bodies lying on the ground by his opponent's feet. He wasn't looking forward to the conversation he would be having with their superior the following day. This kind of thing wasn't supposed to occur on US soil. But then again, all kinds of things that normally didn't occur were about to. "You know, those men had families."

"They chose the wrong line of work."

Stenson paused one final time. "I hope you have an army. Because I do." And with that, he ended the call.

((•))

Hogan remained silent as he moved through the shadows away from the Stenson house. His footsteps barely made a sound. He wore a black backpack, which contained his Glock 17 along with several other weapons, a dozen extra magazines for each, several different sizes of blades, and two grenades for good measure. It was quite like Butler McHenry's bad-day bag, only the extreme version.

Back in the day, Lawrence Walters would have told him to use nonlethal force on the boys sent to guard Stenson's house. Or perhaps it was Hogan's own sense of guilt. Either way, he could hear Lawrence's voice inside his head as he continued walking, and he felt compelled to respond. *I don't tell you how to do your job; don't tell me how to do mine.*

It was not unlike how Hogan had spoken with Lawrence when he was still in charge of the American Heritage Foundation and they had disagreed on an operation. Hogan was the first independent contractor to ever speak to the legend this way. Rather than take offense, however, Lawrence seemed to appreciate the younger man's candor. The two developed a genuine chemistry, what some today might refer to as a "bromance."

They recognized something in each other. Hogan had a determination and ferocity beyond anything the older man had ever seen, except within himself. Hogan was a killer without peer. His physical skills and intelligence were unmatched. But even more than that, he was loyal. If Lawrence called, Hogan dropped everything. He would do anything in his power not to fail, and given the man's abilities, that was saying quite a lot. He was the fiercest weapon any intelligence operative had ever had at his beck and call. And he worked for only one man.

That was, until Hogan's young son developed acute lymphoblastic leukemia.

When the symptoms first appeared, they looked like nothing more than a common cold. A mild fever and chills, but nothing any parent would be overly concerned about. Then the boy started to lose weight. And developed persistent nosebleeds. He started bruising so easily that his nursery school teacher became concerned that he might be showing signs of abuse. They received the diagnosis shortly thereafter.

Hogan took a leave of absence to battle with his insurance carrier regarding treatment coverage. They were denying each procedure as experimental because it was new. The cost of care was well beyond anything he could afford. His only child was dying, and there was nothing he could do.

Hogan felt utterly impotent for the first time in his life.

Then, everything changed. Out of the blue, his insurer informed him that every requested procedure, experimental and otherwise, that had previously been denied would now be completely covered. When Hogan asked how this was possible, the company representative replied with a sentence that still rang in his ears: *We should all have such a good friend.* Five years later, his son was cancer-free and had remained so ever since.

Hogan had known right away that it was Lawrence. The two men never discussed the matter, not then or anytime since. They didn't need to. But Hogan knew there would come a time when he would be asked to return the favor, and that time came right before Lawrence retired. That favor was to head up tactical operations if and when his daughter ever initiated an Alpha Reset Protocol. And until that time, he was to keep the safe site in a state of readiness.

Hogan would have said yes even if there was no compensation involved, but as it turned out, the old man had stashed enough foundation money aside to fund the facility in perpetuity, including reasonable compensation for Hogan's time, which included excellent health benefits, of course. There was no way in hell he would fail the old man, even if Lawrence no longer had any idea who he was or what the Alpha Reset Protocol entailed.

Hogan had already demonstrated that he would kill for his benefactor. What only he knew was that he was also willing to die for him. And that made a dangerous man even more so.

CHAPTER 53

David's Place

Woodsdale, Maryland

June 2, 5:22 a.m.

Butler had slept in his clothes, which was nothing new. In fact, he'd done it so often, both in the military and as a civilian, that he was well accustomed to it by now. All he needed was a place to rest his head, and he could pass right out. He could be sitting upright in a chair, semi-reclined in a car, or curled up on a hard linoleum floor—it really didn't matter. And while it was nice to have a pillow or some other kind of cushion, it wasn't necessary.

His ex-wife had always found it loathsome, and she wasn't afraid to tell him so. *What kind of a person doesn't sleep in proper pajamas? Or even a bed, for that matter?* She found it understandable that this was something soldiers did while in the field, but she could see no good reason why they couldn't adopt a less bestial manner of living upon return to civilian life.

Butler had tried to change for her, particularly after she became pregnant with their first child, but he couldn't seem to break himself of the habit. Well, that one and a great many others that equally incensed his beloved bride. A second baby was supposed to further motivate him into becoming the more civilized version of himself, but the beautiful little darling only made matters worse. There seemed to be no way to coax, prod, or guilt Butler into remaking himself into the man he was supposed to be, at least according to his ex. Their marriage never reached year five.

She moved to Colorado shortly thereafter and took the kids with her, leaving him to sleep in his clothes wherever and whenever he felt like it. Over the last ten years, this often meant the station house or any number of unmarked department vehicles, which had given him a competitive advantage over his peers, as far as he was concerned. Sleeper cars had gotten their name because they were "all show and no go," but Butler had taken the term more literally. The department psychologist had repeatedly expressed her professional concern for his psychological status, but Butler had made it clear on more than one occasion how much he didn't care.

Currently, it meant that he had gotten a hell of a lot better night's sleep than Skylar had, even though he had given her the only chair in the room while he had slept on the floor next to Eddie's bed. Four hours was plenty for him when he needed it to be.

((•))

Skylar, on the other hand, hadn't slept much at all. She was too uncomfortable and much too anxious about her present circumstances to have given herself the luxury of any kind of meaningful REM. Having heard Butler snoring soundly at various times throughout the night, she vacillated between being happy for him, jealous of him, and concerned that he might wake up Eddie. Thankfully, Eddie slept peacefully through the night, so she focused on being jealous. At least, until the most glorious smells started wafting under the door.

Butler smelled them, too. He sat up abruptly, taking a long, deep breath through his nose. He glanced at Skylar, who could only be seen in silhouette. She raised her finger to her lips, motioning for him to remain quiet. He nodded, then stood up silently and moved into the hallway, where he found Lolo and four trolley carts full of breakfast foods: fresh-baked muffins, including chocolate and date nut; croissants; banana bread; a bowl of fruit that did not include blueberries; buttermilk pancakes and waffles; bacon and sausages and slices of ham; eggs that were scrambled, over easy, and in a soufflé; hash browns; a variety of juices; coffee; and several different types of milk. "Good morning," Butler said.

"Good-good morning," Lolo stammered.

Butler continued surveying the breakfast offerings. "Wow, have you been busy."

"Well, you are guests and all." She paused awkwardly. "Do you think, I mean Eddie, will he be able to find something he'd like to eat? Because I can make something else. I can make many things. I had to guess. I don't like to guess. Too much chance. I don't know. I made a whole bunch of different things."

"I'm sure he'll be able to find something to like," he said with assurance.

"Here, Butler, this is for you." She handed him a plate that included the items he had mentioned the night before. "Pancakes and bacon and hash browns, bacon not too crispy."

He was embarrassed as well as a bit flabbergasted. "You really didn't need to do all this."

"Well, I knew you weren't talking about Eddie last night. I know you thought I didn't realize, but I did. I know more than people think I do. I watched you eat. Could tell how hungry you were. I thought you would like a nice breakfast of your favorite things. Breakfast is the most important meal of the day, you know. Breakfast is."

For a man who could be reasonably described as emotionally distant, he was sincerely touched. "Lolo, this is the nicest thing anyone has done for me in as long as I can remember."

"That is a long time. Well, food never did anyone any good just sitting on a plate getting cold. That's what my mother used to say. She would. You should eat while it's hot." She handed him utensils and a napkin, then motioned for him to return into the room.

While he hesitated, the door was opened from the inside. Skylar poked her head out. "Guess who's awake?"

"Is it Eddie?" Lolo asked expectantly. "We didn't wake him, did we? I hope not. That would be bad. I would feel terrible. I mean, it's early. Quite early for most people. I mean, I am not most people, so I don't really know about them, but that's what Dr. Davenport says."

"No, you didn't wake him up. Eddie's stomach did."

"Oh, good, he's hungry. That's a good sign. Very good." She sounded like she was repeating something she had heard her doctor say.

Skylar glanced around at all the breakfast foods Lolo had prepared. "Did you make all this?"

"If it's not enough, just tell me, and I can make more of anything you'd like."

Skylar shook her head with appreciation. "No, I'm sure this is going to be plenty." She turned back inside the room and flipped on the lights. "Eddie, we have quite a nice surprise for you—"

Eddie was no longer connected to the IV. His expression was priceless as the four food carts were wheeled into the room. He looked like a young boy on Christmas morning who had discovered he was getting everything on his list. And then some. "If this food tastes as good as it smells, I may have to revise my entire food-rating system. That will require a great deal of effort on my part. And I may even have to add smell as its own category." He paused to inhale deeply. "I have never smelled anything like this."

"Wait until you taste it," commented Skylar. Butler had already started devouring his plate of food.

As Eddie watched Lolo enter, he looked like a child who was now seeing Santa himself. He stared in wonder. And utter disbelief. It was as if he was having some kind of religious experience, what Buddhists call "that which cannot be communicated."

And then, without warning, he slapped himself.

CHAPTER 54

EDDIE'S ROOM

DAVID'S PLACE

June 2, 5:31 a.m.

Skylar rushed to Eddie, expecting him to continue slapping himself. "Eddie, stop!"

To her surprise, he did. "It wasn't that kind of a slap, Skylar. There is no need for you to be alarmed."

"What kind of slap was it?"

"I wanted to be sure I am awake and not dreaming."

"Oh." She breathed a sigh of relief, although she was still puzzled. "Why would you think you're dreaming?"

He rolled his eyes, as if the answer should be obvious. "She's real. My angel. She's standing right there." He pointed toward Lolo, repeatedly glancing over at her. He then struggled to speak to her. "You're. Real."

"Well, I hope so," Lolo replied sheepishly. "I mean, I think I am." She pinched herself to make sure she felt something. "Yup, I'm real, all right. Ouch." Momentarily embarrassed, she turned her attention back to Eddie. "So you remember me, then? From last night? You were kind of out of it. I mean, not in a bad way, but after all, you had been in a car accident."

"It was not a car accident. It was a van accident," Eddie corrected her. "I thought you were only someone from one of the dreams I had."

Lolo blushed. "Wow, nobody has ever told me that before. I mean, about being in one of their dreams. Wow."

"That is not a bad thing, is it?" Eddie asked.

"No, not at all. I mean, I don't think so. It's really kind of amazing. More than amazing, if you know what I mean. Does that make sense?"

Eddie smiled briefly, then turned to Skylar. "How would I know if I was hallucinating?"

Skylar answered, "Just ask me. I'm a pretty good judge of reality, and I can say with near certainty that you are not hallucinating right now."

He looked down at his arms. "Then why do I have goose bumps?"

Skylar smiled, marveling at what she was witnessing. "I'll explain it to you after you eat."

"And my palms are sweaty. I don't like how it feels. They're slippery."

"Trust me, it's a good thing." She smiled warmly at him. "Let's enjoy the food while it's hot. After all, Lolo went through a lot of trouble to make all this for us."

Eddie looked amazed. "She did?" He turned to Lolo. "You did?"

She nodded, pushing the carts closer to the bed so he could reach some of the baked goods. Two of the wheels SQUEAKED unpleasantly. Eddie cringed. Lolo replied, "No, no trouble. I like to cook. A lot. And you all are visitors. Visitors are special because we don't get many. Not many visitors."

Eddie surveyed the choices, then selected a croissant and quickly took a bite. His eyes went wide with surprise.

Skylar smiled as she bit into one of the chocolate muffins. "Pretty good, don't you think?"

He took another bite as if to confirm what he had discovered during the first one. He spoke with his mouth full. "No, I don't." Lolo began to look upset. Eddie looked quite serious and then he swallowed.

"It is not pretty good. That would be a three or a four, and this croissant is definitely not a three or a four."

Unsure of what Eddie was talking about, Lolo asked nervously, "Then, what is it?" She seemed to be holding her breath.

"The very best score I have ever given any food is a five-plus, but this croissant is so much better than any other one I have ever tasted that I have to give it a six, which is a rating I have never given any food before. Not ever."

Butler chimed in from the corner, where he was devouring his breakfast. "Try the eggs."

"Which kind?" Eddie surveyed his options.

"All of them." He gleefully swallowed another bite.

Eddie extended his fork and took a bite of the egg soufflé. His eyes bugged out with disbelief. "Six." He then quickly took a bite of the scrambled eggs, a waffle, a sausage, and the hash browns. He shook his head. "I don't know how this is possible, but they are all sixes." He pointed to the different food offerings. "Six. Six. Six. Six."

"You seem upset," commented Lolo, who looked confused.

"Now that I know how good food can taste when prepared by a genuine chef, I will never be able to forget it."

"Is that what I am? A genuine chef, really?" If someone had told her she was a fairy who could fly and would live forever, she couldn't have looked any happier.

"Yes. I don't know what else you could be."

"I think so, too," chimed in Butler. "Definitely a genuine chef."

"Ditto," added Skylar.

Lolo teared up and turned to Eddie. "I hope you don't ever forget how good food can taste. Do you want to know why? I will tell you. Because then you won't forget about me, Lolo."

There was an extended pause in the conversation. It was perhaps the most beautiful moment of silence that Skylar had ever heard. Even Butler seemed to appreciate it.

"Even if you weren't such an excellent cook, Lolo, I could never forget you. I have an excellent memory. I will be able to recount every detail of this morning if anyone asks. I don't know very many people, but if someone does ask, I will be able to." Eddie paused, considering something new. "I will be sad if I never get to eat a meal as good as this again."

"I don't want you to be sad, Eddie. Not ever."

He studied her. "You are telling the truth." This seemed to surprise him.

"Of course I am telling the truth. I don't think lying is nice."

Eddie nodded. "I don't think so, either. Lying is something that nice people shouldn't do." He glanced at Skylar. "Unless they absolutely have to."

Skylar jumped in. "Eddie, stop talking and eat before your food gets cold and you decide to downgrade your ratings because of it."

"No-no, I wouldn't want that," Lolo said.

He began to eat as if he hadn't in days, which wasn't far from the truth. And with every bite, he mumbled "six" to himself. And repeatedly glanced at Lolo, who never took her eyes off him. He would smile at her, then look away. Then sneak another glance.

Skylar pretended not to notice but watched every moment closely. There was no denying something wonderful was happening.

If only it could last.

CHAPTER 55

Dulles International Airport

West of Washington, DC

June 2, 6:17 a.m.

The international killer's plane had arrived thirty-four minutes ahead of schedule, but there were no available gates, so Mr. Elliott and the rest of the Lufthansa passengers had been sitting on the tarmac for the last half hour. If the crew had only known what he had done to people for far lesser offenses, they might have operated with a greater sense of urgency.

He normally didn't fly first-class but decided that he could justify the splurge this time. After all, it wasn't every day he received $2.5 million as an initial payment for an assignment. *And if the world's highest-paid assassin can't fly first-class, who can?*

Mr. Elliott hadn't set foot inside the United States in nineteen years. There was good reason for that. The number of governmental agencies hunting him was large and included pretty much all of them. He had made no attempt to hide his horrendous deeds, and in fact had publicized them—without ever showing his face. No one had any idea what he looked like, particularly now that his face had been so thoroughly modified. Little did the plastic surgeons who had performed the work realize that his was the last face they would ever change.

He waited patiently in the customs line to present his identification. He stood behind an attractive German couple who were holding hands. The rings on their fingers appeared to be new. Perhaps this was their honeymoon, Mr. Elliott thought. He smiled at them politely as he imagined their screams while he tortured them. The more barbarous his thoughts, the more pleasant his smile became. It was a little game he played whenever out in public. Which was why he didn't go out much. It was too tempting.

He was traveling under the name of Manfred Engels, just one of several identities he had at his disposal. As he handed his German passport to the customs agent, the man glanced at him perfunctorily. "Good morning."

Mr. Elliott responded with a slight but authentic German accent. "Good morning."

"The purpose of your visit to the United States?"

"I'm visiting an old friend."

"How long will you be with us?"

"Only a few days, I'm afraid. My daughter has a recital I have to get back for."

"Piano?"

"Violin."

The agent nodded with the understanding of a fellow father as he stamped the killer's passport and turned to the following person in line. "Next."

"Manfred" collected his luggage at baggage claim and waited patiently while the bags were opened and the contents inspected. Nothing appeared out of the ordinary. In fact, his clothing and other personal items all looked very German, just as they were supposed to. Mr. Elliott was meticulous.

He cleared customs in less than twenty minutes, making his way out of the secured area, where he paused to check the text messages on his phone. He had one new message from an unknown sender. It read:

4-RED-219 90875. It was a parking garage location. Fourth level. Red section. Space 219. The car parked in it was a blue Ford Fusion, as boring and forgettable a vehicle as has ever been manufactured. Which made it perfect for Mr. Elliott's purposes, along with its keyless entry system.

When the correct five-digit code was entered in a concealed keypad in the driver's door panel, the car would unlock. He pressed *9-0-8-7-5*, and presto, the car was his. His birthday was September 8, 1975. At least, so the passport he was carrying said. He placed his luggage in the back seat, then reached inside the center console, locating the car keys and parking exit ticket. He moved to the trunk and unlocked it, revealing several large nylon bags.

One contained the clothing he planned to wear on the trip. Mr. Elliott prided himself on a casual but elegant sense of attire that could have been featured in the pages of any number of men's fashion magazines.

The other bags contained a small arsenal of international arms: a suppressed Austrian sniper rifle called a Steyr Scharfschützengewehr PIV, commonly known as an SSG PIV; a Belgian machine gun, the M24E6, made by Fabrique Nationale Herstal, which was favored by several branches of the US military; and several American-made hand-guns, including a Smith & Wesson .44 Magnum and a Kimber Micro 9. He had enough ammunition to last for days.

But it was the smallest bag that contained the items he cared most about: knives and cuffs and garrotes and needles and other instruments of torture, both exotic and common. There were several rolls of duct tape and dozens of zip ties because, well, he never failed to find good uses for them.

There were also tactical hoods and other masks, as well as several GoPros and a Canon XA11 compact video camera to capture all the action for posterity. Given what he was being paid for this job, he felt compelled to share the deed with future clientele in multicamera high definition.

Mr. Elliott paid the parking attendant for the seven hours the car had been parked in the facility, then drove away from the airport, heading south. Facing an hour drive, he tuned the FM radio to his favorite classical station, WETA, which broadcast at 90.9 megahertz. He often streamed this station over the internet wherever he happened to be in the world, but listening to it over its native radio waves somehow made the notes sound that much sweeter. A Rossini sonata was in progress, which he found soothing.

It made the thought of what he had to do later that day slightly more palatable. The problem was not the killing or torture that was on his agenda. Goodness, no, those were the rewards. The problem was the building he would be required to enter. Mr. Elliott's father had contracted early-onset Alzheimer's and had lived in a nursing home for the final two decades of his life. Mr. Elliott had found the place depressing as hell because, among other reasons, it smelled like death—and not the good kind. It had the odor of infection and decay. The kind of death that was pathetic: slow and inevitable. There was nothing whatsoever appealing about it.

He accepted that it was a small price to pay. He had a fish to catch, but an elusive one. He knew that he would never find her directly; he'd have to draw her out. And he had found the perfect bait to do so.

CHAPTER 56

Safe House

Gilberts Corner, Virginia

June 2, 6:49 a.m.

Caitlin had already been up for hours. She was able to function on only a few hours of sleep when she needed to, and on this day more than any other, she needed to.

She plotted strategy while maintaining satellite surveillance on her family's location in Harvey, North Dakota, as well as Edward Parks's location in Woodsdale, Maryland. There had been no sign of unusual activity in either location, so she focused on her assault plan. Which had to be executed as soon as possible. She knew the longer this game went on, the more likely she would be forced to play defense, which included bearing the unthinkable. Caitlin had told herself that she would not relent under any circumstances, but if that time came, saying it and doing it were two different things.

She called Butler, who answered on the first ring. "Good morning."

"Why do you sound so cheerful?" Caitlin asked.

"If you'd had the breakfast I just had, you would, too."

"I've had a protein bar and freeze-dried coffee."

"Both are items I am plenty familiar with. Which is what made the breakfast I was served this morning so special."

She paused briefly to let him know the chitchat was over. "You ready to get to work?"

"Copy that."

"Will Edward Parks allow you to take possession of his device?"

"That is unlikely." He said it in a way that let her know this conversation was not currently comfortable for him to have.

"Is he within earshot of you?"

"Affirmative."

"Step away."

She heard a door opening, followed by footsteps down a hall. "If you're going to ask why I don't just take the box, the answer is I don't know how to work the thing."

"Get him to teach you," she responded, suggesting the obvious.

"He will ask why I want him to do that, and he'll know if I don't tell him the truth."

"So tell him the truth."

"Then he won't teach me."

Caitlin was becoming frustrated. "Will he teach Skylar?"

Butler paused. "That's a good question."

"Find out and call me back." She hung up.

((•))

Lolo was no longer in Eddie's room. Neither were the breakfast plates. She'd apparently taken them back to the kitchen for cleanup. Eddie cupped his hands behind his ears the moment Butler walked out of the room. He closed his eyes to focus all his concentration on his powerful hearing. Skylar studied him, speaking quietly. "Can you hear what he's saying?"

Eddie nodded. "He is continuing his phone call with someone who knows about the echo box." He turned to her. "I hope I get to make a phone call one day."

"Then I will make sure that happens."

He smiled briefly, then turned back toward the door, repeating Butler's side of the conversation with Caitlin. "'If you're going to ask why I don't just take the box, the answer is I don't know how to work the thing . . . He will ask why I want him to do that, and he'll know if I don't tell him the truth . . . Then he won't teach me . . . That's a good question.'"

Skylar watched him closely. "What's a good question?"

"I don't know, but you can ask Detective McHenry. He is walking toward us."

Eddie sat back on the bed as Butler entered the room. "Eddie, I have a question for you."

"It's a 'good question,' isn't it?"

Butler gawked at Skylar. "I was all the way down at the end of the hall. Really?"

She nodded. "What did she want you to ask him?"

He took a breath. "If he would teach me how to use the echo box."

Eddie shook his head. "No."

"What if I said please?"

Eddie did not hesitate. "No."

Butler turned to Skylar. "Uh, I could use some help here."

"No." Eddie stared out the window.

Skylar addressed Butler, shaking her head. "I'm not going to force him to do something he doesn't want to do."

"No."

"I'm on your side, Eddie," she said.

He looked confused. "I didn't know I had a side."

"I'm in agreement with you," she clarified.

He paused. "So I don't have to teach Butler how to use the echo box if I do not want to?"

She replied reassuringly, "No, not if you don't want to."

"I don't want to." Eddie continued staring out the window.

Skylar turned to Butler. "There you have it."

Butler paused, realizing he would need to raise the stakes. "What if I told you it could save both of your lives?"

Eddie stared at him. "True." The expression on his face made it clear he wished Butler had been lying. Eddie started to feel uncomfortable. His hand began to twitch, like he was about to start slapping himself.

Skylar saw this, and she interjected quickly, "Eddie, I have an idea."

"What is your idea?"

She took a breath. "Would you be willing to teach me how to use the echo box?"

He paused, surprised by the question. "Yes, but why would you want me to teach you?"

"Because if anyone is going to use the echo box other than you, it should be me."

CHAPTER 57

JESSUP FIELDS'S ESTATE

PARADISE VALLEY, ARIZONA

June 2, 5:01 a.m. Mountain Standard Time

Jessup Fields was sound asleep in the four-thousand-square-foot master bedroom of his $27-million home in the most expensive enclave of the Grand Canyon State. Given the twelve acres of lavish lawns and lush greenery surrounding the twenty-bathroom home, it was hard to imagine that arid desert lay beneath it.

Having played cohost to an event in honor of the president of the United States the night before, he had gone to bed much later than he preferred. Such were the sacrifices in entertaining the leader of the free world. But the night had gone well, and his many well-heeled friends had kicked in admirably, so this was going to be a morning to relish the accomplishment. A scheme he and his brother had set in motion shortly after the president had taken up residence in the West Wing was going precisely according to plan. They were ensuring his future as well as their own. It would last for generations.

Jessup's plans did not include being awakened by his cell phone, particularly not at this hour. Only a handful of people in the world had this number: the president, his brother, and his three ex-wives. If it didn't involve one of his eight children, his exes were forbidden from disturbing his sleep. *One of them must have gotten themselves into another situation* was all he could think as he struggled to reach for the device. Too tired to check the caller ID, he guessed it was his brother because it usually was. "Yes?"

The woman's voice was friendly but assured. "Good morning, Mr. Fields. I'm terribly sorry to wake you, but this is a matter of some urgency."

He did not recognize the voice, and he sat up abruptly. No stranger had ever called him on this phone before. "Who is this?"

"Consider me a friend." She sounded sincere.

"A friend wouldn't be waking me so damn early in the morning."

"When you hear what I have to say, you'll understand."

"You didn't answer my question, friend. With whom am I speaking?"

"Call me Eleanor."

"And just how did you come by this number?"

"The same way I know that your arrangement with the president to ensure his victory in the upcoming election is about to be exposed."

He paused to make sure he had heard her. "Excuse me?" Now he was certain that he had; it was a lot to unpack. The hairs on the back of his neck were standing up.

"If he hasn't already, the president will be receiving a call from Bob Stenson of the American Heritage Foundation, threatening to bring the house down."

"You've lost me." She hadn't, but Jessup wanted the unknown caller to spell out in greater detail exactly what she was saying.

"Stenson will replay a conversation you had in the Oval Office earlier this year, in which you convinced the president to use the services of you and your brother instead of continuing to rely on the American Heritage Foundation for his reelection purposes."

"And you know this how, exactly?"

"Let's just say I have direct inside knowledge."

Jessup now understood that if this caller was to be believed, Bob Stenson had an insurrection on his hands—which could become useful later. "Assuming such a conversation did take place, how would Mr. Stenson have come by this recording?"

"You poked the bear. When you usurped his authority with the president, Stenson took it as a declaration of war. He intends to make an example of you both. He has made it his priority to bring down this administration and to destroy your company in the process so that no one ever dares to challenge his authority again."

Like everyone else in the circles of power, Jessup had heard the stories about Bob Stenson and his foundation but never fully believed them. "I thought Mr. Stenson was one of the president's strongest supporters."

"Not *one of*, sir. *The* strongest. The American Heritage Foundation was the primary reason he won the first election, which is why it was viewed as an act of disloyalty when he decided to rely on you instead."

"You seem to be discounting the excess of thirty million dollars my brother and I contributed through various channels to put the man in the Oval Office."

"Forgive me for saying so, Mr. Fields, but if you thought money was all it took, you and your brother would have stayed on the sidelines, throwing your cash at the ponies as they raced by."

He had to give this woman credit, whoever she was. She was sharp and well informed, and she didn't pull her punches. *Why the hell doesn't she work for me?* "Now that you have my attention, what exactly is the purpose of your call?"

"I have a plan that will help us both achieve our desired goals."

"Do tell."

She paused just a moment to let him know she was in complete control. "The president will be calling you in a panic fairly soon to say that Bob Stenson intends to force him to resign and that you will be going to prison. After he finishes blubbering, tell him that he has nothing to worry about. Then hang up and call me back." She paused again to allow everything she had said to sink in. "But please, don't try to trace this number. If you do, I will know, and if there's one thing you need to appreciate about me, it's how much I value my privacy." She hung up.

Jessup sat for a moment, staring at the phone. "Lord, you work in mysterious ways."

CHAPTER 58

DAVID'S PLACE

WOODSDALE, MARYLAND

June 2, 8:08 a.m.

Lolo returned to Eddie's room to find Eddie instructing Skylar in how to operate the echo box, which was tethered to his laptop computer. Lolo was mesmerized by the device's eight one-inch satellite microphones as they performed their synchronized ballet, acoustically mapping the room. "What is that?" she asked with eager curiosity, pointing to the device.

"It is an echo box," Eddie answered without looking up.

"I like how they move together. It looks like they are doing a dance. I like dancing." She mimicked the movements with her fingers.

"They are not dancing. They are satellite microphones acoustically mapping the room."

Lolo's expression made it clear she had no idea what that meant. "I have never seen an echo box before, because I would remember if I had."

He still didn't look up. "I know you have not seen one. That is because nobody has seen one. Well, except for Butler and Skylar and several staff members and residents of Harmony House."

She leaned in more closely to get a better look at the microphones.

He only saw her out of the corner of his eye, but he panicked, blurting out, "Don't touch them!"

Lolo immediately backed away, looking like she was about to cry. "I didn't. I didn't touch anything. I'm-I'm sorry. I didn't. I've just never seen one before. I'll leave now."

Skylar turned to Eddie. "That was uncalled for. There was no reason to raise your voice like that."

"I thought she was going to touch one of the satellite microphones. She could have damaged them."

"But she didn't, did she?"

He shook his head, clearly starting to feel guilty. His hand began to twitch.

Skylar pointed to Lolo. "Can you see that you made her cry?"

Eddie now looked up and saw her weeping as she backed toward the door. "Those are not happy tears, are they?"

"No, they are not," Skylar answered somewhat tersely.

As Lolo reached the door, Eddie glanced at her, then lowered his gaze to stare at the floor by her feet. "I apologize for raising my voice. That was wrong." His tone softened considerably. "Please don't leave."

She paused in the doorway. "You yelled at me."

"I should not have done that. I am sorry." He glanced up at her briefly.

Lolo managed to collect herself. "I was-was yelled at a lot when I was younger. Even when I didn't do anything wrong. I didn't. Just like now. Makes me sad. I don't like it."

Eddie clasped his hands together, interlocking his fingers. "If I promise not to do it again, would you stay?"

She took a moment to study him closely. "You know, a promise is a promise."

He nodded, smiling ever so slightly as he stared at the floor. "Yes, I do know."

"Well-well, how do I know you're not just saying that?"

Eddie looked confused. "I am saying it."

"Do-do you mean it?"

"Yes, I mean it. Why else would I say it?"

"Lots of people say things they don't mean."

He nodded again, appearing to understand now. "I am saying it. I am saying it I because it is the truth. I never lie."

"Never?" she asked dubiously.

"Well, almost never. The only exception is in very specific circumstances that Skylar explained require people to sometimes not tell the truth, but this is not one of those situations."

Skylar couldn't help but chime in. "He's not exaggerating. He pretty much never lies."

He nodded in agreement. "Pretty much."

Reassured, Lolo moved back toward them, where she could see the computer screen. The three-dimensional graphic representation of the room was nearing completion. Her eyes went wide with curiosity. "What is it doing?"

CHAPTER 59

June 2, 8:14 a.m.

The sun had already been up for a while. Enola Meyers and Charlie Johnson had been up the entire night, looking for a digital needle in an electronic haystack. And gotten nowhere. They had done just as instructed, putting themselves in the perspective of Eddie's rescuers, and imagined every single escape route they could have taken. Enola and Charlie had been methodical and thorough. And every single promising path had either gone nowhere or run into a brick wall. To describe them as frustrated and exhausted would be using both adjectives mildly.

Each had consumed more caffeine than either usually did in a week. Charlie had tossed back a pot and a half of coffee, which his stomach was showing signs of rebelling against. Enola had started with black tea but had moved to Red Bull by one a.m. and then sports energy chews—each of which contained fifty milligrams of caffeine—by four a.m. Such chews were typically used by endurance athletes well into long-distance sporting events to keep their bodies functioning beyond normal limits of exhaustion. Searching for Edward Parks had become her Ironman.

"Tell me you've got something," pleaded Charlie.

"If I did, you would have been the first to know."

He put his head in his hands with frustration. "Do we just suck at this, or what?"

She pointed to her screen. "None of the best trackers operating on the East Coast has found him, either. None of them has less than eighteen years of experience. We have less than eighteen months, so I wouldn't beat ourselves up too much yet."

Charlie pointed toward their door, referring to Trotter and Greers. "What about our friends down the hall?"

"If they had found Edward Parks, they would be dancing on our desks and rubbing it in our faces."

((•))

Daryl Trotter had nodded off just after five o'clock that morning. He slept with his head on his desk. He awoke just as the sun started streaming in through the windows. It took him a moment to get his bearings.

Nearby, Jason Greers continued to work his screens, glancing over briefly. "Good morning, sunshine."

Daryl stood up, stretched, and moved groggily to the window, where something caught his attention. "How long have there been armed guards outside our building?" He was referring to the six black-clad men who were visible, patrolling nearby.

"Not sure. They must have arrived sometime during the night." Greers sounded completely nonchalant.

Trotter walked over to him. "And this doesn't concern you?"

"Why would it concern me? It means we're safe."

"Safe from what?"

"Ask the boss." He motioned to Stenson's car as it arrived in the parking lot with two other vehicles. One in front of him, one behind. There were two men inside each vehicle. Two escorted him inside the American Heritage Foundation and took up positions in the entrance while the other two checked in with the armed guards patrolling the perimeter.

Stenson arrived in their office moments later. "The newbies haven't found much of anything yet. Either of you done any better?"

Greers replied, "We found the first vehicle, the one Drummond and McHenry had stolen in Philadelphia and used to remove Edward Parks and his device from the scene of the accident."

"Show me."

Greers brought up the location of the urgent care facility where Skylar had acquired the medical supplies Caitlin had purchased for her the night before. "A nurse at the facility reported her vehicle as stolen at six this morning, so now all teams are looking for a late-model Jeep Wagoneer."

Stenson processed the information. "You're saying every one of our teams spent most of the night looking for the wrong vehicle."

Reluctantly, Greers responded, "Unfortunately, yes, sir."

Stenson turned to Trotter. "We need you to do what you do best, son. Clearly, somebody's got to come up with an entirely different approach, and nobody does that better than you."

"I'll do my best," Trotter responded, although he was somewhat distracted.

"What is it?"

Hesitantly, Trotter motioned out the windows. "Sir, what's going on out there?"

"You mean the men with the automatic weapons?"

"Has there been a threat we should know about?" He was clearly nervous.

"The threat occurred yesterday, the moment Caitlin McCloskey walked out our door. Make no mistake, she's declared war on you, me, and everything this institution stands for. Until the risk is neutralized, I am not taking any chances. And neither should you." He continued down the hall, seeing no reason to mention that five well-trained, well-armed men had been murdered in his backyard the night before.

((•))

Stenson entered the conference room, where Carter Harwood had worked through the night. The duplicate echo box and laptop were surrounded by several empty Rockstar Energy Drink cans and protein-bar wrappers. "You have something to play for me yet?" he asked impatiently.

"Yes, indeed I do, sir. Sorry about the delay. The process was quite a bit more involved than I had anticipated."

"Play the conversation I want to hear and all will be forgiven." He sat across the table from Harwood, clasping his hands in front of him.

Harwood looked at the rendering of the Oval Office on the screen of his laptop, which was an exact duplicate of Eddie's. The date read: *July 23, 2016.* "The first voice you hear will be Jessup Fields." Harwood clicked "Play."

JESSUP FIELDS: *The back door is embedded in such a way that it would take today's best code-breaking system ten thousand years to crack it. Only the original programmer and my brother and I know how to access it.*

PRESIDENT: *We're talking about tens of thousands of voting machines. How can you manage all of them in such a short amount of time?*

JESSUP FIELDS: *We don't need to. The actual number is less than six percent of all devices. We'll see the votes as they're cast in real time, but only change the ones we need to swing the critical precincts.*

CHIEF OF STAFF: *What about post-election auditing against paper records?*

Harwood quickly interjected, "The next voice is the older brother, Clayton."

CLAYTON FIELDS: *We'll know in advance which precincts are being audited. The ballots to match the modified electronic records will be swapped for the originals the moment they are picked up.*

There was a slight pause.

PRESIDENT: *How much am I going to win by?*

Followed by another pause.

CLAYTON FIELDS: *How much do you want to win by?*

PRESIDENT: *As long as I win the popular vote, I don't care.*

There was now a longer pause, as there often is before the final deal point is reached in any agreement.

JESSUP FIELDS: *Congratulations on your second term, Mr. President. I know we're going to do great things together.*

Harwood clicked "Stop." He looked across the table at Stenson as his boss processed what he had just heard. "You've outdone yourself, Harwood."

"Thank you, sir."

Stenson stood abruptly. "Send a copy of the conversation to my secure account."

Harwood deftly executed several quick commands on his keyboard. "Done."

"Now I want you to keep digging. It's my understanding there have been a number of rather unsavory late-night meetings in our commander in chief's office. Seems to be some kind of fetish. Search for anything that occurred after midnight."

"Yes, sir," Harwood replied, doing his best to hide his exhaustion.

Stenson exited the conference room, pausing in the doorway. "I have been looking forward to the phone call I'm about to make for quite a while."

CHAPTER 60

June 2, 8:21 a.m.

The president was sound asleep beneath a blue quilt embroidered with the presidential seal when there were several knocks on his door. He stirred but didn't awaken until the knocks became louder. Through the door, he heard the voice of his chief of staff, Ted Christian. "Sir, I'm sorry to wake you. It's Ted."

The president was clearly annoyed. "It had better be important." He slowly got up and put on his robe as he made his way to the door. He cracked it open slightly. "What?"

"Bob Stenson is on the phone."

This gave the president pause. "Did he say it was urgent?"

His chief of staff chose his words carefully. "He said it was a matter that couldn't wait."

"Shit."

Two minutes later, he was sitting behind his desk in the private office. Christian sat across from him. The president answered the call on speakerphone. "Good morning, Bob."

"To you too, sir. How's the flight?"

"It would be better if I was still asleep. What the hell's going on?" He tried not to sound panicked.

"Who else is with you?"

"My chief of staff, Ted Christian."

"Well, gentlemen, I'm afraid I have some bad news for you."

"I gather your guys found something?" Christian asked dubiously.

"The satellite surveillance system is real, I'm afraid," Stenson lied with conviction. "It appears to be the North Koreans fronting the Chinese, but we're still confirming that part of it. We were able to interrupt their satellite signal, which should prevent ongoing surveillance for the time being, but it won't last long."

Christian chimed in. "I checked with our best tech guys at NSA, NRO, and NGA, and all said space-based surveillance is years away, and probably decades." He was referring to personnel from the National Security Agency, the National Reconnaissance Office, and the National Geospatial-Intelligence Agency.

"Then it appears you need to get some better tech guys," Stenson snapped. "Why don't you listen to one of the conversations we were able to pull off their servers and then tell me how far away this technology is."

He played the conversation that had occurred inside the Oval Office on the morning of July 23, 2016. Both the president and his chief of staff immediately recognized their own voices. There was no mistaking the authenticity of what they were hearing. Both men slumped in their chairs, turning similar shades of white. The president placed his palms on his desk to steady himself. He gasped breathlessly, "Jesus Christ."

"Mother of . . ." Christian mumbled almost inaudibly. It was a rare moment in his career when he had been completely surprised. This was a man who was widely considered one of the best political strategists in the game. He never missed a trick, because he considered every possible angle of a situation beforehand.

The president struggled to speak. "Why haven't they threatened to use this against us yet?"

Stenson responded with a poker reference. "In hold 'em, when you have their nuts on the flop, you don't push all in right away. You slow play it, as if waiting to see what the other guys are going to do before making your move."

"And sometimes, you push all in right away to make the other players think you might be bluffing," Christian commented suggestively.

"When you have the cards, it doesn't really matter, does it?" Stenson asked, clearly gloating.

The president seemed to recognize that his chief of staff and Stenson were having a separate conversation buried within the one he was participating in, but he was too overwhelmed to draw attention to it. His head was spinning. "If word of this gets out, it would not only be the end of my administration; it could rattle the very foundation of our democracy itself."

"Let's not go quite that far down the rabbit hole," Christian said.

"I'd say this time it's justified," Stenson answered. It was now obvious that he wanted to put the chief of staff in his place.

"Bob, is there any way to fix this?" The president sounded defeated and desperate. Like a man willing to do anything he was told.

"Unlikely, but I'll pursue some back channels that may be open to us. I'll let you know if I get any traction."

((•))

Christian knew that "back channels" meant he would be having a separate conversation with Stenson sometime later that day. Because the director of the American Heritage Foundation had given him a similar call shortly after the president and he had first met with the Fields brothers almost a year ago. Before then, Christian had heard of Stenson and his outfit. Hell, everyone in Washington had. But like most people, he considered the incredible stories attributed to Stenson as nothing more than political ghost tales that politicians and lobbyists liked to tell each other late at night to scare each other. There simply wasn't any way a private entity could wield so much power and influence, and he had told the president as much. *This is the United States of America we're talking about here.*

It was only then that the president had finally admitted the extent of his relationship with Stenson. The AHF apparently knew things from the president's past that they shouldn't have, and they had miraculously made the most potentially damaging of the matters disappear. It was all quite mysterious, and almost mythical.

Christian saw the world through a quantitative lens, which meant he didn't trust those who used a more qualitative prism. He preferred measurable data, like the kind presented by Jessup and Clayton. The brothers had presented him a business proposition, which he then shared with the president, who voiced his concerns about how Stenson and his organization would feel about "going outside the family" for something as important as rigging the next election.

The chief of staff had reminded his boss that the president of the United States didn't have to fear anyone, especially not some privately funded, self-proclaimed intelligence don whose feathers might be ruffled by making a deal with a competitor.

Apparently, he did.

Christian didn't believe that space-based surveillance was possible, but he also had no plausible explanation for how Stenson was just now able to play a conversation that had occurred inside the Oval Office nearly a year ago. The room was electronically swept for surveillance devices daily, so he knew that couldn't be it. There had been no one else in the room during the meeting, but clearly, someone had recorded it. It wasn't the president, and it wasn't him. The only other two people who had been in the room were the Fields brothers, Jessup and Clayton. But why would either of them have recorded the meeting?

The chief of staff hypothesized about a brewing split between the brothers that had somehow gotten out of hand, and one intended to destroy the other without regard for collateral damage. Or that one of them had become overly paranoid and recorded the conversation purely out of precaution, but had unwittingly lost possession of the recording or allowed it to be duplicated, which meant anyone with access to it could be behind this. There were too many scenarios with too many variables to significantly narrow down the list of possibilities, which was incredibly frustrating for him.

Two things were certain: Christian had significantly underestimated Stenson and his American Heritage Foundation; and instead of being guaranteed a second term, the president might not be able to complete his first.

And it was Christian's fault.

CHAPTER 61

David's Place

Woodsdale, Maryland

June 2, 8:28 a.m.

The expressions on Lolo's face vacillated from joy to bewilderment to confusion to sadness and fear as she listened to the last conversation she'd ever had with Helena, her deceased friend who had previously inhabited the room Eddie now occupied.

The voices came from Eddie's laptop, which he was operating. It was connected to the device Eddie called the echo box, which he had explained to her, but the name was about all she was able to comprehend. It was based on a science called acoustic archeology, which was difficult for her to follow.

She understood that matter can change form—that ice can be melted into water and then heated into steam and then cooled back into ice—but that didn't help her much with the concept of sound waves decaying into inaudible energy waves that could then be turned back into sound waves. In fact, the whole business of inaudible sound waves bouncing around the room made her feel claustrophobic. She imagined a thousand people talking all around her, making it difficult for her to hear her own thoughts, much less what anyone was saying. She pressed her hands to her ears, trying to make it stop.

"I don't want you to feel bad," Eddie assured her, just like she had previously said to him. "Not ever. Most people don't understand the science, even after I explain it as simply as I can."

"Don't worry, there are a lot of things I don't understand. I've gotten kind of used to it." To make sense of the device, Lolo had decided to think of the echo box as "the play-back-anything box," because that's what it did. It could play back anything you wanted to hear. And right now, that was the voice of her beloved friend whom she could no longer speak with.

HELENA: *I'm scared, Lolo. Really, really scared.*

Her speech was slightly slurred, evidence of her cerebral palsy.

LOLO: *Don't be scared, Helena. Because we're friends and friends protect each other, don't they?*

Butler and Skylar were awed by what they were hearing. They glanced at each other briefly, apparently realizing they shared a similar bond between them. Friends did protect each other.

HELENA: *I don't think you can protect me from this. Not even Dr. Davenport can. He said the tumor is inop . . . inop . . . inop . . .*

LOLO: *Inoperable.*

"She had trouble saying that word, *inoperable*," Lolo commented as she listened to herself. "I don't know why. It was just one of those things, I guess, but we all have some of those things, don't we?"

Eddie didn't respond. He was too focused on the graphical representation of the echoes appearing on his computer screen.

Lolo nodded, as if recognizing this was one of Eddie's "things."

(((•)))

Helena was curled into a fetal position on the bed. It was the middle of the afternoon, but she hadn't gotten out of bed yet. She clutched a pillow tightly to her chest. Her forehead was beaded with cold sweat. The young woman did not look well.

Lolo sat beside her, dabbing her forehead with a cold washcloth. "Do you want to sing a song together like we sometimes do, me and you? We can sing any song you want."

"Not right now," Helena struggled to answer. "My head kind of hurts."

"I can sing to you if you tell me what song you want to hear."

Helena shook her head no. "Can you just hold my hand a little?"

"Of course I can," Lolo answered. She took Helena's hand and held it tightly. "It's cold. Your hand."

"I know," she said, starting to shiver.

"Are you hungry? I can make you something to eat."

Again, Helena shook her head no. "I'm not hungry."

"I want to help, Helena. I really do. But I don't know what to do."

"You just being here helps. More than you know."

(((•)))

As they continued listening to the echoes of the heartrending scene, Skylar studied Lolo and smiled, almost imperceptibly. Mostly to herself, she said, "You understand more than you think." Her expression made it clear that she was increasingly fascinated by Lolo and looked forward to learning more about her.

As the echoes continued, Helena started to cry loudly. It was gut-wrenching.

HELENA: *Ow! It really hurts! My head!*

LOLO: *Do you want your medicine?*

HELENA: *I took the last of it. I don't have any more. Make it stop. Please, make it stop. Please.*

LOLO: *I'll find Dr. Davenport. He has more medicine. Don't go anywhere. I'll get some for you.*

Her footsteps could be heard as she raced out of the room.

Lolo stared at the floor as Eddie pressed "Stop." The room grew very quiet. "When I came back, she couldn't talk, Helena. Coma. She was in a coma. It's when your brain won't wake up. She looked dead, Helena. I felt bad. Then she died for real. And I felt more bad." Tears ran down her cheeks, which she wiped on her sleeves.

"You are crying sad tears, aren't you?" Eddie asked as he finally looked up from the computer screen.

She nodded. "Helena was my friend. I miss her. I liked talking to her. She was always nice and very clean. This room, very empty until you got here. Now not so empty inside." She looked down as she placed her hand on her chest, then carefully looked up at Eddie, who had turned back toward his computer screen.

Butler's burner phone began to vibrate on the shelf where he had been charging it. He glanced at the caller ID. It was Caitlin, of course.

"I'll be right back." He grabbed the phone and stepped out into the hallway.

Skylar moved to Lolo. "Would it be all right if I gave you a hug?"

She nodded, sniffling back more tears. Eddie watched as Skylar embraced Lolo warmly. His hands imitated Skylar's as they wrapped around her. He seemed to be practicing the movement. Skylar saw this and smiled, then turned back to Lolo, looking her directly in the eyes. "You make my heart sing."

Lolo stared at her a long moment and asked, "I do?"

Skylar nodded. "Has anyone ever told you that before?"

"I don't think so, and I probably would have remembered something like that." She smiled, looking gentle and bright.

"Skylar, you are a doctor," Eddie interjected. "You should know that hearts cannot sing."

"It's an expression," Skylar answered.

"I don't like expressions."

Lolo chimed in, "Eddie, I'm sorry to disagree with you on this, but you are wrong. Hearts can sing. They sure can."

He studied her with curiosity, knowing that she was telling the truth, but also that what she was saying was false. "Internal organs cannot sing. It is physically impossible."

"Maybe yours just hasn't learned how. Your heart. To sing, I mean."

"Maybe you can teach him, Lolo. I'm going to check on Butler. I'll be right back." As she stepped out of the room, she looked over her shoulder at Eddie.

In his twenty-seven years of life, he had never been alone in a room with a woman who was neither a doctor nor a nurse. The expression on Eddie's face was priceless.

CHAPTER 62

Safe House

Gilberts Corner, Virginia

June 2, 8:34 a.m.

Caitlin smiled as she heard the distinctive ring of a video call coming in. She answered it to see her daughter's face on-screen. "Good morning."

"What's good about it?" Marissa snapped. She was inside the truck.

"A little grumpy, are we?"

"If you were about to eat breakfast at some place called JW's Restaurant, Lanes, Bar & Grill, you wouldn't be thrilled about it, either." She panned the phone across the street to give Caitlin a view of where they were going to eat.

"I don't know, I think the name has kind of a nice ring to it." She smiled, hoping her daughter would join her.

Marissa didn't. "I want to come home."

"I'm afraid that's not possible right now."

"When will it be?"

"I'm working on it," Caitlin answered.

"You're not coming here, are you?"

After a slight pause, she asked, "Can I talk to your father, please?"

Marissa handed the phone to Peter as they got out of the truck and walked toward the entrance. "You're really missing out, you know," he said. "After breakfast, we're going to bowl a few games and then grab a couple slabs of baby backs to bring home with us."

Mikey leaned in front of the phone. "It's better than school, I'll tell you that."

Inside the front door, a sign read "Please Seat Yourself." Peter led the kids into a booth and handed them each a menu. Marissa touched something and cringed. "Ew, gross." She quickly grabbed a paper napkin from a dispenser and wiped off her fingers.

"What was it, boogers?" Mikey chuckled.

"Cut it out," Peter snapped. "It's not boogers. It's probably just syrup or something."

"How do you know what it was?"

"I don't. I'm guessing."

An older waitress came over to them, order pad in hand. The white collar of her uniform was slightly yellowed. She noticed the phone Peter was holding. "You're not gonna put me on candid camera, are you?" she asked, somewhat expectantly.

"No, nothing like that," Peter said. "My wife can't be with us, so, you know, next best thing."

The waitress waved to Caitlin on the phone. "Don't you worry, there, Mom. I'll take good care of them."

Caitlin nodded her appreciation toward the screen. "Thank you kindly."

The waitress turned to the kids. "You two had a chance to decide yet?"

"Do you have anything that might be gluten-free?" Marissa asked.

"Why, yes we do, sugar. My cousin, Shirley, has celiac disease. Is that what you have?"

Marissa made a face like she'd just been asked something completely inappropriate. "Uh, no, I just don't do gluten."

"That's fine. All our eggs are gluten-free, so you should be safe there."

Mikey chimed in, "All eggs are gluten-free."

"We are in complete agreement," the waitress commented, realizing that this was going to be *that* table. Every shift had one.

"Do you know if the eggs are organic?"

"They are. And the farmers who raise the chickens even play classical music over loudspeakers at night, which helps them to sleep better." She winked at Peter and then at Caitlin, making sure both were in on the joke.

Mikey didn't know any better. "Really?"

"Don't be a jerk," Marissa snorted.

"He's not the one being a jerk here," Caitlin snapped.

Marissa shook her head in disbelief. "What did I do?"

Peter decided he'd had enough. "I'll have the large stack of buttermilk pancakes. My son will have the short stack, and we'll share a side of bacon. The young lady will have the two-egg special with fruit instead of potatoes and no toast." He turned to Marissa. "How would you like your eggs?"

"Over easy. I can't believe you don't know that."

"Well, I do now," he responded with a strained smile. "Eggs over easy, please."

"She heard me the first time, Dad," the thirteen-year-old said.

The waitress smiled, took down the order, then got on one knee so she could look Marissa evenly in the eye. "Sweetie, I can tell you're having kind of a rough morning, and whatever is going on, I feel for you, but it isn't right to take it out on your dad. See, my dad was in the army, and one day when I was just about your age, these two men showed up at our door and said he had died in a training exercise. The helicopter he was being transported in went down in a ball of flames. He was charred to a crisp. Do you have any idea what I would give right now to spend one more day with him? Heck, one more meal?"

She paused dramatically, never breaking eye contact. "So the next time you feel the need to be real nasty to someone, come find me, 'cause

I can take it, but don't take it out on your dear old dad, because he don't deserve it. No daddy does."

Marissa was clearly affected by the poignant story and nodded sincerely. She had clearly learned a lesson. She looked to her father sheepishly. "Sorry."

He nodded his acceptance. As the waitress stood up, she glanced at Peter to give him another wink, making sure he knew her story was completely fabricated for his benefit.

Peter glanced down at the phone to read the message Caitlin had texted him during the waitress's story. It said: *GIVE HER A HUGE TIP!* He smiled and nodded again.

As Mikey watched the waitress walk back to the kitchen, he turned to his father. "You know, maybe this isn't gonna be so bad after all."

((•))

Outside the restaurant, Coogan looked on from the cab of his truck, wondering what the heck all that chitchat with the old waitress had been about. Probably wasn't anything for him to be concerned about, but then again, you never knew. He reached into the glove box and double-checked that his Smith & Wesson was good to go. It was. So were the three speed loaders. Just in case he suddenly found himself in a serious firefight.

CHAPTER 63

David's Place

Woodsdale, Maryland

June 2, 8:45 a.m.

Lolo and Eddie were alone in the room. He sat on the edge of the bed, staring at the floor. She leaned against the closet door with her arms crossed, thinking about what she should say. She started to say something, then stopped herself. Then started again and stopped. She was struggling to find the right words. "I don't know if I can teach you, I mean your heart, like Skylar asked me to. I'm afraid I'm not a very good teacher."

"Why are you afraid?"

"I don't like to fail," she said. "People make fun of me. Laugh. I feel bad."

"I don't like it when people laugh at me, either." He continued to stare at the floor.

"Then we have something in common." She smiled warmly.

Eddie's gaze turned out the window. "Do you have a criminal record?"

"No." She rolled her eyes, more surprised than offended.

"Have you ever been fired from a teaching position?"

"No."

"Then there is no reason you cannot be a good teacher." He paused, adding, "In fact, I think you would be an excellent teacher."

"Really?" She smiled brightly. "You know, just you saying that makes my heart sing."

"No, it does not." His gaze remained downward.

"How do you know?"

"A heart is designed to pump blood, not produce sound."

"It makes a thumping sound."

"That is not singing."

Lolo had a sudden revelation. "You are very smart, aren't you?"

"The last time it was tested, my IQ was 193."

"Is that good? I mean, I guess it is, 193, from the way you said it. Is it?"

"A genius IQ is above 145. An IQ between 180 and 200 is considered to be highest genius," he said.

She was clearly impressed. "I don't think I have ever met a 'highest genius' before. Or any kind of genius." She continued, "I also think that's the problem, Eddie. You're too smart."

Eddie looked confused. "It is not possible to be too smart."

"Most smart people think that. Because they think too much and don't feel enough. Not nearly enough."

Eddie's eyes went wide as he remembered his conversation with Skylar on their most recent walk to nowhere in the Harmony House yard, which was only the day before, but already seemed like a very long time ago. "There are some things you know because you feel them, aren't there?"

"Yes, exactly. Like cooking. Not for everyone, but for me, I mean. It can be on a stove, or on a grill, or in an oven, or even in a microwave; it really doesn't matter. I just love to cook. I don't know why, but I know that I do, which is why it was so great that I got to cook breakfast for you and Skylar and Butler, my new friends."

Eddie took a moment to process what he was hearing. "Do you know it with your whole being, more than just your brain?"

"Funny, nobody's ever asked me that before. But yes, I think I do. My whole being knows I like to cook. My hands. My eyes. My stomach. Even my toes. Yes, my whole being does."

Eddie became lost in thought. "That is how I feel about my mother's voice."

"Is it beautiful?"

"Yes, I think it is the most beautiful thing in the world," Eddie replied. "Last week was the first time I got to hear it."

"Why did you have to wait so long?"

"Because she died a long time ago, and it took me almost as long to get the echo box to work."

She studied his face. "This is another thing in common. We have both had people we love die."

Eddie stared at the wall. "My mother died giving birth to me, so I never got to talk to her."

"If you could talk to her, do you know what you would say to her?"

He smiled at the thought. "Hi, Mom." After a long pause, he turned briefly to Lolo with the expression of someone about to share his most sacred possession. He asked, "Would you like to hear my mother sing?"

CHAPTER 64

Embassy Suites Hotel

Alexandria, Virginia

June 2, 8:58 a.m.

Mr. Elliott had reserved a suite on the top floor of the eight-story hotel because he wanted a kill room with a view. He wanted his audience to see that the heinous deeds he was going to commit were done on United States soil. It was to be a statement, all right. He hoped that it would drive federal investigators mad knowing they had almost certainly missed their one and only shot to capture the most notorious killer on the international stage in the last ten years.

Having changed into clothing more suited to his personal taste, he moved around the room like a Hollywood film director, putting his thumbs together and forming an imaginary viewfinder with his hands. It had to be just right. Finding the desired location for his master shot of the upcoming scene, he began to move the furniture around the living room, creating a more open space for his talent to perform, if you could call it that.

He positioned his tripod, then affixed his high-definition video camera atop it. He looked through the viewfinder, zooming in and out on his imaginary subject. *On her screaming, tortured face. Bloodied.*

Pleading. Begging for mercy—if not for herself, then for the bait I used to lure her. What a performance she was going to give.

Mr. Elliott then adjusted the strap of the GoPro head mount he was going to wear. One of the visual techniques he intended to employ was to share his own point of view. To let people see what he saw while doing his thing. He thought this was quite generous of him, actually— a gift no one else on earth could give. While in truth it was only an approximation of his true perspective, he was quite certain that he would be redefining the phrase "shock value" for the foreseeable future.

Deciding that his set decorations were complete, he left the room, hanging the "Do Not Disturb" sign from the door handle. He rode the elevator down to the lobby with a young family of Korean tourists who were spared from knowing the horrendous thoughts he enjoyed in their presence. Mr. Elliott's expression gave nothing away.

He walked across the parking lot and got into his rental car, where he took out his phone to check the drive time to the Kelman Nursing and Rehab Center. It was nineteen minutes away. Mr. Elliott started the engine, turned up the volume of his favorite classical station, and drove off.

CHAPTER 65

DAVID'S PLACE

WOODSDALE, MARYLAND

June 2, 9:03 a.m.

Skylar watched Butler as he paced back and forth across the hallway with the phone pressed to his ear. He was talking to Caitlin, who remained bunkered in her subterranean safe house. "How well do you know this guy?" He was referring to Hogan.

"He was a close friend of my father."

"Allegiances can change."

"My father gave him access to six hundred million dollars fifteen years ago with no oversight. He never touched a dime."

Butler paused to take this in. "That's impressive."

"His background and skill set are similar to your own, if not even more remarkable."

He paused, staring at his phone like he couldn't believe what he'd just heard. "You said that last part just to piss me off, didn't you?"

"Who, me?" she replied with exaggerated innocence.

"Okay, if that's how you want to play, I'll play," he answered with a smile.

Skylar tapped Butler on the shoulder, motioning to Edgar, who'd been watching them from his doorway.

"That's Edgar," Butler told her. "I met him last night."

She gave him a friendly wave. "Hi, Edgar, I'm Dr. Drummond."

He glared, responding inaudibly.

"Don't worry, he's harmless."

"What he is is overmedicated. You see the way his joints are all swollen? If I had to guess, he's being given way too much anti-seizure medication."

Caitlin continued through the phone. "Hogan wants you to meet his team in Alexandria. How soon can the two of you be there?"

"What about Eddie?"

"Is he in any shape to travel?" Caitlin asked.

Butler cupped the phone and repeated the question to Skylar. She answered, "I would prefer that he not."

Butler relayed the answer. Caitlin asked, "Would she feel comfortable allowing him to remain in your current location?"

Skylar was close enough to the phone that she heard the question. She responded, "The question is, would *he*?"

(((•)))

Caitlin watched a satellite view of David's Place and the surrounding area. A medical supply van was making its weekly delivery. Several nurses were arriving for their eight o'clock shift. But there was nothing out of the ordinary that she could see. None of the five search teams hired by the American Heritage Foundation were close enough to be concerned about. Not yet, anyway.

She switched her satellite view to one looking down upon the American Heritage Foundation. The incredible array of advanced technology on its roof did not look like much from this angle, which she knew was precisely the idea. What did catch her eye, however, were the vehicles parked around the building's perimeter, along with the armed men patrolling it. She zoomed in closer to see that they were carrying automatic weapons.

Instead of becoming concerned, she felt insulted, as if Stenson was underestimating her. "You really don't appreciate what you're up against, do you?"

CHAPTER 66

Various Locations

Maryland

June 2, 9:18 a.m.

The five search teams looking for Edward Parks had initially been assigned designated areas by their handlers at the American Heritage Foundation. Enola Meyers and Charlie Johnson had divided up the five-hundred-square-mile area surrounding the site of the accident into five distinct territories. Each team was instructed to respect the other teams' boundaries, and to not cross lines until there was a confirmed sighting of the target subject. Then it would be a free-for-all. It was not unlike an eight-hundred-meter race in track and field, where runners must remain in their assigned lanes through the first turn, after which they could break for position on the inside.

It seemed that the five seasoned teams of bounty hunters and skip tracers had abandoned the rules somewhere after two o'clock that morning. Each thought the others had overlooked something and started going back through territories already covered. There turned out to be a considerable lack of respect for each other among the teams. It began to seem like part of each group's motivation was to embarrass the others. This was now a no-holds-barred cage match.

Team One, the O'Brien brothers, were in the process of hacking into yet another Wi-Fi network within range of their current location. At present, there were seventeen. The brothers used some DIY hardware along with an app they had purchased with Bitcoin on House of Lions, one of the smaller dark-web marketplaces. The software had cost them the equivalent of $8,000 at the time. Expensive, but well worth it, considering the app had already paid for itself many times over.

The O'Briens had found great success locating subjects by illegally but untraceably tracking outgoing communication from coffee shops, restaurants, bars, bowling alleys, motels—pretty much any establishment that offered free Wi-Fi to their customers. People on the run frequently used such places as temporary offices, conducting whatever business they deemed essential. Such transactions were often the last ones they would make.

In the course of their illegal snooping, their specialized technology afforded the O'Briens the opportunity to collect random credit card numbers and PINs, which they would then sell on the House of Lions. It turned out that this was the primary use of the app for most purchasers. Even as a little side business, it was incredibly lucrative.

Team Two, led by Cobra Kelly, capitalized on her firsthand knowledge of living on the run, from having done so as a child with her mother. It seemed that her father had intended to kill them both if he ever got his hands on them, so Kelly spent the better part of her teenage years learning how to hide and whom she could trust. It didn't help that her dad was a respected Detroit cop.

Along the way, mother and daughter had got into several scrapes with physically stronger adversaries that left them bloodied and battered, and worse. That was when Kelly vowed to overcome her lack of size with training and skill. Her discipline and commitment in the gym had led to a ferocity that became legendary, personified by the large cobras she had tattooed on both her forearms.

The legend of Cobra Kelly grew dramatically the day she returned to Detroit and went to her father's home, where he was having a backyard barbecue with friends. In front of them, she proceeded to beat the living shit out of her father, breaking his arm, dislocating his shoulder, and blackening both of his eyes. She announced that if she ever saw him again, she would kill him. That was fourteen years ago, and she hadn't seen him since.

During that time, Kelly used her unique combination of skills and experience to become one of the most respected skip tracers east of the Mississippi. Her specialty was rougher types—bikers, gang members, organized crime figures—which Eddie most certainly was not one of, which explained her current lack of progress. To catch a runner, you had to think like one, and while she found it easy to think like a Hells Angel or a lieutenant in the Sinaloa Cartel, she was clearly having trouble thinking like a savant with a rare scientific gift—or like his doctor. Because in this race of five competitors, she was currently in last place.

Team Three was led by the oldest of the five trackers hired by the AHF. His company was called the Ray Dupre Location Company, but he was better known among his peers as Big Ray, because he had grabbed some of the most famous runners to jump bail in the last twenty years. His name was also a reference to his stature, which was five feet two in lifts. Bounty hunters, it seemed, were known for having a sharp sense of humor.

What Ray lacked in height, he made up for with meanness. And in children. He currently had five of them working for him, and each was determined to succeed in the family business. After all, there would only be room for one of them in their old man's seat when he finally retired, and sibling rivalry could be a hell of a motivator.

Team Four was the other all-female team. Known as the Sheilas, Sheila McCourt and Sheila Bryce were both Ivy League–educated, and both had been account executives before a fateful cocktail party conversation led them each to admit they were looking to be their own boss and they decided to join forces. Their two strengths were financial tracking and their suburban-housewife appearances. When questioned, they were never suspected to be trackers, and people often gave up information they wouldn't have otherwise.

Last, but not least, was Team Five: Ray Guthrie and Donald Nance. They were private detectives who had performed services for the American Heritage Foundation on several prior occasions, which meant each man had already been exhaustively vetted. The two men usually worked separately, for purely economic reasons. Teaming up meant losing half a hard-earned fee to a partner, which made no sense to either one of them, except on certain jobs like this one. The AHF was paying both men their full standard rate.

There was also the additional incentive of a $25,000 bonus for whichever team delivered the three individuals in question. Thanks to three ex-wives between them, both Guthrie and Nance really needed the money.

Currently, they were flashing authentic-looking Immigration and Customs Enforcement badges to a Pakistani couple who had purchased the Red Roof Inn in Edgewood, Maryland, by pooling the financial resources of a dozen extended-family members, the majority of whom still lived in Lahore, their homeland's second-largest city.

Guthrie and Nance as ICE agents were asking for permission to search every room in which guests had been staying for less than twenty-four hours. The Pakistani husband said that was most of their current guests—they simply couldn't. His wife, who clearly wore the pants in the family, demanded to see a search warrant. Nance didn't seem to take that too kindly and got right in her face, claiming to have incriminating information on the immigration status of several of the relatives they employed.

It was, of course, an absolute bluff. He had no idea if any of their relatives worked there, but every staff member in view seemed to be of Pakistani descent, so it was a good bet. The ruse was effective; the couple acquiesced after a quick discussion in Urdu. They seemed aware that he was bluffing but couldn't afford the risk. For all they knew, one of their recently arrived cousins might indeed have a lingering immigration problem.

And thus, they allowed two men with questionable federal identification to begin disturbing most of their motel guests, one room at a time. Complaints would be lodged at the Red Roof corporate office, and their Yelp rating would be decimated.

It would hurt their business for years.

CHAPTER 67

David's Place

Woodsdale, Maryland

June 2, 9:27 a.m.

In his room, Eddie finished playing the echoes of his mother's recital on July 26, 1987, which she had performed inside St. Christopher's Episcopal Church in Saylan Hills, Pennsylvania. That day she had sung not only "Amazing Grace" but also "In the Garden" and "It Is Well with My Soul." Each one sounded more beautiful than the last. It was easy to understand why Eddie would never grow tired of listening to them over and over again.

Lolo only had to watch Eddie's face to appreciate the importance to him of what she was listening to. She hoped that one day she would know the same level of happiness that he appeared to be experiencing. "The people who told you she had the voice of an angel were right."

"Do you want to listen to it again?"

Lolo shook her head. "No, thank you."

He stared at the three-dimensional representation of the sound waves his mother had produced that day in the church, as if he could see her. He traced one of the waves with his finger. "She was my first angel," Eddie said, beaming. "Do you know who my second angel is?"

"No, I don't."

"You are my second angel."

She momentarily stopped breathing. "Really? I am? Are you sure?"

"Yes, I am sure."

"Because, really?" She practically squealed, grinning from ear to ear. "Do you have any idea how good that makes me feel?"

"No."

"Well, for someone who doesn't think that hearts can sing, you sure made mine sing."

He stared out the window. "Hearts cannot sing."

She moved toward him. "I bet if you put your ear right here, next to my chest, you could hear mine." She pointed to her sternum. "Listen."

He shook his head as he looked away from her. "I am not comfortable with most forms of physical contact."

She continued toward him. "That's okay, we don't have to touch. No contact. Just put your ear real close. Come on, just try it."

Eddie shook his head, looking increasingly uncomfortable as Skylar and Butler returned. Eddie started to blush.

Skylar recognized that she and Butler had interrupted something intimate. "Excuse the interruption. Sorry for barging in. Would you two like some privacy?"

Eddie was confused by the question. "Some privacy for what?"

Butler shook his head. "Oh, brother."

Eddie shook his head, imitating him. "Oh, brother." After a brief pause, he continued, "That is one of many expressions that confuses me because I don't understand what people mean when they say it. What did you mean, Detective McHenry?"

Butler hesitated, in part because of the scowl he was receiving from Skylar.

Lolo seemed to understand exactly what he meant, so she jumped into the conversation. "It's not like we were having sex or anything like that. Not at all. We weren't even kissing. I was only trying to show him that my heart was really singing. It was."

Eddie started to blush even more, awkwardly repeating, "It's not like we were having sex or anything like that. Not at all. We weren't even kissing."

Butler couldn't help himself. "Well, you are both adults . . ."

Skylar whipped around. "Why don't you go play with your new friend, Edgar. I'll be with you in a moment."

"Yes, ma'am." He couldn't suppress his smile as he exited the room.

Eddie stared out the window, shaking his head. "Hearts cannot sing."

"Eddie said I was his second angel."

Skylar turned to him. "You did? You really said that?"

He nodded. "Yes, I did. My mother was the first. She will always be my first angel. But Lolo is my second because I thought I might be dying when I first saw her."

Skylar was clearly touched. She turned to Lolo and said, "No wonder your heart was singing. Mine would have been, too."

"I know, right?" Lolo shrugged. "I wanted him to listen to my heart. You know, thump-thump-thump. But Eddie isn't comfortable with most forms of physical contact."

Skylar nodded. "I've come to understand that about him."

Eddie glanced at Lolo. "I told you I never lie."

Skylar moved to him. "You know, most people aren't lucky enough to have even had one angel in their lives, much less two."

"I am very lucky, then." He scratched the stitches in his head wound. Considering what he'd been through during the last twenty-four hours, it was quite a statement.

"It is nice having visitors. Everything is so much more special. It is not so lonely in here now. Definitely not."

Skylar took a deep breath, then said, "Eddie, Butler and I need to go somewhere with the echo box for a few hours. Would you mind staying here while we do that?"

"You mean, all by myself?" he asked nervously.

"You won't be by yourself," Lolo reassured him. "I will be right here with you. Except when you go to the bathroom. Then I will be outside the door."

"I can go to the bathroom by myself."

"Me too," she replied. "But if you leave the facility, I cannot go with you because I am not supposed to leave the grounds. I got in trouble once when I walked across the street. There was a dog and he was not on a leash. I wanted to help him. Dr. Davenport was not happy. Not one bit."

"What kind of dog was it?" Eddie asked.

"He was big and white and very slobbery. I didn't mind, though. His owner thanked me. He drove a truck."

"He was probably a Great Pyrenees," Eddie offered.

"Who was?"

"The dog. If he was large and white and slobbery, he was most likely a Great Pyrenees."

"You sure know a lot about a lot of different things."

Eddie turned to Skylar and asked, "How long do you mean by a few hours?"

Skylar thought about how best to answer. "We'll be back by the end of the day."

"That could be eight or ten or twelve hours from now. That is more than a few."

"You're right. I was trying not to unnecessarily concern you."

"If I don't want to unnecessarily concern you, is it okay for me to lie to you?"

"It was a slight exaggeration, not a lie," Skylar corrected.

"An exaggeration is not the truth. If something is not true, then it is a lie. That is deductive reasoning."

"Things aren't always black or white, Eddie," she reminded him.

"No, they are not. Things can be many different colors. The visible spectrum ranges from violet to red, with wavelengths of 380 to 750 nanometers and frequencies of 400 to 789 terahertz."

Lolo added, "And every color in between. Every color can have many different shades."

"The truth is also on a spectrum," agreed Skylar. "On one end is absolute truth. On the other end is total fabrication. Most statements fall somewhere in the middle."

Butler, who'd apparently been listening just outside the door, cracked it open and said, "Here is an absolute truth. We need to go."

Skylar handed him a notepad and pen. "Write down the number for your phone." She then turned to Eddie, pointing to the notepad. "If you need to reach me for any reason, call that number." And she headed for the door.

CHAPTER 68

EDDIE'S ROOM

DAVID'S PLACE

June 2, 9:32 a.m.

Eddie's eyes followed Skylar as she moved toward the door. "Skylar, wait," he blurted out.

"You'll be fine as long as you stay right here with Lolo."

"I don't know how," he replied. He seemed embarrassed.

Skylar was confused. "You don't know how to what?"

"To make a phone call. I have never called anyone before."

Skylar immediately felt bad. She should have known this. At least, that's what she told herself. "No, of course not. Dr. Fenton wouldn't have permitted it."

"Don't worry," Lolo said. "I can call you if Eddie needs to reach you. I make phone calls all the time."

"You do?" Skylar asked.

"I make at least one call every week. I call my mother. On Sundays. Usually at noon. That is the time I am supposed to call. Noon. Sometimes I get her answering machine, but then I just leave a message."

"Does she call you back?" Eddie asked.

"Yes, always. Sometimes it takes her several hours, and sometimes several days, but she always does call back." She paused, seeming to reconsider her answer. "Most of the time."

Eddie stared at the floor, looking sad. "I have not spoken to my father in seventeen years, one month, and nineteen days."

Lolo looked very sad, as if there could only be one reason for this. "Is he dead?"

"I don't know." He didn't look up.

"Why haven't you talked to him?"

Eddie shrugged. "I don't think he wants to talk to me." The statement hung heavily in the room for a moment.

"Well, then he doesn't know what he's missing," Lolo said cheerfully. "You are fun to talk to. Even more than Helena." She looked up, as if toward Heaven. "Sorry, Helena."

Lolo then stepped toward the notepad in Skylar's hand, memorizing the number. "You don't have to worry about me remembering the number, because I have a photographic memory."

"I have a photographic memory also." Eddie smiled.

"That is something we have in common," she said encouragingly.

"Yes, it is." He stared at the floor.

Lolo then wrote a different number on a different piece of paper, which she handed to Skylar. "That is my cell phone number in case you want to call me."

"You have a cell phone?"

"Of course I do. How do you think I call my mother?" Lolo took her phone from her pocket and showed Skylar. "I also have my own Instagram and Twitter accounts. I have eight followers. My mom and dad, my brothers and sisters, and Dr. Davenport. That's eight."

"You are a true modern woman, aren't you?"

"Yes, I am." Lolo beamed with pride. "A true modern woman."

Skylar grabbed Eddie's laptop and echo box and headed for the door. "Eddie, I promise to take good care of the echo box."

He listened to her closely and gave her a brief nod. "I believe you."

"And I promise to take good care of Eddie," Lolo declared.

Skylar imitated Eddie's expression, appearing to listen closely, then gave Lolo the same type of brief nod. "I believe you, too." She winked at Eddie, then exited.

((•))

"She winked at you," Lolo noticed.

"Yes, she did. Skylar does that sometimes."

"Why?" She sat down next to him.

"I am not sure."

Lolo now realized how close to him she was sitting. She stared at the small gap between them but did not move. "Is it okay that I am sitting next to you? I didn't ask, and I should have. I'm sorry. Is it okay?"

"Yes, it is okay. No, you didn't ask, but you didn't need to. You don't need to be sorry, either. Yes, it's okay."

As they sat together quietly, a smile slowly spread across Eddie's face.

"You are smiling."

Eddie nodded, looking out the window.

"That means you're happy."

Eddie nodded some more, still staring outside.

For the first time in his life, he had a friend. And it felt good.

CHAPTER 69

DAVIS FAMILY ESTATE

CARMEL, INDIANA

June 2, 9:48 a.m.

Frequently named the most livable city in the entire United States, this northern Indianapolis suburb was the fifth-largest city in the Hoosier State, as well as its most expensive. A fitting place for a US senator to raise a family, at least according to Corbin Davis's wife, whose family money had paid for not only the home but his campaigns as well.

Melanie Wentworth Davis was the only heir to a billion-dollar pharmaceutical-distribution fortune. Her father, a onetime corner-store pharmacist, had built his company into a nationwide network. Shortly after the company had achieved a billion-dollar valuation, however, he suffered a fatal heart attack and never got to enjoy the lavish lifestyle he had so looked forward to. That was left to his daughter, who had just graduated from Northwestern.

The truth was, she never really had much interest in the family business, so she promptly sold the company to the highest bidder and had lived happily ever since, with a few notable exceptions. After Corbin had failed in his first two attempts at public office, Melanie funneled enough money into his third campaign to make certain he didn't fail again. He outspent his opponent four-to-one, and it worked.

This morning, Corbin and Melanie were flying to New York, which they did several times a year. There was always government business to be conducted in the Big Apple, but more importantly, there was shopping. Melanie refused to buy her clothing anywhere else, except for Paris. Laying out Corbin's outfits for the trip, as she always did before he traveled, she decided it was time to pick up some suits for him as well. Left to his own devices, the man would still be shopping at Macy's.

From downstairs, she heard her husband yell, "Honey, we're forty-five minutes late. We have to go."

"It's not like the plane will leave without us."

((•))

In his home office, Corbin sat with Bob Welker, his chief of staff. "We can't be late for the dinner tonight," he called to his wife. "Bob says we're already cutting it close as it is."

"Tell Bob he's a pain in the ass," she yelled in response.

"He's well aware of that fact."

"Hi, Melanie," Bob yelled up to her. "Need any help packing?"

"I thought you were meeting us at the airport?"

"Too much work to do on behalf of the great state of Indiana."

"I'll bet you're hungover and came here to brag about your latest conquest."

"Not since we won the election. Zero."

"Poor baby. Maybe you'll get lucky in New York."

"That's the plan."

"I'll be right down."

Bob turned to Corbin and spoke quietly. "Have you told her anything yet?"

"I didn't think there was anything to tell."

Bob nodded. "Good idea. Probably better not to get her hopes up just yet."

Corbin studied him. "What aren't you telling me?"

Bob clasped his hands on the table in front of him and leaned closer. "First thing this morning, I got news there's a real a shitstorm brewing in the West Wing."

He had Corbin's attention. "Interesting. How bad is it?"

"The president canceled the rest of his day and won't take calls from anyone."

"That's bad," the senator said, smiling.

"It gets better. My guy at the network just told me an emergency press conference is being scheduled for tonight. Topic unknown."

"Holy shit," Corbin said, a bit too loudly.

"Exactly."

Melanie whisked in. "Exactly what kind of holy shit are we talking about?"

CHAPTER 70

David's Place

Woodsdale, Maryland

June 2, 9:53 a.m.

Skylar followed Butler across the mostly empty lot at the rear of the building. "You think Eddie will be okay?" she asked.

"He's safer here than he would be with us."

She considered her own physical safety as they arrived at a rusted-out 1988 navy-blue Ford Bronco. The tires were bald, and one of the side-view mirrors was cracked. "You sure can pick 'em."

"I didn't. Caitlin did." He revealed a set of car keys attached to a gold-plated emblem that read *Roberto*. "She rented it for us." He unlocked the trunk.

Skylar placed the echo box and laptop inside it. Butler slammed the trunk closed. As she got in the passenger seat next to him, she said, "Too bad. I was looking forward to riding in another stolen car."

"Careful what you wish for. I have a feeling you may get another opportunity before this is over." He put the key in the ignition and started the engine. He put the car in gear, then paused. "You don't have to do this, you know."

"Do what?"

"This. It's going to get hairy, and you don't have the training for it. You could teach me how to use the echo box and just wait for me here."

"I told Eddie no one else would use it."

"I know what you told him."

She paused to consider his offer, then spoke emphatically. "I won't lie to him. Not ever."

He shrugged. "Just wanted to put it out there."

"Do me a favor, Detective," she said sharply. "Never insult my integrity again."

"Yes, ma'am." He tried not to smile as he drove out of the parking lot, looking out the window to hide his expression from her.

They drove in silence for over a minute until Skylar finally said, "Remember yesterday when you said Jacob's death wasn't my fault? You were wrong. It was."

He smiled as if this was something he'd been waiting to hear. "Did you push him onto the tracks?"

"No, but I did push him away. If I hadn't kept him at such an emotional distance, he wouldn't have tried to pry into my work life."

"I guess he didn't have much choice. Sounds like you made him invade your privacy."

"God, I'm starting to hate you," she said with exasperation.

"Good. I think that means we're making progress."

It was now her turn to hide her expression by looking out the window. Because she was cracking a reluctant smile that she seemed not to want him to see. "I really miss him, you know? It hurts in every part of my body."

"It will for a while," he said knowingly. "But eventually, it gets better."

She nodded, continuing to face out the window. "I look forward to that."

((•))

The satellite view of the Bronco was clear. From inside the basement of the safe house, Caitlin tracked them from the GPS signal in Butler's burner phone. She also knew the vehicle's license plate and VIN from her transaction with Roberto. She had made certain there were no outstanding warrants on the owner, nor any unpaid liens on the vehicle itself. There could be no reason why anyone would have any interest in this old Bronco.

Butler checked in via speakerphone, just as she thought he would. "We're on the move."

"Copy that. I have eyes on you." She watched them heading south on I-95.

"How close?"

"Closer than you'd probably be comfortable with."

To test his theory, he put his hand out the window and held out four fingers. "How many fingers am I holding up?"

She zoomed in on his hand. "Four."

Butler closed his fist, then held out two fingers.

"Now two. And if you stick out your middle finger, I will call your mother and tell her that you're disrespecting the manner in which, I am quite certain, she raised you."

"You don't have to bring my mother into this. I just wanted to understand what level of tech we have access to."

Skylar said, "How long have you two known each other again? Because it sure seems like a lot longer than twenty-four hours."

Caitlin zoomed in even tighter on his hand. "You bite your fingernails, don't you?"

"You're right, that's more than I'm comfortable with."

Skylar chimed in, "There go my plans for nude sunbathing anytime for the rest of my life."

"That's what I said after having kids." Caitlin smiled and then got down to business. "Are you in possession of the echo box?"

"We are in possession of the device," Butler answered in a similar tone, "but we felt it best to leave Parks behind."

"No disagreement there. I'm just surprised he let you take the box without him."

"We found something that should keep him occupied for the time being . . ."

CHAPTER 71

Eddie's Room

David's Place

June 2, 9:57 a.m.

Lolo and Eddie continued sitting together quietly. Neither had spoken a word for several minutes. She glanced at the pillow where her friend Helena used to sleep, and then at the different corners of the room. She occasionally glanced at Eddie, but never for very long. He just sat there, seeming at peace as he stared out the window.

She tapped her feet, then clasped her hands together when she finally broke the silence. "This is nice. Just sitting here. Nice. It's quiet. We are enjoying each other's company, aren't we?"

Eddie stared down at the floor, repeating something he had heard Skylar say to him in one of their earliest meetings. "We are actually doing far more than that."

"We are?" She sounded both astonished and confused.

"For one thing, we are nonverbally communicating with each other." He said it exactly like Skylar had previously—or at least he gave his best imitation of her. Which was mechanical and somewhat inauthentic. He glanced at Lolo briefly.

Lolo had the look of a student who was eager to learn. "What are we saying?"

"I don't know what you are saying, but I am saying that I care about you and want you to know I am here for you."

Her eyes brightened. "Wow, really? That is far more than just sitting here. Like you said. A whole lot more. Are you sure you mean it? It's okay if you don't."

He nodded as he stared out the window. "I have never had a friend before." He paused. "We are friends, aren't we?"

"Yes, most definitely. We are friends. I was friends with Helena and I know. You will, too. You will see. It feels better than not having a friend. Much better." She paused as if having a revelation. "You must have been sad for a long time, I think."

He didn't respond at first. After a long moment, he nodded some more and then turned toward the window. His hand twitched. He was starting to become uncomfortable. He didn't like the feeling, particularly as the sensation grew. Eddie knew that he should think about something else, so he did so as quickly as he could. "I like birds."

The statement clearly caught her by surprise. "I like birds, too. Well, kind of. I think. Why do you like them?"

"I like birds because they are beautiful to look at and even more beautiful to listen to. They also never lie. That is important. I think birds are some of the greatest animals in the world. Maybe the greatest."

"Those are good reasons," she replied. "Yes, very good. Do you have a favorite one? I mean, kind? A special favorite?"

"If I could only pick one, I would have to say a blue-winged warbler. That is not to take anything away from the green-winged teal, or the black-capped chickadee, but if I could only pick one, I would say the warbler."

She nodded, as if completely understanding his choice. "I like sea lions."

"They are not birds."

"No, not at all."

"What do you like about sea lions?"

"I like to swim, and sea lions seem like they would be fun to play with in the water."

Eddie looked down at the floor. "I do not know how to swim."

"Then it would be a good idea for you not to play in the water with sea lions until you learn how."

He nodded again. "There are a lot of things I do not know how to do." He paused to consider just how long the list was. He had never flown in a plane, been on a boat, driven a car, eaten sushi, chewed gum, had sex, seen a naked woman's breasts, or even kissed a girl. He had also never ridden a horse, or a skateboard, or a motorcycle, or even a bicycle. He had never been to a beach or a lake, or fished in a stream. He had never played any kind of team sport or even witnessed a game in person. Not one. He had never gone bowling, played horseshoes, attended a barbecue, or been to a carnival. He had never traveled outside the United States, nor even to the Eastern Seaboard. And he had never told anyone that he loved them.

But of all the many things he had never done, there was one thing in particular that he was thinking about. One thing that Eddie had been considering with increasing frequency since he had become a teenager, especially in the last several years. He decided that finally, at long last, this might be the time. In fact, the perfect time. "If I asked you something, would you promise not to laugh?"

Now it was her turn to nod. "I don't think that laughing at someone is nice, so it is something I never do. Laugh at someone. No, never. People laugh at me, sometimes. I wish they didn't. They are mean when they do. The people who laugh. I don't like the way it feels."

"I don't like the way it makes me feel, either." He rubbed his hand on his pant leg, comforted by the friction.

"Feels bad," Lolo concurred.

Eddie nodded, looking down at his shoes.

"You see, you do have feelings sometimes. You do. You know what they are."

He nodded again, glancing at her, then looking away.

She continued, "If most of the feelings you have don't make you feel good, that is why you think all the time. That's what makes you so smart. You think so you don't have to feel bad feelings."

He stared out the window, taking a deep breath. "I do not feel bad right now. Sitting here with you."

"I do not feel bad, either." She smiled.

He looked at the goose bumps on his arms, curious about them. "I feel kind of tingly."

"I think that is good, feeling tingly. You have goose bumps."

"I usually only get goose bumps when I am cold."

"Are you cold?"

Eddie shook his head.

"They are good goose bumps, then."

"I did not know there were good goose bumps." He nodded, accepting her explanation. He then realized something. "You did not answer my question."

"Which question?"

"Do you promise not to make fun of me?"

She nodded. "Oh, yes, of course, I promise. I would never-never make fun of you."

"And a promise is a promise."

"Yes, it is," she replied. "You are not just copying me because I said that before, are you?"

"No, that is something I have said at least thirty-seven times before I met you."

"Thirty-seven, really? Are you sure?" She seemed a little dubious.

"Yes, at least thirty-seven. It is probably much more than that, but I didn't want to exaggerate, because that would be a lie."

"I have never known anyone else who says, 'A promise is a promise.'"

"Well, now you do know someone." He smiled briefly, remembering just a few of the many times he had previously made the same statement.

"Then that is another thing we have in common."

He paused a moment, trying to collect his thoughts. "I like knowing someone that I have so many things in common with."

It was Lolo's turn to smile. "Friends have things in common. Sometimes, more than you know." She hugged herself, which was clearly an expression of joy. She then scooted just a little closer to Eddie. She was now right beside him.

He didn't move away from her. She turned to him slowly as he continued staring out the window. "What was the question that you wanted to ask me?"

CHAPTER 72

SAFE HOUSE

GILBERTS CORNER, VIRGINIA

June 2, 10:03 a.m.

Caitlin recognized the number as the phone rang. It was Jessup Fields. She had guessed he would be calling her no later than ten thirty that morning. Once again, she had guessed correctly. She took a deep breath and settled herself before answering the phone. "Good morning, Mr. Fields. How was your chat with the president?"

"First, enough with the formality. My friends call me Jessup."

"So we're friends now?" she asked. Her tone was playful, not threatening.

"Of course we are, just like you intended. And I have a strong feeling that you and I are about to become very good friends." He almost sounded like a man with a crush.

"If we can solve each other's problems, I believe we will be." Already tired of the chitchat, she wanted to get down to specifics. "How *was* your conversation with the president?"

"He was blubbering like a little bitch, just like you said he would be. He went on and on about some satellite-based surveillance system the Chinese or North Koreans now have and how they know everything."

"Rest assured, they don't. It's a cover invented by Stenson."

"You're entirely sure about this?"

She responded without equivocation. "Yes."

"You mind telling me how?"

"Because I am the one who suggested the story to Stenson in the first place."

"So what brought about your change of heart?"

"He let his emotions get the better of him."

"I would appreciate a little more specificity, if you don't mind. After all, you are asking me to trust you with my entire life's work."

"No, Jessup, what I am offering is a way out of the situation you and your brother put yourselves in. You are the ones who put your life's work at risk. You knew that when you walked into the Oval Office. At least, you should have. Now you're seeking some reassurance as you consider trusting a complete stranger to help you out of this mess."

"You got me there." His tone of voice made it clear how much he enjoyed her brinksmanship.

She paused to emphasize the sincerity of what she was about to say. "The American Heritage Foundation was founded on a set of principles that require an inordinate amount of self-discipline to maintain. I know because my father was one of the founders. When Stenson started deviating from those principles, I couldn't let that continue."

((•))

Jessup massaged his chin between his thumb and forefinger as he nodded slightly. Now it all made sense. This was about protecting her father's legacy, as well as her own future. And if there was one thing Jessup Fields understood, it was the importance of family. "Which of the founders was your father?"

She hesitated momentarily. "Lawrence Walters. My name is Caitlin."

Jessup chortled, shaking his head. *Of course!* "I should have been able to guess you were his kin."

"And why is that?"

"From the first moment you called, I've been trying to figure out where someone of your gender and youth got the unique combination of intellect, charm, bravado, and fortitude you seem to possess. The only other person I ever met with a similar combination was your father. I was only a young man at the time when I met him, and to tell you the truth, he intimidated the shit out of me."

"He had that effect on a lot of people."

"And I admired the hell out of him for it." His fondness and respect for Lawrence immediately gave him an even stronger emotional connection to Caitlin, which he knew was precisely the reason she had revealed her identity. *Damn, she's good. At least as good as her old man, and possibly even better. If she survives, that is.* "To state the obvious, this is one hell of a risk you're taking."

"I appreciate your understatement," she said wryly. "But I have taken every possible precaution. This is something I had to do. If I'm going to win, I need a powerful ally, so I turned to you."

He respected the positioning of her argument. She needed his help, which was why she called him, offering her assistance in return. It was a move he'd made many times in his career. He responded with his best Humphrey Bogart impersonation. "Caitlin, I think this is the beginning of a beautiful friendship."

"Let's hope it's a long and prosperous one."

"So tell me, how can we help each other?"

CHAPTER 73

David's Place

Woodsdale, Maryland

June 2, 10:11 a.m.

Eddie sat next to Lolo, staring at the floor. He thought very carefully, like what he was about to ask was a big deal for him. And most certainly it was. This was clearly something he'd thought about for a very long time. It took him a moment to muster his courage. "Lolo?"

"Yes."

He glanced at her briefly. "Would you teach me how to use your phone?"

Lolo had expected him to ask something else. "Of course I would. Yes-yes."

"You don't have to if you don't want to."

"Why would you think I don't want to?"

He closed his eyes for a moment to focus completely on what she had just said. "It is not that I think you are lying, but I also don't think you are telling the truth. Not one hundred percent truth. I think this is what Skylar meant about most statements being in the middle of the true–false spectrum."

"I thought you were going to ask me something different," she said somewhat reluctantly.

"What did you think I was going to ask you?"

"Don't want to say." Now it was her turn to stare at the floor.

"Your cheeks are red."

She nodded. "Sorry."

"Why are you sorry, Lolo?"

"Don't know."

Eddie made his BUZZER sound. "Not true."

"Confusing."

"What is confusing?"

"Don't know."

Eddie made his BUZZER sound again. "Lolo, do you say 'Don't know' when there is something you don't want to talk about but you are not sure what else to say?"

She nodded again.

"Okay. I understand now." He paused, then asked, "Are we still friends?"

"Yes, of course. We are. Friends are friends through thick and thin. This is only thin."

Eddie nodded, not quite sure what she meant, but he liked the way it sounded. "Only thin." Ordinarily he would have asked her to further explain, but he was preoccupied with her phone. It seemed to have a magical draw for him, as if it were a sacred chalice.

He carefully picked up the device, not sure how to hold it. "Please teach me."

CHAPTER 74

American Heritage Foundation

Alexandria, Virginia

June 2, 10:16 a.m.

Sixty-nine miles south of David's Place, Daryl Trotter climbed onto his desktop. He was not trying to fix an overhead light or swipe away an annoying cobweb dangling from the ceiling. He stood on top of his desk with his hands in his pockets and stared out the window.

Greers was stupefied. "What the hell are you doing?"

"Getting a fresh perspective." He glanced down at his peer as if he was doing nothing out of the ordinary.

"If you say so." Greers couldn't decide if he wanted Stenson to enter their office at this exact moment or not. If their boss poked his head in, Trotter would look like an idiot. Unless, of course, he had developed a new approach to their current mission of locating Dr. Skylar Drummond or Edward Parks. Then he would look daring, or possibly even brilliant.

The fact was that neither had made any progress in several hours. It was frustrating. Greers wasn't about to join Trotter and stand on his own desk, but he instead paced back and forth. "This shouldn't be so difficult."

Trotter stared down at him. "Yes, it should. We're trying to locate people who have already demonstrated an uncanny knack for eluding capture. And this time, we don't have the entire New York office of Homeland Security at our disposal."

"It's time to start throwing out bad ideas. The very worst ones we can think of. Once those are out of the way, then we stand a chance of finding a decent one."

Trotter nodded, thinking this was a good approach—one that he remembered reading about recently in a self-help book, though he couldn't remember which one. "Contact Homeland. Get whatever personnel we need from the DC office."

"After last week, Stenson wouldn't dare risk any more public exposure."

"Agreed. You've got to admit: that was pretty bad."

"No disagreement there. You're up, one–zero," Greers said, announcing the score of their "bad idea" game.

"Tee it up, hotshot. Let's see what kind of bad you've got." Trotter bent down to wipe off a layer of dust that had collected on top of his computer monitor.

Greers said the first thing that came to his mind. "Local cops? We could call in a missing-persons report."

"Only if we wanted to get Homeland involved. They monitor local radio traffic. Anything involving recent federal fugitives would certainly be brought to their attention."

"Which means that was a really bad idea. One–one."

"Does one of them have a particular favorite food?" asked Trotter.

"Unknown. But we do know Parks won't eat anything purple."

"What he won't eat is of no help."

"None whatsoever." Greers nodded in agreement, looking smug. "Damn, I'm good. I'm up two–one."

Trotter didn't like losing at anything. "Have we gone through her boyfriend's apartment?"

"With a fine-tooth comb. We know which side of the bed she slept on, what type of milk she drank, and which channels she got her news from."

"We might have missed something."

"Our guys? Fat chance."

"No disagreement there. Which means we're all tied up again, two–two."

Greers disagreed. "That wasn't bad enough. It was only somewhat bad. Even the best teams sometimes miss something."

"Our guys?" Trotter replied sardonically. Then he had another idea. "You know what a complete waste of time would be?"

"Personally walking every street in Maryland?"

"Checking social media."

Greers shook his head. "I have to give you credit, that is fantastically bad."

"Unless they ran into someone who didn't know any better."

"Which is exactly why I checked Facebook, Snapchat, Twitter, and Instagram last night for every possible combination of their names."

"And?" Trotter asked after jumping down from his desk.

"Individually, their names returned over eleven thousand mentions. Way too many to be useful. Who knew there were so many Skylars, Butlers, and Eddies."

Trotter sat down in front of his computer. "What about combinations of their names?"

"Zero. That's why I didn't mention it."

"What time was it when you ran your search?"

Greers checked his computer. "Ten seventeen."

"And you haven't run another one since?" He was already typing commands into his keyboard.

"It was a stretch even the first time."

"It's still a stretch, but if they did find some Good Samaritan to help them, this person would have acted first, then thought about it later. Eddie Parks needed emergency medical treatment. Who knows how long it might have taken. They needed supplies, a location to treat him, a place for him to recover, and a vehicle to transport him out of the area as soon as he was capable of travel. Perhaps this person jumped in to assist, and then only after the crisis had passed decided to share their heroics."

"Like I said, it was a stretch the first time."

Continuing to multitask, Trotter typed as he talked. "The more I think about it, the odds are pretty good that they're getting help from someone out there. Caitlin didn't have time to reach out through established channels, so who knows what she might have told some Good Samaritan."

"Have we exhausted every one of them, by the way? Traditional channels."

"No one in our network would risk being disloyal. Even if only vaguely, they're aware of the potential consequences." Trotter started furiously typing a series of commands into his computer. "Unless our trio stumbled upon an abandoned house chock-full of supplies, which is highly unlikely, somebody is giving them aid."

"Somebody who probably has no idea who they are," added Greers.

Trotter initiated a search covering all social media platforms and major cell phone carriers for six names during the last twelve hours: *Skylar, Drummond, Butler, McHenry, Edward,* and *Parks.* He then added a seventh: *Eddie.* The search returned 11,673 mentions, far too many to be useful.

Greers shook his head. "That's about the same number I got last night. It's useless."

"I was only being thorough. It's the combination of names that might yield a different result."

CHAPTER 75

TROTTER AND GREERS'S OFFICE

AMERICAN HERITAGE FOUNDATION

June 2, 10:21 a.m.

Trotter revised his search to include various combinations of two names: *Skylar* and *Eddie*; *Skylar* and *Butler*; *Butler* and *Skylar*; and so forth. The search returned three mentions. All from the same Instagram account: @LoloLikesToCook.

"Who the hell is @LoloLikesToCook?"

"Apparently someone who likes to cook breakfast." He pointed to three photographs of various breakfast plates, with a description: *Breakfast for my new friends Butler, Skylar, and Eddie.*

Greers stood behind him, patting both his shoulders. "I could honestly kiss you right now."

"Please don't," Trotter responded without looking away from his screen.

"Tell me you've got a location."

Trotter pointed to coordinates that appeared in the map of Maryland on his screen: N 39.4621°, W 76.3052°. He zoomed in to the location until the street address became visible. "Woodsdale, Maryland."

"How far away is our closest search team?"

Trotter called up the location of each of the five teams in the area. Two were over thirty miles away. One was twenty-one miles and another twelve. However, one team was less than three miles away in a town called Edgewood. "Team Five is two point eight miles away. They can be there in nine minutes."

"Who is Five?"

"Guthrie and Nance."

"I will never again complain about you standing on your desk."

"That is all I've ever wanted in life." Trotter texted all five teams the details, ending the message with the instruction: *GO!*

The text was also received by the other two parties in the group, Charlie Johnson and Enola Meyers, who were just down the hall. They immediately rushed into the office. "How the hell did you find them?" she asked.

"God bless social media," Greers responded. "But I can't take any of the credit. It was all him." He motioned to Trotter, who nodded his appreciation. He had fully expected Jason to take the credit.

Enola couldn't believe it. "You're kidding."

Charlie was also in disbelief. He moved to look over Daryl's shoulder at his screen. "How could they have been so dumb?"

"They weren't. It was somebody who made them breakfast. She clearly has no idea who they are." Now Trotter looked up at Enola and Charlie. "You two want the credit?"

"Are you serious?" Charlie asked with disbelief.

"I'm not one to joke around very often."

Enola stepped toward him, answering for both of them. "Hell, yes."

Trotter turned around in his chair to address them both. "Then it's yours. Go down the hall and tell Stenson you realized Parks had to be getting help. Your search for various combinations of their names yielded three results—all from the same account."

Neither needed to be told twice. They raced out the door. Charlie glanced back, saying, "Thanks, man. We owe you."

"That's correct." Trotter grinned slyly as they exited.

Greers shook his head, applauding quietly. "Well played."

"I thought you would appreciate it."

"And here I thought you didn't understand shit about people."

"I don't, really. I just realized it's what you would have done, so I did it before you could. Now they owe me and not you."

Greers moved over and leaned on Trotter's desk. "You don't really think that's how this is going to play out, do you?"

((•))

Enola and Charlie walked briskly down the hall to Bob Stenson's office. The two of them could count on one hand the number of times they had set foot in this space. The first time for each was their final interview before being hired, during which he had made it clear that working at the AHF wasn't just a job. It was a way of life. A calling. A mission.

Each of those meetings was perfunctory. Stenson trusted the opinions of his lieutenants and wanted to sign off on their picks. It was also one last opportunity for these young would-be world changers to embarrass themselves as well as their sponsors. Such a disaster had only happened once before during Stenson's tenure, but that one time was enough to remind him never to take any decision for granted, particularly when it came to hiring.

Once officially on board, however, employees needed a reason to see him. A good one. Enola and Charlie were both confident that they had one. Enola knocked on Stenson's open door.

He didn't look up from his screens. "Only speak if you have good news. Otherwise, turn around and don't come back until you have some."

"We have located Edward Parks and his doctor."

Stenson now looked up. "Have you now?"

Charlie jumped in. "He's in a home for special-needs adults in Woodsdale, Maryland. Five search teams are en route. One will be there in less than ten minutes."

"Which team?"

"Guthrie and Nance. They happened to be closest."

"I like those two. Good choice to have them work together."

"Thank you, sir." Charlie resisted the temptation to smile. He knew the importance of restraint with their boss.

Stenson directed his next question to Enola. "How did you find them?"

"Social media," she answered. "One of the residents in the facility made them breakfast and posted about it on social media."

"Thank you, Facebook."

"It was Instagram, actually."

"It's all the same to me," Stenson said, turning back to his screens. "Nice work. Let me know when we are in possession of Parks and the device."

CHAPTER 76

HOLIDAY INN EXPRESS

EDGEWOOD, MARYLAND

June 2, 10:25 a.m.

Guthrie and Nance only had to walk across the parking lot of the Red Roof Inn to reach the next hotel in the area, where they were in the middle of the same routine, presenting the same fake ICE identification to the owner of the establishment, when they simultaneously received Trotter's text.

The two men paused, glancing at each other. "That's less than three miles from here," Guthrie said, looking at the location on Waze.

Nance responded, "Time to put your new ride to good use."

$$((\bullet))$$

As they bolted out the door, the owner, who was white and originally from Texas, turned back toward his office and said in fluent Spanish, *"Puedes salir ahora. Se fueron." You can come out now. They're gone.*

As the door cracked open, three terrified women of Mexican descent poked their heads out. Each wore a maid's uniform. *"No me parecían agentes reales,"* one woman said. *They did not look like real agents to me.*

"*Yo tampoco,*" the owner responded—*Me either*—as he reached for a sawed-off shotgun he kept beneath the counter for just such situations. "*Por eso estaba a punto de presentarles a mi pequeño amigo aquí.*" Which is why I was about to introduce them to my little friend here.

((•))

Outside the hotel, the two private detectives jumped into Guthrie's Dodge Hellcat, which he'd recently acquired from a client who wouldn't be needing it for the next three to five years. Among the unique features of this vehicle was its dual-key fob system: a black key and a red key. The black key limited the output of the engine to a maximum of 500 horsepower, while the red key unleashed the full potential of the engine, all 707 horsepower.

Guthrie inserted the red key into the ignition and started up the engine. It sounded angry, snarling like a mechanical dragon. He squealed out of the parking space in front of the Red Roof Inn and punched the accelerator. Their heads were thrown back against the headrests as the tires squealed, leaving smoke and rubber behind. Nance grabbed on to whatever he could and pressed his boots against the floor. "I have got to get me one of these!"

CHAPTER 77

Kelman Nursing and Rehab Center

Alexandria, Virginia

June 2, 10:26 a.m.

Mr. Elliott was enjoying the overture to Beethoven's only opera, *Fidelio* (op. 72), broadcast over his favorite radio station as he pulled into the parking lot of the Kelman Nursing and Rehab Center. He happened to park next to Caitlin's Subaru, which had been there since the day before. There was an open space next to it—the one previously occupied by her father's Olds Cutlass—and Mr. Elliott decided to take it.

There he sat for a moment, finding it amusing that he was listening to an opera about a heroic wife who disguises herself as a guard to rescue her husband from certain death in a political prison while he was, in fact, about to pretend to be a long-lost nephew of a man he would soon be torturing to death.

Of all the many victims he'd subjected to such treatment, none had ever been geriatric, much less mentally incapacitated. Seemed like a waste of his rather well-honed talents. Then again, this upcoming performance had little to do with its subject and more to do with its intended audience. This show was meant for one person and one person only. And it would go on for as long as it needed to.

Mr. Elliott intended to take every imaginable precaution to make certain he did not kill the old man quickly. Because he needed Lawrence alive if he was going to flush out his desired rabbit from what was certainly a well-fortified hole. He needed the old man screaming and pleading and begging incoherently. It could not stop until she arrived, when he would begin doing the same things to her.

Only worse.

CHAPTER 78

Interstate I-95 South

Approaching Baltimore, Maryland

June 2, 10:27 a.m.

Butler was nearing the home of the Ravens at eighty miles per hour when his burner phone rang. The number was Lolo's. Skylar quickly answered the phone, pressing the speaker button. "Is everything okay?"

"Yes, everything is okay," Eddie answered. She was surprised to hear his voice through the phone and not Lolo's. He continued, "Skylar, I recognize your voice. It's not as pleasant as it sounds in person, but I can tell that it's you."

"Yes, it's me."

"This is Eddie."

"Yes, I know it's you. I recognize your voice, just like you recognize mine."

"This is the first phone call I have ever made."

"Well, I'm honored that you chose to call us."

"I don't know anyone else's phone number."

"Hello, Eddie," Butler chimed in.

"Hello, Detective." There was a brief pause. Neither seemed to know what to say next.

Butler finally asked, "You're being a gentleman, aren't you?"

Eddie sounded confused by the question. "How do I know if I'm not being a gentleman?"

"Ask Lolo. She'll tell you."

"Detective McHenry wants me to ask you if I am being a gentleman."

"Oh, yes. Definitely a gentleman. Definitely," replied Lolo. "Because I know. There were boys in my school. They were not gentlemen. Some of the boys were mean and said bad words. Made me do things. Eddie is nothing like them. No, not at all. He is a true gentleman."

Eddie took a moment to process what he had just heard. "She said yes."

"That's a good thing, young man," Butler replied. "I better not hear otherwise."

"Why would you hear otherwise?" Eddie asked.

"Tell the detective not to worry. I will post for all my followers what a gentleman you are being," Lolo said.

Concern immediately ripped across Butler's face. "Tell her not to do that!"

His tone clearly scared Lolo. "Why-why not?"

"Eddie, put her on the phone."

"He wants to talk with you." Eddie handed the phone to Lolo.

"Are you-you angry, Detective? With me?" she asked apprehensively.

"Listen to me very carefully. Do not post anything about Eddie, or Skylar, or me on social media or anywhere else. Is that clear?"

It took Lolo a moment to respond. "Please don't be mad."

Skylar jumped in, using a more restrained tone. "Lolo, did you already post something?"

She answered reluctantly, "Only-only about the breakfasts I made this morning. You liked them. Sixes, remember? That-that is all I posted. Nothing else, I promise."

"Did you include our names?"

Lolo paused to remember. "Well-well, you are visitors. We don't get many, you know. Not many. It's kind of a big deal."

Butler answered abruptly. "Both of you listen to me. You need to get out of there. Right now." He pulled onto the dirt median, where he slammed on the brakes and cranked a U-turn in a cloud of dust.

CHAPTER 79

David's Place

Woodsdale, Maryland

June 2, 10:29 a.m.

Sitting next to each other on the bed, Eddie and Lolo listened as tires SCREECHING and cars HONKING could be heard through the phone. Lolo reacted with serious concern. "Uh-oh. Tires screeching is not a good sound. Never good. Bad-bad."

Eddie commented, "That is what it sounded like when I was in the back of the van yesterday, just before there were gunshots and we were in an accident. There was lots of screeching and honking and metal scraping and other shrill sounds that hurt my ears. I did not like the gunshots, either. But I don't remember anything more because I became unconscious when we crashed. Did you also get into an accident?"

((•))

Inside the Bronco, Skylar could not respond. She was too busy being thrown hard into the passenger-side door as Butler swerved directly in front of several oncoming cars in the fast lane. "Look out!"

Lolo started to panic. "Are-are you okay? This is bad. Very bad. Are you okay? Say something. Please, say something!"

"We're fine," Skylar managed to breathlessly reply through gritted teeth.

Eddie made his BUZZER sound. "Not true. Definitely not. Not true at all."

Skylar attempted to gather herself. "We're okay. We did not get in an accident. Butler just had to make a sharp turn, and it scared me a little."

"True," Eddie said.

On the interstate, the passing motorists HONKED loudly as they veered around Butler and Skylar, screaming at the top of their lungs through their windows. The number of profanities far outweighed the number of words more commonly used in polite company.

Eddie counted them. "Why are so many people yelling bad words at you?"

Butler punched the accelerator, rapidly catching up with the flow of traffic heading north. "That's how people say hi in Baltimore."

Lolo imitated Eddie's BUZZER sound. "That is not true, Detective. My family lives in Baltimore, and that is not how people say hi."

Skylar turned to Butler. "You drive. I'll talk. Deal?" He nodded.

Eddie returned to a previous topic. "Butler, when you said, 'Both of you listen to me. You need to get out of there. Right now,' where did you mean we should go?"

Skylar answered with as much restraint as she could muster. "Butler and I think you and Lolo would be better off if you moved to a different location."

"I have seen most of the rooms here, and they're all pretty much the same," Lolo replied. "Of course, each room has different pictures on the walls. Some have drawings, because that's one of the activities we do every week. Make drawings with crayons or sometimes with paint. I like paint better than crayons because you get to use brushes. I like yellow paint the most."

Eddie said, "I like yellow paint, too."

Lolo responded. "You do?"

"But I don't like purple."

Butler held up his hand and moved his finger in rapid circles, signaling for Skylar to get on with it. "Eddie, do you remember the game of tag we played in New York City?"

"Yes, I do remember," he replied. "I did not like that game. Chess is more fun."

"You played tag in New York City?" Lolo said. "I haven't been there since I was a little girl, but I never got to play any games there."

"It was much too loud. New York City hurt my ears."

"I don't know how to play chess," Lolo added.

"I could teach you."

"You could?" Lolo sounded very excited by this prospect.

Skylar grew frustrated. "Eddie, you don't have time for that. Right now, you both need to leave that facility."

Lolo answered matter-of-factly. "Oh, that is not possible. I cannot leave the building. Dr. Davenport said so."

"Lolo, I am a doctor and I am telling you it's okay."

"But you are not my doctor. You are Eddie's. My doctor is Dr. Davenport."

Skylar struggled to remain calm. "Eddie, there are men coming there right now to play tag with you."

"Please tell them to go away. I don't want to play tag."

"I'm afraid I can't. And even if I could, they wouldn't listen. Which is why you both need to leave right this instant."

Eddie asked, "Why are you afraid, Skylar?"

"Because you're going to have to play tag again whether you want to or not. Please don't ask why. Just trust me. Can you do that?"

Eddie paused for a moment to consider his options. "Yes, I can do that."

Butler spoke under his breath to Skylar. "First, they have to dump the phone. Have her toss it in the john."

Eddie heard every word. Of course he did. "Detective, what's a john?"

"A toilet."

"Why didn't you just say that?"

"I wasn't talking to you." Butler shook his head, reminded how frustrating it could be to talk with Eddie.

Lolo sounded concerned. "A toilet is not a good place for a phone. They do not belong there."

Skylar jumped in. "Eddie, Detective McHenry is an expert at playing tag. If he says Lolo should toss her phone in the toilet, that's what she should do."

"No-no, I don't want to. It won't work anymore after-after that." Lolo was on the verge of tears.

Butler couldn't help himself. "That's the idea."

"My mother wouldn't like it. No-no. Not one bit. I lost my phone once. She became angry. Very angry. Yelled at me. Said I don't deserve one. I don't like being yelled at. Scary. I do deserve one. A phone."

Skylar tried a different tactic. "Lolo, if I asked you to trust me, do you think you could do that?"

"I am sorry, Skylar. You are very nice. You are. But I need to know you better. Before I can trust. Because that is what trust is."

Eddie asked Lolo, "Do you trust me?"

She paused briefly. "Yes, I think so. I am your number two angel. You told me. Nice. I trust you."

"I trust Skylar. I trust her more than anyone I have ever known. If you cannot trust her, you can trust me to do what she says."

Lolo seemed torn. "But-but phones don't belong in toilets. No, they don't."

Skylar turned to Butler, silently asking for an explanation. He gave it a shot, knowing that Eddie and Lolo could hear him. "If they have her number, they will use her phone to track them. It'll lead very bad people directly to them. And if they get ahold of that phone, they will use it to find this number and track us. Skylar, you will be in danger."

Eddie heard every word. "If they know where we are, we will lose the game."

"Yes, we will," replied Skylar. "And we can't let that happen."

((•))

"I understand now," Eddie said, nodding. He turned to Lolo but was unable to look her in the eyes. "Sometimes Skylar asks me to do things that I don't understand, but I do them because I trust her. If she says you should put your phone in the toilet, which is sometimes called a john, I think you should do it."

"Skylar is not my doctor. Dr. Davenport. He's my doctor."

He looked her briefly in the eyes. "I am asking you to trust me. Can you do that?"

Lolo hesitated, then reluctantly handed him the phone. "I can't. You do it."

"Thank you." Eddie stood up as he accepted the phone.

Butler quickly added, "Eddie, after you get rid of the phone, find a good place to hide until we can get there."

Lolo said, "I know many hiding places. Yes, many good ones."

"Great. Just pick one and stay there."

"How do I know which one I should pick?"

"Which one is the best?" Skylar said.

"I would say the best one is behind the empty milk crates inside the old freezer in the kitchen. It doesn't work, but most people don't know that."

Butler said, "Great. That sounds perfect. Get there as fast as you can."

Eddie listened. "I can hear that you are driving very fast. It is not safe to drive in excess of the posted speed limit."

Butler ignored him. "Eddie, when you go into the bathroom, don't put the phone in the toilet bowl. The people you are playing tag with might find it there if it doesn't go all the way down the drain. That would be bad. Lift the porcelain top of the tank where the water is stored and drop it in that water. Then put the top back on."

Eddie walked into the bathroom and paused. He closed his eyes and rotated his head from side to side, making sure he felt comfortable with the acoustics. He heard water dripping from the faucet, and Lolo breathing in the next room. There was muffled vehicle noise from cars passing the facility, but nothing unduly disturbing.

He nodded and then proceeded. Following Butler's instructions, he lifted the lid of the toilet tank, then spoke one last time into the phone. "You are very good at this game, Detective. I don't know all the rules yet, but I can tell you are, because this is one place I would never think to look for a phone. Goodbye." And with that, Eddie dropped the phone into the toilet's water tank and replaced the lid. The phone instantly shorted out and ceased to function.

A moment later, four tires could be heard screeching to a stop not more than twenty yards outside the window.

CHAPTER 80

FRONT ENTRANCE

DAVID'S PLACE

June 2, 10:33 a.m.

Smoke wafted around the Hellcat's tires as Guthrie and Nance jumped out of the vehicle and raced toward the entrance. The skid marks behind the vehicle were eighteen feet long. They rushed into the lobby, where no one was present to greet them. The receptionist's desk was empty aside from a small, well-worn bell, discolored from use. "Hello?" Guthrie rang it repeatedly with increasing frustration. "Hello?!"

Nance glanced at Google Maps on his phone, where he'd been tracking the GPS signal coming from the phone of the party they were searching for. *Dumb shits. Don't they know that cell phones are the single easiest way to track someone?* Apparently they did, because the signal then disappeared. "Just lost the signal."

Guthrie scanned out the windows to make sure they weren't missing anything. "Means they know we're here." He continued ringing the bell.

"Wonder how that happened?" Nance remarked sarcastically, glancing out the windows at the skid marks behind their car.

The older of the two orderlies, Roberto, appeared from around a corner, limping toward them. "Be right there. I'm moving as fast as my legs will carry me." By the time he reached Team Five, he was breathing heavily. "Sorry . . . about that . . . How . . . may I . . . help you?"

Guthrie and Nance presented a new ID, this time from the Department of Homeland Security. Roberto's eyes bulged with concern. Guthrie took the lead. "We're with Homeland Security. We have reason to believe four federal fugitives may have taken refuge on these premises."

"Oh my goodness," Roberto responded. "Here? Are they dangerous? Why would they be here?"

"No idea," replied Nance. "There's no explaining the minds of criminals."

"Are we in danger? What did they do?"

"It's a matter of national security. We're not at liberty to discuss the situation. But for the personal safety of you and the rest of the staff, we need to conduct an immediate search of the facility."

Roberto studied them closely, as if suddenly beginning to doubt their legitimacy. "You guys got a search warrant or something?"

"Matters of national security don't require one. Step back."

Roberto did so, raising his hands in surrender. "If you say so." The two men charged down the hall toward the patient rooms, methodically entering each one with well-rehearsed precision. One would knock, and the other would burst through the door without waiting for any type of response. Some of the patients gasped, others cried, but none put up any kind of resistance.

(((•)))

Looking on, Roberto smiled. He had seen Lolo and Eddie head toward the kitchen, and with all the time she spent in there, Roberto figured she probably knew a good hiding place or two. He was rooting for them. Not merely because they were clearly the dogs in this hunt, or even because of the two payments he had already received from the woman he knew only as Eleanor.

His rooting had increased due to the call he had just received from her, completed only moments before these men claiming to be agents had arrived. She had correctly predicted what they would say and had told him exactly how he should respond. She then asked if he had any friends or family members who might be available to make some quick cash. He told her that as a matter of fact, he did.

CHAPTER 81

Safe House

Gilberts Corner, Virginia

June 2, 10:30 a.m.

Five minutes earlier, Caitlin had been sitting at her command center, looking like a master church organist as she worked her multiple screens and keyboards. Her hands moved with experienced dexterity as she multitasked with ease, including answering a call from Butler's burner phone. On-screen, Caitlin could see from a satellite view that the Bronco had turned around and was now heading north on I-95. "You're going the wrong way."

"Eddie isn't safe," Skylar answered urgently. "We left him with a patient who appears to have posted about us on Instagram."

Caitlin couldn't believe it. "I don't even allow my own kids to have social media accounts. For God's sake, what does a special-needs patient need one for?"

Skylar responded, "I could give you a clinical answer, but right now, all that matters is keeping Eddie safe. We can't let anything happen to them."

"I get it," Caitlin responded, thinking of her own family. "If either one has a cell phone, they need to get rid of it."

"Already taken care of. It's at the bottom of a toilet."

"Good. That was smart." Caitlin worked the screens that were tapped into the American Heritage Foundation, trying to access the locations of the search parties. "Rest assured, there have been teams out there looking for you since you first grabbed Eddie and his device. Might be as many as six."

Butler asked, "You got eyes on them?"

"Negative. My former employer uses independent contractors for this kind of thing. They keep track of their locations via personal cell phones, which means I won't be able to see them until they arrive."

"Who the hell is your former employer, exactly?"

Caitlin took a deep breath, realizing she had nothing to lose by revealing the information. "The American Heritage Foundation."

"AHF," Butler said, remembering something from a long time ago. "I remember seeing those initials on some documents years ago, but I never knew what they stood for."

"Now you do," she said matter-of-factly. She quickly brought up a satellite view of David's Place. The Hellcat and its skid marks in front of the facility were plainly visible, as were the two men running inside. "Drive fast. I'll call you back."

Caitlin hung up and called Roberto, who answered on the first ring. "I got company. Can I call you back?" he asked.

"That's why I'm calling. The two men who just entered your facility. They will claim to be federal agents. They are not who they say they are."

"How can you be sure?"

"Because I have five grand that says so."

"You need something bad, huh?" It was clear he was sensing real opportunity.

"I need bodies and vehicles there. Right now."

"What kinda action are we talking about?"

"Whatever it takes to get my friend out of there safely."

"I got a nephew. Rides with a rough crew. Boy's a Pagan."

"The motorcycle gang?"

"They don't ride tricycles."

"Call them."

"Ten grand."

"Fine."

"How many you want?"

"All of them."

CHAPTER 82

KELMAN NURSING AND REHAB CENTER

ALEXANDRIA, VIRGINIA

June 2, 10:37 a.m.

Mr. Elliott walked up the stairs to the front entrance of the building, pausing to take one last breath of fresh air before entering. He thought of his father and glanced up toward Heaven, wondering if the old man might be looking down on him at this very moment. The thought gave him a chuckle, because if his father could see him now, it would mean he'd been watching him all this time performing his many heinous deeds. *I hope you've been enjoying the show so far, dear old Dad, but pay attention, because today is really going to be something special.*

He decided then and there to make this event even more gut-wrenching by imagining that Caitlin's father was his own. *Yes, old man, this one's for you.* Mr. Elliott shook his head in disbelief that he had not thought of this earlier. It was only now that he was certain he would be able to perform at the top of his game.

He walked through the glass entry doors and approached the Formica-covered front desk, which was currently unoccupied. In a perfect German accent, he called out, "Hello? Is anybody here?"

The front desk clerk waved through the dingy window of an office behind the desk. "Be right with you!" He tried to sound as courteous as he could, given that he appeared to be managing several other matters.

Mr. Elliott nodded, waiting patiently. He occupied himself by imagining what the clerk would look like if he was missing his eyes.

CHAPTER 83

David's Place

Woodsdale, Maryland

June 2, 10:39 a.m.

The two freezers sat side by side in the kitchen of David's Place. One functioned properly and served its intended purpose. The other did not and functioned more as a combination pantry/storage closet. There were mops and cleaning supplies next to stacks of canned tomatoes and five-pound bags of refined sugar.

Eddie and Lolo positioned themselves behind empty milk crates in the back of the defective unit. They sat on the cement floor with their legs crossed, facing each other. There were only a few narrow streams of light by which they could see. It was nearly pitch-black. Eddie tilted his head from side to side, then rotated it left to right.

They spoke in hushed tones. "What are you doing?" Lolo asked.

"I'm acoustically familiarizing myself with this space."

"I don't understand what you just said."

"To be comfortable in a new space, I have to listen from a variety of different angles."

"Okay." She nodded.

"It's very dark in here," whispered Eddie.

"Yes, it is," she responded. Her voice quivered ever so slightly. "Very dark. I-I can barely see you."

"You are scared. I can tell by the way your voice sounds. The pitch and timbre are different from your normal speaking voice." He looked directly at her because she could not see that he was doing so. In the darkness, he studied her face and its every feature—at least, as best he could. Her hairline. The shapes of her ears. The silhouette of her eyelashes. And the more he looked, the more he was certain that he had never seen anyone so beautiful in his whole entire life.

She nodded again. "Aren't you scared?"

"Yes, but I am pretending not to be."

Lolo paused for a moment. "Isn't that lying? Pretending, I mean."

He took a moment to consider his response. "Yes, but I think in this circumstance it is okay."

"I thought lying was bad and-and something you never do." She tilted her head with curiosity.

"I think it's okay if you are scared and you are trying not to be."

She nodded, accepting his explanation. "Can you pretend for me? Most of the time it doesn't work. When I try to pretend. To be a famous ballerina. Or-or a pretty fashion model. Or a five-star chef. It doesn't work. No, it doesn't."

"You don't have to pretend to be pretty. Because you are. Very pretty."

If it wasn't so dark, he would have seen that she was blushing. "No-no. Not true. I'm not."

"Yes, you are. You can believe me. I am being accurate."

"I think you must need glasses."

"No, I do not. I have very good vision. It is not as good as my hearing, but it was measured to be twenty-twenty at my most recent optometrist's visit, which is considered excellent except for combat pilots. They must have twenty-ten vision, but I do not want to be a combat pilot."

"I don't want to be a combat pilot, either," she said.

"I have never flown in an airplane," Eddie said.

"I have never flown in an airplane, either. That is another thing we have in common."

Eddie nodded. "Our list of things we have in common is longer than I have ever had with anyone else."

"I hope it gets longer. Much longer." She leaned toward him. "Eddie, why are you so nice to me?"

He carefully considered his answer. "I don't know how not to be." She was close enough that he could feel her breath on his face, and he immediately leaned back and turned away. He looked at the floor next to them. The metal shelving behind her. And the aluminum ceiling above them. "How did you know about this hiding place?"

"Because I come back here sometimes when I am sad."

"When are you sad?"

"More than sometimes. Too much, I think." She rocked back and forth, which seemed to comfort her.

"You are not sad now, are you?"

"Oh, no, I am not sad. No, not sad at all. I am scared. But with you. You help me feel not so scared."

"How am I helping you feel not so scared?"

"The way you talk to me. Like you care. And notice. Not everybody does that when they talk to me. Notice."

He smiled, but then his ears perked up. He closed his eyes to help him focus exclusively on his hearing. "The men. They are coming."

CHAPTER 84

Down the Hall

David's Place

June 2, 10:42 a.m.

Guthrie and Nance methodically advanced down the hallway, checking the last of the patient rooms. Guthrie knocked on the door, and Nance rushed through it. All he found was an old man snoring soundly in his bed. His teeth and hearing aids were on the nightstand next to him. Nance checked the closet, the bathroom, and under the bed, just to make sure. No one else was there.

He backed out of the room. "Think they took off?"

"Possible. Could have doubled back on us, too," Guthrie responded. "You want to take off or retrace?"

"Let's split up. You retrace. I'll check the common areas, then work back toward you from the other side."

Guthrie nodded. "I like it. Except you retrace." He took off into the recreation room before Nance could protest. Nance started going back through the rooms they had already searched. Guthrie checked the recreation room, startling the handful of residents who were busy working on their daily arts-and-crafts project.

The young nurse supervising their work did not appreciate the interruption. "Can I help you?"

"Have you seen a man and a woman who do not belong here?" Guthrie asked.

"Well, I see you," she answered pointedly, crossing her arms across her chest.

"It's a matter of national security," he stated sharply. "Have you seen them or not?"

She looked him in the eyes. "I have not."

He checked inside the room's two storage closets, then moved on to the medical examination rooms.

After a moment, the nurse mumbled under her breath, "National security, my ass." It was only now that the gaunt woman she was helping with her painting of a donkey cracked a smile. A great big one.

CHAPTER 85

I-95 North

Four Miles South of Woodsdale

June 2, 10:44 a.m.

Racing north on I-95, Roberto's vintage Bronco was barely holding together. Minor problems like poor wheel alignment and lack of tire tread became big ones when traveling over one hundred miles per hour. The vehicle shook so much that Butler had difficulty holding on to the steering wheel. All he could see in the rearview mirror was a blur.

Skylar looked concerned. "This doesn't feel safe."

"It's not," he answered matter-of-factly. He kept his eyes on the road.

She gripped the door handle tightly. "This is not how I want to die, Butler."

"This is not how you're going to die. Try meditating. It'll make you feel better."

"Is that what you're doing?"

"Fuck, no. I live for this shit."

Butler's phone rang. It was Caitlin. Skylar jumped, hitting the speaker button halfway through the first ring. "Hello." Her voice quivered along with the car, sounding like she was standing on one of those vibrating platforms chiropractors use.

"Your voice sounds strange. Everything okay?"

"Never better," Skylar lied.

"You still on I-95?"

"Copy that," answered Butler. "Passing an exit called Mountain Road."

"Get off," Caitlin instructed.

"When?"

"Right now."

He slammed on the brakes, skidding to a stop in a cloud of dust along the shoulder. Skylar closed her eyes, dropped the phone in her lap, and braced her hands against the dashboard. "I hate roller coasters!"

"Then you're certainly not going to enjoy this." He put the car in reverse and backed up rapidly toward the off-ramp. To the phone, he asked, "Now what?"

"Go north on Mountain Road," Caitlin answered.

"Where are we going?" Skylar asked.

"Rendezvous point."

"How's Eddie getting there?"

CHAPTER 86

David's Place

Woodsdale, Maryland

June 2, 10:46 a.m.

Inside the broken kitchen freezer, Lolo was rigid with fear. Her breathing was shallow. She spoke rapidly. "Now scared. Really-really scared. I am. Don't like this. Not at all. No-no."

Eddie whispered, "We should not talk if we don't want them to find us."

She clenched her teeth, as well as the rest of her. She spoke as quietly as she could. "I don't know if I can. I'm sorry. I'm sorry. I'm really scared."

"Would it help you not to be scared if I held your hand?"

She nodded, reaching out for his hand. At first, he flinched and pulled back his arm. He didn't mean to, it just happened.

"Sorry-sorry-sorry." Her breathing was becoming more rapid. Her hands were starting to shake. Tears streamed down her face. She was on the verge of complete panic.

Eddie recognized her desperation because it reminded him of the moment when Homeland Security agents had surrounded him outside his childhood home. He had never been so scared in his life. He remembered breathing very rapidly and thinking he was going to die, right before he went into shock. Then everything went black until he woke up in Children's Hospital of Philadelphia. He didn't want that to happen to Lolo. Not now, or ever.

He spoke soothingly. "It's okay." He then took a deep breath to muster his courage and reached out for her hand. At first, he overshot and grabbed her wrist. She quickly adjusted her arm and grabbed his hand. She squeezed it tight. So tight that Eddie grimaced. "You're hurting my hand."

"I-I can't help it," she whispered. "Sorry."

"Is it helping you?"

She nodded again.

He then whispered very quietly. "You can squeeze all you want, then." He paused, then added, "One of them is in the kitchen." He pointed toward the door.

CHAPTER 87

KITCHEN

DAVID'S PLACE

June 2, 10:47 a.m.

Guthrie rushed into the kitchen, methodically scanning the room. He quickly moved around prep tables, getting down on one knee to check beneath them. Finding nothing, he moved behind several stacks of canned goods, which appeared to have been just delivered. He advanced toward the freezers, first checking the one that was operational. It was ice-cold. He moved inside briefly, quickly determining his targets were not there.

He turned toward the adjacent freezer and put his hand on the door handle, when his phone buzzed inside his pocket. He answered it quickly. "What?"

"We have company. Meet me out front."

((•))

Inside the freezer, Eddie listened to the man exit the kitchen and move down the hall. "He's gone now."

Lolo continued squeezing his hand. She was breathing fast. "Are you—are you sure?"

"Yes, I am sure. Another man called him on his phone and said, 'We have company. Meet me out front.'"

"Eddie, are you okay? You don't sound right. In pain."

Grimacing, he couldn't take it any longer. "My hand. It really hurts."

She released her grip on his hand. "Sorry-sorry. I forgot. Didn't realize. Sorry."

"I believe you." He paused to massage his hand. "You were scared. I understand. I did not mean to put you in any danger, either, but I did. It was wrong."

"Oh, it's not your fault. No, not at all."

"Yes, it is. It is my fault. Those men came here because of me. I do not want anything bad to happen to you because of me."

"That's okay, Eddie. I don't mind."

He did not make his buzzing sound because she was telling the truth. "But I do mind." He stood up.

"Where are you going?"

"I am leaving so that you will be safe."

She stood up quickly next to him. "But I don't want you to go. I don't get many visitors. Please don't go."

"I don't want to. You are my one and only friend. But I know it's the right thing to do."

"Eddie, how do you know? How?"

With the protection of the darkness, he looked her in the eyes. "I know with my whole body. This is only the second thing in my life that I have known with more than just my head. I do not know how I do, but I do."

"Will-will I ever see you again?" Lolo asked haltingly.

"Yes. Unless I die, but I will try not to."

"Try very hard not to. I would be sad. So sad."

He began moving slowly toward the door, stepping carefully, feeling in front of him for objects that might block his path. Upon reaching the door, he cracked it open just enough to allow a sliver of light to stream in. The narrow band illuminated her face. "You should go to your room. Like the other patients. Pretend you are asleep. In this circumstance, it's okay."

She nodded. "I will miss seeing you, Eddie. It was nice having visitors."

"I will miss seeing you, too."

"I am your second angel."

"Yes, you are." He paused to consider what he was about to say. "I will see you again."

"Do you promise?"

He nodded. "Yes, I promise."

"And a promise is a promise."

"Yes, it is." He opened the door the rest of the way, unaware that a man was standing on the other side of it.

CHAPTER 88

FRONT ENTRANCE

DAVID'S PLACE

June 2, 10:50 a.m.

Sheila McCourt and Sheila Bryce, better known as the Sheilas, walked briskly toward Nance as he came out of the building. "Fancy meeting you ladies here," he said.

"Nice to see you again, Don," Sheila B. said as cordially as she could. "Thought you partnered up on this one."

Behind him, Guthrie charged out of the front doors. "He did. With the best there is. Sheilas." He offered a courteous nod.

Sheila M. nodded back similarly. "Ray. Any of the others here yet?"

"We're the first," answered Nance. "You're the second. But the others won't be far behind."

Sheila B. looked back and forth between the two men. "So you haven't found them."

"Their signal died when we walked through the door," Guthrie replied.

"Sounds like they saw you coming," Sheila M. said with a smirk.

Nance clearly didn't appreciate her tone. "Or somebody tipped them off."

"Believe that if it makes you feel better," Sheila B. countered.

Nance shook his head. "You know, I was gonna see if you two were interested in joining forces, seeing as how Dupre's gonna show up with like five of his kids. But now I'm thinking, nah."

"Aw, we didn't hurt your feelings, did we, darlin'?" Sheila M. said with mock sincerity.

Guthrie stepped forward, pausing for a moment. He spoke with cold menace. "Just remember, we offered to play nice. Now, if you happen to find 'em first, don't be surprised when we take them from you."

He and Nance turned to head back inside the building, when a sound grew rapidly in the distance. It was the low-decibel rumble of motorcycles being ridden at high speed in their direction.

"You boys expecting company?" Sheila B. asked as she watched the bikers in their ninety-mile-an-hour approach.

Nance tracked the motorcycles closely. "Pagans. Son of a bitch. What the hell are they doing here?"

"Ain't no coincidence," his partner responded.

"Somebody called them," Nance said, eyeballing the Sheilas.

Sheila M. spoke with a tone that was more concerned than it was defensive. "Wasn't us, that's for damn sure."

Sheila B. didn't hesitate. "If you two are still interested in teaming up, we just changed our minds."

"Yeah, good idea," Guthrie replied, completely distracted as the Pagans pulled into the parking lot.

CHAPTER 89

KITCHEN

DAVID'S PLACE

June 2, 10:52 a.m.

Inside the kitchen, Eddie exited the broken freezer and bumped into Roberto, startling him. Eddie panicked. "Please don't shoot."

Roberto held up his hands to show he was not in possession of a weapon. "What are you talking about? I'm here to help you, man."

Listening closely, Eddie nodded. "I believe you." Eddie looked down to Roberto's feet, studying them. "I wonder why I didn't hear you?"

Roberto lifted his pant leg to reveal the soft-soled shoes he was wearing. "Lots of our patients have real good hearing. I used to wake 'em up all the time. Wasn't worth the hassle. So I got these special shoes and learned to walk real quiet."

"That is very impressive. Because I usually hear everything."

"I think you might have also been distracted." He motioned to Lolo, who was peeking out from behind Eddie.

She waved sheepishly. "Hi, Roberto. It's me, Lolo."

"Yes, I know." He nodded. "You're Eddie, right?"

"How do you know my name?"

"A lady named Eleanor is paying me to help you."

"I don't know any lady named Eleanor."

"Well, she knows you."

"How much is she paying you to help me?"

"None of your damn business." Roberto turned to Lolo. "You should go on up to your room now and get under the covers."

"For how long?"

"Until I say so."

She nodded, then headed for the door, where she paused and turned to Eddie. "You won't forget your promise, will you?"

"I will not forget." He spoke with absolute conviction. As he watched Lolo exit, he heard the rumble of the arriving motorcycles. "Roberto, what is making all those loud engine noises? It hurts my ears."

"Man, if your ears are hurting now, you're gonna have a serious problem." He reached into his pocket and pulled out rubber earplugs. "My wife snores like a freight train. I can't sleep a wink without these, but you're gonna need them a whole lot more." He offered them to Eddie.

He examined them. "These look like excellent earplugs."

"Put them in your ears. It's about to get way louder around here."

Eddie took the earplugs and placed them in his ears. He tilted his head from left to right, then rotated his head back and forth. "Yes, these are much better than tissue paper."

"Follow me." Roberto led him out a delivery door.

CHAPTER 90

Kelman Nursing and Rehab Center

Alexandria, Virginia

June 2, 10:55 a.m.

The front-desk clerk finally scurried out of the office to the desk, where Mr. Elliott was waiting impatiently.

In his German accent, he asked, "Is it common in this country to keep family members waiting so long to see their loved ones?"

"I'm real sorry about that. I just had three major situations get dumped in my lap, but you don't need to hear about that, do you?"

"No, actually, I do not."

"Your patience is greatly appreciated." The clerk smiled tensely. "How can I help you?"

"I am here to visit my uncle Lawrence. Last name Walters."

"Lawrence is your uncle? How about that. I didn't know he had any European relatives."

"Do you know the complete ancestry of all your patients?" Mr. Elliott asked a bit sharply, as any good German would.

"No, I can't say that I do, but I do know some," the clerk said, clearly eager for this conversation to be over. "May I see your identification, please?"

Mr. Elliott handed over his German passport, which identified him as Manfred Engels. The clerk studied the document. "German, huh? I guess you must be related through his wife."

Again with appropriate German disdain, Mr. Elliott replied, "How very astute of you." He let the insult linger in the air along with the dreadful stench of hospital-strength antiseptic. "My mother was Anna's older sister, Marie. She passed on twelve years ago. Apparently, they both carried the BRCA gene. One can only hope my cousin, Caitlin, is not also a carrier."

"One can only hope," the clerk replied as he wrote down the man's name in the official visitor's log. He then pointed down the hall. "Lawrence's room is that way, last door on the right."

"Thank you." Mr. Elliott nodded and walked down the hall. He glanced into each room as he passed, since the doors were all open—not unlike a gawker passing the scene of an accident who just couldn't help but take a gander. It was only human nature to be curious about damage and decay. Because one day, it happens to everyone.

Mr. Elliott arrived outside Lawrence's door. He knocked gently. "Hello? Uncle Lawrence, are you awake?"

CHAPTER 91

David's Place

Woodsdale, Maryland

June 2, 10:57 a.m.

The four private investigators looked on as the Pagans circled around the front parking lot in a menacing ritual. It was a motorized dance of primitive territoriality. Each of the beasts rode atop a Harley-Davidson with no less than nine hundred cubic centimeters of engine displacement. These rides were not for the faint of heart, nor for the inexperienced.

The bikes on display included a vintage Ironhead, a Forty-Eight Special, a Dyna, several Road Kings, and a matte-black Sportster. Each was among the baddest bikes on the road, and each commanded respect—even before an observer would notice the Pagan logo proudly worn on the back of each rider.

These jackets were not worn casually. They were a badge of honor and could not be purchased in any store at any price. They had to be earned through blood and commitment, as defined by each group's leader. When a motorcycle gang wore their colors, it was akin to pirates of a different era raising the Jolly Roger. It meant they were on official business. The question currently on the mind of each tracker hired by the American Heritage Foundation was, *What the hell brought the Pagans here?*

As his brethren continued riding around the immediate area, including two carrying passengers on the backs of their bikes, the leader sped directly toward the four private investigators. They didn't move. They knew to hold their ground.

The Pagan screeched his bike to a stop within two feet of them and turned off his engine. He removed his helmet and got off his machine. It was only now that his full size could be appreciated. He was six feet four inches tall and 260 pounds, but it was the scars across his neck and face that gave him a truly menacing look.

Guthrie stepped forward. "Can we help you with something?"

"You dicks are upsetting some of the residents here. That ain't right."

$$((\bullet))$$

As the Pagans continued riding about in seemingly random fashion, it would soon become apparent that there was nothing haphazard about it. It was a well-orchestrated distraction. One of the two riders carrying a passenger sped off around the back of the building. He rode up to the kitchen loading area, stopping beneath a covered overhang, where they could no longer be seen from satellite view. This was where Roberto and Eddie were waiting.

Eddie kept his hands over his ears until the rider switched off his engine and got off the bike. The Pagan removed his helmet, revealing a beard and unruly shoulder-length hair. "What's up, Uncle?"

"Hey, man, thanks for coming," Roberto answered, then gave his nephew a hug.

"We're family." The biker eyed Eddie as the passenger also dismounted. "This the dude?"

Roberto nodded. "This is him. Eddie, this is my nephew, Lobo. Lobo, this is Eddie."

"Lobo means *wolf* in Spanish," noted Eddie. "Did you know that?"

"You don't fucking say," he replied sharply.

"Yes, I do fucking say," Eddie replied. "I just did say."

Lobo's female passenger removed her helmet and Pagans jacket. She was striking, particularly because of her gold teeth and the small lightning bolts tattooed on her cheeks. She offered the jacket and helmet to Eddie. "Put these on."

Eddie shook his head. "Those are not mine."

"No, shit. Put 'em on, fool." She was clearly not one to suffer nuisance lightly, nor those outside the neurological norm.

Roberto intervened. "Eddie, they're here to help you. She's giving you a disguise so the men looking for you won't recognize you."

Eddie thought for a moment, then nodded. "In that case, thank you." He put on the helmet and jacket. His face was hidden behind a tinted face shield. "Everything looks very dark now."

Lobo studied him, then turned to Roberto. "He does realize what an honor it is to be wearing our colors, don't he?"

"Nephew, he ain't got a clue," his uncle responded. "Please remember he's got . . . issues."

"I have Asperger's syndrome," Eddie corrected him. "But I have learned it is now more commonly referred to as autism spectrum disorder."

"I couldn't give a shit. Get on." Lobo motioned to the back of his bike, where his girlfriend had been sitting.

Eddie did not move. "I have never ridden on a motorcycle before."

Roberto stepped toward him and spoke intensely. "If you ever want to see your friends again, get on the damn motorcycle and keep your mouth shut."

Eddie nodded and got on the back of the motorcycle. Lobo mounted the bike in front of him and started the engine. As he put the hog into gear and ROARED off, Eddie was thrown back into the sissy bar and nearly fell off. He instinctively grabbed onto what was in front of him, which happened to be Lobo.

Eddie was terrified. He desperately wanted to let go of Lobo because it was most definitely physical contact, and with a stranger, no less—but he was more afraid of falling off the motorcycle. Not sure what else to do, he closed his eyes as tightly as he could and started to silently repeat every word of the conversations he and Lolo had had earlier. He started with a conversation that included Skylar.

"'You make my heart sing . . . I do? . . . Has anyone ever told you that before? . . . I don't think so, and I probably would have remembered something like that . . . Skylar, you are a doctor. You should know that hearts cannot sing . . . It's an expression . . . I don't like expressions . . . Eddie, I'm sorry to disagree with you on this, but you are wrong. Hearts can sing. They sure can . . . Internal organs cannot sing. It's physically impossible . . . Maybe yours just hasn't learned how. Your heart. To sing, I mean . . . Maybe you can teach him, Lolo.'"

It was only now that he realized she had. Eddie's heart was singing. Yes, it really was. *Thump-thump, thump-thump.* He could feel it. He really could. Sitting there on the back of a Harley-Davidson motorcycle, clinging for dear life to a man who looked like a wolf, Eddie finally understood what Lolo and Skylar had been talking about. *Thump-thump, thump-thump.*

Of course hearts could not sing literally! It was a metaphor used to describe the sensation of bursting with joy. Which meant it was an expression, a type of language he had always disliked because he found them confusing. But for the first time in his life, he understood an expression. Because he could feel it. He could hear his heart singing. *Thump-thump, thump-thump.* Not just beating but singing.

For the rest of Eddie's first-ever motorcycle ride, this was what he focused on. Not the incredibly loud two-cylinder Harley-Davidson engine revving beneath him. Not the sound of the wind whipping past him at over seventy miles per hour. Not even the terror he felt every time Lobo leaned the motorcycle into a turn. Eddie listened to the music of his heart. *Thump-thump, thump-thump.*

And it was beautiful.

CHAPTER 92

Kelman Nursing and Rehab Center

Alexandria, Virginia

June 2, 11:01 a.m.

Mr. Elliott entered Lawrence's room slowly. "Uncle Lawrence, can you hear me?" He saw the old man sitting in his easy chair, which was pointed out the window. He must be sleeping, the assassin figured. *It's what old people spend most of their time doing. What a waste.*

"How would you like to take a little excursion today?" he asked, not expecting a response. Which explained the surprise on his face when he received one.

"Sounds good to me." The man sitting in the chair, clenching a dart gun in his right hand, was not Lawrence. He was wearing a white wig cut just like the old man's, but it was not him.

He stood up suddenly and fired a dart into Mr. Elliott's abdomen. Mr. Elliott quickly removed the dart, but not before whatever drug it contained had entered his bloodstream. It was nearly instantaneous. His body sagged as he desperately tried to fight off its effects.

Dropping the German accent, he spoke in his regular voice as the man stepped out of the chair to face him. "Who the hell are you?"

The man removed his wig. "Someone who has been waiting to meet you for a very long time."

"I gather this is personal for you, then," Mr. Elliott replied as he reached toward the small of his back, where he had concealed a Ruger beneath his shirt. But he did not reach it quickly enough.

The man kicked him squarely in the chest, sending him flying backward into a nightstand holding several framed photographs of Lawrence and family members. The glass frames shattered as the Ruger escaped from Mr. Elliott's grasp and slid across the floor. Mr. Elliott grabbed one of the broken frames and threw it at the man. Then another. And another.

Several of the flying shards of glass cut into the man's flesh: one in his forearm, one in his chest, and one in his cheek, which just stuck there like some new type of adornment that might accompany a nose ring or a tribal ear stretching. He showed no emotion at all as he removed the glass from his face. Blood streamed from the wound. As he dropped the shard to the cold linoleum floor, it made a distinctive *plink* sound.

It was only now that Mr. Elliott realized what he was up against, particularly as his motor functions grew increasingly impaired from the tranquilizer. He desperately started throwing anything he could grab. A lamp, which his assailant managed to duck, smashed into a cinder-block wall behind him; a desk chair sailed through the window with a loud crash; and a brass-handled derby walking cane, he effortlessly caught in midair with one hand.

((•))

"My turn." Holding the bottom of the cane, Hogan wielded it like a club and slammed the brass handle into the side of Mr. Elliott's head. His skull shattered. The sound was distinctive. "That was for a friend of mine."

Mr. Elliott immediately dropped to all fours, bleeding profusely but still struggling to maintain consciousness. He desperately tried to crawl toward his weapon. "Who . . . was your friend?"

"I won't give you the satisfaction." *Her name was Kindra Ogletree.* The thought only seemed to further fuel Hogan's rage.

Mr. Elliott was defenseless against the next strike, a front kick to his face. His nose was completely shattered. He went down in a heap and did not get back up. "That was for my other friend who tried to help the first one." *His name was Lyle Murphy.*

Quentin, the front desk clerk, appeared in the doorway. He was pushing Lawrence Walters, who sat in a wheelchair, looking very confused. "Is this my room?"

CHAPTER 93

Lawrence Walter's Room

Kelman Nursing and Rehab Center

June 2, 11:05 a.m.

Quentin picked up Mr. Elliott's Ruger from the floor and looked at Hogan. The two men had clearly developed a relationship through Hogan's regular visits over the years. "This wouldn't be yours, would it?"

"I believe it's yours." He grabbed a towel from the bathroom and wiped some of the blood off his face.

The clerk pocketed the weapon, then looked around the room at all the damage, shaking his head. It looked like the place had been hit by a tornado. "Just who in the hell do you expect is gonna clean all this up? Not me, I hope."

"I'll pay you a week's salary."

"Two weeks. Plus damages."

Hogan nodded his consent.

Bewildered, Lawrence looked up at Quentin. "What in God's name happened here?"

"Ask the man standing over there." He pointed to Hogan.

"Who is he?"

"He's an old friend of yours named Hogan. He's visited you every few months since you got here."

The old man studied Hogan. "I remember knowing a Hogan once, a long time ago. I believe we worked together. Is that you?"

Hogan nodded. "Yes, sir."

"Did you owe me something? I can't remember."

"That's why I'm here," Hogan said. "I'm settling accounts with you."

The old man only now noticed Mr. Elliott lying unconscious on the floor. "Who is that man and why is he bleeding all over my floor?"

"He was here to do you harm. I wasn't going to let that happen."

"He ain't dead, is he?" the clerk asked.

"Not yet."

The clerk smiled, as did Lawrence. "I liked you, didn't I?"

"I believe so, yes, sir."

Lawrence turned his gaze toward Mr. Elliott and pointed his shaking hand. "Get that piece of shit out of here."

((•))

A few minutes later, Hogan used Lawrence's wheelchair to remove Mr. Elliott from the premises. His hands and wrists were now zip-tied together tightly. Hogan was taking no chances. He placed Mr. Elliott in the back of the assassin's rented Ford Fusion and then opened the trunk. Hogan was appalled by the breadth of weaponry it contained. The torture devices included specific apparatus that had been used in the gruesome snuff films that featured his former colleagues, Kindra and Lyle.

What was done to them was horrible. And inhumane. The images that were streamed from Mr. Elliott's dark-web site had haunted Hogan for years. And because of it, he had vowed that no matter what it took, or how long he had to wait, one day he would kill the man who had perpetrated the deeds.

At times he had considered going abroad himself and hunting the man down before age began to diminish Hogan's talents. After all, this type of mission was among his specialties. But the risks involved were difficult for him to justify, given his family obligations. He had allowed himself a window of two more years. If an opportunity didn't come up during that time, he had committed to making the trip.

Hogan realized his wait was over the moment Caitlin decided to proceed with the Alpha Reset Protocol. He was certain that Bob Stenson would go after any vulnerability that she had, and the most obvious one was Lawrence. As the unofficial godfather of most currently working assassins in the United States, Hogan had maintained contact with most of them over the years, providing training or advice whenever requested. So it was easy for him to reach out to the teams before Bob Stenson could. Hogan told them to decline Stenson's offer, or simply not to answer. Each complied. Which left the American Heritage Foundation director only one choice: Mr. Elliott.

Hogan was a man who had spent a lifetime cultivating methods to moderate his emotions. *Never get too high; never get too low. Just get the job done and move on.* Especially when it came to killing. Any emotion distorted the deed. "Kill without joy" was his professional mantra, because he had seen too many in his profession become obsessed with the rush. They got addicted to it. He was certain this was what had happened to Mr. Elliott, only in the extreme. Like those who try heroin or oxy or fentanyl for the first time—once you experience it, you cannot unexperience it. And with some things, once is all it takes. They grab hold of you and gradually begin to consume you. Ask any real alcoholic.

Hogan suddenly realized that his intention was to torture Mr. Elliott with the same horrible instruments the man had used on Kindra and Lyle. He wanted the sick bastard to scream like they had. To beg like they had. And to suffer like they had. He was going to settle the score Old Testament style. An eye for an eye. Then an ear for an ear, before moving to his hands and other body parts. Hogan intended to keep Mr. Elliott alive for as long as inhumanely possible.

And that was when it hit him. He had lost it. He wanted to inflict as much suffering as possible and enjoy it. *Enjoy it!* The revelation made him shudder. This was how easy it was to go over the edge. *If you can justify this, there is nothing you won't be able to.* Hogan knew he had nearly gone down a road there would be no returning from. And that everything he was devoted to in his life would have been placed in jeopardy.

He did not hesitate. He slammed the trunk shut and opened the door to the back seat, where he placed his weapon against Mr. Elliott's chest and fired. The sound of the gunshot was muffled. The human torso makes an excellent silencer when a weapon is fired directly against it. So, it turned out, does the human skull. Because when Hogan fired a second bullet into Mr. Elliott's forehead, it was similarly muted.

Hogan did not relish the moment or revel in any retribution. He was back in control. The job was done and that was that. He returned the wheelchair to Quentin and thanked him again for his assistance. Then he drove off in Mr. Elliott's rental car, which he abandoned only a few blocks away, but not before sending a group text to his contacts within the CIA, DIA, Homeland, and the FBI. It read: *First come, first served.* It included an image of Mr. Elliott's fingerprint after it had been pressed against one of the rental-car windows, and the GPS coordinates of the vehicle. He wondered how long it would take for the news to reach Bob Stenson.

As it would turn out, not long at all.

CHAPTER 94

ELECTRONIC VOTING SYSTEMS

PHOENIX, ARIZONA

June 2, 9:31 a.m. Mountain Standard Time

Jessup Fields and his brother stood in front of the world headquarters of EVS as they addressed a dozen reporters and their cameras. "Ladies and gentlemen of the press and good people of this country, my brother and I just learned of a hostile and brazen attack committed by a nefarious group of Russian hackers—not only on our voting-machine business, but on the very sanctity of our American way of life . . ."

((•))

Flying in their G6 somewhere in the clouds above New York State, Corbin Davis and his wife and chief of staff were watching the live newscast in disbelief. Jessup Fields continued: "These foreign hackers went so far as to splice together random pieces of conversation from our great president to make it appear as if he were somehow involved in their nefarious scheme. Well, I am here to tell you that this is all fabrication. Pure and simple fabrication."

Corbin Davis turned to Bob Welker. "What the hell do you make of this?"

"The president had him go on the offensive," responded Welker. "Get the fake news out there first, and that's what the people will believe. When the real news comes out, it will seem bogus."

"The spin has always been what matters, not the story," Melanie concurred.

"It's a sad commentary, don't you think?" asked Davis.

"It's the world we live in," responded his chief of staff, looking out the window at the farm fields twenty-three thousand feet below them.

"God, I hope you can make things better," Melanie said to Corbin.

"It's why you married me, isn't it?"

CHAPTER 95

AMERICAN HERITAGE FOUNDATION

ALEXANDRIA, VIRGINIA

June 2, 11:34 a.m.

Bob Stenson watched two separate screens. On one was the breaking news about Russian hacking of Electronic Voting Systems. On the other was a satellite view of the Pagan motorcycle gang circling around the Maryland facility where Edward Parks had been located. Stenson heard footsteps walking quickly down the hallway toward his door. It was Greers, who was panicked. "Sir, have you been watching the news?"

"No, I thought I'd catch up on the last few episodes of *The Bachelor* that I missed." He paused. "My goodness, boy, will you kindly relax?"

"What are we going to do, sir? How can we possibly use the echoes from the Oval Office now?"

"I'm already having Mr. Harwood pore over every date since he's been in office. It won't take long to find something we can use."

Momentarily appeased, Greers then pointed to the satellite view of David's Place on-screen. "But what about the Pagans?"

"I've got to admit, using them was rather clever. I've watched at least five of them head off in different directions, and for the life of me, I couldn't tell you if Parks was on the back of one."

Greers remained rattled. "And I assume you've heard that Mr. Elliott was found dead in his car less than twenty miles from here."

Stenson clenched his jaw. "Excuse me?"

"Mr. Elliott. The operative who supposedly doesn't work inside US borders. Apparently, he does."

"I know who Mr. Elliott is," the older man replied carefully. "Who found him?"

"Every agency with initials," Greers answered anxiously. "Whoever took him out made sure they all knew exactly where to find him." He then asked the question that was really on his mind. "Sir, what do you think he was doing in Alexandria?"

"I doubt it was to admire the view from the Masonic Memorial."

"Yes, I doubt that also." He was clearly in no mood for joking around.

Stenson wanted to hear what his subordinate was thinking before he offered up any details. "What do you think he was doing here?"

Greers answered like it should have been obvious. "I think Caitlin hired him."

This took Stenson by surprise. "To come after me?"

"Not just you, sir. He may have been hired to come after all of us."

Stenson rubbed his chin, thinking about the irony that in fact he had hired Mr. Elliott, and not Caitlin. At least now it was clear why Greers was acting so emotionally. He had the access codes to Mr. Elliott's dark-web site and had seen too many of his "promotional films."

"It would've been a hell of a move on her part, don't you think?" Stenson said.

Greers remained gravely concerned. "No, sir, I don't. It would mean she's gone off the rails, and that anything is now possible."

Stenson stopped rubbing his chin. "Why do you say that?"

"There's a reason we have never once hired him. The man is a psychopath. It's like making a deal with the Devil. Anyone willing to go that far is unstable. They are capable of absolutely anything."

Stenson struggled not to take the statement personally. "Not if the Devil is now dead."

Greers paused, still anxious. "That's the other thing that concerns me. If one of ours had put him down, you would have been the first to know. If we didn't do it, who did?"

"The entire law-abiding world was hunting the man. If he was dumb enough to set foot inside US borders, he was clearly dumb enough to get caught."

Greers shook his head. "Bit of a coincidence, don't you think?"

"I don't believe in coincidence. You know that."

"Neither do I. Because you taught me not to."

Stenson nodded. "I'll reach out to the agencies and see what they know. When I find out who put him down, I will let you know."

"Thank you, sir."

"In the meantime, relax. You seem rattled. What you need to do is find Edward Parks and his goddamn device. Are we clear?"

"Yes, sir, I'm on it." Greers collected himself and exited even more quickly than he had entered.

After making sure his subordinate had gone down the hall, Stenson shook his head in frustration. Two and a half million dollars had just gone down the drain. There was no way he would ever get back his down payment to Mr. Elliott. Such were the risks in hiring psychopathic international killers.

As if to Hogan, he said, "Well, you son of a bitch, you may be good, but you can't be in two places at once." He picked up his phone and dialed the number of another phone currently located in Harvey, North Dakota.

CHAPTER 96

"MONTGOMERY" FAMILY HOME

HARVEY, NORTH DAKOTA

June 2, 10:38 a.m. Central Daylight Time

Peter, Marissa, and Mikey were sitting around the vintage kitchen table, playing a game of Scrabble. It was one of several board games Peter had discovered in a closet after they'd returned from breakfast. Peter played the word *corpus*. "Corpus. With the *c* on a triple letter, that's sixteen points. Read 'em and weep." He added sixteen to his score.

"Corpus? Is that even a word?" Marissa asked.

"Of course it is."

"Oh yeah? What does it mean?"

Mikey jumped in. "Boy, are you dumb. Corpus means a core of pus. Corpus. Get it?" He cracked himself up.

His sister rolled her eyes. "That is so not funny."

"Yes, it is. You just don't get it 'cause you don't have a sense of humor."

Marissa turned to Peter. "Dad, I'm serious. What does it mean?"

"It means the main part of something. In accounting, it's what you start with, or the principal of a fund, which is separate from the income or interest it earns."

"Exactly," chimed in Mikey. "It's the core of something. But usually, it's pus." He laughed even louder, particularly when his father chuckled as well.

Marissa shook her head, rolling her eyes again. "I can't believe you're encouraging him."

Mikey reached into the canvas tile bag to select three letters, but he apparently didn't like his selections, so he quickly put them back and picked out three others.

"You are such a little cheater," his sister commented.

"I am not," Mikey answered.

"Are too. I saw what you did. Don't try to deny it."

"What is it that you think he did?" asked Peter.

"He repicked his letters."

"Well, Mikey, is that true?" asked Peter.

With awkward hesitation, his son answered, "No."

"Mikey—"

"I'm getting killed anyway. What does it even matter?"

"It's the principle of the thing." Peter crossed his arms across his chest in a father-knows-best pose.

"She always wins. It isn't fair."

"I'm older than you," said Marissa. "I'm supposed to win."

"You may be older, but I'm smarter."

"Are not."

"Are too."

"Wanna bet?"

A voice they had never heard before then joined their conversation. "I'll put my money on the little guy." It was Coogan, the man who'd been watching them from the moment they had landed at Minot International Airport. He was standing just inside the front doorway, looking down the barrel of his Smith & Wesson.

Marissa screamed. Peter immediately stood up from the table, moving in front of his children as he addressed the intruder. "What the hell do you want?"

Coogan eyed Marissa menacingly. "Ain't about what I want."

"Then what are you doing here?"

"You do what I say, ain't no one gotta get hurt, and this'll be over real quick. But you and your wife don't do what you're told, well, it'll be another story."

"My wife isn't here. I have no idea where she is."

"That's the miracle of technology. It don't matter where she is. We're gonna have us a little conference call just the same."

Peter glanced at his satellite phone and desperately wished he hadn't left it in plain view.

Coogan held up a dozen large zip ties, which he tossed onto the Scrabble board, scattering the tiles. He addressed Marissa. "Girly, you know what these are?"

She nodded, completely terrified. "Daddy, I'm scared."

Peter tried to sound as reassuring as he could. "Just do what he says."

"Use them ties to fasten your old man's wrists and ankles to the legs of his chair. Then do the same for your brother there. If you try to get cute and tie them too loose, I'll make them so tight they'll have to amputate their hands and feet. You wouldn't want that now, would you?"

She shook her head as tears streamed down her face.

"Well, get to it, then."

She picked up one of the zip ties and moved to her father, who pushed his chair away from the table so that Coogan could see what Marissa was doing. "Daddy, I'm sorry."

"It's okay, honey. Make them tight like the man wants." He paused to lock eyes with her. "We're going to get through this."

She nodded, wiping the tears from her cheeks as she tied his legs to the chair.

CHAPTER 97

TRAILER PARK

JARRETTSVILLE, MARYLAND

June 2, 11:45 a.m.

Speeding along in the rusted Bronco, Butler pulled up quickly to the entrance of a dilapidated trailer park, where he paused uneasily. "You sure this is the right place?"

Skylar held up the phone, which showed their location on a map. "They're the coordinates she sent. Why, what's the matter?"

He motioned outside the windows, where they were being surrounded by Pagan gang members, who clearly didn't care for outsiders entering their compound. "Because if this is the wrong place, we're in deep shit."

A menacing-looking biker approached the driver's side of the vehicle. "You lost?"

"We're looking for Lobo."

"Never heard of him."

Butler maintained his gaze. "He's expecting us."

Across a weed-filled courtyard, Lobo stepped out of his trailer and gave a nod to his Pagan brother. The first man stepped back from the Bronco, allowing Butler and Skylar to proceed. They parked next to

Lobo's Harley. He eyed them with suspicion. "Ain't that my uncle's ride?"

Butler nodded. "We rented it from him."

Lobo studied them. "Who the hell are you people?"

Butler didn't answer. "Is our friend here?"

Lobo looked toward his trailer. "He's chillin' inside. What's wrong with him?"

Skylar answered, "He has Asperger's syndrome. He's on the high-functioning end of the autism-disorder spectrum."

"My kid's got it. Autism. It's real messed up. Kid don't say shit."

"How old is he?" asked Skylar.

"Six." Lobo's voice was a mixture of sadness, resignation, and disgust.

"Have you tried getting him any kind of occupational therapy?"

"Any kind of what?"

"Training to help him cope with his sensory-processing issues. Most kids with autism have difficulty filtering out extraneous stimulation, which prevents them from developing the same way as their peers."

Lobo looked her up and down. "You a doctor or something?"

Before Skylar could answer, they heard an urgent female voice inside the trailer. "Lobo! Get in here!"

"Yes, Auntie!" Lobo immediately ran back inside. Butler and Skylar followed cautiously. Upon entering the mobile home, they discovered Lobo's aunt staring at Eddie, who was on the floor, playing with Lobo's young son. The small boy was laughing. And not just a little. He was laughing hysterically.

Upon seeing Lobo's reaction, Butler looked confused. "What's wrong?"

Lobo sat down quickly. His knees practically gave out beneath him. "He's . . . never laughed before."

Skylar looked on with compassion. "Never?"

Lobo shook his head. "The only sounds he's ever made are these strange chirps and grunts. Screams a lot, too. Throws tantrums all the time." He paused to take in the moment. "This is the first time the kid's ever seemed happy."

"He is happy," Eddie confirmed. "You can tell because he is laughing."

Lobo's aunt shook her head, dabbing at the tears welling in her eyes. "I had given up hope that something like this could happen."

Lobo turned to Eddie. "How did you do it?"

"How did I do what?"

"Get him to laugh like that," the aunt replied.

"I spoke his language." Eddie made several chirp sounds, followed by grunts and other guttural utterances. After a moment, the little boy laughed even harder. It was infectious.

"What did you just say?" the aunt asked.

"I am not entirely certain, but I believe I just told him that I passed gas."

The little boy then made a similar series of chirps and grunts.

"He just said that he passed gas, too." Eddie paused. "He also needs his diaper changed."

The aunt stared in amazement. "He told you that?"

Eddie shook his head. "No, I can smell it."

As the aunt got to her feet and picked up the little boy to change him, she turned to Eddie. "Young man, thank you."

"You are welcome." After she carried the boy into the bedroom, Eddie got to his feet and turned toward Skylar. "Lobo let me ride on the back of his motorcycle. It was loud and scary."

She smiled. "I'm sure it was."

He removed the earplugs from his ears. "Roberto gave me earplugs, so it did not hurt my ears. They are still golden like William Tuthill's." He paused, listening to something the others could not hear. He turned to Lobo. "Mr. Lobo, did you know there is a woman standing outside your door?"

Lobo spun around to see Cobra Kelly standing on the front porch with a shotgun in her hands. "When I heard the Pagans had gotten involved, I had an idea you might bring him here."

Butler studied her and Lobo. "You two know each other?"

Lobo nodded. "Bitch is a bounty hunter."

"Bad word," Eddie chimed in.

She addressed Lobo. "I have no beef with you or anyone you ride with. I'm only here for him." She motioned to Eddie.

Butler stared at her coldly. "You really don't want to do this."

"You're wrong about that, tough guy. I've been given all kinds of incentive." She took a step toward Eddie.

"What is a bounty hunter?" he asked.

"Someone who wants to play tag," Skylar answered.

"I don't want to play tag with her or anyone else."

Butler protectively stepped in front of him. "You should really reconsider."

Cobra Kelly held out her weapon threateningly. "Or what?"

Directly behind her, she heard the sound of a revolver's hammer being locked back into firing position. CLICK-CLICK. The gun was held by Lobo's aunt, who had slipped out a back door. "Or I will blow your head clean off your shoulders."

The older woman's tone gave Cobra Kelly no doubt. She knew she was beat and held her arms out to the sides, allowing Lobo to grab her weapon.

He turned to Butler and Skylar. "Time for you to go."

"I couldn't agree more," Skylar said. She led Eddie and Butler out the front door and into Roberto's Bronco.

"More cars are coming. They are driving faster than the posted speed limit." Eddie pointed through the windows as four sedans

SCREECHED to a stop in quick succession in the entrance to the trailer park, blocking the Bronco's exit.

"More asshole bounty hunters. That's Ray Dupre and his kin," Lobo said.

In his car, Big Ray spoke into a handset, which was amplified through a loudspeaker mounted under the hood. *"Y'all ain't goin' nowhere."*

Three rifles simultaneously opened fire from different locations around the trailer park's entrance. BOOM! BOOM! BOOM! They were fired by the Pagans who had initially greeted Butler and Skylar. Two tires in each of the bounty hunters' vehicles went flat. Each of the sedans now sat at a severe angle.

The gunshots hurt Eddie's ears, so he quickly placed the earplugs back in.

Lobo stepped toward Dupre and his sons. "I wouldn't get out of your cars if I was you. Keep your hands where we can see them."

Big Ray nodded compliantly and placed his hands on his dashboard. His family members followed suit.

Lobo approached the Bronco, pointing behind them. "There's a back way. Go."

Butler hit the gas, spraying gravel as he sped out of the trailer park. Eddie and Skylar were both thrown against the backs of their seats. After a moment, Eddie said, "When we get back to Harmony House, I don't ever want to play tag again."

Skylar smiled. "That's a deal."

CHAPTER 98

SAFE HOUSE

GILBERTS CORNER, VIRGINIA

June 2, 11:58 a.m.

From her subterranean bunker, Caitlin watched via satellite as the Bronco sped away from the trailer park. She answered the call from Butler on the first ring. "Did you have a nice visit with your new friends?"

"Did it have to be Pagans?" Butler asked.

"Given the time frame, I didn't have much choice."

From the back seat, Eddie asked, "Who are you talking to?"

Skylar answered, "Her name is Caitlin. She's the one I told you about who is helping us."

"Hi, Eddie," said Caitlin.

"I know that Skylar said you are helping us, and I know your name is Caitlin, but you are still a stranger. I don't talk to strangers."

Butler chimed in, "Eddie, Skylar would be dead if it wasn't for Caitlin."

Skylar said, "Could you be a little less dramatic, perhaps?"

"He is telling the truth, Skylar. One hundred percent. In light of the circumstances, I think it would be okay if I talk with Caitlin." He paused a moment. "Hi, Caitlin. Did you know that this is only my second phone call?"

"No, I did not know that."

"Lolo taught me how. She helped me make my first phone call. She is very nice. She is my friend. I know because she said she is."

"Then I think you should believe her."

"Caitlin, why are you helping us?"

She was taken aback for a moment. "Because I did not think you were being treated fairly."

"How did you know?"

"I'll explain that when this is all over."

"When what is all over?"

Caitlin glanced at another monitor, where Hogan appeared on-screen. He made a circular motion with his finger, meaning for her to wrap it up. "Guys, you'll have to excuse me, but I have to go. Butler, proceed to the previous rendezvous point. You'll be given further instructions there."

"Copy that," Butler replied before hanging up.

Eddie asked, "Butler, what are you copying?"

((•))

Inside her bunker, Caitlin turned to Hogan on-screen. "Is everything set?"

He nodded grimly.

"You know how much I hate this, right?"

He nodded again. "If you didn't, there would be something wrong with you." He paused, checking another screen in his location. "It'll be over soon enough."

"Hogan, if this thing goes sideways—"

"It won't. Everything is covered. Just do your part."

Her phone rang. It was a Skype call, so it rang on both her phone and one of her computer screens. The call was from her husband. "Is that him?"

He nodded. "Answer it."

She clicked the camera icon on the screen. A handheld view of her terrified family appeared. Peter, Marissa, and Mikey were each tied to a chair. Marissa and Mikey were gagged so that they couldn't speak. Coogan's face could not be seen, but his voice could be heard. "Hold on one second there, Mrs. McCloskey, there's somebody else who would like to speak with you."

((•))

Inside the modest home in the lesser end of Harvey, North Dakota, Coogan pressed the "Conference" button for another party to join the call. After a moment, Bob Stenson appeared in split screen from his office at the American Heritage Foundation. "Sorry it's come to this, Caitlin, but you didn't leave me much choice."

CHAPTER 99

June 2, 12:02 p.m.

Down the hall from Stenson's office, four separate cell phones rang simultaneously with Skype calls. Inside Trotter and Greers's office, the two men turned to each other quizzically as their phones rang in unison. Greers said, "What the hell?"

Trotter studied his phone. "The call is from an unknown sender."

"I thought that wasn't possible on Skype."

"It's not supposed to be. Whoever this is knows what he's doing. He also knows who we are."

Greers clearly found this unsettling. "You don't know that."

"Yes, I do. Listen." They could hear two other phones ringing down the hall. The sounds were coming from the office shared by Enola and Charlie.

"Well?"

"Duh," responded Trotter as he pressed the icon to answer the call. Greers immediately followed suit.

((•))

Down the hall, Enola and Charlie had arrived at the same decision. Each pressed the icon to receive the call. On their screens, three views appeared: one of Peter, Marissa, and Mikey held hostage, looking terrified; one of Caitlin in her subterranean safe house; and one of Stenson sitting in his office down the hall.

In the text window at the bottom of each screen, the following message appeared:

Stenson does not know you can see this. He cannot hear you or see any comment you make. Decide for yourselves which side you should be on.

There was a slight delay in the transmission, much like the seven-second delay in a network's live broadcast to prevent profanity or other obscenities from going out over the air. Then they heard what Stenson had said a few seconds earlier: *"Sorry it's come to this, Caitlin, but you didn't leave me much choice."*

((•))

"Each member of my family is a complete innocent!" Caitlin screamed from her bunker. "Look at them!"

"You brought this on yourself."

"That's bullshit!"

"And don't even try to claim your father is an innocent," Stenson said abruptly.

"Have you seen him lately?" she asked in disbelief.

"You know I have."

"He was your mentor!"

"He helped you initiate the Alpha Reset Protocol. I don't know how, but don't try to deny it. You would never have gotten this far without his help."

"He always knew you were a vindictive little man. Why do you think he prepared for this so many years ago?"

Stenson briefly bit his tongue. "You hold him on such a high pedestal. If you only knew——"

She exploded with pent-up emotion. "You son of a bitch, you hired Mr. Elliott—the pure embodiment of evil—to torture him until I gave myself up."

Stenson remained frighteningly calm. "Obviously, that never came to pass."

"So what is this, your backup plan?"

"I always have a Plan B. You know that. Return the six hundred million, give yourself up, and nothing will happen to your family. You have my word."

Caitlin steeled herself. "And if I don't?"

"My man, Coogan, up there will start with your daughter. The things he is going to do to her will occur right in front of your husband. And if that doesn't work, Coogan will then do the same things to your son."

Caitlin clenched her fists tightly. She seemed barely able to contain herself. "You are absolutely vile."

"Desperate times require desperate measures."

Caitlin paused as she adjusted the position in her chair. She now sat more upright. Her expression seemed to change dramatically. She no longer looked disgusted and beaten. She appeared confident. Even certain. "I guess the key would be never to get that desperate, then."

"This is your last chance, Caitlin. Tell me where you are right now, or this will become rather distasteful."

CHAPTER 100

"MONTGOMERY" FAMILY HOME

HARVEY, NORTH DAKOTA

June 2, 11:06 a.m. Central Daylight Time

Coogan was not literally licking his lips, but he might as well have been. As he pointed the satellite phone's camera at his three frightened hostages, he locked his eyes on the girl. The one he'd been instructed to attend to first. He couldn't stop thinking about what he would soon be doing to her. His hands trembled.

Caitlin then said something that confused the other parties on the call, except for one. "Hogan, now."

For the first time during the call, Hogan spoke from his unknown location. "Damien, go."

((•))

Damien Davis was one of the eight assassins Bob Stenson had previously attempted to hire before being steered in Mr. Elliott's direction. Unfortunately for Stenson, Hogan had reached him first. He was currently standing in the backyard of the modest Harvey residence, clad completely in black, as Hogan had been the night before.

Eric Bernt

The weapon in Damien's hands was a Springfield Armory M1A, one of the finest sniper rifles in the world. In the proper hands, it was accurate to within a quarter of an inch at a thousand-yard range. The .308-caliber spitzer bullet fired from it traveled at 3,100 feet per second. In other words, it could travel the length of ten football fields in just over a second, which meant it flew the distance from gun barrel to Coogan's skull in approximately three one-hundredths of a second. It happened so quickly, it was difficult to differentiate the sounds of the gunshot, the window shattering, Coogan's head exploding, and the bullet puncturing two additional interior walls before exiting the house and lodging in a telephone pole.

Moving only the essential parts of his body, Damien efficiently chambered a second round and fired again, this time puncturing the center of Coogan's chest before his body had even started to collapse to the floor. If the sniper's camouflaged outfit wasn't enough to suggest that Hogan had trained him, the double tap most certainly was.

Coogan somehow managed to maintain a grip on his phone as he dropped to the floor. As luck would have it, the phone had twisted around, allowing those still on the Skype call to see his now-lifeless eyes in close-up.

Damien communicated into a headset. "Target is down."

"Double tap?" Hogan asked.

"Is there any other way?" Damien entered the house through a back door and used a switchblade to cut through Peter's restraints, then handed him the knife to free his children. By the time Peter looked up to thank him, Damien was already gone.

Peter hugged his two children long and tight. Tears flowed from all three.

Over the phone, Caitlin could hear him saying how much he loved them. Loudly, she asked, "Peter, is everyone okay? Peter?!"

Peter eventually made his way over to his phone, on the floor next to Coogan's body. He stared at his wife's image on the screen. Stenson had already left the call. "I'm here. The kids and I are fine."

"Thank God." She touched her screen as if to touch him.

"Caitlin, how did they find us?"

With tremendous guilt, she answered, "I wasn't careful enough."

He searched her eyes as best he could on the small screen. "Tell me the truth. Are we safe?"

Caitlin looked him squarely in the eyes. "I have one last thing to take care of, and you will be."

"Then we can come home?"

"Then you can come home." It was only now that she realized Stenson no longer appeared on-screen.

"Hurry up about it, would you?"

CHAPTER 101

June 2, 12:09 p.m.

Inside their office, Enola and Charlie finished watching the last of the Skype call. Enola shook her head. "I can't believe he was going to do that to her kids."

"I can't believe what a badass Caitlin is," Charlie said. "I totally underestimated her."

"Because she's a woman?" Enola asked pointedly.

"Because she looks like my middle-school algebra teacher."

"I'll tell you what, the woman has stones. Can you imagine being that cool when some asshole has a gun pointed at your family?" She gave her best impression of Caitlin, repeating her line: "'I guess the key would be never to get that desperate, then.'"

He paused. "I'm sensing a bit of a girl crush here."

"Hell yes. Woman is my hero. Where she leads, I follow." On-screen, she reread the earlier text:

Decide for yourselves which side you should be on.

She typed: With you.

"I'll be right beside you." Charlie typed a similar response.

They both received the same reply: Shelter in place.

((•))

Down the hall, Trotter watched Greers pace around their office. "I can't believe he hired Mr. Elliott."

"I can't believe she stole six hundred million dollars from our accounts," Trotter said. "I would love to know how she did it."

Greers suddenly stopped pacing. "What I want to know is: Who the hell is Hogan?"

"If I had to guess, he's an old friend of the family."

Greers nodded. "You were right about family connections." He paused. "What are you going to do?"

"My choice is easy," said Trotter.

"Why is yours easy and mine isn't?"

"I'm not the heir apparent." He let that hang there for a moment. "I'm no threat to her. All I am is a quant, whether I'm his or hers. But honestly, can you imagine yourself taking orders from her? Or more importantly, her trusting you to be her dutiful lieutenant?"

Greers stood there frozen for a moment. "Shit." He grabbed whatever personal items he could fit into his backpack and headed for the door, where he paused. "Have a nice life."

"You too." Trotter listened to him walk down the hall. "For as long as it lasts." Turning back to his screen, he typed a response similar to Enola's and Charlie's: With Caitlin. He received the same reply: Shelter in place. Trotter muttered, "Well, I guess that answers that."

((•))

In the conference room, Carter Harwood sat at the conference table, wearing headphones. He was hard at work cleaning up the latest set of echoes from the Oval Office. It turned out there was a real art to it, which would come as no surprise to any sound engineer. The job of cataloging the tens of thousands of conversations that had occurred in the space over several decades was massive. Completing the effort would take months, if not years.

As instructed, Harwood had started with the conversations occurring after midnight since the current president had taken office. In total, there were fewer than two dozen in that time period. Most were brief and inconsequential, but three of these sets of echoes were, quite simply, shocking. Harwood had read about various fetish practices, but he wasn't entirely prepared for listening to them as they took place. In fact, one incident in particular had nauseated him. He found it rather upsetting that this type of behavior had occurred inside the Oval Office. Utter depravity, it seemed, was practiced even in the most hallowed of confines.

As distasteful as these were for him to hear, they were also good opportunities for Harwood to practice removing harmonic distortion and other white noise from the re-created sound waves. It was similar to a baseball player taking batting practice. As with most jobs, the more he practiced, the more efficient he became. He figured by the time he started working on April, reconstructing each set of echoes would take less than a third of the time it currently took.

He was so focused on his efforts that he was startled when Stenson entered the room. "Sorry about that, sir. I wasn't expecting you."

Stenson was all business. "I need the box and the computer. Now."

"Yes, of course. You were right about the meetings after midnight. If you could just give me a minute to finish up what I'm—"

"Now." Stenson pushed the lid of the laptop closed, forfeiting whatever work Harwood hadn't saved.

He grabbed the laptop as Harwood unhooked the echo box. "Right. There you go. Sir, while you're off campus with the device, is there anything you'd like me to be working on?"

"Go get some rest. We'll regroup tomorrow." And he walked out the door.

His tone was unsettling. Harwood knew something was wrong but decided not to dwell on it. "The man said, 'Go get some rest.' Then that's what I'll do." He grabbed his shoulder bag and started packing up his things.

CHAPTER 102

June 2, 1:03 p.m.

Butler parked next to a man standing alone in the shadow of a building in the adjacent office park. Butler opened his door. "Stay here."

Eddie and Skylar remained in the Bronco. "Who is he?" asked Eddie.

"I'm not sure," answered Skylar.

"He reminds me of the mystery man who used to work at Harmony House."

(((•)))

Hogan kept his eyes on the American Heritage Foundation offices, particularly the eight armed guards surrounding its perimeter, as Butler approached. The two men nodded but did not shake hands. "Caitlin sent us," Butler said.

"I know who you are," Hogan replied. He motioned to Eddie. "The kid all right?"

Butler nodded. "Considering."

"What his box can do—changes everything."

"No question."

"Not sure that's a good thing," Hogan said.

"In the wrong hands, it's very dangerous."

"I've got an idea. Would you like to hear it?"

Butler listened to Hogan's plan as he counted the armed guards across the street. "Does Caitlin know about this?"

"Not yet." Hogan smiled. "She'll find out soon enough."

Butler nodded in agreement. "I count eight armed hostiles."

"Two more inside. Ten total."

"How many on our side?"

"Plenty."

Butler knew what that meant. "Ghosts?"

Hogan gave a slight smile, providing Butler his answer.

Butler looked around, guessing where the snipers might be set up, but knowing he would never see them. "When's the party start?"

"Soon as they start coming out the door," Hogan said.

"I want the guy in charge."

"You sure?" He glanced over to the two civilians Butler had brought with him.

"It's something I have to do."

"In that case, two birds, one stone." Hogan handed him a large hard-shelled case.

CHAPTER 103

FRONT ENTRANCE

AMERICAN HERITAGE FOUNDATION

June 2, 1:09 p.m.

Jason Greers exited the building and moved quickly to his car. As he reached for his door, he never heard the suppressed sniper's bullet fired from the office-complex rooftop several hundred yards away. His head exploded, spattering his car window.

The armed guards surrounding the building immediately sprang into action. All took up defensive postures. Their only problem was that none of them was sure where the enemy was located, or how many shooters there were. Both questions were addressed in short order.

More suppressed gunfire came from two other locations, making a total of at least three snipers. Each was positioned over fifty yards from the other. The entrance to the American Heritage Foundation had been triangulated; to defend against one direction was to be exposed to two others. The guards started dropping like flies.

((•))

Inside the Bronco, Eddie said, "That is gunfire, Skylar."

"Yes, it is. Close your eyes and cover your ears," she instructed urgently.

"I still have earplugs in, Skylar."

"Do it anyway."

Eddie did so but could still hear the gunfire clearly. He counted gunshots. "Two. Three. Four. Five-six-seven."

Watching the action in the distance, Skylar was both relieved and horrified. She had never rooted for people to be killed before.

"Is our team winning?" asked Eddie.

"Yes." What she didn't say was that the battle was completely one-sided. The AHF guards didn't stand a chance. Neither did the geeky-looking man with the shoulder bag. He barely made it out the door.

"Eight."

Six guards were down. Stenson exited the building with four armed guards in a tight formation, rushing to their vehicles. Stenson carried the duplicate echo box and laptop with him.

Skylar recognized the devices, glancing down to the originals sitting on the back seat next to Eddie. "Son of a bitch."

"Bad word."

She pointed to the devices in Stenson's hands. "Can you see what he's carrying?"

"It looks like the echo box and my laptop. They must have made copies." The two guards behind Stenson suddenly went down in unison. "Nine-ten."

Just as they reached their vehicles, the two guards in front of Stenson were hit as well.

"Eleven. Twelve."

Skylar rolled down her window and yelled to Butler, who was standing in the distance. "He's got another echo box!"

((•))

Stenson jumped into his vehicle, still carrying the duplicate devices. He started his car and roared out of the parking lot. He seemed to be getting away. That was when Skylar saw Butler standing in the street directly in his path. "I didn't mean you should get run over!"

CHAPTER 104

Parking Lot

American Heritage Foundation

June 2, 1:11 p.m.

As Stenson accelerated directly for him, Butler stood calmly, holding the RPG-7 missile that had been in the case Hogan had given him. He positioned the weapon on his shoulder and took aim. It was clearly not the first time he had done so. "This ends now." He pulled the trigger. FWOOSH!

Munitions of this type had two sections: a booster and warhead/sustained motor. The booster contained a small strip powder charge designed to propel the grenade out of the launch tube. The sustained motor then ignited, rocketing the warhead toward its target at 660 miles per hour.

Stenson's car was only one hundred feet away. The impact was nearly instantaneous. And completely devastating. Had anyone bothered to count, the pieces would have totaled over one thousand. Several of them rained down on Butler, who didn't seem fazed.

((•))

Inside the Bronco, Skylar could barely believe what she had just witnessed. *As if this day hasn't included enough!*

"That sounded like a rocket," commented Eddie.

"You're right, it was."

"Can I open my eyes yet?"

"Yes, I think so."

Eddie did, marveling at the flaming debris raining down from the sky. "I have never seen fireworks, but I think they must look like this."

They were startled by a knock on the window. Hogan was standing next to the car.

Skylar rolled down the window. "Is it over?"

"For the moment. If you want to end this permanently, you need to follow me. Bring the device."

Eddie chimed in, "He is telling the truth. One hundred percent."

Skylar got out of the car. "Eddie, wait for me here. I'll be right back."

He shook his head, grabbing the echo box and his laptop. "No, Skylar, I am coming with you."

She pointed out the window. "Look, Butler is right there. I promise you'll be safe."

"I am not afraid, Skylar. That is not why I want to go with you."

"Then why?"

"You are not the only one with someone to protect now." He was referring to Lolo. "If we can use the echo box to stop the bad guys permanently, I am the best person to make sure it is done properly."

Eddie got out of the car, pausing to rotate his head from side to side, then forward and back. "Hey, wait for me!" He quickly jogged after Skylar and Hogan as they walked across the street and entered the American Heritage Foundation.

((•))

Moments later, three yellow vehicles arrived: two vans and a large flat-bed truck. Each had a large Superior Cleaners logo stenciled on its side. The personnel inside each immediately went to work removing the evidence. Several started removing bodies while others doused the flaming wreckage of Stenson's car and began sweeping up debris.

Within minutes, the area would have no evidence of what had occurred.

((•))

In Stenson's office, Hogan watched in silent amazement as Eddie recorded the echoes bouncing around the space. The eight microsatellite microphones moved in unison, performing their familiar dance. Eddie kept his eyes on the screen as the acoustic three-dimensional rendering of the room was completed.

"It's all right to speak, you know." Skylar commented. "It won't hurt anything."

"I'm just trying to imagine everything that's been said in this room over the years," said Hogan.

"Scary, huh?"

"You have no idea."

"True." Eddie continued watching the progress bar on-screen reach *100 percent.* "All done."

Hogan handed Eddie a portable storage drive. "Put all the echoes on that, then erase them from your machine."

Eddie did so. He handed the drive to Hogan. "I have erased the files from my computer. You now have the only copy."

Skylar studied Hogan closely. "You mind if I ask what you're going to do with that?"

"I'm going to post the files to a couple dozen dark-web sites in encrypted form. If anything ever happens to either of you, or anyone tries to steal the box, the encryption key will be automatically mailed to every news organization in the world."

"How will you know if anything happens to us?" asked Eddie.

"I will send you both a number that one of you must text every day. If a message is not received in any twenty-four-hour period, the key will be released."

Eddie turned to Skylar. "In order to ensure one of us sends a text every day, I think it would be a good idea if I got my own phone."

"You make a good point."

"I will need you to teach me how to send a text message, of course."

"Of course," she responded. "Would there happen to be any other reason you'd like your own phone?"

Eddie blushed. "Yes, there would."

Clearly eager to change the subject, he turned to Hogan and motioned to the portable drive in his hands. "You're not going to listen to the echoes, are you?"

Hogan shook his head. "The world needs its secrets."

"Why are you doing this?" Skylar asked.

"To be sure Caitlin doesn't make the same mistake her boss did. He wasn't always a bad man. He just turned into one when he became obsessed with the device. I'm making sure she won't come after you."

"I am obsessed with the device," Eddie said. "Does that mean I am a bad person?"

"No, Eddie, I think you are unique," Hogan said. "You are probably the only person in the world who can handle a technology that powerful."

Eddie smiled. "That is a very nice thing for you to say. My heart is singing. Would you like to hear it?"

Hogan eyeballed him, then headed for the door.

Skylar called after him. "Thank you. For everything."

He paused in the doorway. "Check the Harmony House bank accounts when you get back to your office. You won't ever have to consider selling the echo box to the highest bidder to make ends meet."

She looked at him in wonder. "Wait, I don't even know your name."

"Yes, I know." And with that, he was gone.

After a long moment, Skylar turned to Eddie. "Oh, by the way, the answer is no."

Eddie looked confused. "The answer to what is no?"

"The question you asked me yesterday that I promised to answer in no more than forty-eight hours."

He nodded. "Yes, I remember."

"You do not need to share the echo box with anyone unless you want to."

Eddie smiled with relief. And then his ears perked up. "There are sirens approaching in the distance, Skylar. Seven of them."

"Then it's time for us to pack things up and get out of here."

As they left the building, there were no dead bodies anywhere. No disintegrated car. No yellow vans. In fact, there was absolutely no sign that anything out of the ordinary had occurred. Eddie paused and said, "Skylar, where did all the dead bodies go?"

"I have no idea. And I hope I never do."

Butler pulled up in the Bronco. They jumped in quickly, and he drove away just moments before the first police vehicles arrived on scene.

The authorities would conclude it must have been a false alarm.

CHAPTER 105

June 2, 2:47 p.m.

Caitlin stared at Hogan on-screen a short while later. "What the hell did you do?"

"The Alpha Reset Protocol is complete. You are now in charge of the American Heritage Foundation. Your family is flying back from North Dakota as we speak. I wish you luck and hope you honor your father's legacy. This is the last time you and I will communicate."

"And the echo box?"

He leaned back in his chair and crossed his arms on his chest, preparing to tell a story. "I like a good martini. Sometimes, I even enjoy two. But I never shoot heroin. Would you like to know why I don't? Because it would change me. I would start thinking I need it, and I don't. Just like you don't need the echo box. Your father did just fine his entire career without it, and so will you. You will already know plenty of the world's secrets. You just might have to work a little harder to uncover new ones. And that's not a bad thing."

"You want to tell me what happened to the one hundred million dollars that were transferred out of our accounts?"

"About that . . ."

((•))

The first thing Skylar did when she arrived at her desk back at Harmony House, later that evening, was to check the account balances. Her eyes opened wide as she stared at a number in excess of one hundred million dollars. She looked at Butler, who had entered with her. "Hey, I could use a new head of security. Think I could interest you?"

He was staring at her flat screen mounted on the wall, where the president's emergency press conference was just starting. "Possibly. Doubt you can afford me, though."

She smiled slyly. "I'll bet you I can."

He picked up the remote control and turned up the volume. "Would I be able to hire my own guys?"

"Of course. What do I know about security?"

"I'll think about it."

On-screen, the president addressed the country with grim-faced stoicism. "My fellow Americans, I want to reassure you all tonight that the very foundation of our great democracy has withstood the most insidious attack in our nation's history . . ."

((•))

The Embraer Phenom touched down at Potomac Airfield later that night. When the plane came to a stop, Caitlin rushed out to greet Marissa and Mikey as they scrambled out of the aircraft. "I am so glad to see you guys!" They embraced like they were never going to let go.

Marissa looked into her mother's eyes. "Mom, I will forgive you under one condition."

"What's that?"

"I never want to go to North Dakota again."

"Deal." She turned to her son. "How about you? Do you forgive me?"

"I think so. As long as that's not the last time I ever get to fly in a private plane."

She turned to Peter as he made his way down the ladder. They hugged for quite a while. Tears streamed down her face. "I am so sorry to have put you through that."

"You are going to tell me everything. And I mean everything."

She nodded. "I promise."

"Then you are going to have somebody really high up in the government inform my company board that the reason I had to leave so abruptly was a matter of national security so important that the future of the country depended on it."

"You know, that's actually not far from the truth."

He smiled. "And don't forget, you owe me a new car."

"I was hoping you forgot about that."

"Oh, and one more thing. I'm enrolling the kids in public school tomorrow."

"You're joking."

"Do I look like I'm joking?"

CHAPTER 106

HARMONY HOUSE

WOODBURY, NEW JERSEY

June 4, 8:07 a.m.

Eddie slept soundly under his Batman sheets. It was the second consecutive morning he had slept in past eight o'clock, which was rather unusual for him. Then again, the last few days would have been atypical for anyone. There was a light knock on the door. "Skylar, I am still sleeping. Can you come back later?"

From the other side of the door, she said, "I'm sorry to wake you, but I have a surprise for you."

"What kind of surprise?"

"Open the door and I will show you."

Still in his pajamas and wiping the sleep from his eyes, he opened the door to find Skylar holding a cell phone. He suddenly looked wide awake. "Is that for me?"

She nodded. "It is."

He took the phone in his hands, practically caressing it. "This is the very best surprise I have ever been given."

"You were right. I think it is important that you have your own phone."

"Is it okay if I make a call?"

She beamed. "It's your phone. Go right ahead."

He immediately dialed one of the two phone numbers he knew. He put the phone to his ear and listened.

Lolo answered the call. "Hello."

He smiled at the sound of her voice. "Hello, Lolo, this is Eddie."

"Hi, Eddie. This is Lolo."

"I am calling you because I wanted you to be the first person I have ever called with my very own phone."

"You make my heart sing, Eddie."

"You make my heart sing, too."

She exclaimed with disbelief, "Really? You're not just saying that?"

"You helped me understand what I did not understand before. I know this with my whole body and not just my head."

"Can I tell you a secret?"

"Yes, of course you can."

"Would you mind stepping outside your door?"

Eddie did so. Standing in the hallway, he looked in one direction, but there was no one there. He turned around and looked in the other direction, but there was no one there, either. Until somebody walked around the corner. He immediately recognized her footsteps. It was Lolo. "What are you doing here?" he asked excitedly into his phone.

She quickened her pace. "I live here now."

"You do?" he said eagerly.

Into her phone, she said, "I'm hanging up now because I would rather talk to you in person." She ended the call as she approached him. "I'm your new neighbor."

Listening to her closely, he stared at the floor, looking amazed. "True."

She pointed to the door next to his. An index card was taped to it, which read *Lolo*. "This is my room. It's right next to yours."

He turned to Skylar, who joined them in the hallway.

She nodded tearfully. "And you don't need to ask. These are happy tears. Very happy tears."

He smiled. "I knew that, Skylar."

"Dr. Drummond, I would like to ask Eddie something in private. Would that be all right?"

"By all means . . ." Skylar motioned inside Eddie's room. As Lolo walked through the doorway, she gave Skylar a knowing glance.

Eddie followed Lolo into his room. "What did you want to ask me?"

Lolo paused, as if trying to muster her courage.

Skylar jumped in, saying, "I'll be outside if you need me." With a smile, she pulled the door closed. A great big smile.

ACKNOWLEDGMENTS

I would like to express my heartfelt gratitude to everyone who read my first book, *The Speed of Sound*. Thank you for taking a chance on a new writer. To everyone who reached out, your comments and criticisms were invaluable. I learned a great deal from each of you. I would like to thank the community of veteran authors who have taken me under their wings. Your acceptance has meant the world. I remain blessed with the support of the incredible team at Thomas & Mercer and Amazon Publishing, led by the irrepressible Jessica Tribble. I don't know where I'd be without the wisdom of Paul Lucas at Janklow & Nesbit. Lastly, the following is an incomplete list of those I feel compelled to mention: Kevin Smith for his inspiring collaboration. Adam Levine and Karl Austen for always having my back. David Moore for his wisdom. My wonderful friends from Gladwyne, Pennsylvania; Madison, Wisconsin; and Northwestern University for their continuing embrace. And the good people of Agoura Hills, California, for our glorious bubble. Community is everything.

ABOUT THE AUTHOR

Photo © 2017 Conner Martin

Eric Bernt was born in Marion, Ohio, and raised in Gladwyne, Pennsylvania, and Madison, Wisconsin. He attended Northwestern University, where he learned that journalism was not for him—but storytelling was. Upon graduation, he moved to Hollywood, where he wrote seven feature films including *Virtuosity* (starring Denzel Washington and Russell Crowe) and *Surviving the Game* (starring Rutger Hauer, Gary Busey, and F. Murray Abraham). He has also written for television (*Z Nation*) and is the author of *The Speed of Sound*. Eric lives in Agoura Hills, California, with his wife and three children. For more information, visit www.ericbernt.com.